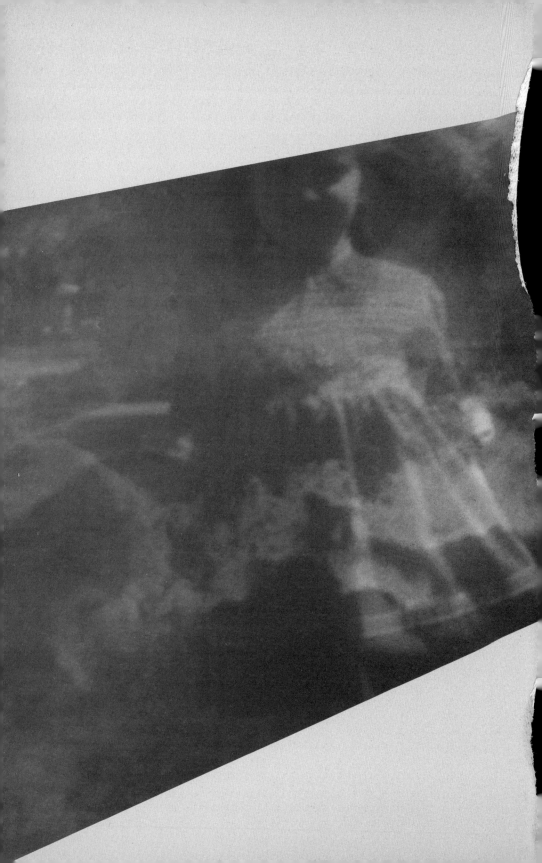

Also by Judith Kelman

After the Fall

Fly Away Home

More Than You Know

One Last Kiss

If I Should Die

The House on the Hill

Someone's Watching

Hush Little Darlings

While Angels Sleep

Where Shadows Fall

Prime Evil

Summer
of Storms

Summer of Storms

Judith Kelman

G. P. Putnam's Sons
New York

G. P. Putnam's Sons
Publishers Since 1838
a member of
Penguin Putnam Inc.
375 Hudson Street
New York, NY 10014

Library of Congress Cataloging-in-Publication Data

Kelman, Judith.
Summer of storms / Judith Kelman.
p.   cm.
ISBN 0-399-14674-1
1. Murder victims' families—Fiction.   2. Sisters—Fiction.
I. Title.

PS3561.E39727 S8   2001   00-045728
813'.54—dc21

Printed in the United States of America

10 9 8 7 6 5 4 3 2 1

This book is printed on acid-free paper.♾

BOOK DESIGN BY MEIGHAN CAVANAUGH

Acknowledgments

I am eternally grateful to my friend and agent, Peter Lampack, and to Sandy, Ren and Rima of the Lampack Agancy. Warm thanks also to Natalee Rosenstein, my first and foremost editor, and to Leslie Gelbman, wise counsel and consummate professional.

For their generous advice and input, I thank photographer Robin Bowman, author Marilyn Wallace, author Mickey Friedman, author Lia Matera, Dick Lavinthal of APB News, Lieutenant Phillip Panzarella of the Brooklyn Cold Case Squad and the inspiring members of the Vidocq Society.

And, of course, thanks to Ivan, my incomparable partner in all things.

For Linda, John, Elissa, and Danny

and in loving memory of

Flora, George, Gert,

and Zach

Summer of Storms

Chapter 1

I have secret pictures from the night of my sister's murder. The shots are crude composites, caught at the skewed perspective of a small, frightened child. Bodies lean at a curious tilt. Faces stretch in grotesque disbelief. Everything has the feel of a universe gone dangerously awry.

Elements of these images have come to me in dreams. Others wafted up the stairs in tantalizing scraps when my parents presumed I was asleep. Still others I have plucked from historical records in an attempt to fill the disquieting blanks. But my pictures remain grainy and indistinct. No matter how I try, I cannot bring the events of that night into clear, comprehensible focus.

It was on a Tuesday, the fourth of August, during an endless, oppressive season that the media had dubbed the Summer of Storms. Sixteen tropical disturbances had pummeled Caribbean islands and Atlantic seaboard towns since the National Weather Center began its annual six-month count in early June. Twelve of those had grown into full-fledged hurricanes, and six, triple the normal number, had intensified to the most lethal categories, with winds in excess of 111 miles an hour, leaving thousands injured and hundreds dead. Property damage was enormous, and among people living along the beleaguered East Coast, there was a pervasive sense of apocalyptic doom.

A week earlier, meteorologists had announced that yet another tropical storm, this one named Queenie, had been upgraded to full hurricane status. She was shaping up to be a bad one, feisty and temperamental, and some predicted that she might turn out to be the biggest and most devastating of all, weighing in at a cataclysmic Category Five on the newly invented Saffir-Simpson Hurricane scale.

When, late that weekend, broadcasters with grave, weary voices announced that the storm was expected to make landfall in the Manhattan area, even the staunchest, most unflappable New Yorkers flocked to the supermarkets to stock up on bottled water, canned goods, masking tape, batteries and candles.

That Tuesday happened to be my third birthday, and my parents decided to go ahead with my party despite the storm. By the time they realized that we were out of birthday candles to set atop my cake, even those had been stripped from the shelves by desperate, irrational shoppers. My mother was forced to improvise with a squat white votive candle, which she carved with a carrot peeler into a ragged numeral three. In one of my pictures of that night, the melted stump of the candle rests amid a scatter of chocolate crumbs and one large sugary pink rosette on the folding table around which everyone had gathered for a hasty celebration late that afternoon.

I have seen the headlines from that day, and they were filled with dire predictions about the monster tempest that was bearing down on the city. I imagine that a jittery current must have underscored the forced festivities. Everyone was worried about flooding and power outages and the pitiless havoc that nature can wreak, and the subject must have been central among the grownups at my party. It's likely that they attempted to douse their flaming nerves with a greater than normal quantity of wine and beer, which would account for the platoon of empty cans and bottles clustered in tidy rows near the kitchen door. The half-dozen children in attendance, including my sister and me, likely caught the adults' tension and reacted with loud, churlish behavior. One of my mental images of the room that night shows swirling track marks in the pale mauve carpet, probably made by my ten-year-old cousin Alan, who, like Queenie the hurricane, had a fearsome wild streak that was nearly impossible to contain.

My party broke up quickly as the sky darkened to an ominous ash and the first feral growls of distant thunder sounded hours earlier than expected. After the guests left, the living room was scattered with crumpled wrapping paper, cone-shaped hats and lolling pink balloons. A broad banner, scratched in red crayon in my sister's childish hand, sagged above the couch. "Happy birthday, Anna," it read, with one of the two Ns drawn backward.

Against this innocent tableau, the storm outside raged in stark, disturbing relief. Rain fell in quicksilver sheets and a ponderous haze shrouded the city.

Our building, a slender spire of dun-colored brick, crouched like a timid child behind the flared skirt of the Queensboro Bridge. In the dark of the storm, the span was nearly obliterated by the suffocating fog. The soaring towers to the north appeared to have been decapitated. The bumpy distant coastline disappeared.

Newsmen had warned against unnecessary travel, and in that season of violent destruction, most elected to heed the advice. Once the storm began in earnest, few people walked the streets. Those who dared to venture out scurried along with arms perched defensively and downcast eyes. Few cars, except emergency vehicles, rode the slick, flooded streets.

Based on the weather reports, my parents had expected my party to be over long before the hurricane struck. Though none of our guests had far to travel, my folks suffered guilt pangs for getting people out in such miserable conditions. Anxiously, they called to make sure that everyone had arrived home safely. Then they put my sister and me to sleep in our adjacent rooms and went to bed themselves.

Normally, my mother would have restored the apartment to perfect order before she turned in for the night. Bertie has always been a devout believer in pristine appearance. Even when things were wrong, especially then, she strove to keep the surface deceptively clear and smooth. But that one fateful time, reasoning that it would not make any difference, she yielded to tense exhaustion and put off the cleanup until morning.

She had no way of knowing how obscene that cheery mess would appear in the light of the next grotesque day. She could not have foreseen that sometime during that tumultuous night, while the sky blazed with giant javelins of lightning and thunder howled like a stuck beast, someone would steal into my sister's room unheard.

From the deep circle of moisture on the carpet, police concluded that the killer stood inert for several minutes, dripping rainwater from his sodden shoes and clothing, as he watched my sister sleep. Then, for some reason, he drew closer.

My sister, Julie, or "Jewel" as my parents call her now, must have sensed the intruder's presence and come awake. She made no sound, at least none that could be heard above the screaming wind. But, by all indications, she did not go gently. Though she was only five years old and small for even that tender age, she struggled hard enough to tear a ragged gash in her bedsheet. She raked her killer's flesh, trapping his skin cells under her fingernails and drawing blood.

Storms have always put me hard to sleep, as if someone were holding my head underwater until my brain went limp and spongy. And that night, I'm told that my whole family slept that way, oblivious and insensate, like the dead.

The next day dawned preternaturally still as it often does in the aftermath of a raging tempest. Nature, having staged a toddler-quality tantrum, backed off to rest and repent. A hazy sun baked the sprawl of ragged debris: tree limbs, downed power lines, an astonishing crop of umbrellas with snapped, twisted spokes. Widespread power outages caused many businesses to close for the day. The city came awake at the plodding pace of an invalid.

So did my family. Normally, I was up at first light, but that morning I slept until almost eight, then barreled into my parents' room to belly flop between them on the bed. Given my unusually late awakening, no one gave a thought to my sister's failure to appear at the breakfast table. It was past nine when my mother finally declared that the time had come to rouse her. I can still picture the fan of wrinkles that furled from Bertie's soft gray eyes as she smiled in bemusement, "Think I'll go and give that little lazybones a shake."

The rest plays through my mind in a garish slide show. Scenes shift with a jarring click and flash of dislocating light.

The air rent with my mother's ungodly scream. My father bolted from the kitchen and raced down the hall to Julie's room. His frantic words came like ax strikes. "Get my black bag, Bertie. Call the ambulance. Wake up, Julie. Come on, sweetheart. Take a breath now. *Breathe!*"

Soon, a fleshy fence of strangers circled my sister's bed. When they parted, two grim-faced men emerged, ferrying a lumpy sheet-wrapped form on a strange metal rig. One of my sister's honey-colored curls poked out, as if she were playing hide-and-seek.

My sister loved to play games. She delighted in unexpected twists of circumstance and broad infant ironies. Though I was too little to provide reasonable competition, or maybe because of that, she would often recruit me for games of giant steps or Simon says or jacks. She also loved to tell riddles and jokes, so I suspect she would have been delighted for a time by all the questions and musings and desperate, dark humor her killing provoked.

But eventually, I know she would have grown weary of this particular game. Like me, she would have had no greater wish than to have the mystery solved. The time was long overdue for all of us to lay the grisly matter to rest and try, as best we could, to be done with it.

Chapter 2

Every spring, my hometown of Charleston, South Carolina, hosts a two-week cultural celebration known as Piccolo, or "Little," Spoleto, after the larger Italian event after which it was modeled and named. For most local citizens, the annual festival means an exhilarating influx of tourist dollars along with a heady round of parties and performances. But I anticipate those particular two weeks with dread. During that time, my boss, Palmer Pruitt, offers his dollar ninety-nine portrait special, inviting a stampede of bargain-seeking subjects to our photo shop.

Mr. Pruitt is a dear, gentle, charmingly misguided soul, who sees his portrait sale as a sacred Piccolo Spoleto tradition. When I tried in the past to coax him out of it, he seemed stunned, as if I'd suggested retiring Santa or sentencing the Easter Bunny to the chair.

Having worked at Pruitt's Photos for almost a decade, I am keenly aware that not everyone is easy to shoot. But for some reason, the annual rock-bottom offer attracted the least captivating faces and most repugnant personalities in town. Naturally, they expected perfection and consumed an absurd amount of time. Many had been memorably exasperating. But the worst of the bunch looked marvelous when compared to my customers this morning.

For the past two hours, Mrs. Cecelia "Ceecie" Warburton and her twin baby girls had taken turns ruining a record number of exposures. In shot after shot, one or the other of the toddlers would scrunch her eyes or spew a thread of drool or topple on her small round rump and bawl. The more temperamental twin, "Miz" Melanie, had a Sarah Bernhard–quality aversion to the camera. "Miz" Ashley appeared to be suffering from baby narcolepsy. Suddenly, without warning, she would hang her head like a weary commuter and nod off.

The wasted rolls lay like spent ammunition at my feet. Normally, I had almost limitless forbearance where a camera was involved. Normally, small children recognized and accepted me as one of their kind. But this session had run my patience hard to ground. Worse, I could not afford to displease "Miz" Warburton, a self-styled Southern belle from the South Bronx, whose husband happened to own the building in which the photo shop was housed. Ceecie had not come because of the dollar ninety-nine special, but despite it. In her endless perversity, she had decided that this morning, today, immediately, even though it required my canceling a packed roster of appointments, she absolutely had to have a birthday portrait taken of her girls. No matter that she'd never even bothered to pick up the shot she'd had me take of them six months before. No matter that their birthday was two months away. Mr. Pruitt, whose lease would soon be up for renewal, was in no position to refuse her outrageous demands.

Neither was I. I needed the paycheck, and Pruitt's was one of a precious few photographic jobs in town. My true passion was photojournalism, which I pursued on a freelance basis with near missionary zeal. Since college graduation, I had spent much of my free time and most every spare nickel in pursuit of stories that caught my stubborn interest.

From the first time my father handed me a camera, I was captivated. Growing up, I carried my hand-me-down Ricoh everywhere, like a security blanket. Behind the lens, I found refuge and freedom, distance and connection, an intoxicating way to tame the huge, chaotic world. Pictures had the power to expose the essence of the truth, to bring things into sharp, clear perspective, and that was what I desperately wanted to do.

But I was not there yet. Some of my best shots had been published, and I had won inclusion three times in the prestigious annual photographic edition of *Communication Arts*. Unfortunately, plaudits would not pay the rent or cover the student-loan payments. Despite my regular round of calls and applications, I had not been able to land a job with a newspaper or magazine. Until I did, I was stuck at Pruitt's, coaxing dogs and debutantes, begging for smiles.

A nervous twitch strummed the lid of my lens eye, and my shutter finger threatened to cramp. Time to haul out the big guns.

I dropped to all fours and treated the Warburton girls to my finest puppy imitation. I yipped and chuffed and balled my hands in paws. With the fine sandy hair trailing from the tortoise clip at my crown, my round blue eyes and chunky compact form, playing Shih tzu was not all that much of a stretch. Turning, I scampered about and wagged my denim-clad tail section. Finally, from behind came a chortle of delight. Peering over my shoulder, I caught sparks of amusement in the twins' emerald eyes. They clapped their pudgy hands and sported matching gap-toothed grins.

I kept up the pooch act, holding the camera out of sight to avoid terrorizing Melanie. All I needed was one decent shot. At best, Miz Warburton would hang it on the wall, overwhelmed by a garish frame, in her outrageously overdone Charleston manse. More than likely, the witch would never set eyes on the picture again, except to admire her own insipid image in the glass. With any luck, I would not have to hear Ceecie's pig-squeal voice or see her freeze-dried face again until it was time for the twins' next portrait emergency.

Slowly, I brought the camera around. For head shots, my weapon of choice is a Mamiya medium format, which provides a larger negative and crisper image then the standard single-lens reflex. Unfortunately, it's also heavier and harder to conceal than the Canon EOS I use for fieldwork.

With a clandestine peek through the lens, I set the shutter speed and tweaked the focus. Soft light suffused the space. The composition could not have been more pleasing. The little ones posed like chubby bookends on the antique Kashan rug that their mother had brought in for the shoot. They wore matching green velvet dresses with smocked bodices, lacy white socks and black patent Mary Janes. Green velvet headbands bound their fine jet hair.

I caged the camera behind an arm and brought it level with the girls. As I was about to expose the lens and snap the shutter, a shriek pierced the magic moment, "Wait, stop!"

Ceecie teetered toward the babies on stilt-heeled lime-green pumps. She wore a clingy silk dress splashed with cabbage roses. A broad-brimmed straw hat perched on her teased platinum bob like a giant potato chip. "Come now, Miz Melanie darling. Mama has to fix your hair." This last word stretched to nearly three-syllables, though Ceecie's flat Bronx accent poked up sharply through the drawl.

Melanie cringed as her mother approached. Ceecie attacked the child's scalp with a paddle-sized brush as if she were currying a horse. The little girl's face bunched in red, wrinkled piles and her lower lip slid out like a tiny cash drawer.

"Please, Mrs. Warburton," I said. "Her hair is fine."

"Why, the nerve!" Ceecie drew up larger than life, as if she had mounted her husband's millions to make the point. "Who are you to tell me about my baby's hair?" This time, she taffy-pulled the word to four syllables: hayuh-ayuh, like an Indian chant.

"Please. I didn't mean anything by it. I'm trying to take their picture. That's all. The twins are tired. Everyone's tired. I was only suggesting that we get the picture done."

Melanie's lips quaked and her face flamed with burgeoning rage.

So did Ceecie's. "You were only suggesting? Well, let me remind you, missy, that suggesting is not your job. If you can't manage to take a decent picture of these two magnificent baby girls, I believe you should consider finding yourself a more suitable line of work. In fact, I have half a mind to go into Palmer Pruitt's office and suggest that to him right this very minute."

I ached to agree aloud that Ceecie Warburton had half a mind, at best. But I knew the price I would pay for that fleeting satisfaction. "You're right. It is my responsibility. Give me just a few more minutes, and I'm sure I can get a wonderful shot of the twins."

"You'd best do exactly that." Ceecie set her truculent jaw and tottered to the rear of the studio. "And be quick about it."

I knelt before the toddlers and placed myself at their miniature mercies. "Okay, you guys. Here's the deal. All I need you to do is smile for one little second, and then you get to go home with your mommy. What do you say?"

Melanie's reply was the piercing shrill of an emergency vehicle. Ashley took up the cry, bowing to pummel her head on the rug. For good measure, she overflowed the banks of her disposable diaper, and a dandelion-yellow stain spread around her on the pricey antique carpet. Ceecie shrieked at the sight, and all three Warburton girls devolved into howling, florid lumps of inconsolable grief.

"Now look what you've done," Ceecie railed as if I had befouled the rug personally. "That's it. I've had quite enough. We're leaving." She plucked a cockroach-sized cell phone from her Chanel purse and cupped her ear to blunt the cacophony. "Bring the car around, Hector, and send Nanny Rebecca in to fetch the girls immediately!"

Hanging up, she scorched me with an acid glare. "The trouble with you, missy, is you don't know your rightful place."

I longed to take up my camera and fight back. If only I could snap close-ups of Ceecie's back-alley sneer and distribute copies to the membership committees of Charleston's more desirable ladies' auxiliaries.

"You're a useless little no-talent, old-maid shop clerk. That's what you are, Anna Jameson. It so happens I only bring the girls in to have their portraits done here because I thought it might boost the reputation of this cheesy little place. That'll teach me to be charitable."

My tongue came unglued. I matched her phony drawl and raised her one. "You are absolutely right, Miz Warburton, ma'am. I don't know what I could have been thinking. Please, please forgive me. I will stay in my rightful useless little no-talent, old-maid shop-clerk place from now on and thank my lucky stars for big-hearted, generous souls like you, Miz Ceecie. As God is my witness, I'll never be sassy again."

"Don't you dare be sarcastic with me. I'm warning you, I will not stand still for that."

"Go, then," I suggested.

The twins continued to screech as Nanny Rebecca, a dour, rawboned woman in a funereal dress, slam-dunked them into a double stroller.

Ceecie shrilled above the din. "What did you say?"

Thinking of Palmer Pruitt, I reined in my runaway temper. "Nothing. Look. I'm sorry things didn't work out today. Why don't you bring the girls back another time?"

"Not on your life, you cheeky twit. I won't allow you to upset my precious babies ever again. What I will do is talk to Palmer Pruitt and see he cans your nervy ass before you ruin his pitiful business altogether. Otherwise, my husband can surely find a far more suitable tenant for this space."

"Look, I was out of line. You're right. I'm sorry."

"You certainly are. Sorriest thing I've ever seen."

She stomped out and slipped into the stretch Fleetwood idling at the curb. Her dragon breath fogged the glass as they pulled away.

I headed for the back office. Palmer Pruitt deserved to hear about my terminal foul-up firsthand.

I knocked at the door marked AUTHORIZED PERSONNEL ONLY. Mr. Pruitt's tremulous voice rose in incomprehensible response. When I poked my head in, I discovered my boss on the phone. "Sorry, I didn't mean to interrupt."

He motioned for me to enter. "Not at all. Phone's for you, in fact, Anna. Your uncle Eli."

Pruitt, a slight, bespectacled widower of indeterminate age, rose and patted his chair. He buttoned his concrete-colored cardigan and shook down the legs of his drab, droopy corduroy pants. "Sit, Anna. I'll step out and let you have some privacy."

"That's not necessary."

"Please. I need to go check on something in the darkroom anyway."

"Thanks, then. I'll only be a minute."

"Take your time. Knowing Ceecie Warburton, I canceled all your appointments until late this afternoon. How did it go?"

"Actually, I need to talk to you about that."

"Sure, whenever you like." His face pinched with kindly concern. "I hope she didn't give you too hard a time. She's some piece of business, that one."

I waited for the door to close behind him. "Hi, Uncle E. What's up?"

"What's up with you, sweetheart? You sound terrible."

I swallowed a bitter lump. "Just a little work problem."

"Maybe it's time for a change, then."

"Definitely. The minute *Life* comes knocking, I'm out of here."

"How about Burlingame Media?"

"I suppose if they really twisted my arm, I might consider it. But I'd think all those breaking stories and Pulitzer prizes could get tedious."

"You can let me know after you've been there for a while."

"Don't tease, Uncle E. It's been a bad morning."

"I'm not teasing. I've been in discussions about a paper-importing co-venture with Stewart Burlingame. We had a meeting at my office this morning, and he noticed your work on my wall. He was so impressed, he asked how he could reach you to talk about your coming to work for him. I wanted to check before I gave him your number. Would that be okay?"

"No, it would be incredible. The best I've been able to get from a place like that is a Dear Applicant letter with an offer for a discount subscription. I can't believe it, Uncle E. It's a miracle."

"Wait, Anna. Before you go into orbit, I'm afraid there's a hitch."

In the ensuing silence, I pictured him settled behind his desk, worry lines scoring his broad, ruddy face. I imagined him selecting his words with extravagant care like a scrupulous cook at a fruit stand. My uncle balanced sharp intelligence, keen wit, boundless wisdom and the engaging guise of an outsized elf. The combination had served him well in his shipping business, which he had grown from a failing family firm into a thriving international conglomerate. And it had helped sustain him through overwhelming personal tragedy.

Eli's wife and only son had been killed almost twenty-five years ago when their car spun out on an ice slick during a family vacation in Spain. Irene and Alan were sent plunging into a ravine, where raging flames consumed the car. Eli, who had been thrown clear on impact, survived, though he suffered multiple fractures that required almost a year of rehabilitation at a Swiss clinic.

A syncopated limp was the only visible remnant of his unthinkable ordeal. Eli jokingly referred to it as his time-step. My parents had wrapped themselves in a steel cocoon of grief after my sister's death, but Uncle Eli found the means to embrace life. Through him, I understood that this was possible.

"What kind of hitch?" I asked.

"The media group is headquartered in New York City. Burlingame would want you to work for him there."

"New York, for God's sake. Why couldn't it be someplace more acceptable, like Sodom or the dark side of the moon?"

"I know. Your folks will not be pleased if you go, to say the least. Not with you or me, but that's how it is."

I groaned. "Now what am I supposed to do?"

"You're supposed to live your life, Anna," he said gently.

"You don't think it would be horrible of me?"

"Not at all. Frankly, given how long you've wanted this, I think it would be sinful to pass it up. Anyhow—"

"Anyhow, what?"

I heard him filling his chest, gearing up to say something difficult. "New York is not the enemy, honey. A sick person murdered Julie. It could have happened anywhere."

It felt odd to discuss the forbidden subject, especially with a close relative. At my mother's insistence, I had been tiptoeing around the monstrous fact of my sister's murder for as long as I could remember. Now I had the chance to follow my dreams and confront the family demons at the same time. The possibility filled me with a disquieting combination of longing and dread.

My uncle was right. Blind fear was the enemy, not New York.

"Logic has nothing to do with what my mother believes."

Eli chuckled. "She's a strong-willed lady, your mom. Takes after her daughter, I suppose. Which is exactly why I know she'll be just fine."

"It's so incredible. My head is spinning." My throat was dry and my chest was pounding, too, but I tried to ignore that. Beyond the career opportunity, I understood that I needed to do this. I would never be free of the past until I faced it dead on.

"Enjoy the ride, sweetheart. I'll call and put things in motion."

Chapter 3

My parents lived in a classic "single" house on Wentworth Street. The construction layout, one room wide by three deep and three stories tall, was devised to thwart the tax laws in seventeenth-century England, where assessments were based on street frontage. Early colonists had imported the style, and it stuck as most things did in Charleston. Citizens of this town prided themselves on a studied aversion to change. The running joke claimed that it took three Charlestonians to change a light bulb: one to change the bulb and two to sit around pining about how much better the old one used to be.

A tidy line of palmettos cast claws of shade over the pristine, pale amber facade. The shutters and trim were Charleston green, a near-black tone that revealed its true nature only under bright light and close scrutiny.

The same was true of this house. It had a cheery surface that struck me as mildly embarrassing, like a lie that, once told, could not be gracefully retrieved.

Once in seventh grade, in a misguided play for status and attention, I invented a boyfriend from out of town. I dubbed him Paul, after my favorite Beatle, and endowed him with an exotic missionary family who traveled the world. I wrote myself flowery love notes from the mysterious young swain, working left-handed in tortured strokes to mask the penmanship. When my friends clamored for a photograph, I rummaged through trunks in the attic until I found an acceptable picture of my dad at about my age. I snipped off his Boy Scout cap and neckerchief and trimmed his ears, which billowed like pale parachutes from his close-cropped hair. What a relief it had been months later to admit the duplicity to my best friend and discover that Shelby, in similar fashion, had fabricated the thrilling tale of her "discovery" by a scout from the Ford Modeling Agency.

Much as I loved and admired my parents, much as they were good people blessed with rare and remarkable abilities, no one would accuse them of being anywhere near lighthearted. The beckoning plastic hand in the window was a misleading prop. So was the thick jute doormat that read: "Welcome prize committee. Please slip check under the door." This house, these people, were relentlessly, religiously sad. Grief ran beneath their lives like a toxic stream, tainting everything. You couldn't draw a decent breath in this house without catching a bitter whiff of it.

Crossing the side porch to the entry door, my heart sank. Through the window, I spied the gleam of company silver on the dining room table. My mother had set out the stemmed crystal and white charger plates rimmed in a dainty blue floral chain. The ecru linen cloth had been pressed smooth. Matching napkins posed in graceful fans around an arrangement of dahlias and zinnias from my mother's garden. The last time the table had been festooned like this was after Great-Aunt Lucy's funeral in July. My mother reserved her finest things for the most solemn occasions. It was one of Bertie's more perplexing little quirks.

When I called earlier to say I had something to discuss with them, I had taken great care to keep my tone bright and unrevealing. But my mother had an uncanny knack for seeing through my most artful masks and miscues. Perhaps my sister's death had heightened her ability to anticipate trouble in the same way that blind people can develop a heightened sense of hearing or smell. Years ago, I had dubbed this disquieting aptitude *Mom-niscience,* the all-knowing, all-seeing scrutiny of the wary mother hen.

Bertie bumped through the swinging door from the kitchen, ferrying a tray heaped with my favorite childhood foods: barbecued chicken, mashed sweet potatoes, biscuits and gravy, homemade applesauce, roasted corn. My father trailed behind, balancing a pitcher of water in one hand and iced tea in the other. My stomach churned from the Last Supper feel of it all.

"Sit, dear. Everything's nice and hot. Now what is it you wanted to discuss?" Bertie asked as she laid out the last of the bowls.

"Why don't we eat first? Relax."

"Might as well get whatever it is out in the open," she insisted. "No one enjoys being kept in the dark. Isn't that so, Frank?"

My father shrugged, which was as close as he ever came to taking sides in a domestic debate. Pop was a man of few select words, unlike me, with my unfortunate tendency to shoot from the lip.

Braced for a storm, I told my parents about Stewart Burlingame admiring my work. I explained how honored I felt not to mention amazed. "The job is in New York. I know how you feel about the city, but there's honestly nothing to worry about."

Bertie dabbed her tight-pursed lips with a napkin. Whatever the situation, she maintained the studied, unruffled look of a model room. Today, she wore a graceful lavender silk dress with a pale scarf bound in a complex knot at the neck. Her pewter hair fell in tidy waves. Half-moon earrings framed her face like single quotation marks, and a small watch on a gold mesh bracelet circled her fine-boned wrist. Her eyes offered the sole hint of her crushing dismay. They darkened like the stone in a mood ring from feathery gray to the menacing charcoal of a thunderhead.

Her voice remained tuneful and light. "I can certainly understand how flattered you must be by the offer, dear. But when you've taken the time to think things through, I'm sure you'll realize that it's simply not a sensible idea." She passed this across the table along with the mashed sweet potatoes.

"Why not?"

"A million reasons. Your family is here. Your friends, your home." With a sweep of her hand, she embraced the relevant universe: this house, this town, everything that was comforting and familiar and presumed to be safe.

I prodded my untouched food around the plate. "I can't pass up a chance to work for Burlingame, Mom. It's what I've wanted to do forever. You know that."

"Taking pictures is fine, Anna. I just don't, for the life of me, understand why you can't do it here." She plucked a wing from the chicken plate and snapped it so sharply I suffered a sympathetic twinge.

"There's no work here."

"What do you call your job at Pruitt's?"

"Just that: a job. Time served. A way to pay the bills."

"That's what work is, dear. If it were all fun and excitement, they would call it something else. Wouldn't they, Frank?"

My father slathered strawberry jam on a biscuit chunk and stoked his mouth. "Delicious lunch, Bert. You've really outdone yourself."

She fired a killer look at him, and then fixed me in her cold, determined sights. "I saw Livvy Barndollar's oldest girl last week when I went to play bridge. Poor thing spent six months in New York and couldn't wait to come back home. I hardly recognized her, she was so thin and haunted-looking."

"Kate Barndollar was always thin and haunted-looking, Mom. Her nickname in school was Morticia."

"She was nothing like this," Bertie insisted. "Living in that horrible place all but did her in. Livvy tells me it's gotten so you can hardly walk from here to there without having to step right over a criminal or a crazy person. Poor Kate couldn't sleep nights on account of the screams and sirens. She felt so threatened, she took to walking around with one of those pepper sprays. And she stayed in after dark altogether."

I piled more potatoes on my plate, building a soft, squishy wall. "Sounds as if I'll have plenty of fascinating subjects to shoot."

Bertie puffed her exasperation. "I will never understand you, Anna. I swear. Don't you have any regard at all for your own safety?"

"Of course I do. I like myself a lot. Try not to worry, Mom, please. I promise. I'll be fine."

"You can't make that promise. Some things are simply beyond your control. I mean, as if going off to the jungles of Mexico wasn't bad enough."

"It was Mexico City, Mom. The closest I came to a jungle were plants in the hotel lobby."

"And what about running off to take pictures of that crazy bunch out in Idaho? They had guns, for Lord's sake. Bombs."

"They had no gripe with me. The worst threat I faced on that shoot was bad food. Place was the Spam capital of the universe. Everything in the town's only restaurant was made of Spam or a Spam substitute. I kid you not."

"El Salvador, then."

My cheeks flamed. "We've been over and over that one. Rick Marks was a friend of mine. The political mess he stepped in was over years before we went. Anyway, all I did was take pictures so the family could try to document what happened to him down there. You make it sound as if I joined the local guerrillas."

She took up the stone-handled silver carving knife and, with one brutal stroke, hobbled a chicken leg.

I blurted the rest. "I have an appointment to meet with Mr. Burlingame on the twenty-third. I've given notice at the shop and to my landlord. I'm going to fly up to New York next week. Shelby's invited me to stay with her until I find a place of my own."

Bertie's eyes dulled to slate. "Why did you tell us you wanted to come over to discuss this if you've already made up your mind?"

"I didn't come over to discuss it. I came to tell you that I'm planning to go. This is something I have to do, Mom. Please try to understand."

"I understand perfectly. You simply do as you please. What we think doesn't matter in the least."

"That's not true." I could not begin to express how far from the truth that was. Despite the uncanny talent I had for disappointing my mother, I craved her approval like a deep, painful thirst.

Her face drew in thought, and then brightened. "I've just had a wonderful idea. I bet if you went to the *Post and Courier* and told them you had an offer from that Burlingame place, they'd climb over themselves to give you a position right here in Charleston."

"Garden parties. Fund-raisers. Beauty pageants. I don't know if I could stand all the excitement."

"Are you suggesting there's something wrong with those things?"

"They're wrong for me. I've been trying for years to get a job working for a serious publication, doing serious stories. I simply can't pass up a chance like this."

My father frowned at his watch and pushed back from the table. "I hate to leave you lovely ladies, but I've got a meeting downtown at two."

"That's fine." I stood for his warm, engulfing hug.

Pulling back, he brushed the wispy strays from my forehead. His sad puppy look caught me like a sucker punch to the ribs. "We're going to miss having you nearby, Annie girl."

"New York isn't far, Pop. We'll see each other all the time."

He cleared his throat and wheeled away quickly. The screen door squealed shut as he trudged across the porch with his hands jammed deep in his pockets.

I trailed my mother into the kitchen. With sharp, angry moves she ripped plastic squares from the wall-mounted dispenser and wrapped the remains of the food. She scraped the dinner plates and scrubbed the porcelain until it squeaked in surrender.

"Can I help?" I ventured.

"No need. I'll just finish up here, then, if it doesn't interfere with all your big, important plans, maybe you can drop me off at the store. Better to keep busy. Not think about things."

My mother did not drive. Both of my parents had sentenced themselves to certain deprivations after my sister's death. Bertie let her driver's license expire, stopped tinting her hair and gave up her cleaning help. My father ceased taking pictures, a lifelong passion he had passed along to me. Sadly, the last shot he ever took was the one that ran in the national press for months beneath lurid headlines about my sister's unsolved case. It was taken right after my birthday party. Julie posed while Pop finished the last frames on the roll. His practiced eye captured a smiling little beauty with party-flushed cheeks, a wide blue stare and sun-shot ringlets, very much the angel in training she turned out to be.

I had been anything but. My mother's standard description of me as a little girl was *handful,* and I know that in her view, I remained a stubborn, willful, exasperating child. I could read the crushing disappointment in the set of her jaw and the Tupperware seal of her lips.

"Don't do this, Mom. Please. Being angry with me is not going to solve anything."

Bertie shook out a choking fog of Ajax and took out her frustrations on the sink.

"Who says I'm angry?" She took up the sprayer and hosed the bowl as if she were trying to quell a riot. With a resolute nod, she folded the dish towel. "I'll run up and get my purse."

"I'll get it for you."

"You needn't bother."

"I want to, Mom. Please stop."

The upstairs hall had the cool, closed-in feel of a cave. My old room was first on the right. At the doorway, I paused to scan the artifacts of my muddled adolescence: Guns N' Roses posters, paper pom-poms, prom souvenirs. Photographs I had taken over the years were tacked everywhere. Studied family portraits, crude candid shots, quirky bits that had caught my seeking eye.

My sister's room was next on the right and held the honored place closest to the master bedroom. Though the door was always locked and the windows shuttered, the space served as a nagging reminder, like a shard of shrapnel lodged too close to my heart to be removed safely.

Sibling rivalry was hard enough in a normal case, but Julie held an impossible advantage. How I longed for a standard-issue mortal sister, one who got pimples and PMS and disappointing grades. How I yearned to borrow my big sister's clothes, spill her secrets and tattle in delectable spite when she misbehaved. But Jewel was beyond misbehavior, untouchable, perfect in perpetuity.

Soon after the murder, my parents fled New York for Charleston, where my uncle Eli had settled with his wife, Irene. My folks moved in an attempt to leave the gruesome notoriety and the rest of the nightmare behind. Aunt Irene's family had deep roots in Charleston and useful connections. They helped my dad, who lacked the will to establish a new medical practice, find a good job as a consultant to a pharmaceutical company. They arranged for this house and helped set my mother up in the store.

My parents had a chance to make a new start here, but they had been unable or unwilling to leave the past behind. Early on, they had vowed to preserve Julie's things until her murderer was brought to justice. If it took forever, which now seemed to be the case, they were determined to keep that promise.

My sister's room in this house was a precise replica of the one she'd had in New York. That building had been torn down years ago, consumed by a giant high-rise. But here, the shrine was inviolate. There was the same brass bedstead and white wicker chest; the same rose-toned quilt and floral wallpaper. The identical bisque dolls and battered teddy bears perched on the windowsill. Her yellowing storybooks and antique games lined the shelves. Thirty-year-old party dresses gathered dust in the closet and ancient play clothes filled the dresser drawers. A pair of small red sneakers with rainbow laces lay akimbo beside the bed, exactly as they had on the night of the murder. Even the water glass my sister sipped from that night still rested on the nightstand.

Once, many years ago, I slipped the key from the bottom of my mother's lingerie drawer while my parents were out for the evening. I sneaked into Julie's room and pressed my lips to the rim of that glass. I ran my tongue across the cool smooth edge, searching for some trace of my sister. I braced for the taste of her spit or a hint of her breath, rank and musty with age, but I could not detect a thing. It occurred to me that my mother must have cleaned the glass thousands of times. Still, for weeks I felt guilty and ashamed, as if I'd committed some unforgivable sacrilege.

A pale yellow glow leaked out from under the door. Thirty years after the murder, the Snow White night-light beamed on. Every three months, my mother changed the bulb so that it would never burn out and strand my sister's delicate spirit in the dark. Every Friday afternoon, Bertie shut herself inside for an hour to dust and vacuum and set everything back in precise order. If I pressed my ear to the door and tuned out the buzz of cleaning noise, I could hear her singing Julie's favorite song, "Someday, My Prince Will Come."

For as long as I can remember, I have prayed for the killer to be caught. Surely, someday whoever did this would confess or make a mistake and my parents could convert the room into a study or a guest room or a den, anything but that gruesome shrine.

As a kid, I scanned the morning papers compulsively, convinced that the very next breaking story would be a solution to my sister's killing. Over the years, I've had the secret conviction that somehow, if I worked hard and long enough, I could clear up the mystery myself. My parents know nothing about this. They would never, in a million years, understand.

The first attempt, when I was about thirteen, began as an angry outburst, like hitting back at a bully who has finally crossed an inviolate line. But it quickly blossomed into a serious obsession. I spent every spare moment at the library, reading everything I could find about the "Sleeping Beauty Murder," as my sister's killing came to be called.

I ignored my friends and neglected my schoolwork and grew so pale and preoccupied, my mother hauled me to the pediatrician for a complete checkup though only four months had passed since the last one.

After ruling out a physical illness, Dr. Gotthelf advised my parents to take me to a child psychologist, a kindly snow-haired man named Dr. Eiseman. We played checkers once a week for a couple of months, which was somehow supposed to heal the unspecified emotional bruise. I remember taking exceptional care to keep my fears and feelings to myself. All Dr. Eiseman could possibly have learned about me in those months was that I liked to sit with my legs curled under my rear, that I preferred red disks to black and that I refused to move, under any circumstances, in reverse. We never talked about dead sisters or unsolved murders or obsessions that made a person come perilously close to flunking math. But somehow, slowly, my total absorption eased.

I have never fallen into quite that sorry a state again. But my sister's murder is never very far from my mind. Sometimes, in the middle of the night, an ancient question will bubble up to haunt me. Why had the cops let the handyman, my prime suspect, go? Why hadn't they tracked down and questioned that crazy man who'd startled Julie as she got off the day camp bus on the day of the murder? And what about that vagrant who'd exposed himself to several little girls in a nearby playground days earlier? Was he still in custody on the night when my sister was killed?

In my mother's view, the worst thing was knowing that the perpetrator still walked free, that he might have been anyone, the smiling counter man at the pizzeria down the block, Greg, the avuncular doorman, or Lenny, the giant slug who'd delivered the mail. The killer might have been a friend or a stranger, a random assailant or a cunning stalker who had been watching my sister and planning the murder for months. There was no one you could trust, not completely.

To me, the worst thing was the secret I held deep inside and showed to no one. Irrational though it may be, I have always felt responsible for my sister's death. I have tried to chalk this up to survivor guilt or some other facile excuse. But words are worse than useless, like trying to douse an electrical fire with water.

In one of my mental pictures from that night, I am striding barefoot along a hard, cold pipe. Julie, bound in a blindfold, has followed me into the danger unaware.

My toes curl with the struggle to hold my balance and my arch cramps hard as though cruel hands are squeezing my feet. Paralyzing terror trails a minuscule step behind. I feel its heat at the back of my neck and the pained kicking flutter of my heart. My ears fill with a breathy rush and the shrill of my own strangled cries. I must keep my focus fixed straight ahead. An errant blink, the slightest lapse and both of us might go plummeting into the void.

I take another step. One more. We are close to the end of the pipe, nearing safety. Then I hear my sister's voice.

What do you think you're doing, Annie Fanny? You're supposed to be in bed.

For a second, I forget myself. *Don't call me that. My name's not Annie Fanny, it's Anna Lee.*

Anna Banana. Annie Fanny.

Stop!

I stumble. My arms flail in comical rounds, seeking purchase in the vast, empty air. Somehow, I regain my footing. But when I glance back, my sister has vanished.

I understand that I have made her disappear, and I know with chilling certainty that the trick is irreversible.

Chapter 4

My mother broke her brooding silence as I angled to the curb in front of Bertie's Bridals. "A big shipment came in late yesterday for the Wilson wedding. If you have a couple of minutes, I could use some help getting it unpacked."

"Sure."

"I wouldn't ask, but my back's been acting up."

"I'm glad to help, Mom. Really. It's fine."

As a little girl, I adored spending Saturdays at my mother's King Street shop. If I was extraordinarily good, which was rare, or if my dad was tied up and no sitter could be found, which was blessedly common, my mother would dress me up, prime me with a long list of rules and warnings and take me along.

While Bertie practiced her best dress-rack diplomacy, I would crouch beneath the *peau de soie* and satin gowns and dream. On summer days when the air hung like steaming towels, I imagined that the puffy white skirts were great mounds of fresh-fallen snow. In the dreary dark of winter, I conjured broad-winged gulls circling a sun-washed beach. I was not permitted to snap real pictures in the shop, but I caught the best shots in my mind. In a blink of my imagination, the bridal frocks were transformed into beneficent ghosts or floating angels. Whipped cream. Plump roosting birds. Clouds.

Back then, before I had become—in my mother's eyes—a potential customer, I loved everything about the place. Bertie's sales voice seemed possessed of magical properties. So did her genius for pairing the bride and her attendants with perfect costumes for the stellar event.

Whenever the bell trilled, my mother would smooth her dress and hurry to the door to greet her customers. For ten minutes or so, they would sit in the circle of flowered chintz easy chairs at the back of the store. They would sip my mother's fawn-colored sun tea or fresh-squeezed lemonade and chat about the wedding plans.

Bertie listened raptly, cooing in delight as if she had never heard of anything quite so elegant and original before. Hundreds, maybe thousands of times, she exulted with undiminished passion over the idea of six-tier cakes with butter-cream rosebuds and fountains filled with pink champagne punch. No one would have imagined that all the while she was making complex, almost acrobatic calculations, involving geometry, physics, mechanical engineering and biometrics, which required precise analyses of the ways in which human bodies and the physical universe interact.

"Now then," Bertie would say, patting her thighs in punctuation. "Let's try a few things, shall we?"

She would pluck several fluffy confections from the racks and direct the bride to the dressing room, a peach-walled square with blush-colored carpeting and the very kindest light. I would peek through the gap between the frame and the door and take imaginary snapshots as my mother bunched the fabric in careful puffs and draped it over the bride-to-be.

In moments, every girl emerged from the dressing room transformed. The mousy ones stood straighter so their parts fell smoothly into place. Squat girls seemed to stretch and rangy ones waxed delicate and even perfect beauties were enhanced. Outsized bosoms shrank to gentle swells and curves were coaxed from chests flat as landing strips. Excess years fell away, and pregnant bulges vanished amid the frothy waves like tiny ships at sea.

My mother's powers of persuasion and observation had always been awesome to behold. But I did not wish to be the object of them, especially now.

With crisp moves, she unlocked the shop door and flipped the sign so the OPEN side faced out. As we crossed the threshold, the automatic bell trilled a greeting. Bertie worked the slim venetian blinds, fussed with the window display and flipped through the mail.

I searched for the pile of cartons. "Where's the shipment?"

"It can wait. Sit with me for a minute, Anna. There's something we need to discuss."

Reluctantly, I trailed her to the circle of flowered chairs. I braced for a sales pitch, maybe a curve ball, definitely something low and outside.

Bertie sat opposite me and smoothed her lavender skirt. "This is about Kevin, isn't it, sweetheart? Wanting to run away after a thing like that is perfectly natural. A broken engagement is such a disappointment. Believe me, I understand. I don't know if I told you this, but your father and I had a falling out just weeks before our wedding. Can't even remember what it was about, but at the time, I was simply devastated. I remember telling my folks that it was over, that they should go ahead and cancel the wedding and send back the gifts."

"It has nothing whatsoever to do with Kevin."

"You two have had fights before, Anna. You'll kiss and make up, just like always. Don't worry."

"Listen to me, Mom. Kevin is history. And even if he wasn't, I would still take this job."

"Certainly, dear. Of course you would."

"Please try to understand how important this is to me. It's been my dream for as long as I can remember."

Her gaze softened and strayed to the gowns. I imagined her sizing me up as a low bodice with long slim sleeves, a full skirt and cathedral train. I could hear her mental calculator: add height, emphasize the waistline and camouflage the well-upholstered butt. Sometimes, I suspect that my mother started mentally fitting me for a wedding gown *in utero*.

"There's no point in my talking if you don't bother to listen, Mom."

Bertie snapped alert as if I'd slapped her. "My word. What on Earth are you so angry about? I'm just trying to be supportive."

"Then support what I want to do."

"I'm sorry, Anna. I can't do that." She straightened the bow of her scarf, smoothed her hair. When her gray eyes fixed on me again, they were honed steel.

"Why not?"

"I don't know if you remember my mother. You were still pretty young when she died."

A murky picture formed in my mind. "Some things. I remember she smelled like medicine and always had a wadded tissue stuck in her sleeve. And she made these sniffling noises." I envisioned the old woman's arched nose twitching mouselike with something between curiosity and distaste.

Soon, another ancient memory bubbled up. It was a dinner at my grandmother's house, a dark oppressive railroad flat on the Upper West Side of Manhattan crammed with untouchable knickknacks and plastic-shrouded furniture. I sat on a wooden highchair in footed pajamas dotted with sailboats. Julie was beside me in a white organdy dress and party shoes. She was teaching me to sing the alphabet song. My tongue tickled with the curly run of *l-m-n-o-p*.

Suddenly, my grandmother clutched her chest and fluttered her eyelids and groaned. There was a rush of frantic response. Phone calls, shrill voices, angry rebukes. My sister and I were silenced sharply, wrenched from the table as if we'd committed some grievous sin.

Bertie's lips pressed in a grim line. "That's your grandmother Myrna, to a tee. Most of the time, she moped around the house or took to her bed with some dire ailment or the other. But every Sunday, rain or shine, she would get dressed up and meet with her lady friends downtown to have lunch and exchange complaints. My mother would talk about her weak heart and delicate stomach; the other women would discuss their fragile nerves and female problems and crushing headaches. My father used to call it the ladies' Sunday organ recital."

"Organ recital. That's priceless."

"You wouldn't think so if you had to live through it. Everyone considered my mother a frail, sickly soul who might shatter like one of her porcelain figurines if she weren't protected from bad news. I understood this from the time I was a very little girl. Even when I was sick or hurt, I knew not to burden her."

"That must have been tough."

She shrugged. "It was simply the way things were. I like to think I'm stronger for it. That I can deal with things. I know I give that impression, anyway. People seem to view me as the sort who always has everything pretty much in hand."

"That's true."

"If you want the real truth, my image is no more accurate than my mother's. She was no weakling, and I'm no tower of strength. That business—" This was her code for the unspeakable subject of my sister's murder. *That business.*

"I understand, Mom."

"No you don't. You can't possibly understand."

"All I'm doing is making a career move. This is a good thing, not some horrible catastrophe."

She stared at her hands. "I have a bad feeling. I can't explain."

"Because it's just that: a feeling. Nothing more."

"There is nothing more." She looked up and held me in her determined sights. "In the end, you need to trust yourself. Do what you absolutely know to be right."

"That's exactly what I am doing."

"Are you, Anna? Sometimes I honestly wonder."

A bell sounded at the front of the store. Customers entered in a rush of mild spring air and a trill of eager conversation.

My mother rearranged the scarf at her neck and tucked away her unruly emotions. "That must be Lily Pendleton. Her daughter just got engaged to the Larwin boy. She said she might stop by."

Chapter 5

A sea of revelers filled my uncle Eli's large Federal-style house on Battery Street. They spilled through the French doors and onto the lawn overlooking the concrete seawall. It looked as if the dam holding back Charleston's tide of social movers and seekers had collapsed.

Much of the enormous turnout was a tribute to the man. My uncle was well loved and universally respected. Intelligence and charm had garnered him acceptance in Charleston's most exclusive circles. He had been admitted into the Hibernians, an honor normally restricted to those whose familial taproots spread wide and deep. Most impressively, a place had been reserved for him in the "friends" cemetery at St. Philip's Episcopal Church. Under normal circumstances, anyone whose ancestors had not been born, bred, schooled and buried in Charleston for several generations at a minimum was relegated to burial on the "strangers" side across the road.

Everyone who was or wished to be anyone had accepted the invitation to this bon voyage party in my honor hastily recast from a Piccolo Spoleto celebration. My uncle's longtime secretary, Laurette Macon-Gray, had packed the list with friends, relatives, old school chums, neighbors and countless others I could not begin to place.

Everything had been organized with my uncle's typical generosity. Waiters in white jackets threaded through the crowd passing champagne and gorgeous hors d'oeuvres. Others whisked about to spirit away empties and discards. A galaxy of tiny lights twinkled in the magnolia trees and lavish bouquets graced the tables. An eight-piece orchestra accommodated requests, including half a dozen reprises of "Dixieland" and an equal number of "New York, New York."

A steady stream of guests pressed close, offering overwrought praise and good wishes. I forced myself to smile and dispense pleasantries like a Martha Stewart Pez machine.

As the cocktail hour drew to a close, Uncle Eli mounted the third step of the broad mahogany staircase. Looming over the crowd like an affable giant, he clacked his glass with a spoon.

"Most everyone knows I have a talent for making a short story long. But tonight, I'm going to keep it brief and to the point. The real talent in our family is my lovely niece Anna. Stewart Burlingame has recognized her gift, as those of us who know and love her have for years. I thank you all for coming out to help me toast her success and wish her a fine adventure. To Anna."

"To Anna!" roared the throng. Moist and waxen lips pressed my cheeks. Hands groped and passed me along in a game of human hot potato. I was showered with yet more exuberance. "What a marvelous thing!" "I'll be able to say I knew y'all when." "*Carpe diem,* honey." "Way to go!"

I caught a glimpse of my parents, huddled in the corner. My mother, who normally favored jelly-bean or cotton-candy colors, wore black. My father's expression was weary surrender.

"So, Anna honey, how long before we get to see one of your pictures on the front page of *USA Today*?" asked a squat, stocky man whose face flamed with bourbon and branch.

I searched my memory bank for the inquisitor's name, but I was hopelessly overdrawn. "We'll see," I said with all the faux Dixie coyness I could muster.

"You simply must look up our cousin Roy Jollette when you get to the Big Apple," said the towering copper blonde at his side. "We mentioned you were coming, and Roy said he'll be pleased as punch to show you around. That boy's made a positive killing in farm futures. Quite a catch." She pressed a business card into my palm and winked broadly.

"Jollette Consulting, Grains and Cattle," read the peacock blue italic. My imagination served up a weird hybrid, a good old boy in a Hermés tie and denim coveralls. I pictured Cousin Roy stuffed in a Ferrari with a prize sow at his side. I had no desire whatsoever to be that sow. "Thanks. I'll try."

"I'd do better than *try* if I were you, darlin'," the tall woman breathed. "Goin' after your little career is fine, but time keeps on ticking, if you catch my drift."

I did, and it reeked of cloying jasmine perfume. When a hand from behind clamped my shoulder, I seized the excuse to turn away.

My relief evaporated at the sight of Kevin Moultrie, my first love and former fiancé. He was sorely underdressed for the festivities in a T-shirt, dark jeans and running shoes. His sandy hair looked tousled, as if he'd just stumbled out of bed.

I winced at the unwelcome association. Somehow, Kevin always inspired me to think of bed and its more athletic connotations. No matter how I worked to reset the focus, this man still brought to mind galloping hormones and the risk of imminent discovery by the police patrol at Shem Creek's lovers' lane. He still caused me mild palpitations and a warm flush, which I had come to recognize as allergy symptoms.

"I thought you were out of town courting investors," I said. Kevin was a modern gold-miner, who did his panning with a business plan and fax machine, working with start-up Internet and biotech firms. His parents were outraged by his stubborn refusal to join them in a thriving furniture manufacturing business or, at the very least, to work in the family foundation. But as I had learned the hard way, Kevin was a hard steer to break.

"I came back early to see you before you left, Anna. We have to talk."

The party din had risen again to a roar. The caterer circled like a sheepdog, trying to herd the guests toward the triple tent where dinner was about to be served.

"This is not exactly the ideal time for a chat."

"I understand. Just give me five minutes."

He led me out through the kitchen, where half a dozen people in floppy toques scurried about. "Remember the diced cilantro," barked the head chef. "Baby carrots to the left."

Crossing the lawn, we were stopped by a group of celebrants.

"Look who's here. Our star. We're sure going to miss you, sugah," gushed a woman whose streaked red hair swirled atop her head like a cherry parfait.

"Thanks," I muttered.

"Who's that?" Kevin asked when we were safely out of range.

"No idea. I can't tell you how much I'm looking forward to some genuine, in-your-face, Northern hostility."

We had circled to the blind side of the garage. "That's what I wanted to talk about. You can't go. It's a terrible idea."

"Why is that?"

"I've done some asking around about Stewart Burlingame. You don't want to work for a guy like that. He's a shark."

"My uncle does business with him. If Burlingame had too many sets of teeth, Eli would be the first to walk away."

"Your uncle is in a different league. He's got enough muscle to put a guy like that on his best behavior. You go in unprotected, vulnerable. I know you. It's not going to work."

I had to smile. "My, my. Listen to you. I'm not a classic Mustang or a Harley-Davidson or even a boutique brewery beer and still, you seem genuinely concerned. I have to tell you, I am touched, Kevin, not to mention amazed."

"Can't you be serious for once?"

"Why would I want to do that?"

"Because I'm asking you to. Because I *am* genuinely concerned."

The swell of affection rose from ancient habit. I had been connected to this impossible character for much of my postpubescent life. Since the spring of eighth grade, we had functioned as an idiomatic phrase. We were invited together, thrown together, linked like parts of a chain. Nearly everyone, myself included, had presumed that we would someday get married, make a grown-up life together and have kids. But after a brief, disastrous engagement six months before, I had abandoned the fantasy and faced the truth. We already had the only kid we ever would, and it was Kevin. He suffered from a condition I've come to call Intention Deficit Disorder. Any time we came close to a permanent attachment, he ran like hell, stopping only when he hit someone else's mattress.

I kept telling myself that he didn't matter anymore, but a stubborn, irrational piece refused to listen. I hated that I still felt anything for him; I hated that the bruises he'd inflicted still throbbed as if they were raw and fresh.

I looked him straight in the steel-blue eyes. "Okay, here's the serious answer. Thanks for the concern, but it isn't necessary. I'm a big girl. I'll be fine."

His look hardened. "There's more."

"What?"

"This is not the time to talk about it. Just please trust me, Anna. It's the wrong thing to do right now. Delay it for a while at least. That's all I'm asking."

A nasty thought crept into my head. Could elusive Kevin be angling for reconciliation? Talk about wrong timing.

"Hear me, Kevin. I'm going to New York, and I'm going to work for Burlingame. Nothing you or anyone else says is going to change that." I hammered home the point with a hard glare.

"I'm telling you, it's a mistake."

"And I'm telling *you,* I've made up my mind. Now all I want to hear is good-bye and good luck."

"Good-bye and good luck." He pulled me close and kissed me deeply. I tasted his spicy breath and felt his probing tongue. He played me like a well-practiced instrument, stroking, coaxing and raising a rich crop of goose flesh.

I melted against him. Kevin hiked my skirt and cupped my rear and pressed hard against my crotch.

"Don't, Kev. No."

His fingers found the elastic of my panties and slipped beneath. He knew the control panel—start, warm up, go.

"I said *no.*"

I wrestled loose, smoothing my rumpled black linen dress as I strode away. Kevin's tirade trailed me as I hurried toward the house. "Would you stop acting like such a damned fool, Anna? Why can't you listen?"

Most of the guests had drifted into the tent. Unprepared to face them, I slipped into the house. I climbed the stairs to my uncle Eli's bedroom, a blue-walled oasis of calm filled with fine art and lovely antiques. The armoire was country French, and a Louis XIV chair perched beneath the bay window astride a pale Aubusson rug. In the bathroom, I doused my burning face with cold water and scowled at my shaken image in the mirror above the sink.

Back in my uncle's room, I paced angrily. My heart was galloping like a spooked horse. Damn Kevin.

I sought distraction in the family photo gallery over the fireplace. Eli's wife, Aunt Irene, had been a doe-eyed, raven-haired beauty with a high brow, sharp chin and patrician features. Her family had settled in Charleston in Colonial times and risen to local prominence. An infant daughter, who'd died of crib death, was a tiny replica of Aunt Irene. Their son Alan had favored Eli with his strapping build, wild cinnamon hair and ruddy, puckish face. But the resemblance, as I sharply recalled, ended with the physical similarity. Alan had been as loud and churlish as Eli was warm and dear. With a guilty twinge, I remembered my reaction on hearing about my young cousin's death all those years ago. My horror at the tragic accident had been blunted by the guilty, spiteful realization that I would never have to deal with that horrid budding terrorist ever again.

Stiff period portraits of the ancestors on both sides, dating back to the dawn of photography in the late 1830s, surrounded Aunt Irene and the children. I had an enormous family, if you counted the dead.

Hearing my uncle's limp in the hall, I turned away quickly, but as he entered the room, his eyes strayed to the pictures as if he sensed what I had been thinking.

"Remembering is good, sweetheart," he said gently. "It's what we do to honor the ones we've lost."

I allowed my eyes to drift back to the portraits. "I remember Aunt Irene's sugar cookies and her wonderful voice, so deep and throaty. I always wished I could sing like that."

"You have a lovely voice."

"Come on, Unc, the only way I can carry a tune is in a shopping bag."

"Well, it's lovely to me."

I traced the baby's face with a finger. "I was thinking how much Maggie looked like Aunt Irene. Such a little beauty."

"Yes. She was, and so sweet-natured. She barely ever cried and never showed the least bit of temper."

My gaze lit on Alan. "It's amazing how different kids can be."

"Yes." His face tensed with an odd look that I could not read.

"I'm sorry, Uncle E. I just meant that Alan was a strong personality."

He forced a brave smile. "Nothing to be sorry about. It's true. Please, sweetheart. Don't give it another thought."

Clearly, the painful subject needed to be changed. "It's a beautiful party, thanks."

"I'm glad you're enjoying it, Anna. And we should be getting back. But first, I wanted to see you alone, to give you this." He limped to his armoire, opened the door and retrieved a gift-wrapped box.

"You shouldn't have, Uncle E. All of this is too much."

"It's not a gift, just something I'd like you to have."

The box felt oddly heavy for its size. Beneath the silver paper was a red leather case inlaid with a scrolled gold-leaf border. Inside lay a shiny, snub-nosed pistol with gold engraving and a mother-of-pearl handle.

"It's a Lady Derringer, thirty-eight-caliber special. Looks dainty, but it's made for serious business."

I stared dumbstruck at the thing, trying to mask my revulsion.

"What, sweetheart? You look upset."

"I'm going to New York, not Dodge. I thought we agreed that the city is not the enemy."

"This has nothing to do with New York. It's about being prudent, taking care of yourself. I believe everyone should have a means of self-defense, just in case. Think of it like carrying an umbrella on a cloudy day. Best way to guarantee against rain."

I did not believe in umbrellas. A treacherous storm would wrench one out of your hands. Next thing you knew, you'd be poked in the eye with a jagged spoke and injured by your own laughable notion of defense. I held the gun gingerly, like a vial of lethal gas. I would feel better when it was safely packed away at the bottom of some hiding place I would elect to forget.

He took the pistol back and passed me a slip of paper with a hand-lettered name and address. "I'm going to have it shipped to this dealer I know in Manhattan. He'll take care of getting you the permit and all. All I'm asking is that you agree to have it around, sweetheart. Consider it a favor to me."

"All right, if it'll make you happy."

"It will, Anna. The world is unpredictable. People are unpredictable. The plain fact is you simply never know."

Chapter 6

Ted Callendar stared into Kelly Anson's kohl-rimmed eyes and willed the young woman to reveal herself. Four hours of hard probing had gotten him nowhere. He had asked all the necessary questions, studied every maddening detail. In a way, make that several ways, he had been more intimate with this woman then anyone else in long memory. Still, Callendar barely knew her any better than he had when the evening began.

True, he called her *Kelly* now. But that hardly counted as reasonable progress considering that he had seen her naked form from every conceivable angle. He had mapped and traced every mark on her milky suede skin, every scratch, every mole and patch of discoloration. She had a small butterfly tattoo on her right ankle, evidence of chronic intranasal irritation, a wormy appendectomy scar and a chipped right front tooth.

Callendar had seen her laid open, splayed and revealed, so her body was in many ways more familiar to him than his own. Her heart weighed 190 grams and was slightly enlarged. Her lungs were smooth, fluffy pink and unremarkable. Her gallbladder contained 10 cc of bronze-colored bile. She had evidence of chronic vaginal trauma and scarring of the fallopian tubes consistent with pelvic inflammatory disease. The cause of her death had been blunt injury and asphyxia. The manner of her death had been homicide. Her last meal was a burger with ketchup and mayonnaise, which she washed down with 10 mg of Valium and most of a bottle of cheap red wine.

One thing Kelly had not been was a health nut.

Callendar looked up from the autopsy report and rubbed his weary eyes. His attention drifted to the tube, where he could focus on a different sort of homicide, this one in progress. Top of the eighth, and the Indians were trouncing the Yanks, 10–zip. His beloved team had slid in the last two weeks from first place to underwater.

Ted Callendar took the whole thing very seriously and very, *very* personally. He blamed the twenty-five-million-dollar man: Daryl McKecknie. The highest paid player in baseball history, hired out of free agency during the offseason, had struck out his last ten times at bat. When he wasn't swatting flies, he was fumbling puffballs, acting as if he was afraid to break a nail. The only thing the clumsy oaf seemed to remember about the game was how to chew his cud and hawk great globs of bilious phlegm at the plate. For that, Callendar had to admit, his aim was still pretty remarkable.

Callendar found the remote under a takeout pizza box and stabbed the off button. More than the team, he was disgusted with himself. His was a prime field for burnout, and he was showing all the signs. His passion for the work had run out of juice. He found it tough to get up and out in the morning and even harder to keep going through the day. His energy level had sunk to emergency reserve. At this point, he was running on fumes and necessity.

Beside two crumpled cans of Heineken was a two-year-old picture of his daughters. Madison had bloomed since then from a scrawny, clingy ten-year-old into a self-possessed, frighteningly independent adolescent. Cody, a year younger, had always been a smart, cheeky kid, and her teenage rebellion promised to register a big number on the Richter scale.

The divorce didn't help, though it had been an unquestionable necessity. He and Janice had started out like most couples: in deep, twirly-eyed love. Then, when their vision cleared about a year into the marriage, they found that they disagreed on just about everything.

By that time, Madison was a fact and Cody an impending reality. Callendar winced remembering the endless battle he and his ex-wife had engaged in over every issue from the color of the nursery walls to what the babies would be called. He leaned toward classical or biblical names that had passed the test of social hiccup and endured. Also, he had wanted to name at least one of the girls in memory of his father, as was Jewish tradition. But Janice had detested the old man, who had died the year before, and she refused to have her kids saddled with anything to do with him.

His ex was determined to ride the crest of any current wave. Place names were in, so their daughters would be named for cities in Wisconsin and Wyoming, where they had never even been. Janice won that round as she did most of them. Callendar had only so much fight in him, and he had exhausted most of that early in the match. He had taken what he could until he was incapable of bearing any more. The marriage had ended eighteen months ago in a TKO.

At least, two excellent things had come of it. He smiled at the picture of his girls and found the will to pick up the Kelly Anson case file one more time.

Again, he read through the preliminary facts. Three years ago last month, the manager of a no-tell hotel in Times Square had discovered the body. Kelly normally checked out less than an hour after she showed up with her latest trick, but this time she had spent the night. When the manager went to collect what she owed him in overtime the following morning, he found her nude corpse on the floor. Livid bruises covered the body and circled her neck. The furniture, such as it was, had been trashed.

The case was no mystery. Everyone knew that Kelly's pimp, a vicious punk known as "Gorgeous Jorge," had murdered the girl. The motive boiled down to a simple multiple choice. Either she had threatened to quit, lied about her take or failed to turn enough business. For the Gorgeous Jorges of the world, any of those was more than sufficient grounds for murder.

The case had gone cold for the usual reasons. Jorge had the power and pockets deep enough to buy top-notch legal help. Kelly lived on the edge of the fringe. Few people in the Deuce, as the neighborhood around West Forty-second Street was called, had more than a passing awareness of her. Most, including the homicide squad that caught her case, could not get it up to care very much when she died. They viewed it as a basic occupational hazard or a street-cleaning operation. No major loss, either way.

In the crime-scene shots, Kelly looked every bit her part: a low-end whore with a burgeoning coke habit and precious little self-respect. She already looked ten years older than the eighteen she was.

Most murders came down to gangs, drugs or greed, and in Kelly's case, all three had been operative. In addition to his string of girls, Jorge ran a pack of teenage terrorists out of the South Bronx.

What had Callendar stumped was Kelly Anson herself. Detectives on the case had tracked down her family through her driver's license. The Ansons still lived in the house where Kelly grew up, a gracious four-bedroom Colonial on a large wooded lot in Stamford, Connecticut. Neighbors, teachers and friends had corroborated her parents' account, that Kelly had been a sweet, solid kid. Never any trouble. By all accounts, she had been raised with all the meaningful advantages. Her parents were fine, caring people, active in the community, loving and good to their kids. Her three siblings—two boys, one girl—had turned out fine.

Kelly had shown academic promise and considerable artistic talent, garnering prizes and several scholarship offers for her sculpture. The girl had chosen to go to Pratt, where she would have access to New York's great galleries and museums. Her folks had delivered her to her dorm room for orientation along with the standard complement of personal and electronic student paraphernalia. But for reasons that remained the major mystery in the case, she had failed to register and moved out before classes began.

Kelly had called home to report that she was all right, but had decided against continuing her education. She would tell her parents nothing more, not even where or how she planned to live. Worried sick, they begged their youngest child to come home, but the girl would not budge. Afterward, they tried several times to find her, but failed, even with the aid of a private investigator and several desperate calls to the NYPD.

Their only comfort was that Kelly had given her word that she would call home every Saturday. For six months, their daughter kept that promise religiously.

Then suddenly, she did not.

A week later, two city cops rang their bell and informed the Ansons that they need not worry about their daughter anymore.

As a forensic psychologist, Callendar took a cold, clinical view of situations like this. He had seen all kinds of lives, even seemingly strong and solid ones, shattered on the rocks of whim and circumstance. The human psyche was a fragile, highly complex mechanism that could break down in a staggering variety of ways. In the worst case, the damage led to a refrigerated drawer in the morgue and a toe tag.

But as the father of two little girls, his professional detachment collapsed. The Kelly Anson case made him furious and scared him to the bone. How could he protect his own kids from a monstrous end like that? All it took was one tiny step in the wrong direction followed by another and another, and then—

Callendar speed-dialed his former home. His stomach fisted at the sound of Janice's phony, maple-syrup voice on the answering machine. Her anti-Semitic phase had been followed by a stint at Buddhism, which preceded her ovo-lacto vegetarian, anti-fur activist period. Her latest kick was vintage seventies universal love, which of course did not include peace and forgiveness for him. Along with the indigent gypsy wardrobe, she had adopted a Romper Room voice and a smiley-face personality.

Please, please, don't hang up. We're delighted to hear from you and we're going to call you back just as soon as we can! Leave a message for Janice, Madison or Cody after the beep. God bless, and have a wonderful day.

Callendar hung up, thankful that he wasn't diabetic. He was also grateful that he didn't have to leave a message. Cody always checked the caller ID as soon as she walked in the door. The girls would call him back.

He flipped on the set again in time to watch McKecknie bumble an easy get in left field. On his next at-bat, the ape registered his eleventh consecutive strikeout, ending the game though not the misery. Daryl the dud had a five-year deal. Callendar seriously doubted that his high-powered agent and army of lawyers had left any dangling loopholes. He shot the bird at McKecknie's retreating back as the station cut to commercial. He killed the set and made for the kitchen. He was about to drown his sorrows in a pint of chocolate mint chip ice cream when the phone rang. He dashed for it, anxious to speak to his girls. They liked to call together, conference him in.

"Hey, my little honeys, what's up?"

There was no one on the line, nothing but a dial tone. Then the ring blared again, and he traced it to the phone across the room. That was a tie line to the

Arcanum, a volunteer group of diverse forensic experts that investigated long-unsolved homicides. When he took over as head of the intake committee six months before, Callendar had agreed to have the line installed at home, but most of the requests for their help came by mail. That was how they came to consider the Kelly Anson case. The rare phone call he took on the group's behalf normally came during reasonable business hours.

He picked up, allowing only a trace of his annoyance to seep out.

"I'm sorry to bother you. I wanted to leave a message for the Arcanum. I didn't expect anyone to answer at this hour."

Callendar's irritation evaporated at the caller's brittle tone. "That's okay, ma'am. How can I help you?"

As her story unfolded, Callendar's heart started thwacking like a jack-hammer. It felt like waking up after a long, long sleep.

Chapter 7

The approach to New York's La Guardia Airport is cleverly designed to snap one's hair follicles to attention. Planes stream in a mere heartbeat apart, then swoop onto runways set on a harrowing collision course with Flushing Bay.

The move and my mother's dark predictions had my nerves on screaming red alert. I couldn't shake the conviction that I was doomed to pay mightily for my good fortune in landing a job with Burlingame. I envisioned fate hanging around with a smirk on its face, waiting to crush me with some giant cosmic joke.

At times, the superstition took on eerily human form. For several days, I'd had the disquieting sense that I was being watched. Even today, as I trudged through the airport lugging my motley possessions, I thought I spied a large, shadowy figure out of the corner of my eye. He vanished, as imaginary threats tend to do when confronted squarely, but that did nothing to quiet my galloping neuroses.

On the descent I plucked the safety card from the seat and read about emergency exits, life vests, inflatable slides. I read the German, Spanish and French translations and tried the Japanese. I even counted the exclamation points, which abounded. *Remain calm!! Place oxygen mask on children first!! Life vests under seat!!* Anything to distract me from thoughts about the substance abuse rates among pilots and air traffic controllers or the fallibility of radar. Words like *human error* trounced through my mind. *Scattered wreckage. Dental records. Next of kin.*

The woman seated beside me had her bronzed legs crossed at mid-thigh. She sported three-inch heels, thin as bug feelers. Vividly, I imagined them puncturing the emergency slide, trapping the rest of us in this giant sardine tin full of highly flammable fuel. I was tempted to pull the shoes off her stupid feet, but before I had time to assault the reckless twit, we bumped down and jolted to a terrifying stop.

At first, I failed to spot my friend Shelby, who stood amid the cluster of limousine drivers beside the baggage carousel. As I wandered around, bug-eyed with the commotion, she called my name and rushed up to me, waving a hand-lettered welcome sign on a Popsicle stick. We embraced with noisy fervor. Her dark curly hair tickled my nose.

"You didn't have to come, Shel. I was all set to hop in a cab."

"So you'll hop in mine. I promise not to overcharge you or get you lost."

"Damn. I was hoping for a real taste of the Big Apple."

"Fine. We'll go to Central Park later and get you mugged. How's that?" Her huge brown eyes went liquid. "I can't believe you're actually here."

"Believe me, neither can I. I was fully expecting my mother to hijack the plane and force us back to South Carolina."

I hugged her again. Three kids had not thickened Shelby's lithe body or modified her signature mode of dress: black shirt, black slacks, black purse, belt and shoes. As far back as junior high school, her closet resembled a total eclipse. Shelby knew how to read the various garments by touch, how to distinguish between a dozen nearly identical skirts, slacks and blazers. Like so many things about her, it was truly impressive.

"Come. Let's grab your bags."

With her usual efficiency, my friend negotiated the luggage crush and the people push and the perilous crossing to the parking garage. She seemed unfazed by the kamikaze cabs and runaway shuttle buses. I was content to tag along like a leashed pet, happily sniffing the engine fumes, jaw gaping with astonishment.

Soon, we were settled in Shelby's black Range Rover with my mongrel duffel bags and camera equipment piled in the rear. She navigated the mazelike airport exit, and in moments we were creeping along the Grand Central Parkway toward the city.

All the anticipatory tension of the flight and the past two weeks drained away. All my complex emotions about being in the city faded to background noise. Being with Shelby felt exactly right. Our brand of friendship offered absolute product reliability and unlimited shelf life. No matter how much time passed between visits or calls, we retained the same easy closeness.

I attribute this to our somber decision as ten-year-olds to adopt each other as sisters. Shelby had four brothers, or as she liked to put it, no one useful. I thought of myself as an inadequate remainder, a less-than-only child.

After several planning meetings in her backyard playhouse, we concluded that the standard pinprick and commingling of blood would not suffice. Our arrangement had to be legally binding. Shelby's dad was a lawyer, so we retained him to hammer out the fine points and draw up a contract. We made a fee-for-service deal, agreeing to bake him a dozen Toll House cookies every week for a year. This turned out to be highly advantageous for us when he started putting on weight and forgave the debt after a month.

Watching Shelby behind the wheel, I had to smile. She was still so like the willowy owl-eyed girl who sat behind me for most of elementary school. Back then, her name was Shelby Jennings, but though she followed me alphabetically, in every other way she had always been light-years ahead.

While I was still grappling with basic geometry and the fundamentals of acne, Shelby breezed through high school in three years and went on to

Yale as a dual major in chemistry and classics. While I was still desperately underfunded for a training bra, Shelby sprouted honeydew breasts and come-hither hips and the kind of endless, lathe-turned legs that turned otherwise rational men into drooling, stumble-tongued buffoons.

Given that, it was hardly surprising that my friend now had a flourishing psychiatric practice, three boisterous little kids and all the appurtenances of an actual adult life while I was still struggling to wrestle my uncertain future out of the box.

I stared out the window, mesmerized by the vast urban sprawl. Despite the tourist glut, runaway development and a booming economy, Charleston retained its laid-back, low-rise, small-town Southern feel. Here, traffic lurched in a cacophony of horns and squealing brakes. Giant buildings huddled close, crowding out the sky. Pulsing, flashing, beckoning signs perched everywhere.

I plucked the lens cap from my Canon and rolled down the window. I snapped a cemetery so crammed with stones, it appeared as if the dead here must be buried standing up. I captured a row of dilapidated factories with shattered windows. Shea Stadium. There was the once futuristic site of the 1964 World's Fair. Clicking furiously, I recorded my first glimpse in thirty years of the famed city skyline, perched in glittery splendor against the dusk. I started to believe that I could know this place, shrink it to manageable size. This was a vibrant, incredible city, not at all the horror central of my mother's worst nightmares. I kept shooting frame after frame until Shelby's silence grew too heavy to ignore.

I set the camera down. "What's wrong, Shel? Speak to me."

She pulled a ragged breath. "I hate to dump this on you at a time like this, but I'm afraid it can't wait. Harvey and I are having problems. Major ones."

"What?" Then, catching the rest, I added, "Who?"

"His personal trainer. Her name is Kim. Harvey admitted the affair a few months ago. Claimed it was a meaningless fling and that he was done with her. We went to counseling, talked things out, and I honestly thought we'd gotten past it." She braced against the seat. "Then last night, he told me he was going to an industry dinner. He said I shouldn't bother to come along, that it was going to be one of those deadly boring things with rubber chicken and interminable speeches. He came home at three in the morning, freshly showered. I guess he expected me to be asleep. Seems as if I've been asleep for months, maybe years. Lord, Anna. I'm a psychiatrist. I'm supposed to be an expert on human behavior. I feel like such a damned fool."

"Harvey's the fool, not you." I had always thought there was far less to Shelby's husband than met the eye, but for the sake of the friendship, I had done my best to like the wormy, overbearing creep.

Shelby fiddled with her wedding band, running it up over the knuckle, then shoving it angrily back in place. "You wouldn't say that if you knew the idiotic things I've done. The gym this Kim person works in is near Harvey's office. One day I went there to have a look at her. I tried to talk myself out of it, but I couldn't. I guess I needed to size up the competition."

I could relate. I had gone that route with one or two of Kevin's side dishes. "Sounds reasonable to me."

"It wasn't even close. I told the manager I wanted to try the place out. I signed in with a phony name and disguised myself with a baseball cap and dark glasses. I used everything but the fake nose, like something out of a Groucho Marx movie. I trailed Kim around for most of a morning, studying her, eavesdropping, fascinated and repulsed. You should see her. She defies gravity this woman, her brain, her body, everything. And you know what she believes in, what she honestly thinks is the secret of the universe?"

"What?"

"Kim has a theory that you can fool your body into losing weight by pairing unlikely foods. She's convinced that if you eat, say, chocolate with anchovies or tuna salad with whipped cream and honey that the pounds will simply melt away. She plans to write a book about it, using herself as a living example. That flea-brained bimbo has no idea that what she's hit upon is a recipe for inducing nausea. I felt like suggesting she call it *The Appetite Assassination Diet* or maybe: *Gag Yourself Thin.*"

"*Gag Yourself Thin,* by Kim from the Gym. Perfect." I had to laugh, and for a moment, Shelby joined me. Then her face warped with pain. "The whole thing seems so unbelievable. How could he break up our family for that?"

"The hell with him, Shel. It's his loss."

"It's not that simple. We've got kids, a home, endless entanglements."

"You are hands down the most capable person I know. You'll deal with this. I know you will."

Shelby squeezed my hand. "Thanks. I need to hear that, early and often. This kind of thing isn't exactly what you'd call a confidence booster."

"I know. Kevin put me in the same spot a time or two. Thankfully, we didn't get related. But there are remedies for that. Do you know a good lawyer?"

"If it comes to that."

"If?"

We were approaching the turnoff for the Fifty-ninth Street Bridge. "I know this may be hard for you to understand, but I'm not ready to give up. We've agreed to go back to the counselor, give it another try."

I was appalled. How could this brilliant, beautiful, accomplished, all-around fabulous young woman subject herself to ego-assassination by that third-rate dick-brained jerk? If word got out that she was on the loose again, hordes of far better men would line up, take numbers. "Whatever's right for you, Shel," I forced myself to say.

I held back the stream of invective and outrage. I couldn't conceive of staying with someone who subjected me to that kind of humiliation. That's why I had finally broken it off with Kevin. His straying was too hurtful, too damaging. Obviously, so was Harvey's, yet my friend seemed willing to put up with it. I love Shelby fiercely, but she is written in a language that I will never fully comprehend.

"I'm trying to do what's right, but it's not just about me. Divorce is hard on everyone. I see it in my practice all the time. Being shuttled back and forth between parents is tough and confusing at best. I want my kids to have the fantasy, the whole Ozzie and Harriet. But then I think I'm not doing them any favor if Ozzie turns out to be a hopeless womanizer and Harriet plays doormat. What kind of role models would that give them? But then I think, it isn't right to just give up. People can change if they put their minds to it."

Shelby followed the signs to the bridge lower roadway. Her building, a rippling brown and tan structure, loomed mere blocks away. "Everything's just such a mess right now." She shot a sheepish look my way, and then glued her giant eyes back on the road.

"Look, Shel. The last thing you need at a time like this is company."

"No. That's okay. I asked you to stay. Harvey has moved into the guest room for the time being, but we'll manage. You can bunk with the girls, or I can move the baby in with me."

"Absolutely not. The right answer is for me to go to a hotel. I'll be more comfortable and so will you."

"You sure?"

"Positive."

Shelby fished in her purse for a cell phone. "I'll call and find you something terrific, then. On me."

"Yes to the call, my phone's about out of battery. No, thanks, to the housing scholarship. It's sweet but not necessary."

"Please let me do that much, Anna. I feel responsible, not to mention guilty."

"Guilt is good. Next time I need an outrageous favor, you get the call."

"Anything. Anytime. You know that."

Shelby dialed several midtown hotels. The Grand Hyatt was the first to boast a vacancy.

The bellhop heaped my duffel bags onto a brass cart and led me into the cavernous lobby. I held the smile until Shelby slipped into the traffic stream on Forty-second Street.

I felt like a lost, lonely kid. I had been looking forward to a couple of days under Shelby's comforting wing, getting to know her little ones better, catching up. But sometimes things simply slip off the careful course you set.

Chapter 8

Griffey was miffed at the duck. From across the table, Clu Baldwin caught the subtle signs. As his wise glance grazed the scrawny breast of fowl on his plate, the man's dense brow drooped a fraction and he issued a minuscule sigh.

Clu alone noticed the rare slump in Griffey's strikingly constant good nature. The three dozen other pairs of eyes in the room were politely fixed on C. Melton Frame, a barrel-shaped man capped by a pale walrus mustache and a black toupee that oozed across his head like an oil spill. Dressed in a Chesterfield jacket and paisley ascot, Frame had commandeered the podium, taken the microphone hostage and spent the past fifteen minutes strafing the group with his standard litany of stellar accomplishments.

Scorsese had optioned his latest best-seller as a feature film. His next book would soon be published to a forty-city tour, featured in an Oprah segment and a million-copy print run. Meanwhile, he had been tapped to chair a special presidential commission on urban crime, short-listed for this and the other thing and elected unanimously for the prestigious Lifetime Achievement Award by the International Association of Forensic Analysts. Sadly, the awards ceremony would conflict with graduation at Stanford University, where Frame had been asked to give the commencement address and receive yet another of those tiresome honorary doctorates people were forever forcing on him. Clu's brain started to fizz like a sleeping foot.

Frame took a promising step away from the podium, but he quickly returned. "I almost forgot. I wanted to share something with you that I've found really life enhancing. I've decided not to give any more autographs. No exceptions. I agreed to do a signing at Barnes and Noble last week. *Quel* mistake. It was scheduled to last two hours, but there was such a mob, I simply couldn't escape for close to three and a half. The fans were so impossibly demanding, I thought my arm would fall off. Honestly."

Clu coughed to mask an unstoppable yawn. Frame, cofounder and self-appointed Chief Muckety-muck for life, held forth like this at the start of every monthly meeting of the Arcanum. The long unsolved murder cases the society took on, chosen from the many submissions received each month, were compelling and fascinating. The results, when a vexing puzzle could be solved and justice served, were gratifying beyond Clu's most optimistic imaginings. Most of the members were seasoned, knowledgeable professionals who brought impressive energy, selfless dedication and boundless intelligence to the collective enterprise. Some were downright brilliant, most notably Solomon Griffey, an internationally renowned forensic scientist, whose DNA testing methodology had changed the face and scope of criminal prosecution.

Clu, who had been inducted into the invitation-only group less than a year ago, remained awed by Griffey's achievements, though she had long since come to consider him a friend. He was a dear, gentle, reasonable, equable soul, qualities which self-important fools like Frame tended to mistake for a kick-me sign.

"I see that we're about to get down to the most serious business of the meeting, which of course is—dinner."

A few people joined in Frame's self-appreciative laughter as the blowhard swaggered to his chair. He carried himself as if he owned the place, if not the universe at large. In fact, Solomon Griffey, and not Melton Frame, had provided the Arcanum's entrée into this magnificent room at the Calibre Club, the international think tank headquartered in an elegant brownstone on Manhattan's East Sixty-fifth Street. Inclusion in the club, which strove to provide a catalyst and forum for positive humanitarian change, was akin to receiving a Nobel Prize or a MacArthur Genius Award. Members like Griffey tended to come up with life-enhancing notions over chess games or casual cups of tea.

As soon as Frame wedged his bulky bottom in the seat, the white-coated waiter appeared, bearing a silver warming dome on a tray. He lifted the dome with dramatic flair to reveal rare filet mignon cradled by bordelaise sauce, asparagus spears and a ring of dauphine potatoes.

"There you go, sir."

Frame kissed his fingertips. "Looks brilliant, Roger. Good man."

Griffey cast one longing look at the steak, which should have been *his* by any reasonable definition of justice. Frame always showed up late, but tonight he had outdone himself, arriving more than an hour after the rest of the group. Lyman Trupin, a charter Arcanum member and former director of the FBI, had finally suggested that perhaps Frame was to be a no-show and called for the proceedings to begin. Griffey had just ordered the filet when Frame sauntered in and claimed his habitual place at the head of the head table.

"I'll have the same," he bellowed before dear Griffey had a chance to punctuate the request with his usual diffident smile.

When the waiter explained that Griffey had just reserved the last portion, Frame dismissed the unthinkable slight with a backhanded swipe. "Tell the chef it's for me."

"I would gladly, sir. But I'm quite sure that's all we have."

Frame sniffed, flaring his outsized nostrils like a bull. "Be a good old chap and have something else, won't you, Griff? A nice piece of duck, perhaps. You'd like that."

Before Griffey had the chance to respond, Frame clapped him painfully hard between his shoulder blades. "It's all settled, then. Make sure you tell the chef I want that steak rare, Roger. Charred on the outside, nice and juicy in."

Now the rotten bully was rubbing it in, making raucous pleasure noises as he chewed. Clu was sorely tempted to march her rangy frame over and dump the plate on his head. She imagined the bloody juices running down his pathetic boot-black rug, staining his stupid mustache.

Ted Callendar rose to introduce the latest case. Half a foot taller than Frame, Callendar stooped to aim his voice nearer the microphone. "We have a rather unusual situation this evening. As most of you know, after reviewing all the new, valid applications, the intake committee had agreed that we would consider the Kelly Anson murder this month, but I had a phone call late last evening that changed my mind. I realize this violates standard procedure, but I'd like to ask the members' indulgence."

Frame sputtered his objections through a mouthful of meat. "You're absolutely right, Ted. It is a *clear* violation. Whatever it is will have to wait for next month."

"Unfortunately, it can't. This happens to be a time-sensitive matter, Melton. Let me explain."

"I simply cannot permit that. The rules are perfectly clear."

Clu smirked behind her long-fingered hand. Frame's frantic protests had nothing to do with the rules. His assistant, a crack researcher, always armed him with detailed crib sheets on the scheduled case, including suggestions for provocative comments and pointed questions that he could make during the Q & A that followed the review of the facts. Frame would never dream of playing on a level field. He might lose.

Griffey cleared his throat and stood—an assertion so unusual that everyone instantly fell silent and strained to hear what he had to say in his quivering filament of a voice. "As I understand it, the Arcanum's charter is to serve justice by investigating the most pressing unsolved homicides that are brought to our attention. If that is in fact the case, I move that we suspend standard procedure and hear what Mr. Callendar has to report."

"Second," Clu said.

The motion carried quickly over Frame's apoplectic cries.

Callendar, an expert in psychological profiling, referred to his notes. "The call came in shortly after ten P.M. on the Arcanum tie line at my home. The caller was a woman who asked at first to remain anonymous. Her identity was blocked on my caller ID. Normally, I would have written her off as one of those crackpot crime groupies who phone from time to time, but something in her tone moved me to take her seriously.

"She told me she had heard of our group and wondered how we went about selecting the cases we agreed to review. What was the oldest murder we had ever investigated, she wanted to know. What was our success rate? Why were we able to succeed where others had failed? Precisely what magical methodologies did we use?

"I engaged her in conversation until I felt that we had established some basic trust. Then I asked if there was a particular case she had in mind."

Callendar cleared his throat. "She became highly agitated. She claimed that she was in a serious, possibly *dangerous* situation. Terrible things might happen if the facts of the matter got out. But I continued to reassure her that everything presented to the society is held in strictest confidence, that we protect our subjects and sources. Eventually, slowly, she began to open up.

"She told me that her daughter was murdered many years ago and that despite an all-out investigation and numerous serious suspects, no arrests were ever made. Now, she is convinced that whoever committed the crime has resurfaced. She believes that the killer is playing games with her, possibly trying to drive her insane."

Callendar consulted his notes again. "Apparently, the victim wore a baby bracelet, which spelled out her name in alphabet beads. She never took it off, even to bathe or sleep, so when it turned up missing from the body, detectives on the case presumed that the killer had taken it as a souvenir. This was one of the details that the police kept from the press to foil false confessions."

"Souvenir collecting is quite common in homicides," Frame observed grandly, as if he alone among the assembled experts had knowledge of that elementary fact.

Callendar ignored him with commendable restraint. "At that point, the caller broke down. When she regained her composure, she explained that she has maintained the little girl's room exactly as it had been on the night of the killing. She is the only one who ever goes inside, and that is only once a week to clean. Otherwise, the bedroom is kept locked and shuttered at all times. She keeps the only key hidden in her dresser.

"Last week, while she was running the vacuum, she heard a strange noise. When she examined the machine, she discovered a small white bead identical to the ones on the missing bracelet. The letter *J* was stamped on two sides.

"The carpet had been moved from the murder scene to her current residence two years after the child was killed. She had cleaned the room countless times since, but she reasoned that somehow, she had never passed the vacuum over that particular place in the carpeting in that particular way. She presumed that the bracelet must have been broken in the lethal struggle, and that the perpetrator had taken the rest of the beads but failed to find the *J*."

"Any outside cleaning help?" asked Mike Saitas from the rear of the room.

"None," Callendar said. "And none of the other usual suspects. No boarders, no houseguests, no recent repair people."

"Pets?" Saitas persisted. "An animal could have picked up the bead from some other, less obvious place and deposited it in the little girl's room."

"I asked that. Negative."

"We have not agreed to take on the case yet," Frame griped. "These tiresome questions are unnecessary and highly inappropriate at this point."

Callendar nodded, conceding the point. "She considered reporting the find to the precinct that's still technically in charge of the investigation, but decided against it. She assumed the police would dismiss her and the news as time-wasting nonsense. No one had taken any particular interest in the case in more years than she cared to consider, though in some ways she supposed that was fortunate. She could not bear the thought of reporters descending again, perhaps casting their suspicions on her or her husband as they had so many years ago when police failed to turned up a credible outside suspect."

Trupin sprang to his feet. "If you're talking about the Sleeping Beauty Murder, hurry up and get to the punch line, Ted. We've been aching to sink our teeth into that one for years."

Clu seconded that, too. Her maternal grandfather, Jimmy Cluny, for whom she was named, had sparked her interest in forensic analysis in general and the Sleeping Beauty case in particular. At the time of the murder, Grandpa Jim had been a detective on the NYPD. Like several others, he had gotten close enough to the botched Julie Jameson murder investigation to have his hard-earned reputation singed by it. Sadly, that happened in the final year of his tenure on the force. He carried the failure with him to his grave.

Unfortunately, no one with valid standing, notably a relative or investigator who had worked on the case, had sought the society's help. Without such a request, the Arcanum could not get involved. None of them was willing to bend that fundamental rule. They could not afford to waste their limited resources trying to knock down brick walls.

Callendar tamped the air. "Bear with me, Lyman, please. I'm almost there.

"The caller told me she got down on her hands and knees and went over every inch of the carpet searching for other parts of the bracelet, but she found nothing. Then, last Friday, when she went in to clean the room, she discovered a bead on the bed stamped with a letter *U* and three more in the upturned paw of a teddy bear on the windowsill that spelled out *L-I-E*. She fled the room in terror and called her husband at work. He rushed home and arrived in under half an hour, but when she led him into the bedroom to show him what she had found, the letters had vanished." Callendar paused and filled his chest. "And yes, the caller identified herself as Alberta Jameson, Julie Jameson's mother. I believe that explains the urgency of the matter."

Clu's expertise was forensic linguistics. During her more than forty years in the field, she had analyzed syntax, semantics and vocal quality to judge a subject's mental state, background and veracity. She had been called in on numerous cases to analyze suicide notes and ransom demands, not to mention written or taped threats from terrorist groups, stalkers and assorted other monsters. She would have given anything to have been on the receiving end of the call Callendar described. She ached to suck up every syllable and nuance. "You're suggesting she sounded suicidal, Ted?"

"In my opinion, it's a very real possibility."

Griffey's dense brow sank. "And if that happens, the truth could die with her. You were absolutely right to bring this to the group's immediate attention, Ted. No victim deserves vindication more than that innocent little girl. Having that case go cold always struck me as the worst form of obscenity."

The force behind his softly spoken words struck Clu. Griffey had a remarkable way of holding listeners in his reticent thrall. "Was there anything you picked up aside from the obvious guilt-induced hallucinations?"

"You can hear for yourself." Callendar produced a small portable recorder, but before he could press the play button, Frame shot up from his chair. "I'll remind you that what you're holding represents the fruit of an illegal wiretap, Mr. Callendar. The Arcanum does not engage in such activities, not as long as I have any say in the matter. I hardly think that justice ignored is justice served."

"What if I told you that I informed Mrs. Jameson about the tape?"

"I'm afraid I'd be forced to doubt you," Frame huffed. "It is hardly believable that a fearful, agitated woman such as you describe would agree to have such a conversation recorded. Now my suggestion is that we proceed with a review of the Kelly Anson case as scheduled and put all this other questionable business aside."

"Mr. Callendar's word is more than sufficient for me. I move that we hear the tape, then open the case to anyone who cares to volunteer," Griffey said.

Frame was overruled again. Clu's heart thumped wildly as Callendar switched on the recorder.

The woman's voice was a desperate shrill. *The monster who killed that little girl has to be stopped before someone else is harmed. I keep thinking that the only reasonable answer is to assassinate us all. Make sure anyone who knows anything about Julie's murder is silenced permanently. Until then we are all in dreadful danger. Please, Mr. Callendar, I can't go on like this much longer. You people are my only hope.*

Clu shuddered as her practiced ear caught the missing beats. The woman was clearly lying. But what was the truth? And how would they get to it before any of her chilling predictions turned to fact?

Chapter 9

The Burlingame office tower spans a midtown city block. The steel gray edifice soars to a glistening glass dome, inspiring locals to dub it the Flashlight Building. The striking spray of light off the roof has caused and averted disaster. In one tragic case, a commercial airline pilot, stricken by a seizure induced by the ferocious glare, swerved off course and collided with a private plane, killing six people and injuring dozens. On a far more fortuitous occasion, a weather helicopter caught in dense fog was able to guide his craft to a safe landing by the Flashlight Building's otherworldly glow.

At the center of the block, a tidy green space frames a soaring fountain, centered by the Burlingame logo, a trio of flying fish, cast in bronze. People stream through the revolving doors at the periphery. Through the chrome-walled lobby, they are funneled toward a two-lane security station. Employees slide their ID badges over an electronic sensor and pass through on the left. Visitors must sign in and explain themselves.

I waited behind a willowy woman who ferried a teacup Maltese in the pocket of her cropped denim vest. The guard, a squat simian in a marine blue uniform, barely looked up before he passed her a visitor's badge and waved her through. When my turn came, he squinted beneath his sloped brow at my signature and went grim. "Wait right here, Ms. Jameson."

My heart raced with nonspecific guilt. Maybe New York had a law against attempting to impersonate a grown-up. I certainly felt like an impostor in the navy suit, cream silk shell and prim pearl choker, all gifts from my mother, who, despite hard evidence to the contrary, clung to the stubborn hope that I was educable. Someday, surely I would take up structured undergarments, assume control of my headstrong hair, learn to apply makeup and develop a sense of style. Bertie could not accept that every one of her elegance and good taste genes had passed me by.

"Is there a problem? I have an appointment with—" Before I could drop the name, a slim, bespectacled man in broad pinstripes and a dotted bow tie scurried up to the desk.

"Good morning, Ms. Jameson. I'm Arthur Selkowitz, Mr. Burlingame's executive assistant. This way, please."

Through a locked door at the rear, a maze of corridors led to a private elevator. My ears popped as we shot to the penthouse executive suite. The doors gaped to a massive expanse of taupe carpeting and lush, exotic plants. A ginger-haired woman perched behind a freeform glass desk in the center of the space. Selkowitz cocked his head like a quizzical dog and waited.

"Management meeting's winding up. You can go right on in," she said.

As we entered, a dozen pairs of curious eyes turned from the conference table to stare. I forced a stilted smile. I had calibrated my courage for a brief pointed audience with Burlingame alone, nothing like this.

Stewart Burlingame was another unpleasant surprise. He was a beefy man with the squashed mien of a bulldog. A thatch of wiry hair bulged from the open collar of his shirt, and his rolled sleeves revealed thick, furry forearms. Sausage lips fenced a fat black cigar that suffused the space with the smell of baked manure. His brow was a scraggly hedgerow over veal-colored eyes. They bounced at me, and then fell away. "Who's the kid?"

Selkowitz cleared his throat. "This is Ms. Jameson, the photographer, sir."

"Oh yeah. Right. Come in. Join the party. *Chronicle* profits for the quarter were up two percent. This bunch has been making excuses for why that wasn't three point five, as projected. Nothing I like better than watching a good tap dance. Very entertaining."

A florid man with silver hair jumped in. "As I was saying, that's because of the *Newsline* acquisition, Mr. Burlingame. If you eliminate the related costs and charges, the earnings are actually up slightly over four percent."

"How about I remove you and *your* related costs and charges?" He fired his words through a blue haze of smoke. "I want you to take a good look at these characters, kid. Memorize them. Every last one represents a perfect example of what not to do." He tipped his head toward the white haired man. "That's Paul Jurovaty, president and chief of lame excuses. Next to him is Rob Cameron, who heads up the Dumb Idea and Bad Execution division. Sylvia Foster over there runs Advertising and Promotion. Runs it right to ground. She's the one we thank every time circulation takes a nosedive. The pretty boy at the end of the table is Skip Kessler. What is it you do again besides combing your hair, Kessler? I always forget."

"Marketing."

Burlingame snickered. "Every time you say that, I think of a little old lady pushing a shopping cart around the A and P. Only difference is, she accomplishes something. Brings home some actual bacon. What we get from you is about the same effect as taking a shower with your socks on. Or maybe, whizzing upwind." He motioned at me. "Sit, kid. It's not every day you to get to watch a crackerjack incompetence team in action. One of you jerkoffs make yourself useful for a change and get the kid a chair."

I shrank in the seat, cheeks burning. The fact that Burlingame treated everyone with equally rude condescension did not make it any easier to take. I cringed as he tossed outrageous insults and epithets around the table, though everyone else, including "Dopey" from Fulfillment and "Dog face" from Research and Development, seemed oblivious. I imagined my mother assuring me that it was nothing personal, that the problem was his. I could hear Bertie's cool, melodic voice, the one she used to try to persuade me that it was mature and prudent to keep my raw reactions to myself.

This is business, Anna. You don't have to like the man. Just deal with him.

The meeting adjourned with a scrape of chairs and the buzz of relieved voices. Burlingame cleared the room with a swat of his hairy hand. Then, abruptly, he turned to me.

"Like your work, kid."

"Thank you."

His eyes narrowed. "No experience, though."

"That's not true. I've covered dozens of stories on a freelance basis, and several of my shots have been picked up by major publications." I placed my portfolio on the black granite conference table, but when I moved to open it, he slapped the cover as if it had committed some unpardonable offense.

"I'm talking real experience. *Hard experience.* Not some pea-green wannabe snapping art shots during summer vacation."

I stood straighter. "You asked me to come here, Mr. Burlingame. You said you liked my work."

"What I *meant,* kid, was that you show potential. You've got decent instincts. A good eye. But that doesn't make you ready for prime time." He chewed the stogie's sodden end. "You want to work for an A-level operation like this one, I'll need to be convinced."

"Then let me show you my portfolio."

He socked the table, so the papers jumped. "Are you hard of hearing or what? I told you, this isn't amateur hour. You want to show me something? Go dig up a killer exclusive. When I send you out, shoot something fresh and original. Don't try to hand me yesterday's crap. This is a news group, not a museum."

I wanted to throw something, preferably him. Furious, I picked up my portfolio and made for the door.

Burlingame called after me. "Whoa, wait up. Where are you going? What the hell is this?"

I faced him down. "You're not interested. Neither am I."

"Not interested? Did I say that?"

"Good-bye, Mr. Burlingame."

As I neared the exit, a lanky young man in a tennis shirt and khaki cargo pants loped in and stood blocking my way. "Sorry I'm late, Mr. B."

"No you're not, smart ass. You're always late. Anna Jameson, meet Dixon Drake, boy wonder. Barely out of diapers, and he already knows how to screw up a story as well as the old-timers."

Drake extended a hand. "Good to meet you." His melon-slice smile framed square glistening teeth. He had the kind of fault-free, colorless face that manufacturers stuck into sample frames and photo albums, the kind you barely noticed as you crumpled it up and threw it away.

"Excuse me, Mr. Drake. I was just leaving," I said.

"Take her down the hall and talk some sense into her, will you, smart-ass? I'm no good at tantrums."

"Correction, Mr. B. You're *great* at tantrums. It's *people* you're no good at."

Burlingame flapped off the insolence, slumped in his throne-sized desk chair and took up the phone. "After you help her collect her marbles, send her back so we can talk terms."

Outside the office, Drake frowned. "You okay?"

"Sure. No big thing. I'll just go back to my hotel room, put my feet up and shoot myself. Take care, Dixon Drake. Good to meet you."

"If it's any consolation, he's like this with everyone."

"To be honest, it's no consolation."

"Let's have a cup of coffee. We can plan ways to bump him off. It'll be fun."

"Thanks, but no thanks. All I want to do is get away from here. From here and him."

"And then what?"

I went mute, struck by the enormity of the mess I'd made. I had given up my apartment, sold my furniture, quit my job. The landlord had rented my place, a bright, spacious, bargain-priced one-bedroom in North Charleston, immediately. My replacement at Pruitt's Photos, a dapper, affable British chap named Todd Johnston, was working out horribly well. From what Mr. Pruitt had reported, even Ceecie Warburton found the guy charming. I couldn't bear the thought of returning to Charleston in slump-shouldered defeat. Where would I live? What would I do? How could I face my friends and parents? How could I face myself?

"Coffee would be good," I muttered.

Drake led me down a narrow hall to the executive dining room: a wood-paneled square lined with first editions and masterworks in oil. A wizened man in a white dinner jacket rushed to greet us.

"A pleasure to see you again, Mr. Drake. You must be Ms. Jameson. Delighted. Mr. Burlingame called ahead and told me to expect you." He ushered us to one of the dozen widely spaced tables. "Now what can I get you folks? A nice omelet, perhaps? A Belgian waffle? Or perhaps you'd prefer an early lunch. I can highly recommend the lobster bisque today, and the seared tuna."

"Just coffee," I said. "Black."

"Please, Ms. Jameson. Allow me to offer you some snacks, at least. I'd be glad to arrange a nice assortment."

"Thanks. I'm not hungry."

The headwaiter's eyes sparked with alarm. "Please. Mr. Burlingame would be most distressed."

"We certainly wouldn't want that," Drake said. "Go for it, Walter. Bring on the wretched excess. Make it a double."

The headwaiter stepped away, beaming like a backup light. "Yes, sir. Thank you, sir. Right away, sir."

"What you're seeing is classic Burlingame. After he slaps you around, he sends you out to get the boo-boos kissed," Drake said.

"How do you stand it?"

He shrugged. "Mr. B may not be Prince Charming, but when it comes to the business, he's the best. Working here means quality assignments and top-notch support. Plus the company name has an abracadabra effect. Say you work for Burlingame and doors magically open. The pay is decent, benefits are good and you can't beat the experience. I'd have a hard time finding anything that ran even a close second."

Walter reappeared pushing a two-tiered silver cart. Soon the table was laden with pastries, muffins, scones, fruit and cheese, hand-dipped chocolates, pots of exotic jam.

"I'm not asking for Prince Charming, but that man is insufferable."

Drake took an eclair and dunked it in his coffee. "He likes to see how far he can push. It's a game with him." He followed the eclair with a napoleon, tipping his head back and downing it like a sword swallower.

"I didn't come here to play games. If that's what he insists on, I'm out."

Drake shoveled a slice of layer cake onto his plate. "I hear you."

I eyed him sharply. *I hear you* was my friend Shelby's stock phrase, the one she used to let me know that she thought I was talking nonsense.

"There's no choice."

"Sure there is. You're making one. The question is whether or not it's the right choice for you."

"I'm a photographer, Dixon, not a punching bag."

He dispatched the layer cake and moved on to the cookies. "Your call. My only suggestion is that you consider this logically. What problem are you trying to solve? What's your goal?"

I sipped the coffee, which was bitter and lukewarm. "My goal is to work for a company like Burlingame. The problem is how to do that without working for a *man* like Burlingame. From where I sit, that looks like checkmate."

"Let me offer you another way to view it. The media group employs many thousands of people worldwide. Burlingame pays no attention whatsoever to an overwhelming percentage of them. When he takes a particular interest, it's because he considers you worth his time, because he believes you have something worth cultivating."

"How does he expect to accomplish that by kicking people around?"

"I believe he sees it as a kind of boot camp. You're the new enlisted kid, promising raw material that needs shaping up. He sets himself up as a combination drill sergeant, commander in chief and killer bee. Going through the process isn't fun. I know that from personal experience. But you'll learn a huge amount and after a while, you build up a kind of immunity combined with grudging respect. Look at what the man has built, what he's accomplished."

I tried to imagine a galvanized version of myself, unaffected and amused, watching the slights and insults bounce away. "I honestly don't think I have it in me to deal with a person like that."

"Sure you do. The question is how to get it out where it will do you some good."

I studied his face. He looked brand new. There were barely any lines, no footnotes. "Can I ask how you got to be so ridiculously grown-up?"

"You want the truth or the Disney version?"

"Truth."

"Five years ago, I caught a cold I couldn't shake. I ignored it for as long as I could, which turned out to be a big mistake. By the time I dragged myself in to be tested, my blood counts were off the charts. Doc diagnosed me with acute leukemia. Told me I had six months, a year—max. I took a week to crash over the news, then realized I had no time to waste moping. Figured I'd go out with flair, big hero. So I said my good-byes, bought a burial plot, even planned my own memorial service. Barbecued burgers and dogs, I thought. Blueberry cheesecake for an appetizer. Instead of eulogies, I decided they should run a few of my favorite Monty Python skits. Definitely 'The Ministry of Silly Walks' and 'The Hundred-yard Dash for People with No Sense of Direction.' I was honestly ready for whatever comes next. But for some unknown reason, I was granted an eleventh-hour reprieve."

I stirred cream in my cup and studied the whorls. "Certainly puts things in perspective."

"Helps. My idea is to enjoy every day, make the most of it. Not let the dickheads get me down. Works pretty well, most of the time."

Walter swooped over to top off our coffees. Drake didn't speak again until the waiter was well away. "If you really believe you don't belong here, run. But if you want the job, my advice is to drink up and go in fighting. Nothing the boss likes more."

"I don't feel in much of a fighting mood."

"Pretend, then. Go cut yourself a deal, and then we can get to work. Desk wants us to cover a protest rally uptown. High-profile police brutality case. Lots of big mouths and hot tempers on both sides. Should be great."

"I don't know, Dixon. I'm a lousy negotiator in the best of circumstances, and these are far from it."

"You can do this, Anna. I know you can. Here. Have some vitamins and minerals." He passed me the plate of chocolate-covered strawberries, but I couldn't eat. My mouth was chalk.

"Thanks anyway."

"Let's go, then. I'll wait outside while you work things out with Burlingame."

"I don't want to do this."

"Of course you don't. Only a lunatic would want to deal with a guy like that. But he likes you. You're one of the chosen. Keep that in mind."

"Chosen for what?"

With a wink and a victory sign, he left me at the door. I knocked sharply and let myself in.

Chapter 10

I trail the portly, copper-haired woman up five flights of stairs. Her rear end swings in wide, chaotic arcs, like a hammock crammed with boisterous kids. I find myself mesmerized by this, thinking it probably violates some elemental law of physics.

My fascination deepens at the peculiar presence of a chunky graphite-colored cat on the penultimate step before every landing. All four are identical in form and position, curled in plump semicolons with their heads pressed against the riser above and their tails drooping nearly to the step below. Once I determine that they are real and breathing, I decide this must represent some obscure good omen. At this point, I am ready to grasp at anything.

The temperature and humidity had climbed to record highs this late May afternoon, and so had I. This was the fifth high-floor walk-up I had come to see in as many hours.

The first, in a ramshackle West Village brownstone, featured a low-hanging fire escape for handy burglar access and a bird's-eye, brick-wall view of the scorched tenement next door. In the next, there were waves in the pea-green linoleum and the walls leaned and bulged at odd angles like a live-in funhouse. The next was in the east sixties over a fast food joint and reeked of rancid grease. The one after that was precisely large enough to hold a junior bed, a folding toothbrush and a half-pint of oxygen.

Drake's friend Marylese Veitch, who worked in Burlingame's classified department, had passed me an early printout of this week's apartment rental listings. I had circled everything in the vague neighborhood of my price range and called to make appointments.

From the outset, it was clear that someone with Orwellian sensibilities had designed the vocabulary. *Affordable* meant uninhabitable. *Cozy* meant claustrophobic. *Charm* referred to depressing disrepair. I did see one fabulous one-bedroom in the Gramercy Park area with an eat-in kitchen, walk-in closets, pleasant views, central air and an English-speaking doorman with only one head. The only spoiler was the published price, which turned out to be a serious misprint.

The copper-haired woman spoke an unidentifiable language that sounded like a cross between Spanish, Chinese and mashed potatoes. She pulled a jangling clump of keys from her paisley Bermuda shorts and worked the locks. As she led me into the L-shaped studio, she fanned her florid bosom and chatted in a ceaseless, indecipherable stream. I wrote my own subtitles. *Here we have the very latest thing in carpeting, pre-stained* and *mildewed for your convenience.*

She pushed aside the filthy curtains and pointed out. *I ask you. How many buildings offer unobstructed Dumpster views* and *the stench to go with them?*

Great porcelain chunks were missing from the bathroom sink, the toilet leaked and the shower stall bore a rust stain in the shape of California. The woman kept smiling and jabbering in a tone that reeked of phony enthusiasm. *Wouldn't take much at all to fix this up good as new, honey. All you need is kerosene and a match.*

Still, I forced myself to consider renting this hellhole. The square footage was more generous than most I'd seen. A coat of paint would make an enormous difference, and the landlord might agree to make some basic repairs. I could replace the carpet with an inexpensive remnant. Maybe there were hardwood floors underneath.

And maybe this year September would come in July.

So it was a dive. What choice did I have? Clearly, I was not going to find a palace in my price range. In this city I could barely afford a slot in a decent parking garage.

My negotiation with Stewart Burlingame had concluded with a nasty new surprise. He would be launching a weekly magazine called *Upshot* in a couple of months. If I proved myself, his plan was to assign me there. Until then, I would be considered a trainee, temporary and probationary, paid by the day, plus expenses. During that time, Dixon Drake would be my advisor, responsible for teaching me the ropes and keeping me from hanging myself with them. I had explained in calm, compelling terms that I needed a reliable, stable income *now*, and for a moment I thought I had him convinced.

"I got the picture, kid. You need to pay bills, buy food. All that."

"Exactly, Mr. Burlingame."

"That would be in the category of *your* problem. My advice is you go deal with it. Chop chop."

The copper-haired woman sashayed to the kitchen and flipped on the light. Over her shoulder, I spotted a flurry of movement near the sink. She shrieked, clutched her heaving cleavage and staggered back to the foyer. I ventured one step closer and stalled in horror at the sight of an enormous mahogany creature with long twitching antennae and legs like Mick Jagger.

The woman stuck to the foyer wall like flypaper. Her black eyes popped in cartoon rounds. I rushed past her and left without a word. I raced downstairs so fast it felt like falling. I was on the street before it struck me that all four lucky cats had disappeared.

The scorching atmosphere wavered with oily currents. Pools of molten tar pocked the roadways. I drew cautious sips of the searing air and slowed to the plodding pace of a trash barge.

Drake and I had agreed to meet at the corner of Eighty-sixth Street and Third Avenue. From a block away, I spotted him slumped against a lamppost, jabbering into his flip phone, jotting notes in the slim black leather journal he carried all the time.

Perspiration had tinged his pale hair military beige, and a Rorschach sweat blot spanned the back of his blue knit shirt. As I approached, he ended the call and snapped the mouthpiece shut.

"Glad you showed up on time. We're supposed to cover a press conference at Gracie Mansion in ten minutes." We started walking east. "Burlingame has had it in for the mayor since the city denied his application last month for a tax abatement," Drake explained. "We cover every sneeze and hiccup that comes out of City Hall, looking for eggs to smear on Hizzoner's face."

"Whatever happened to objective reporting?"

"It went the way of every other noble, unassailable idea that failed to turn a profit. Your job is to take the most unflattering shots you can. First prize would be snapping the mayor with his finger up his nose or fondling the family jewels. A close runner-up would be finding some new and clever way of discrediting him. Catch him copping a feel of Lady Liberty, perhaps. Or maybe find out that he claimed to be a church on his tax return. That would be especially sweet, given how holier than thou Conley is. But Burlingame will be happy enough if you capture him looking angry or clueless."

"That's how the mayor always looks."

Drake chuckled. "Burlingame's not the only media man angry with him. Meanwhile, how did the apartment hunting go?"

"It went."

"You didn't find anything?"

"Not even a decent packing crate. I'm about ready to give up. I can't afford to live in this city—period."

"Sure you can. Problem is you been using a close-up lens when you need wide-angle."

"It's too hot for riddles," I groused.

"Manhattan is one tiny island in a sea of bigger, better opportunity. A short ride over one of the bridges can mean double the space at half the price. It's amazing. That's why I live in Brooklyn."

Despite the melting heat, he moved at an energetic clip with his face tipped to catch an imaginary breeze. I had to shift into higher gear to keep up. The strap of my camera bag nipped my shoulder and my feet were spreading in my shoes like unbaked dough.

"I can't do that," I said.

"Why not?"

"I just can't."

"You know Brooklyn? Have something particular against it?"

"No. I've never been there."

Drake nodded extravagantly. "I certainly can't argue with impeccable logic like that."

We walked a block in strained silence. At the corner, he stopped to buy an orange Creamsicle from a street vendor. I hovered over the freezer compartment and a couple of my brain cells came around.

"I know it sounds dumb, Dixon, but I was counting on living in Manhattan."

"Doesn't sound dumb at all. Just unrealistic, impractical and self-defeating."

"Okay. Maybe you're right. I'll look."

"If you like, I can introduce you to the guy who found me my place. Name's Thomas. He has a line on all the best deals. Are you free tomorrow?"

"Except for worrying about a place to live, I've got nothing on my calendar."

"I'll track him down and give you a call on your portable."

"Thanks."

We had come to Gracie Mansion. The mayoral home was a sweeping, white Federal building with ornate trellis roof rails and a wraparound porch. It would have fit perfectly on Charleston's Battery Street.

Drake tipped his head to the north. "That's Hell's Gate, where the Harlem and East rivers meet the Long Island Sound. George Washington squatted on this property at the beginning of the American Revolution. British cannons wrecked the original house and the owner put the land on the market. A Scotsman named Archibald Gracie bought it and built this place at the end of the eighteenth century. The city took it over about a hundred years later and did their best to run it to the ground. Sanitation department used the mansion for equipment storage and public toilets, if you can believe. Later on, they turned it into a museum for a while. When the museum relocated, the place was rat bait again for a decade or so until the park commissioner lobbied for a restoration. Fiorello LaGuardia was the first mayor to live here in the early forties."

"How do you know all that?"

"Every assignment comes with a detailed cheat sheet. Burlingame has the best research department in the business. Anytime you want to know anything about anything, just ask."

Just ask.

My mind filled with that long-ago night, a silent intruder slipping into my sister's room. I imagined the veils of mystery slipping away, the face of the enemy coming clear.

Firmly, I pushed the dangerous thought away. I would not be drawn down that slick-sided well again. Thousands of professional and amateur sleuths had spent mountains of time trying to unmask my sister's killer. It was insane even to consider that valuable new information might be lying around in some dusty box in Burlingame's research department.

At the press conference, I snapped half a dozen rolls with my Mamiya and another six on the Canon EOS. Unflattering shots of Mayor Douglas Conley came easily. The flagpole behind him appeared to spring like a turkey timer from his skull. The microphones crowded at his mouth gave him the look of a muzzled dog. Even without the props, he had the kind of stern features that would play far better chiseled on a coin than printed on an eight-by-ten glossy.

Dixon and I parted company at the mansion door. He was going home to call in his story. I planned to stop at the Flashlight Building and drop off the film at the Burlingame lab. After that I would go back to my hotel room to call in a story of my own.

I have never been able to lie to my mother, at least not successfully. But Bertie taught me by expert example how to temper the truth. Certain things were too dark or painful to expose without careful filters. Watching her tiptoe around my sister's murder and the thorny feelings that brutal act provoked, I learned how to soften unsavory facts.

I did not want to burden my parents with needless worries. The key was choosing the right words, ones that were true enough, if not exactly factual.

I would tell my mother that I had decided against staying with Shelby, that I had more peace and privacy in the hotel. I would claim that I'd looked at lots of places to live, that I was closing in on a decision. I would report that Burlingame had taken me on and that I'd already had a couple of interesting assignments.

One of my pictures from my first shoot at the protest rally had landed on the metro section front page. I had put a copy in the mail with my microscopic photo credit circled in red. Bertie would show it off at her garden club, boast about me shamelessly at the store. It wasn't as good as being able to announce that I had finally come to my senses and set a wedding date, but my minuscule success might bring her some small measure of compensatory comfort.

New York is a wonderful place and not unsafe at all, I planned to say. Things had improved enormously under Mayor Conley, a strict law-and-order man who had cracked down on everything from aggressive panhandling to spitting in the street. I would leave out the part about how this had created an atmosphere of paranoia and siege.

People were looking over their shoulders, watching their backs. At such times, there's always the danger that you will fail to notice that you are about to trip over a dangerous obstacle that lies dead ahead.

Chapter 11

New York subways strike terror in some, but I find them surprisingly agreeable. Hurtling along, I am treated to a light show, sparks in darkness, rushing spray of scenes. The jolting rhythms of the ride place me in an oddly satisfying state of stunned relaxation. So does the clacking cacophony of metal striking rail.

As a bonus, New York's underground offered certain rarely mentioned extras, such as free entertainment. In less than a week, I had been treated to a staggering variety: cabaret, theater of the absurd, mime and high drama. Today's ride featured a musical comedy. A peripatetic loony in surplus fatigues entered the train from the rear. He dropped on one knee, spread his grimy, scabrous hands and delivered a rousing rendition of "Hello, Dolly." Rising with a grunt, he passed through the car, bowing proudly. A flame-haired woman in tangerine tights and a yellow tunic dropped a quarter in his seeking palm.

To her visible horror, he seized her hand and kissed it loudly. "Thank you, thank you, dear lady. You are most gracious, indeed. In fact, your marvelous generosity will assist me in purchasing my dream retirement home in Boca Raton, Florida. Two bedrooms on the eighteenth hole. Feel free to come visit anytime. *Mi condo es su condo.*"

At Canal Street I changed from the Lexington IRT to the J train, which delivered me to the Marcy Avenue station. Drake had provided detailed travel instructions along with a capsule history of the Williamsburg section of Brooklyn, courtesy of Burlingame's research department. Having arrived twenty minutes early for my meeting with Thomas the real estate man, I sat on a bench at the North Green Park and read.

This fan-shaped slice of the borough had suffered a long string of thwarted hopes and political hard luck. By the 1850s, the former farming community had evolved into a popular vacation spot for the likes of Cornelius Vanderbilt and William Whitney. Then, at the turn of the century, the opening of the eponymous Williamsburg Bridge brought an influx of immigrant families. The upper crust fled, and the neighborhood's economic fortunes plunged. By 1910, Williamsburg tenements had the worst overcrowding and highest infant mortality rates in the state.

The next fifty years saw a slow resurgence in commerce and manufacturing, but just as the area perched on the brink of renewed prosperity, the Brooklyn-Queens Expressway was launched like a spear through the area's heart. The main downtown thoroughfare was obliterated, and five thousand people were displaced from their homes and workplaces. Manufacturing jobs dissolved and property values disintegrated again.

New residents settled in their separate corners. Hasidic Jews moved to the southwest, Italians to the west, Poles drifted north near the area known as Greenpoint. Tensions flared between these groups and the majority Puerto Rican population.

Then, in the 1980s, space-starved Manhattan artists began to venture across the bridge. Words like *creative energy* and *renewed vigor* were tossed about in the local *bodegas.* The city planning commission started toying with ways to revive the decaying waterfront. Insufferably hip perennial insiders started referring to the area as *Billburg,* as if it were a close personal friend.

But Williamsburg remained light-years removed from Manhattan's Chelsea or SoHo or any of the other trendy, astronomically expensive neighborhoods that had exploded out of the economic ashes in recent times. From the look of things, there was no major danger that high-rise travesties by Trump would infest this area anytime soon.

I was still fifteen minutes early for my scheduled meeting with the Realtor. Restless, I walked up Marcy Avenue and turned onto Broadway, a bustling thoroughfare steeped in dappled shade by the elevated train. The area throbbed with an earthy vitality. Salsa music blared from passing cars. The shops were festooned with pulsing signs, bright balloons and grand-opening banners.

Intrigued, I pulled out my Canon and started shooting. I captured a pair of glum-faced men in black felt hats walking stiffly behind a giddy cluster of brash, fleshy girls. A group of Latinos sat on upturned milk crates playing dominoes. A chicken strutted like a security guard in front of a market whose bins were heaped with alien foods. Brown sticklike tubers, odd-shaped speckled fruits, fibrous yellow slabs bursting with seeds.

Turning off the main street, I found more striking scenes. Dilapidated commercial buildings flanked newly constructed garden apartments. Brightly painted storefront churches punctuated block-long spans of shuttered stores.

Down a short, nondescript street, I came upon the waterfront. Through the charred scope of a burned-out building, I sighted on the World Trade Center in lower Manhattan across the choppy water. Standing in a desolate vacant lot, surrounded by rusting machinery and broken glass, I commanded a heady, unobstructed view of the most expensive property in the world. Dixon's description was right. It was amazing. I shot three rolls before I remembered that it was time to meet the Realtor.

Returning to the North Green Park, I found a grizzled man slumped on a bench with his eyes shut and his face tipped to catch the sun. His sparse silver hair was bound in a puny tail, and a dusky beard hugged his chin like low-lying fog. He sported tan Birkenstocks, a tie-dyed shirt and ropes of bright crystal beads, as if he had been frozen in the sixties and recently left to thaw. He sprang to his feet at my tentative hello.

"You Anna? Name's Thomas."

"Good to meet you, Mr. Thomas."

"Plain Thomas will do me fine. I've got *the* perfect place to show you. Come ahead."

He led me through a maze of streets to another section of the waterfront, this one even more depressed and desolate than the first. The neighborhood's prime feature was a sprawling tank farm. Huge beige receptacles crowded behind chain-link fence capped by razor wire. Small signs at intervals warned that we were being videotaped for our own protection.

The heat spell had finally cracked, and the air had the crisp feel of unlimited promise. I caught a briny scent and the melodic trill of a child's exuberant laughter. Thomas's enthusiasm infected me as well. "Best place in the universe. Right here."

We turned onto a block where a mocha-skinned man in an artist's smock and beret stood painting tiger stripes on a three-legged desk. He raised his dripping paintbrush in a salute. "Hey, man. How's it going?"

"Can't complain."

"How come that is? Your complainer's out of whack?"

Thomas laughed. "Guess you could say that."

"Sure I can. Just did."

As we walked on, Thomas told me that the oddball was a homeless man named Bolly, who had lived on the block for years. "Real character, that one. Always up to something brand new and way, way out there."

Farther down, two scantily dressed women strolled in lazy arcs. A tan Chevy Blazer drifted up and paused beside the taller one, a jut-hipped blonde in purple hot pants and a lemon Dynel wig. She strode to the car and leaned in, propping her meaty bosom on the sill. Moments later, she sidled around, slipped in and draped herself like a boa around the driver's neck.

"You'll find all kinds, all shapes and sizes, the sort of mix that made this city great," said Thomas proudly.

"Hookers and johns, you mean?"

"Each to his own. That's the basis of democracy. Anyway, the skin trade is alive and well in every neighborhood. Park Avenue, Fifth, you name it. May not always be in your face like this, but it's there just the same. Dressed up, disguised, whatever."

The remaining girl, a short bulbous brunet in a silver mini dress, flashed Thomas a toothy smile. He smiled back and shrugged his regrets. "You could have far worse neighbors, take my word. Those girls are like anybody else, just trying to get by."

"Get by what?"

A lipstick-red Neon turned onto the street. The driver negotiated terms with the pudgy brown-haired whore and drove off in less time than it normally took me to order lunch.

Thomas was building to a crescendo. "People around here have a sense of community. They honestly care. Look out for each other. Plus, you can't beat the value. You're an artist, Dixon said."

"Photographer."

"There you go. You've got an eye, an imagination. I don't have to show you what's in front of your face."

We had come to a ramshackle building with caged windows on the ground floor. Straps of tar paper drooped like grimy bangs over the stained brick facade. Rusted vans and panel trucks blocked the entrance. Beside the door hung a sign for the Marv-Liss Mannequin Company, Inc.

"How many apartments are there?"

"Marv-Liss operates on the first and second floor. Top level is split into two units. One's a sculptor's studio. Guy works in metal, big pieces with a heavy African influence. Spends most of his time over there in Kenya or Jo'berg, getting inspired."

"How soon will the other one be available?"

"Should be by the end of the day. Tomorrow morning at the latest. Old lady who lived there couldn't hack it alone anymore. The nephew promised to pick up her valuables and vacate tonight."

Thomas worked the building lock. We entered a cavernous hallway crammed with moving dollies, refuse bins and packing crates. The lid had slipped from one of the trash cans, and mannequin parts poked forth. There was a plastic hand with a missing forefinger, an eyeless head, a broken female torso and two mismatched legs.

The elevator, a gunmetal mesh cage, rose through the center of the space.

Thomas flipped a lever to summon the creaky lift. We edged inside between hills of cartons and rose in jerky bursts to the third level. The Realtor worked the heavy latch to release us and led me to the end of a dim, narrow hall.

"Can't show you the old lady's apartment. Nephew's refused to turn over the keys until he has a chance to do a final walk-through. But I got in touch with Don Stillman, that's the sculptor, and got permission to show you his loft next door. Layout's exactly the same, only flipped. Should give you a pretty good idea."

"Great."

"Only problem is we have to go in through the rear. Stillman couldn't get the key to me but he said the back door's always open."

I followed him onto a rickety catwalk. Behind us stretched a flat span of littered rooftop overlooking the river. A passing tug blasted its horn, and a cigarette boat sped by in a roaring streak. A wave of vertigo struck as I side-stepped cautiously toward the adjacent door. My calves clenched and a crawl-ing sensation scaled my neck. Trailing Thomas inside, I inhaled hard to still the queasiness.

The floor-through loft had been divided with the rear half set aside as liv-ing quarters. A hand-painted screen separated the sleeping area from a cozy living room with track lighting and wide plank floors. Bold abstract oils graced the whitewashed walls and samples of the artist's metal abstracts perched everywhere. There were bright primitive rugs, woven throws and a large collec-tion of carved African fertility dolls. The stylized women had proud breasts and huge intelligent eyes like my friend Shelby, and the men's heads were indis-tinguishable from their sex organs, like her husband Harvey. The kitchen was a bright, tiled square with a potbellied stove at its center. The bathroom featured a large claw-foot tub and antique hardware.

Through an archway off the kitchen was the studio, which overlooked a lit-tered courtyard. Across the yard was another ramshackle brick-faced building.

Thomas followed my gaze. "That one's all commercial. There's a machine shop and a furniture manufacturing operation. Not a lot of traffic, which is good."

I looked around the studio. Blowtorches and giant tanks of oxyacetylene fuel lined the wall to the left. To the right were racks of draconian tools and heaps of sharp-edged scrap metal. Sketches and plaster prototypes were scattered everywhere.

"I thought of this place soon as Dixon told me you were a photographer. I knew you'd get the picture, so to speak."

"It's nice. Lots of space." I kept my tone even and detached. Heel clicking or shouts of joy might raise the price. "The other loft is exactly like this only flipped, you said? Same size?"

"Exactly. Only it needs a little fixing up. Old lady Graff lived here since the dawn of time. These past years, she hasn't been exactly all there. Elevator stopped running to the top floor, if you know what I mean." He tapped his temple. "She took to wandering around in the middle of the night, carrying a butcher knife, threatening whoever she happened to see. For a while, everyone thought she was harmless, but a couple of weeks ago, she went after a young woman was out for an early morning jog. Mrs. Graff tried to stab her, but the girl was too fast. Fortunately, she got away with nothing more than a bad scare and a nasty scratch. That's why they finally had to put the old lady away."

A buzzer sounded. Thomas loped to a panel near the door and pressed a button. "Must be Dixon. I told him I'd be showing you this place, and he said he'd try to come by."

"What kind of fixing up does it need?" I asked.

"From what the owner described, it's a little down at the mouth. Probably take some cleaning, coat of paint. But then you'll have yourself a regular dream house, dirt cheap."

"The owner won't pay for any of the repairs?"

"Doesn't have to. Not with space like this at the price he's willing to take."

Dixon ducked in through the catwalk door. He scanned the sprawling loft and whistled low. "How come I didn't rate something like this, Thomas? It's huge."

"Timing, pal," Thomas said. "That and location. You know what they say."

I strode around, fighting back the smile. "What are they getting for dirt around here these days?"

The price he quoted was only fifty dollars more per month than my North Charleston place, which had been roughly half the size. Granted, this was not exactly a modern garden apartment complex with a pool and a laundry room.

And it didn't have anything that would pass, even by my very flimsy definition, as security. My heart started squirming oddly.

"I should probably see some other things before I make a decision."

"Your call, but I have to tell you, this place is going to go and fast. Spaces like this just don't come along every day. Not at this price or anywhere close. Plenty would be willing to take it sight unseen. Tell her, Dixon."

"You don't want it, I'll take it. This place is triple the size of mine. Maybe more."

"The building feels sort of deserted."

"Quiet is good. You'll come to appreciate that in this city. Believe me."

"I suppose."

Thomas tented his hands like a priest. "Hear me. I have three daughters, all about your age. If this place wasn't safe enough, I wouldn't be showing it to you."

"Listen to Thomas. He knows this neighborhood better than anyone," Drake said.

"I'm sure you're right. I'd just like a little time to think it over," I said.

"Fine. No problem." The Realtor frowned at his watch, a mechanical moon face on a beaded silver band. Stars spilled through the indigo sky to mark the swiftly passing time. "Look, I've got to run. Give a call when you are ready, and I'll see what else I can dig up." He started flipping off the lights, shutting doors, closing off the possibility. "Maybe you'd feel better with a roommate or two. There are plenty of shares around."

"No. I definitely don't want that. Anyway, I'm not saying no to this place. Where can I reach you later today?"

He scribbled his number on a paper scrap. "You can try there, but I've got to be honest, I have a bunch of other appointments today and there's not much chance this will still be available. But no biggie. Something else will turn up, sooner or later."

"Can't you hold it for a little while? A couple of hours?"

"Wish I could. But if I don't get a signature on it soon, someone is sure to steal it out from under me. Rental market is red hot right now, and this is one of those rare, really *primo* deals. If the nephew weren't in the way, it would be long gone already. But he's been holding on, hoping he could find some way to take the place over himself."

"Why can't he?"

"Owner doesn't want him, plain and simple. Guess he figures the kid might turn out to be nutso like his aunt." He flipped off the last of the lights. "Okay, then, boys and girls. Let's hit the road."

"No, wait. I've decided. I'll take it."

"You sure? I don't want to pressure you."

"I'm positive. What's the next step?"

"I can turn the keys over tomorrow morning, but there are a couple of things you need to know about. Let's go. I'll explain on the way."

Chapter 12

"It's incredible." Dixon made his third circuit of my new home, skirting the rubble. "Honestly, Anna. I've never seen anything like it."

"No one has. Not if they've had any luck at all."

"All this space. And furnished. You may be sitting on some valuable antiques."

"How would I ever know?" An astonishing mass of litter buried everything. One leg of a sofa poked out beneath the hiked hem of a faded blue skirt. I could see the flared wooden edge of an end table, the soiled fringe on an ottoman, not much else.

I groaned. "I can't get over Thomas saying that all this needed was a little fixing up."

"So it's more than a little. Big deal."

"It's an *enormous* deal, Dixon. I think we could be looking at a potential world record. Biggest mess in history. Ever hear of the Collier brothers?"

"Sure, I used to read their encyclopedia, searching for the dirty parts. The *Britannica* was way better. I remember this picture on page two hundred seventy-eight."

"Not *that* Collier. These men were the original packrats, a couple of reclusive eccentrics who lived together for decades and saved absolutely everything. My mother used them as a cautionary tale when she wanted me to clean up my room. When the brothers died, the undertakers could barely get through the junk to get the bodies out. Wouldn't surprise me if there was a body or two under all this."

"It's just a lot of garbage. You'll get rid of it."

His relentless optimism deepened my gloom. "This isn't *just* a lot of garbage; it's a clutter orgy." Everywhere I looked was another collection. Filthy stuffed animals spewing their cotton guts, yellowed books of ancient trading stamps, candle stumps, matchbooks, crumpled postcards, chipped Depression glass, fragments of junk jewelry, soiled hats, battered dolls. "It looks like the entire universe of useless stuff set up shop here and started reproducing." I slumped on a couch-sized pile of yellowed, crumbling issues of the long-defunct New York *Sun* and tried not to weep. "It's just too much, Dixon. I wouldn't know where to start."

"Give me an hour. I'll round up some friends to help haul out the trash and spruce up the place."

"I can't ask strangers for a favor like that."

"You don't have to, I will. We'll have a modern barn raising. You provide the suds and pizza, and I'll bring the arms and backs. What do you say?"

"I say you're sweet, but it's hopeless."

He looped his hands under my armpits and lifted me bodily. "We'll have none of that. Get thee to a hardware store, Anna Jameson. Pick up a couple of gallons of whatever you like that's on sale, plus rollers, cheap brushes, masking tape, cleaning stuff and tarps. We should be able to improvise the rest. I'll meet you back here by eleven."

In the time it took me to collect the supplies, Dixon corralled a half dozen willing volunteers. Ramon and Hidalgo, his next-door neighbors, commandeered a dolly from the first-floor hall and wheeled out load after load of trash. As they cleared space adjoining the wall, a froth-haired beanpole named Vishnu rolled on a prime coat of ivory latex. Dixon and a silver-blond pixie named Monique scraped, masked and painted the trim a bright glossy white. I trailed behind, sweeping up and dusting away several decades' worth of filth.

Lou, a Fred Flintstone look-alike whose family business was theatrical lighting, repaired frayed wiring and installed ceiling tracks and other fixtures from a failed off-Broadway show.

The last recruit arrived an hour after the rest. He was barefoot in tattered jeans and a grimy T-shirt. His long hair was matted and his obsidian eyes sank in bruise-colored troughs.

Dixon greeted him with outsized enthusiasm. "Hey, look who's here. Glad you could make it, buddy. Anna, this is Sam. Everyone calls him Spook, for obvious reasons. But don't let the Dracula thing fool you. Guy's a mechanical genius. Incredible with his hands."

The hands in question were calloused and webbed with fish-scale scars. Only a nub remained of his left pinkie, which he held curiously aloft. He reeked of stale tobacco and rancid sweat. I struggled to mask my revulsion.

"Why don't you start over there with the kitchen, Spook man? Looks like all the appliances could use your magic touch," Dixon said.

Wordlessly, the mechanic crossed to the end of the space. He swiped debris from the surface of the range and began dismantling the grease-encrusted oven. Despite the stuffy closeness of the long-shuttered apartment, I shivered.

"Spook's the best," Dixon whispered. "A little weird, but a major talent. There's nothing he can't fix."

Weird did not begin to cover the question. My photographer's eye picked up things that disturbed the harmony of a composition, stray disturbing elements that the casual observer might fail to notice.

The mechanic held himself with visible deliberation, as if he feared he might otherwise hurtle out of control. His dark eyes had a rubbery translucence, and they moved in slow, watchful arcs like a stalking predator. Every so often, I felt their heat on me. I sensed him sizing me up, drawing private conclusions.

The others took no special notice of him, and I tried to catch their indifference. I chided myself for being such an ingrate. The creepy guy could be out enjoying the lovely spring day instead of laboring over my filthy, ancient appliances. After a while, his disturbing presence receded, like a dripping faucet. I lost myself in the rhythms of the work and the intense high of single-minded camaraderie.

The last time I could remember being part of a group like this was tenth grade, when the Central High School drama club put on "Guys and Dolls." Shelby played the romantic lead, Sarah Brown, the Salvation Army lady, and Kevin starred opposite her as Sky Masterson. Naturally, I was typecast as Adelaide, the ditsy blonde meant to provide comic relief.

For two months, we spent every free moment in rehearsal. We staged three sold-out evening performances and a standing-room-only matinee. After the final curtain fell, with the applause still echoing in my ears, I plunged into sudden despair. I did not want the play to end. Fevered with stage fright though I was, I loved speaking prescribed lines and drawing predictable responses. I loved the energy of the cast, the total absorption in this thing that was so much more controlled and flattering than real life.

Tonight, I wasn't the only one fueled by manic momentum. Dixon's friends refused to leave until they finished the job. We worked until nearly two in the morning, pausing only for necessary breaks and refreshments. Lunch and dinner consisted of greasy takeout, which we ate standing up on the fly. We went through a case of soft drinks and another of low-end beer, slaking the thirst of eager exertion.

The transformation was astonishing. Without the trash, the space bloomed to double the size. Fresh paint hoisted it up from the gloom. The excavated furnishings turned out to be serviceable, if not exactly precious or antique, as Dixon had predicted.

The near-blue sofa sagged like an ancient horse. The arms on the fat, cozy club chair were rubbed bald, but crocheted doilies provided decent camouflage. The Tiffany-style lamps had only a few chipped glass sections, which I turned to the wall.

Monique had a flair for decorating, and she pushed things around, making the most of the wrought-iron occasional tables, rag rugs and crude patchwork quilts.

Ramon discovered a stack of framed prints and posters at the back of a closet. Dixon hung them under Monique's watchful gaze, and then did the same with a pair of blue moiré curtains. He straightened the final frame and wiped his hands. "I'd say that about does it."

My eyes pooled with emotion and bone-deep fatigue. "I can't believe how great the place looks. I honestly don't know how to thank you."

"When we get a chance, I can take you to some great places around here for plants and things. Finishing touches," said Monique.

"That'll be great."

"I've got some recessed retrofits and picture lights you could use. I'll give a call during the week and throw them in for you. Make those prints look like the genuine item," said Lou.

Besotted with gratitude, I saw my saviors to the door. We traded sloppy sentiments and hugs. I felt enormous affection for these selfless souls. Still, when Spook approached, all my molecules shriveled and crouched, trembling behind my bones.

He held up a filthy metal device. "You may want to hold on to this."

I took it from him gingerly. "Thanks."

As soon as the door shut behind them, I surrendered to the crushing exhaustion that had been threatening to level me for hours. Slumped on the couch, I could barely move. My limbs hung like cement blocks and my mind was socked in a dizzying fog. Mustering the last of my strength, I trudged to the bedroom. I had made the bed earlier with the linens I discovered in a hand-painted hope chest. Unlike the rest of the apartment, everything inside had been kept in pristine condition, neatly folded and wrapped in tissue paper. Bertie had started a similar chest for me at about the time I entered preschool. She still kept it up.

In this case, I was grateful. I couldn't wait to slip between the crisp embroidered sheets and drop my cannonball head on the pillow. But when I drew back the plump comforter, I froze.

On the bed lay a flaxen-haired doll. A rope of gauze circled her plastic neck. One blue glass eye stared at me, the other winked shut under a dense-lashed lid.

The sight sent me reeling back in time. I imagined a faceless stranger standing beside my sister's bed, watching her sleep, dripping a circle of moisture on the rug.

Dizzy, I sank to the floor. I drew greedy breaths until the bristling horror receded. Sharp outrage stomped in to take its place.

As a kid, I had been subjected to vicious pranks like this. Once, when I was away at summer scout camp, some anonymous monster sent me a chatty, three-page letter. Bright stickers festooned the envelope. I was halfway through reading it when curiosity moved me to turn to the final page. There, in flowery script, was the signature: *love and kisses, Julie.*

On another obscene occasion, during my visit to a church-sponsored haunted house at Halloween, a small vampire burst from the shadows with his arms splayed and his fingers bent in claws. He tuned his voice to a spooky tremor and declared, *Anna Jameson, I am your sister's ghost.*

Terrified, I bolted for the exit, trailed by my tormentor's maniacal giggle. On the way, I tripped over some unseen object in the inky darkness and split a three-inch gash in my scalp above the ear. By the time I got home, my hair was matted with blood and I was sobbing in great uncontrollable bursts. It took seven sutures to seal the wound, and I still bear the hard, wormy scar. When I'm burdened by serious stress, I still get stabbing headaches at the site. I could feel one starting now, and I pressed my skull to quash the pulsing pain.

My mother used to claim that kids who resorted to such meanness were sorry souls, drowning in insecurity. I did my best to believe her, to muster some noble sympathy for the irredeemable little brats. But this could not be chalked up to the mindless cruelty of children. A nasty, grown-up perpetrator had culled the grisly props and set the scene.

I tried to recall who had been in the bedroom last. Vaguely, I remembered Ramon ducking in to use the facilities, but I couldn't be sure whether that was before or after someone, maybe Vishnu or Monique, passed through to wash the paintbrushes in the bathroom sink.

I realized that the doll could have been stashed under the sheets at almost any point after I cleaned the room and made the bed early that afternoon.

Dixon's creepy friend Spook was the one I wanted most to blame. But I knew the risk of trusting mere appearances. Any of my eager volunteers could have been responsible.

Whoever it was had a warped mind and a cruel, sick sense of humor, at best. At worst, whoever set it up was testing me, making some unspoken threat.

It occurred to me that my mother might be right. Maybe it was a foolish, dangerous mistake to trust anyone.

Chapter 13

I was wrenched awake by a booming voice from downstairs. "What is it with you, Jake? You didn't sleep last night? Maybe you're sick?"

"I'm fine, Moshe."

"Fine doesn't move in slow motion, Jake. Fine gets the job done *today*!"

"I'm moving. I'm doing."

My bedside clock read five past ten. Horrified, I checked my cell phone, which had run out of juice. When I plugged it in, I found four messages waiting in my voice mail.

The first was from Dixon. He'd been called out to JFK to cover the Pope's arrival for another reporter who'd been leveled by food poisoning. The city desk was trying to track me down and he'd given them the number of my portable phone. I should call in as soon as I got this message. I strained to hear him over the strident drone of jet engines.

"I'd better run, Anna. Looks like his holiness is about to touch down. Oh, by the way, I hope you liked the baby doll. I found her under a pile of paperbacks, and I couldn't get over how much she looked like you."

I had no time to waste feeling foolish. The other three calls were increasingly frantic messages from the office. I was more than an hour late for my scheduled call-in.

Max Kahan answered at the city desk. Dixon had introduced Max to me as one of the good guys, a fair-minded soul who meted work out evenhandedly. Managing assignments was a position of particular power. Abuses and overbearing control were not uncommon.

My voice was a croak. "Hi, Max. It's Anna Jameson. I just got your messages. What's up?"

"Mr. Burlingame wanted you to shoot a crane accident downtown. I called the hotel, but they said you checked out. Drake gave me your cell phone number, but I couldn't get through. Everything okay?"

"Yes, except my battery died. Where's the shoot?"

"Too late now. Sorry. I had to send someone else."

"It's my fault. I moved over the weekend. I should have let you know."

"No problem as far as I'm concerned. But I have to tell you, the boss was not exactly pleased."

"Is he ever?"

He chuckled. "I guess you could say it's a matter of degree. In this case, I suspected he was just the least bit irritated when the firestorm through the receiver scorched my ear. Makes him nuts when someone he requests isn't reachable. One of his menagerie of pet peeves."

"Great. Now what?"

"He said you must need a good long rest. I'm supposed to tell you not to come in until the beginning of next week."

"You're joking."

"Wish I was."

"A week seems like a pretty stiff penalty for a dead battery. What do you get for a typo at that place, the electric chair?"

"It's tough, I know. But that's Mr. Burlingame."

"There must be some way to reason with him."

His voice dropped, and I caught a muffled echo as he cupped the mouthpiece to keep from being overheard. Like most absolute dictators, Burlingame had a full complement of stooges, shills and spies. "Take my advice and don't try to go that route, Anna. The boss *really* hates being questioned."

"But it's ridiculous."

"Maybe so, but it is what it is. Look, I've got to go."

He hung up with a resolute clack, and I sat staring in disbelief, listening to the silence. *A week.*

I spotted the rumpled doll across the room, slumped where I'd tossed it in a fit of pique last night. I picked her up, smoothed the soiled pink dress and set her on the bed.

As I did, the voice from downstairs roared again. "You call that moving, Jake? I've seen mountains go faster than that. Continents, even."

Perched on the sill, I watched two young men ferry a mannequin from the building to a mud-colored panel truck at the curb. They were trout-belly pale and oddly dressed for work and the weather in black mohair trousers, starched white shirts buttoned sternly at the neck and thick-soled black shoes. Both had the limp posture and forceless stride of bodies sorely unaccustomed to exercise. They wore constricting suspenders, dark skullcaps and expressions of beleaguered distaste.

"Hurry it up, for the love of Pete," the voiced begged. "By the time you get there, the customer will be retired. Or dead, maybe."

"We're hurrying, Moshe," the man on the left protested. "It's not our fault if the order wasn't ready on time."

"Ready isn't enough, Jake. You understand? Ready doesn't get the goods to the customer. Ready doesn't get the check written and the bills paid."

"Neither does your harping," said Jake. "Leave us be and we'll get done sooner."

Jake left his partner clutching the bald, naked mannequin in a tango hold and climbed heavily into the cargo hatch. "Okay, Asher. Hand her up."

The second man hoisted the plastic model with a grunt. Jake dragged it inside the truck and placed it in a decorous pose beside several identical figures.

Jake dabbed his brow with an outsized handkerchief as he and Asher trudged back toward the building.

From below came the plaintive voice again. "Would you move? This is a good customer, Jake. I can't afford to lose him. Don't you understand?"

An angry flush relieved Jake's sickly pallor. "I understand that you're driving me nuts, Moshe. Can't you see I'm doing the best I can?"

"Lazy is all I see. Lazy and slow. Where's your pride, Jake? Where's your ambition?"

"You think you can do better, be my guest." Jake tucked the hankie in his pocket and threw up his hands. In a fury, he strode away.

"Where are you going? What are you doing? You can't just walk off like that. Come back!"

Jake kept walking.

"A person doesn't take off in the middle of a job," bellowed the voice. "I'll see to it everyone knows, Jake. Mark my words. If you leave now, you're through. No one will hire you. No one, you hear? Don't you dare come crawling back, you little *putz*."

Breakfast was leftover pizza and a Coke. By the time I showered and dressed, the mud-toned van had left. Across the street, the homeless artist was putting the finishing touches on the tiger-stripe desk. Except for him and a couple of street girls working the early shift, things were quiet.

I grabbed my camera bag, stuffed a dozen rolls of film in a fanny pack and ducked across the catwalk, over the littered roof and down the rickety rear stairs. I fixed my gaze on the building and avoided gazing down from the dizzying height. But still I felt a prickling rash of fear along my legs. The wave of wooziness threatened me all the way to the ground, but avoiding the elevator still seemed to be the more prudent course.

In the mid-eighties, some of Williamsburg's underutilized commercial buildings had been rezoned for partial residential use. But as Thomas the Realtor had explained, Mr. Price, the owner of this property, challenged the change in a long, costly court battle. He had been trying to evict Mrs. Graff, the former occupant of my loft, for years. The irascible old woman was a major thorn in Price's side, and he dearly wanted her tenancy to be judged illegal. She took in stray animals, and then set them loose to roam the mannequin factory, where they chewed on valuable equipment and left highly questionable gifts. She cooked pungent non-kosher food for spite, suffusing the factory with the unthinkable aromas of frying bacon and baked ham. She hung a large crucifix in her window and fitted it with blinking lights that she displayed on the holiest Jewish holidays.

Price accused the old lady of property damage, tortious interference with his business, delinquent payment of rent and being a general *nudnik*.

Mrs. Graff, acting as her own attorney, had countered with charges of age and gender discrimination and every conceivable form of harassment. She asserted that she had lived in the building before the original commercial zoning was put in place and was therefore a legal residential tenant. Somehow, the matter had gotten mired in court delays and bureaucratic bumbling and never been resolved. Price had eventually given up and done his best to ignore the old woman. He had taken in Stillman, the sculptor, who proved to be an ideal tenant: respectful, unfailingly reliable with his rent and, best of all, rarely home.

Technically, the building had never been zoned for mixed commercial and residential use. In other words, despite the rent and deposit checks and a piece of paper that looked very much like a lease, Price could petition to evict me at any time, and he would likely win. Unlike old Mrs. Graff, I was in no position to engage in protracted self-defense or pay a lawyer to defend my dubious turf.

Thomas had advised that the prudent approach would be to keep the lowest possible profile. I slipped out through the back door and made it to the street unseen. Safely away from the building, I slowed to a leisurely, aimless stride. I had nowhere to go, nothing in particular to do. I passed the tank farm and meandered, for a time, along the waterfront.

A few blocks down loomed a giant factory building with blackened windows and a burnt-chocolate facade. A cabin cruiser passed, and from a quirky angle, it appeared as if the boat was towing the building in its energetic wake. I pulled out my Canon and shot several frames before the cruiser steamed ahead, breaking the odd illusion. I continued on, searching for fresh inspiration until a passing couple caught my eye.

They were a stooped elderly pair. The snow-haired man had one hand pressed to the small of his back, fingers jiggling outward in a rakish little dance, and the other planted firmly at his waist. The woman's frail arm looped through his cocked elbow in a tidy hook and eye. They strode in matched rhythm, with their heads tipped together like light-craving plants. Their soft, lined faces showed the ease of long habit and firm belonging. The lens framed them in gauzy sunlight, giving their connection the rich patina of a thing long cared for and lovingly preserved. A brick of loneliness lodged in my chest as I captured them on film.

After they passed, another couple strolled in my direction. The young man had chlorine blue eyes and spiked hair bleached to the yellowed white of mayonnaise. Half a dozen earrings girded his left lobe like razor wire, and a large silver stud pulled his lower lip in a pout. The woman at his side was enormously pregnant, bursting like an overripe peach. Her pale piqué maternity dress had puffed sleeves and a bow at the waist and her flaxen hair was drawn up like Alice in Wonderland's. I read them at first as a near-perfect mismatch. But then they stopped at a corner and stared at each other with a look of intense adoration. I captured their rapturous eye-lock on film and the moment that followed, when the young man knelt and pressed his ring-infested ear against his beloved's gargantuan belly. He listened to their baby swimming in the womb and his smile was sheer bliss and wonderment.

I held the camera to my chest, but for once, I drew no comfort from its familiar company. My stomach cramped with emptiness and fear like a small child who finds herself suddenly lost.

Once when I was four or five, I drifted off while Bertie flipped through a sale rack of summer dresses at Dillards department store. By the time I thought to look for her, she had vanished from the place in which I had planted her firmly in my mind.

I charged around the store in a wild panic, bumping blindly through a jungle of strange legs and sharp-edged displays. Or maybe I heard Bertie tell the story and claimed it as my own. She rushed to the security guard, who reported my absence to the main office. A lost-child alert boomed over the loudspeaker system. Some kindly stranger recognized me by my mother's description, a short, chubby blond girl in a striped red T-shirt and white shorts, and delivered me to Bertie for a reunion filled with tears and bitter reproach.

Don't you ever leave me like that again, Anna Lee Jameson. You had Mommy worried to death.

My cell phone was in the loft, charging in its cradle. I hurried to the nearest stationery store and bought a phone card. It was decorated with Broadway show signs and proclaimed, *I love New York.* Three blocks away, I found a working pay phone.

Like any born-again three-year-old, what I wanted above all—*immediately*— was my mother. But given my current mind frame, talking to Bertie was the worst possible idea. Ditto for my father. My ache for love and comfort was so overwhelming, I would probably have dissolved in a primitive ooze and seeped directly back to Charleston through the phone lines.

Uncle Eli struck me as the next best thing, but when I dialed his office, Laurette, his secretary, told me he'd been called out of town. "Seems a major shipment got held up in some political mess. Mr. Jameson left late last evening to try and straighten things out. How are you doing, Anna?"

"Fine. I just wanted to check in."

"Sure thing. Just hold on."

Before I could protest, she patched me through to Eli's cell phone, a multi-band version that rang all over the world.

"Hello, sweetheart. I'm so glad to hear from you. Is everything all right?"

"Yes, Uncle E. Sorry, I didn't mean to interrupt you in mid-crisis."

"It's my pleasure, believe me. How's the job? How do you like New York? Have you found a place?"

"I have. Everything's going fine, Unc. Honestly. But you sound awfully frazzled."

"I'm just busy. A little distracted, I suppose. That's all."

"You get back to it, then. I'll speak to you when things settle down."

"All right, sweetheart. What's your number there?"

"I can't get a landline for a couple of weeks. You can reach me on my cell phone in the meantime."

"I'll do that. Meantime, you take good care of yourself."

"I will, Unc. You too."

Feeling utterly foolish, I set the receiver down firmly. This was no time for simpering surrender. I had suffered a couple of minor setbacks, a tiny bout of loneliness and self-doubt, nothing more. Lord knew I could put the week to productive use, get my new place in order, familiarize myself with the neighborhood, grow up.

A teenaged boy breezed by on Rollerblades and flashed a toothy grin. As soon as he caught me watching, he commenced a startling series of leaps and turns. He jumped the curb and spun a full three-sixty in the air. Then he backed up in a perfect figure eight. Coming off the curve, he burst in a splay-armed pose and swooped across the street like a broad-winged bird.

I drew out my Canon and crouched to catch him from a more advantageous angle. He escalated his performance in response. Some people shrank from the camera. Others bloomed like parched plants after a healing soak. This kid was fueled by the attention, as if I were operating him by powerful remote. I could have clicked through my entire film inventory, but when I paused to reload, the circuit broke. The boy grew gangly and shy. His eyes fell like a dancer unsure of his feet and he lost his fluidity. In an awkward flurry, he tried to regroup, but the moment was lost. He pushed off and wheeled away with dejection dripping like melted ice cream from his face. Halfway down the block, he looked back and shot me a rueful smile.

I could relate. I had enjoyed the brief, magnetic bond as much as he had. Given the right mix of subject and circumstance, I could lose myself completely in a shoot. There was alchemy involved, the mystical conversion of a fleeting image to something solid and permanent. The camera could wrest smiles from sullen strangers, peek behind their careful public veils. Better yet, in a wink of the shutter, time could be trapped and preserved. Entire stories could be written or rewritten with one swift flare of light. The right shot exposed the truth, told everything.

I reminded myself sternly that this was the point. This was why I pursued this impossible career. This was why I had come to New York and needed to stay.

I had spent much of my life searching for that magical, revealing image, the singular clear vision that had eluded me for thirty years. Something told me I might find the missing truth right here, in the place where my sister was killed.

I had come to a block lined with abandoned warehouses. Fractured windowpanes caught the noon sun like faceted jewels and sprayed glinting light streams along the pavement. I was about to turn away when an unexpected scene at the side of the farthest building caught my eye.

A door opened, and a hulking form in silhouette bloomed behind the screen. A moment later, a scrawny, sallow man stole around from the rear to join him. The pair huddled close, gesturing sharply, then the skinny one took off the way he'd come and the big man drifted back inside.

Nothing happened for a few minutes, but before I had the chance to walk away, a battered car with blackened windows drove up and paused in front of the building. The big man opened the screen, and two young toughs scurried out carrying burlap sacks. They deposited the sacks in the trunk of the battered car and retrieved a torn bulging envelope from the driver. As they hustled back toward the big man, I saw the edge of a thick stack of cash through the tear.

This had to be something big. Probably a drug deal, I thought. I imagined the warehouse stacked with sacks of heroin or cocaine smuggled in from Asia or Central America.

My heart hammered painfully as I ducked behind a silver minivan in the packed line of cars along the curb. I understood the danger here if my instincts were correct, and I was sorely tempted to flee. But if I honestly wanted to be a journalist, I could not run from a potential story. Burlingame's words echoed in my mind. I needed to show him that I was capable of finding something fresh, able to dig something up on my own. If I did this right, I could redeem myself.

Kneeling low, I snapped several more shots of the warehouse. Then, another jittery character approached, working his hooded eyes like a radar-scope. Satisfied, he loped toward the door. Tight black pants bound his butt and a leather vest strained over thick arms and bulging pectorals. I shot frame after frame as he rapped on the door and the lumbering shadow appeared again behind the screen. They exchanged a few words, then the big man passed a brick-sized package to the muscled thug.

I dug into my camera bag for the telephoto lens. I snapped it on and tried to zoom in close enough to get a shot of the package, but no matter how I worked the focus, I was too far out of range to see clearly.

In a crouch, I circled to the side of the van, snapping nonstop, seeking camouflage in the shifting shadows and the sun's capricious glare.

The muscle man wheeled around suddenly and scowled in my direction. I was close enough to see the bulge beneath his vest and the metallic flash of a pistol as the leather slipped momentarily aside. Sinking beneath a shade pool, I held my breath.

The tough hooked his thumbs in his belt loops and flexed his chest in a simian show of physical supremacy. Then he set his jaw and ambled away from the warehouse.

As he started down the block, yet another player approached. This time it was a pout-faced woman in mirrored sunglasses. She wore a short blue shiny dress and slab-thick metallic sandals, laced like a gladiator's, halfway to the knee. Again, the big man poised behind the screen. Again, I watched the nervous, clandestine exchange.

The sun had shifted, casting a broader swath of shade across the roadway. Heart stuttering, I left the cover of the van and drew closer. Spying through the viewfinder, I stole ahead. I planned to bolt at the slightest hint that they had noticed me. A narrow alleyway directly behind me led through to the adjacent street, where a row of shops lured a steady stream of pedestrian traffic. I calculated that I would be able to make it to the company of a crowd before these characters had a chance to overtake me. I struggled to convince myself that this was a reasonable risk.

I had them almost in clear view. I chanced another step, but I was still out of range.

One more.

When I adjusted the focusing ring, the pair at the door loomed in sharp relief against the dark interior of the warehouse. *Perfect.* I set my finger on the shutter release and squeezed, only to find that I had run out of film. Cursing, I reloaded quickly. Then, just as I was about to capture the winning shot, a dark van barreled down the street, bumping on flabby shock absorbers, speeding directly at me. I tried to step out of the vehicle's path, but it swerved in my direction. Bearing down.

I shrank, cringing, against a parked car. The van edged closer, gobbling the meager space between us. I was nipped by the shadow of the grill, breathing the engine's acrid exhaust.

Suddenly, the van cut right, missing me by a wisp. Then, as I slumped in relief, the side door swung open. Massive arms reached out and wrenched me inside. I was wheeled around backward and trapped by steely limbs. A huge hand clamped my mouth and pressing fingers sealed my eyes. I struggled against the suffocating hold and the horrifying darkness.

Flares of panic fired in my mind. Only one clear thought seared through. This must have been what my sister felt. It must have been like this for Julie.

Chapter 14

I strained against my captor's titanium grip. My arms went numb, and a shimmering daze exploded behind my eyes.

Stop. Let me go!

What emerged was a garbled shriek. I wrenched my right foot free and kicked back. My heel struck bone, and the stranger's leg recoiled.

Let me GO!

The voice that answered was surprisingly gentle, like a painless injection. "Calm down now. Easy. No one's going to hurt you."

Slowly, he eased his grasp. "Sorry if I scared you." He showed me a detective's badge, a chunky silver flower in a slim leather case. "Name's Al Elisson. Detective Elisson. NYPD. Are you okay, Ms.—?"

My shock gave way to fuming outrage. I turned in a huff, prepared to face the man down. But he was almost six and a half feet tall with pier-piling arms and a neck you could use to jack up a sixteen-wheeler. "No, I am *not* okay. Since when do the police go around grabbing law-abiding citizens off the streets?"

"Sorry, ma'am. Couldn't be helped."

"What's that supposed to mean? Did I miss something? Have my constitutional rights been revoked? Did I fall asleep and wake up in a George Orwell novel?"

"Nothing like that. How about a nice cup of coffee?" He tipped his giant head toward a thermos. "It's a really good French roast. Fresh beans. Grind them myself."

I thought about the perfect shot that had gotten away. The cops' presence confirmed my suspicions that the strange doings at the warehouse were a big story.

"What did you say your name is again? I want to make sure I have it right for the lawsuit."

"Elisson."

"Listen, Sergeant Elisson."

"Detective," he corrected.

"Fine. *Listen,* Detective, I don't want coffee or anything else from you. All I want is to get out of this truck and go about my business." My camera bag lay at his pontoon-size feet. I hoisted it onto my shoulder and moved toward the hatch. "If I find out that any of my equipment has been damaged, you'll be hearing from me."

His beefy hand cinched my arm. "Sorry, I can't let you go just yet." He spoke into a walkie-talkie. "Drive around, Harry. Looks like we've got a little situation on our hands."

A deep, gruff voice like the detective's crackled back. "Whatever you say, boss."

"I am not a *little situation,* Detective. I happen to be a working journalist, and you have no right to detain me. Now, I insist that you let me go *immediately.*"

"Relax, miss. Please. Have a seat."

"I'm not fooling around, Detective."

"I can see that."

The van turned, then turned again and picked up speed. Below us thrummed the crisp metal mesh of the bridge span.

"I demand to know where you're taking me and exactly how long you plan to hold me prisoner in this truck."

"Calm down and I'll explain as best I can."

Grudgingly, I sat on a narrow bench between several electronic devices.

The cop's blocky face went grave. "What's your name, miss?"

"Anna Jameson. Remember that, Detective. I'll be the one charging you with harassment and unlawful detention. I'll be the one blasting you all over the front page of the *Chronicle* in sixty-point type."

His lips pressed in a weary smile. "I don't blame you for being a little annoyed, Ms. Jameson, but quite honestly, things could be much, much worse. You were about to step into a hornet's nest."

"I can handle myself."

Again he spoke into his transmitter. "I need an update, Harry. Has it gone down okay?"

The driver's voice crackled again. "They've collared Santa Horse and all the elves. Cleanup crew is picking up the take. Looks to be a record snow haul."

"Good deal. Ride around for another ten minutes in case there are any unexpected complications, then you can head back and we can see our guest to her door."

He turned to me. "You live near here?"

"None of your business."

Chuckling, he shook his head. "You're not easy, Ms. Jameson."

"Forgive me, Detective. Being kidnapped makes me just the least bit cranky."

He perched gingerly on the opposite bench, like an elephant trying to hatch a pea. "I'm trying to tell you we had no choice. You heard Harry. What you stumbled on could turn out to be a record heroin bust. As you might imagine, those boys don't take kindly to someone getting in the way of their business dealings, and they're just a wee bit camera shy."

"That happens to be *my* story, Detective. My exclusive."

"Correction. It's not *your* anything. It's a major criminal enterprise we've been staking out for weeks. It's not safe for you or any civilian to be in the vicinity until we have the scene secured. I simply can't allow it."

"What do you mean you can't *allow* it? The public has a right to know about criminal activity, and I have a right to record it."

He sighed. "My job is to protect people, Ms. Jameson, even when that means protecting them from themselves."

"I don't need protecting."

"In this case, you do. So happens the character in charge of that operation is a very naughty boy named Santa Delaguerra. Last guy who ticked him off was a local dealer who turned up a few grand short to pay for a wholesale buy. Delaguerra hacked the guy up and turned him into mulch. Homicide boys found traces of the poor sap on three public golf courses in Queens: bone fragments, a couple of teeth, a little AB-positive dirt and a diamond pinkie ring. Still had the guy's little finger in it. That pinkie was all the wife and kids had to bury. They really ought to make teeny-tiny coffins for times like that. Don't you think?"

The blood drained and pooled at my feet. "That's terrible."

"Actually, the grass on those courses grew particularly lush and green. Unusually disease resistant, too. Even kept down the weeds. Go figure."

I took a probing look at the cop. He had curious puppy eyes and a comfortable lived-in face. His crooked smile threatened airborne contagion. Something about him was achingly familiar, and I scrolled through a number of giant-sized character actors, seeking a match. It was maddeningly difficult to stay as furious with him as I would have liked.

"This is not a nice man, Ms. Jameson. This is a man with a very nasty temper. In fact, I'd have to say he takes crankiness to a whole new level."

"Okay, fine. I understand. You were just doing your job."

He peered at me patiently, expectantly, the way my mother did to signal some serious breach of etiquette.

"And *thank* you for the rescue, honestly. I've wanted to be many things, but never mulch."

His cockeyed smile returned.

"Now, please, Detective. Can't you take me back before anyone else gets the call? Every paper in the city is going to be crawling on this. It would mean a huge break for me if I could get in first. You said yourself that the bad guys have been taken into custody, so it's safe."

He rose wearily to his feet and pressed the intercom button. "Catch me up, Harry."

"I'm listening for it now."

I heard the distant squawk of a transmission over the police band. Then the detective's partner came back on line.

"They're about through checking out the rest of the building. Everything looks nice and quiet so far. Cleanup's under way. Few more minutes, and the paddy wagons will be ready to rock and roll."

"Tell the boys to sit tight until we get there. And tell them to say nothing to the press until I give the word."

"Your wish is my command, esteemed colleague."

"Don't bother being so damned agreeable, partner. Nothing you do is going to get me to forget that poker debt." Elisson clicked off the microphone and hefted his thumb. "I'll have to ask you to buckle your seat belt, Ms. Jameson. Harry went to school in Montana. Majored in rodeo."

Harry stopped at the end of the block. The street outside the warehouse swarmed with cruisers and vans. Most were hastily parked at odd angles like a child's abandoned toys.

Elisson opened the hatch and helped me down. He followed with my camera case, which shrank to a weightless miniature in his hands.

"This means a lot, Detective. Thanks."

"No problem. Listen, I work undercover, so I've got to take off before any of those clowns get a look at me. He handed me a card. "In case you decide to sue or need that cup of coffee or whatever, give me a holler. That's my direct line."

I stuck the card deep in my purse, where I kept the junk. "Sure."

The van drove off. I wandered up the street, snapping frantically. The warehouse plus the tangle of official cars choking the street would serve as perfect set-up shots for the story. I envisioned a front-page lead with a banner headline and a full-page featured jump.

I shot a pair of men hauling out burlap sacks that must have contained the confiscated drugs. I took half a roll of the side of the building, where pelting gunfire had shattered the brick. Idling out front was a correction van crammed with suspects. I counted eight of them, all painfully young, all trying to hide their fear behind flimsy masks of snarling contempt. The next van held three men and two women. I recognized the big chief by his bulky silhouette. His brow was a craggy outcrop over lazy lizard eyes. His skin had the gritty look of a forbidding back road. His lips drew in a threatening sneer around a fence of stained, broken teeth.

I circled the van, trying to avoid the reflective glare and the drug lord's incendiary stare. He tracked the lens, unblinking, and then worked his eyes in a languid stroll over my body. He dawdled awhile at my breasts and slowly brushed his tongue across his lip. He loitered again at crotch level, and smirked.

My face burned fiercely as I hid behind the camera and kept snapping. An armed cop manned the wheel, and another held shotgun position. The prisoners were trapped behind a bulletproof divider, shackled hand and foot. Still, I felt Delaguerra's gaze like an unwanted embrace, a stranger's fingers grabbing me like fruit he meant to steal. That was the downside of a camera's intimate connection. Sometimes, getting too close to a subject is the last thing you want to do.

Chapter 15

The J train pulled out of the station as I raced up the stairs at Marcy Avenue. The next one took forever to come, then stalled beneath the bridge for a full ten minutes. Forty endless minutes later I raced into the Flashlight Building. The elevator stopped at half a dozen floors on the way to twenty-three. I ran down the hall to the film lab, printed detailed instructions and slipped the rolls in an envelope.

I asked to have the first frames on each roll short-clipped. That meant test developing three or four of the exposures in case some processing adjustment had to be made. The Ektachrome professional 200-speed film I'd shot could be pushed several F-stops, if need be. The light at the scene had been tricky.

A portly, pink-skinned man posed behind the desk. His ID proclaimed him Assistant Manager. His name was Earl. He cracked his gum loudly, and exhaled a sugary mist.

I offered my most fetching smile. "This is a really important shoot, Earl. Can I count on you to see that it gets priority kid-glove treatment?"

"Sure thing."

I passed him the film-filled envelope with reverent care. With another gum crack, he flung it blindly backhand toward the packed line of bins.

"How soon can you have it ready?" The processing room was visible behind a room-wide glass partition. At least a dozen technicians scurried about, working the giant machines.

Earl chewed in reflective rounds as his dull eyes bounced from bin to bin. The media group published ten general-interest publications plus at least twice that number of trade rags, and there was a huge mass of pending work for all of them. Nearly all of the visible envelopes were marked *Rush*. Many had the word boldly underlined, circled and framed by frantic exclamation points.

"Couple of hours," he said. "And that's pushing."

"Please, Earl. I've got the jump on this story. I can't afford to lose that."

He leafed through the stack of orders on his desktop clipboard. "Jameson? I don't have anything on it."

"Nobody does. It's something I dug up myself."

He shrugged. "Best I can do is a couple of hours, like I said."

"Come on, Earl. Have a heart."

He ambled toward the back room. "You can wait or come back. Up to you."

"Fine. I'll just explain to Mr. Burlingame that we blew a major scoop because you refused to give it priority. I'm sure he'll understand."

With a sneer, he plucked my envelope from the bin and tossed it on the desk. "You don't like the service here, you're welcome to take your business elsewhere. Maybe try one of those extra-speedy photo places. I hear they give double prints and little cardboard albums and everything."

"Okay, you're right. I shouldn't have said that. I'm sorry. But if I don't get this in quickly, it's trashed. Every minute counts. That's the truth."

He stretched the gum to a membrane and blew a bubble half the size of his head. "Counts for how much?"

I fished two tens and two ones from my wallet.

He examined the bribe with a dubious frown. "Can't light much of a fire with that."

"Can't get blood from a stone, either."

"See what I can do."

"Do that, Earl. I'll wait right here."

With a threatening gum crack, he shook his head. "Bad idea to look over my shoulder, " he chided. "Make me nervous, I might screw up."

"All right. I'll be out in the hall. Let me know as soon as it's ready."

I paced the corridor, dodging the steady flow of reporters headed to and from the research department. A few eyed me warily as if they could see the pressure building inside my skull, threatening to blow and scatter grisly clots of exasperation all over the place. Each time I passed the photo lab, I shot a sharp, meaningful glance through the glass door panel, trying to prod Earl along. But the harder I glared, the slower he seemed to move. Aside from cold cash, the guy was fueled by pure perversity.

I forced myself to ignore him. I waited a full eleven minutes before I broke down and went inside to check on his progress. Earl was perched like a flabby bookend against the wall, in the thrall of a *Victoria's Secret* catalogue.

I tapped my nails on the counter. "How's it coming?"

He flipped the page, turned it sideways and edged it closer to his mud-brown eyes.

"The shoot, Earl? Remember?"

"Shouldn't be long now. Few more minutes," he muttered.

A messenger wearing a purple unitard and a winged black bike helmet bumped through the door. "Got a rush for *Scoop*." He fished a sack of film rolls from his pouch along with a crumpled sheet of paper. "Dispatch says I should wait and make the round trip."

Earl bent the catalogue page to mark his place before examining the routing slip. "You got it, Chief. Take a load off, and I'll turn these babies right over for you."

"After mine, Earl. I was first," I reminded him.

He eyed the clock. "New issue of *Scoop* goes to bed in an hour. Company policy says they get to jump the line."

"But mine is just as time-critical. Maybe more."

"Says who?"

"I do. This story is huge."

"Yeah. Well, let's say this other shoot proves that the world's going to end by close of business."

The messenger whistled low. "You shittin' me, man? World's about to end, I'm sure as hell not doin' it here. I'm going out and get me lots of wet stuff, all kinds."

"Easy breezy," Earl advised. "I was talking hypothetical."

Beneath the helmet, his eyes tensed to slits. "What's that? One of those bad-ass diseases turns your insides to soup?"

"Hell, no."

"Some kind of bomb, then? What, man? Lay it on me square!"

Earl sighed. "Just words, chief. I was trying to make a point for the lady. Show her who's who and what's what. You dig?"

The messenger scrutinized Earl, searching for hints of sincerity. Satisfied, he mopped his sweaty brow beneath the bike helmet. "Hoo-wee! I get to tell you, you had me going there for a minute."

"Lighten up, pal. Life's too short."

"Yeah. That's what I was thinking."

Earl handed him the lingerie catalogue. "Here, check out this mail order. Suck down a little eye candy. Relax."

The messenger flipped to a bathing suit spread and his jaw slumped. "Mail order, you telling me? These guys take Visa?"

"Doesn't everyone?"

"Sign me up!"

I clenched my teeth so hard they hurt. "Please, Earl. I don't have time for this."

He shifted into even slower motion.

"I'm begging you, Earl. I'm pleading with you."

Suddenly, Earl wrenched the catalogue from the startled messenger and jammed it in a drawer. He loaded his arms with film envelopes and raced to the processing room like a Keystone Cop on speed. He rushed back to the bins for another load as the lab door bumped open.

A willowy woman in a boxy gray suit strode into the lab. Fierce opal eyes blazed beneath a Dutch boy drape of blue-black hair. Ivory skin stretched over jutting cheekbones and a firm, square chin. She slipped on the pewter granny glasses dangling from a beaded chain around her neck and took up the clipboard.

"This backlog is still unacceptable, Earl. Frankly, I had hoped for far more improvement by now."

"There has been, Ms. B-briscoe," Earl stammered. "Turnover time's gone *way* down."

"Judging by the number of complaints I've been getting, I'd say your colleagues would disagree."

Earl's pie face went tight. "People just get mad because I refuse to play favorites. That's what they're really griping about."

"That's the truth, Ruth," said the messenger eagerly. "Earl here's a fair ball. The real deal. Liberty and just ass for all."

"Is that so?" She peered through her half glasses at my laminated ID. "I hate to put you on the spot, Ms. Jameson, but I'm a bit confused. I presume you're waiting for a shoot to be processed?"

"I am, yes. A very important one."

Behind her back, Earl signaled frantically. He clutched his hands in prayer position and then drew a slashing finger across his throat.

"May I ask how long you've been waiting?"

Earl aimed a manic pantomime through the glass. "Couple of minutes, and it's coming up right—now." One of the lab technicians tossed him the developed film, which he handed to me. "There you go, Ms. Jameson. Quick as we could do it, like I said."

"Can't complain *this* time," I said. "I don't mean to be rude, Ms. Briscoe, but I've got to run and get this in."

"Of course. Good meeting you, Ms. Jameson. Feel free to call me directly if there's ever a problem."

I cast a pointed look at Earl. "Oh, I will, definitely."

Chapter 16

Dr. Phil Stanton and Professor Sadie Olbetter were in the hall, engaging in one of their frequent rarified intellectual debates. Whatever the issue, if Dr. Stanton was pro, Dr. Olbetter was stridently, vocally con and vice versa.

Their favorite recurrent themes were the death penalty, physician-assisted suicide and genetically altered food, but they could get just as worked up about whether John's or Original Ray's had the best pizza, whether the weather was partly sunny or partly cloudy. Critical matters like that.

This time they were debating the origin and ownership of the diet Snapple iced tea in the staff lounge refrigerator.

"My assistant brought that tea in for me this morning, Dr. Stanton," Sadie snapped. "You might at least have had the courtesy to ask."

"And you might have the courtesy to check your facts before you make false assertions, Dr. Olbetter. It so happens that I purchased this very can at the Venus Delicatessen not one hour ago."

"Then I presume you'd be able to show me the receipt."

"Able, to be sure, but not willing. I have no need to dignify your absurd and insulting allegations. Sadly, Dr. Olbetter, a psychiatric professional would be the one to deal with your particular problem. Delusions of persecution, I believe they're called."

"I'll certainly bow to your considerable personal experience with psychiatric aberrations, Phillip."

"Spare me the spectacle, Sadie. I've seen you bow to the administration far too many times; and the sight is not one I would elect to witness voluntarily."

Clu Baldwin's laboratory at the Latham Forensic Institute was down the hall from Sadie's and Phil's. In her dozen years at the West Tenth Street facility, she had spent countless hours patiently waiting for the pair's intrusive hostilities to end. Normally, she refused to squander her dwindling energies on needless confrontation. But today, she had neither the time nor the patience to put up with their foolishness.

Clu plucked off her earphones, strode angrily out of her office and raised her hands in a "T" for time-out. "Can you two please take it elsewhere? I can't hear myself think."

Sadie, a thin, bookish crime historian, blinked her pale green eyes. "Well, *excuse* us. Come, Phillip. We certainly don't want to disturb Dr. Baldwin. I'm sure she's working on something earth-shattering, as always."

"I'm sure," huffed Phil, an aging Mr. Clean look-alike who ran Latham's evidence department.

Clu watched with immense satisfaction as they made their way out, whispering and giggling like flirtatious seventh-graders. They could find a more suitable place to dip each other's pigtails in the inkwell.

She wanted some time to set her tumultuous thoughts in order before the others arrived. But as she returned to her desk, security buzzed up to announce Solomon Griffey's arrival. Mike Saitas and Russell Quilfo appeared at Griffey's heels, and Ted Callendar and Lyman Trupin showed up five minutes later. Even the chronically, clinically late C. Melton Frame sauntered in a mere ten minutes after the scheduled start of the meeting.

Clu greeted everyone at the conference room door. She had set out the essentials: cups, notepads, pens, a coffee carafe and a large bowl of peanut M&M's, on the scarred walnut table.

Griffey was first to speak. "To begin, I'd like to thank Lieutenant Quilfo for getting us the records so quickly."

Quilfo was a veteran homicide detective on the NYPD who now headed the Cold Case Squad in Queens. "Everyone's pulling together on this for a change. No politics as usual. I've never seen such impeccable cooperation between the DA and the commissioner's office. It's a true miracle. Thank the Lord, folks. Not me."

"Having read the case, it's clear that we have several fertile areas of possible further investigation to explore. But obviously, we need to address the immediate crisis first, " Griffey observed. "What's your suggestion, Ted? How do we reduce the risk you've identified that Mrs. Jameson is likely to attempt suicide?"

"Hard to say. I thought of contacting her husband or physician, but it's risky. Think of a jumper. It's impossible to know what might push her over the edge."

"Isn't there some way to get her into a protective environment? Involuntary commitment, perhaps?" Griffey asked.

"Too risky," Callendar pronounced. "If Alberta Jameson was my patient, I would have her hospitalized immediately. But with the situation as it stands, there are far too many ways such an attempt could go wrong."

"Forgive me for interrupting, Ted. But I've analyzed the tape thoroughly, and I believe we may be focusing on the wrong issue," Clu said.

"Dissension in the ranks so soon?" Frame chuckled. "I knew it was a mistake to take this thing on."

"No need to leap to negative conclusions, Melton," Griffey observed mildly. "Proceed, Dr. Baldwin, please."

"I will, thanks." Clu pulled a breath and tried to settle her galloping heartbeat. "I've examined the tape from several angles, and while I second Dr. Callendar's profound concerns about the caller, my analysis leads me to a different and highly disturbing conclusion."

"Do tell." Frame's tone dripped with sarcastic challenge.

"My first thought was that the woman had developed a guilt-induced pathological response to the crime. Most notably, she referred to the victim as *that* little girl, never using terms such as *my* child or *my* daughter. I see that sort of semantic distancing quite a bit."

Frame snapped his fingers. "So you figured out, that easily, that the mother is suffering from repressed guilt that she is responsible for the killing or knows who is? Remarkable work, Ms. Baldwin. Truly."

"That's far from the only possible conclusion, Melton, though repressed guilt may certainly be a factor. The caller may be unable to deal with some personal sense of responsibility, real or imagined. She may believe that she failed to protect the child or somehow contributed to the tragedy," said Clu. "For example, the parent of a murdered child might suspect that she forgot to lock the door on the night of the crime or that she somehow brought the child to the attention of a dangerous individual."

"In my experience, many parents of crime victims suffer those sorts of doubts," Trupin said.

Clu fished select charts and printouts from the pile of documents in front of her. "True. But there was more. As I'm sure you know, there are reliable vocal markers of a suspect's veracity. When someone lies, especially about an issue that is highly emotionally charged, laryngeal tension increases and respiratory control deteriorates." She pointed to areas of marked slope and flutter on computer-generated representations of the voice from the tape. "There's no question in my mind that the caller was either distorting or withholding significant facts."

Frame puffed his contempt. "That angle was pursued to the death and led nowhere. If the mother was the perpetrator, how do you account for the fact that a left-handed person strangled Julie Jameson and Alberta Jameson happens to be right-handed?"

"That's not—" Clu began.

"How do you explain the absence of defensive scratches on Mrs. Jameson, despite a thorough examination by her personal physician on the day after the crime, when we know the murdered little girl inflicted such wounds on her assailant by the dermal tissue under her fingernails?" Frame beamed with self-congratulatory spite. "And what about the damp footprints on the carpet? The mother wore a size six B; the intruder was a nine triple E."

Griffey broke in. "No one has suggested that Mrs. Jameson committed the murder, Melton."

Frame jiggled a finger in his ear. "My word, I must be hearing things. I could swear Ms. Baldwin just claimed, not two minutes ago, that the caller was lying."

"So I did," Clu said. "But as I'm sure you're aware, there can be many logical explanations for that, as well. One thing that struck me in particular was that the areas of most intense breakdown occurred when the caller made reference to the perpetrator."

"But you just asserted that she is not under suspicion," Frame said. "Have you reached a conclusion or have you not, Ms. Baldwin? I must say, I'm confused."

"As was I. I couldn't make the pieces fit, which is why I tracked down and analyzed an archival TV news clip in which Dr. and Mrs. Jameson made a plea for anyone with information about their daughter's murder to come forward." Clu passed copies of the critical data around the table. "I compared Alberta Jameson's voice and speech patterns from that interview with those of the woman Dr. Callendar spoke with on the phone. There were large, significant differences." She pointed out several gross inconsistencies on her charts.

"That news clip has to be thirty years old," Frame said. "Wouldn't that account for considerable differences? I know I certainly don't sound the way I did at age twenty-four."

Clu also knew that he was having a bit of trouble with his arithmetic. Frame had turned seventy-two last July. "True, the way you sound differs with age, but your basic voice print remains as distinctive and identifiable as your fingerprints. Barring serious illness or surgical alteration, there's only one way to account for inconsistencies like this. The caller was not Julie Jameson's mother."

Griffey's lips pressed in a grim line. "But the woman on the phone did have inside knowledge of the crime. She knew about the missing bracelet, which was in fact a closely held secret."

"That's why I believe the situation is even more urgent than we first believed," Clu said. "Listen." She leaned over and started the recorder. She had advanced the tape to the statement she found most disturbing.

The caller's eerie voice filled the room. *I keep thinking the only answer is to assassinate us all. Make sure anyone who knows anything about Julie's murder is silenced permanently.*

Griffey laced his fingers tightly. "The threat is clear, ladies and gentlemen. Now I suggest we get to work and make sure that no one makes good on it."

Chapter 17

The main elevators terminated on the floor below the executive suite. I raced up the fire stairs, only to find the heavy metal access door locked. No one responded to my shrill hellos or strident pounding. After several maddening minutes, I gave up and went down to the lobby.

Convincing the guard to call up to Burlingame's office consumed more precious time. My message was relayed from security to the reception desk after which it passed through several layers of assistants at the speed of a python ingesting a sheep. I was jangling with frustration by the time the return call came. Mr. Burlingame was unavailable, but if it was truly critical, Mr. Selkowitz would see me for a moment.

On the ride up, I opened the envelope and flipped through the contact sheets. The strips of tiny images looked even better than I had dared to hope. There was the bullet-spattered warehouse wall, the sacks of confiscated drugs, the phony bravado hung like a cheap disguise on one of Delaguerra's young underlings. The drug lord's menacing glare burned back at me.

When the elevator door opened onto the penthouse suite, I found Arthur Selkowitz glancing skittishly at his watch.

"I certainly hope this is as urgent as you suggest, Ms. Jameson. It is not a good time," he said.

I held out the envelope. "This is an early exclusive on a major story."

"I'm afraid whatever it is will have to wait. Everyone is in with Mr. Burlingame, working on a crucial breaking issue right now."

"It *can't* wait. There has to be someone available who can deal with it before we blow whatever lead we have left."

He closed his eyes in weary dismay, but I refused to disappear. "What's the nature of the story?"

"There was a record drug bust in Williamsburg a while ago. I was first at the scene, and I convinced the arresting detectives to give me some lead time before they broke it to the press. That advantage is running out, Mr. Selkowitz. Now what do you suggest I do?"

"I suggest you lower your voice and calm down, Ms. Jameson."

"I'll calm down after someone takes a look at this shoot."

"I can assure you, that isn't necessary."

I watched in sputtering disbelief as he turned and walked away.

"Didn't you *hear* me? This is big, breaking news."

He crossed the broad reception area and ducked down a narrow hall.

Furious, I strode toward the desk. I wasn't about to let that scrawny little man throw away my hard-won break.

The receptionist was on the phone, staring at a solitaire game on her terminal screen.

"Excuse me," I said.

She held up a finger. I was to wait.

"Please. I need help *now*!"

With a scathing silent reprimand, she went on with her call.

Looking around, my eye lit on the metro edition of the *Chronicle*. There, on the front page was Santa Delaguerra's menacing face. NARCOTICS STING YIELDS RECORD HAUL, the headline blared.

Bristling with disbelief, I read the piece through to the center, two-page jump. More shots accompanied the background stories. Several had been taken inside the warehouse before the arrests were made. One showed two young thugs guarding a storeroom packed with sacks of heroin. Another captured a clandestine transaction at the warehouse door. Yet another showed the drug lord hunched like Scrooge over a table stacked with hundred-dollar bills.

The metro edition went to bed at noon. This story had to have been written, edited, illustrated with selected shots and pasted-up before I happened on the scene. Somehow, Burlingame had gotten word of the stakeout and arranged for an inside plant.

The receptionist looked up. With a murmured apology, I turned and skulked toward the elevator.

Halfway there, I was stalled by a voice from behind. "What the hell are you doing here?"

"I thought I had a breaking story, Mr. Burlingame. It was a mistake."

He rolled his rheumy eyes. "A mistake."

"Yes, sir. I didn't know you had the jump on it."

"Actually, you don't know anything about anything."

"I risked my neck to get these pictures for you."

He clipped the end of a fresh cigar. "Here's a breaking story for you, kid. Big news. I expect you to do what you're told."

"You told me to go after fresh, new angles, to chase down exclusives. That's what I was trying to do."

"You were told not to come in for a week. That's seven days, in case they count differently where you come from. One whole hand plus two fingers, if you need the visual aid."

"I understand."

"My ass. You could have screwed up a major lead we've been setting up for weeks, not to mention maybe gotten yourself killed, which is the kind of bullshit aggravation I absolutely don't need. This is my team, my ball, my court and my rule book. You got that?"

I pictured myself on the plane home, dragging it down with the weight of my shame and defeat. "I do."

He lit the cigar with a silver-faced Bic. "You make sure of that, kid. You've got one more chance to get it right. One more strike, you're out."

Chapter 18

I showered quickly and hurried out, late for my dinner with Shelby. I clambered down the rickety rear stairs as quickly as I could, struggling to outpace the pursuing panic. I would not think about the perilous height, the crawling in my legs, the fear slowly snaking around my neck.

Stepping onto firm ground, I filled my lungs. But before I had time to revel in relief, a bearded, little, white-haired man appeared. His arms were tightly woven and his face was an iced challenge.

"You're the new one?"

"Yes."

"I'm Price. I own the place."

"Yes. I know."

"Rent's due on the first of the month. Every month. No excuses."

"I can assure you I'll be a good tenant, Mr. Price. You don't need to worry."

"No pets, no loud parties."

"Of course. Good meeting you, Mr. Price. My name's Anna Jameson."

He recoiled from my extended hand as if I had approached him with a flamethrower.

"I don't touch women."

"Sorry, I didn't know." Thomas had mentioned that my landlord was an extremely Orthodox Jew and adhered rigorously to several volumes of complex rules. But he had not offered any details.

Price eyed me fiercely. "I'm married thirty-eight years. In all that time I never touched a single woman except my wife. You think I'm going to start now?"

"I understand, Mr. Price."

He cocked his head like a curious dog. Despite the studied ferocity, the best word I could think of to describe the man was *cute*. He reminded me of a small child dressed up as a vampire for Halloween. You pretended to be scared, but you ached to smile and pinch his little cheek.

"No subletting and don't try to sneak anyone in. The lease is for you alone. Period."

"That's fine."

"No smoking, no parties, no noise, no mess."

A short, plump woman came up behind him. She wore a cordovan wig, a prim dark dress and a kindly smile. "What about breathing, Moshe? Will you let the girl do that?"

"I'm telling her the rules, Rivka. She wants to live here, she goes along. Not like that old witch."

"Mrs. Graff was crazy, poor thing."

"She drove *me* crazy. How about that?"

"So how come you tried to help her for all those years?"

"Who says I tried to help her?"

"I do. You're a good, kind man, Moshe, no matter how you try to pretend otherwise."

"Okay, maybe I did try to help her. Maybe I'm a little crazy myself. That doesn't mean this strange girl needs to know our personal business."

Mrs. Price winked my way. "Believe me, dear. You're going to love Moshe. Everybody does. Under all that carrying on, he's a regular pussycat."

"Pussycat, my *tuchas*. If you want people to respect you, you show them your teeth."

"Not just a pussycat. A regular *doll*." She lowered her tone to a conspiratorial hush. "Man would give you the shirt off his back. You're in trouble, there's nothing he wouldn't do for you. Regular heart of gold, he has. Platinum, maybe."

He stroked his beard like a faithful pet. "Who asked you, Rivka? I don't remember inviting you to any conversation. You came to walk me home, that doesn't include words."

His wife's smile did not waver. "Welcome to the building, Anna dear. We'd love for you to come to *Shabbos* dinner Friday night."

"That's nice of you, thanks."

"We live five minutes from here, down Marcy Avenue. Moshe will show you."

"I look forward to it. Now, if you'll excuse me, I'd better run."

S helby met me for dinner at the Paradiso Grande on Grand Street. The hostess showed us to the solitary vacant table, a small round at the center of the room.

This was paradise Williamsburg style with plastic ferns and garlic-scented air. Clay pots on the tables held cheap silk flowers in the muddy pink of dried bubble gum. At the center of the room a stuffed parrot perched in an ornate wire cage. When the hostess clapped her hands, the bird's eyes lit up and it twirled around, singing a tinny rendition of "La Cucaracha."

Most everything in the establishment was fried, including the waiter, a scrawny hawk-faced man with dark hair slicked in a vintage fifties pompadour. He stood frowning in exaggerated concentration, with his pencil perched like a dowsing rod above the order pad. His pupils were full moons in total eclipse. He fixed those giant orbs on Shelby as if she were a slice of cream pie and he was starving. "*Que quieres?* What do you want, pretty lady?"

Shelby took no notice when men swooned, as they always did. Inevitably, this inflamed them even more. "What's good?" she asked.

"Place down the street." The laugh shook his jittery frame.

"I'll have the ribs and an iced tea," I told him.

Shelby ordered barbecued chicken with a plantain mush called *mofongo.*

"I'll put that right in for you, *querida,*" the waiter assured.

He went to the kitchen and reappeared with a salad, a bowl of greenish soup, a basket of bread, pats of butter in gold foil, extra napkins and a sugary pink drink with a plastic flamingo stirrer. He crowded all of this on Shelby's side of the table. "On the house, *linda.* Anything else I can get you?"

"No. That's fine," Shelby said.

He waggled his finger at her. "Don't forget to save room for dessert. I'm going to bring you something real extra special."

"I'd like a plain old, ordinary iced tea," I told him again. "If it's not too much trouble."

After he walked away, Shelby locked me in her clear blue sights. "What's wrong?"

"Who said anything's wrong?"

"I could hear it in your voice on the phone machine. That's why I needed to see you tonight."

"That's a technical foul, Shelby. You said you wanted to get together to trash Kim from the Gym."

She swirled her drink with the plastic flamingo. "I do, absolutely. We'll get to that. Now spill."

"It's nothing. A little trouble with the boss. You have your own problems right now. You certainly don't need mine."

"What kind of little trouble?"

"Nothing much. Stewart Burlingame is a pompous, overbearing, unreasonable, rude, detestable, manipulative, horrid, small-minded, raisin-hearted man."

"Sounds as if you don't like him very much, either."

The waiter came back with a plate of fried chicken wings and set them in front of Shelby. "For you to nibble until your dish comes out, *querida*. I don't want you should be too hungry."

"Iced tea?" I asked again with little hope of satisfaction. I was accustomed to being ignored around Shelby. People noticed the painting, not the wall.

"Maybe you should consider changing jobs," Shelby observed.

"If everyone else can deal with him, why can't I?"

She nibbled a wing. "Good question. Why can't you?"

"I don't know. I keep stepping on my own feet. Fouling things up."

"And why do you think that is?"

I knew what came next. Every so often Shelby donned her shrink hat and urged me to muck around in the cesspool between my ears.

I shrugged. "You're the doctor, Doctor. You tell me."

"I can't tell you what I don't know. But this does seem to be a pattern of yours, Anna."

The waiter reappeared with our dinners. Shelby's plate held an entire flock of chickens. Mine was mostly white space around sauce-covered bones.

"Everything okay?" the waiter asked.

"You forgot my friend's iced tea," Shelby said.

His hand flew to his mouth. "Oh my God. I'm so sorry. I'll get it right away. This minute."

She pushed her plate to the center of the table. "Eat."

"What do you mean by a pattern?"

"You're like a runner who always trips at the finish line. Whenever you get close to what you want, you seem to find some way to screw it up."

"For instance?"

"Fourth-grade spelling bee, final round. There you were, a word away from glory, and you flubbed up on *adamant.*"

I gnawed defensively on a scrawny rib. "That's a tough word for a fourth-grader."

"Maybe so, but it's a tough word that we happened to have practiced. I even remember you saying that if there was an Adam ant, there ought to be an Eve ant, too."

"So I forgot. Maybe I had stage fright. Anyway, that's ancient history."

"Fine, then let's look at more current events. You and Kevin, for example."

"We're not an example of anything, Shel. That relationship simply wasn't meant to be."

"Only because you were determined to make it so. Every time he got too close, you pushed him away."

"Not true. He and I have been way too close plenty of times, sometimes several times a day."

"I'm not talking about *sex.* I'm talking about happily ever after and 'Here Comes the Bride.'"

I pressed the frosted glass to my cheek. "When it comes to a lying cheat, those two don't necessarily go together."

Shelby stared at her plate.

I set my hand over hers. "Sorry, Shel. I was talking about Kevin, not Harvey. But that was a dumb, insensitive thing to say."

"No. It's the truth. But it also happens to be true that you are forever finding ways to ruin things for yourself. Take that business with Senator Bedell."

"Come on. How was that my fault?"

I was a few years out of college at the time and had what appeared to be a promising start to the career I craved. Some of the first shots I submitted, snapped at a battered-women's shelter, sold to *The Atlanta Journal*. My naïve head swelled with visions of Pulitzer prizes, fascinating assignments in exotic locales and men in trench coats with clothing underneath.

Then one night, I was in a bar with some friends. Leaving the ladies' room, I spotted Senator Tom Bedell in a rear booth. The girl he was with looked young enough to be his daughter, but his behavior toward her was far from fatherly.

I could not resist taking a picture, even though it meant sneaking out front to get my camera, then hiding behind a potted fern like something out of a bad sitcom.

The shot was intended for my personal collection only. In those days a politician's sexual peccadilloes were not considered fit to print. One did not discuss or display presidential privates in public. Even if such things had been deemed acceptable, Bedell was a powerful, hugely popular, zillionth term untouchable. Trying to humiliate or harm him was a lose-lose proposition.

"You're the one who sent the picture to the *Charlestonian,* Anna."

"That frame happened to stick to the back of the shot I was trying to sell. It was an accident, pure and simple."

"You know what Freud says about accidents."

"Yes, and you know what I say about Freud."

She gave me her ultra-tolerant smile, the one that told me I was getting nowhere at warp speed. "Don't you think it's more than simple coincidence that you happened *accidentally* to send that particular shot to that particular publication at that particular time? It was common knowledge that the senator's family owned the magazine and that he was gearing up for a run at the Oval Office. Of course the Bedells would suppress your picture and then do everything in their considerable power to slap you down for trying to get in their way."

I fished through Shelby's French fries for the crispest one and ate it with a loud, spiteful crunch. She had some nerve, attempting to confuse me with clear, unassailable logic. The Bedell fiasco had caused countless job rejections and ten years of hard time at Pruitt's Photos. The senator had called in markers all over the industry to ensure that my professional name would be mud.

"It was an accident," I muttered lamely.

Shelby's adoring waiter circled our table like a ravenous fly. The instant Shelby sipped a molecule of water he raced over to replace it. He kept brushing away her crumbs and asking if she needed anything. The hostess, who needed him to wait on other tables, kept clapping to win his attention. This triggered the stuffed bird to sing. *La cucaracha, la cucaracha, ya no puede caminar.*

Shelby remained unflappable, but my nerves were starting to fray. "Let's get out of here."

"Sure, I can't wait to see your new place."

"That's sweet, Shel, but not necessary. I'm sure you're anxious to get back to the kids." I signaled for the check. Shelby's waiter stared through me as if I were made of mist.

"Actually, I'm not. Harvey's home for a change, and the nanny has the night off. I want him to spend some time with the kids alone. Maybe he'll realize that even the baby's conversational level is light-years above Kim's."

"How's that situation coming along?"

"I've got it almost resolved. The only open questions are which poisons and who goes first." She motioned vaguely and the waiter bounded toward the table.

"What can I get for you, *querida*? Ready for dessert?"

"Just a check, please."

"Nothing else, you sure?"

"Positive."

His face drooped like hot wax. I knew the look. He would have done anything to delay her departure. Many years back, I was visiting Shelby in her college dorm when a repairman came to fix her broken phone. Poor guy fell for Shelby instantly and hard. He insisted on rehanging everything on her walls with phone anchors. When she started fiddling with scraps of bright-colored connector wire, twisting it absently into rings, the man went out to the truck and returned with giant spools of the stuff, enough to string together a whole community of gossips, enough to lose his job over, to be sure. Shelby had turned the misguided gift away with gentle tact. My friend had the most impeccable sense of right and fairness. It was one of the reasons that my love and admiration for her generally outpaced my seething envy.

We walked awhile in companionable silence, chasing our stretched out shadows toward the waterfront. We passed the tank farm and turned onto my block.

I shrank a bit, seeing the seedy strip from Shelby's sanitized East Side perspective. Bolly, the homeless artist, slept in an upended cardboard wardrobe on the corner. Only his feet poked out, dirt-soled and spattered with paint. Surrounding him was the tiger-striped desk and other curbside finds: the spring mechanism from a convertible sofa, the cracked porcelain bowl of a sink and the mournful head of a broken parking meter.

A fat-lipped working girl, one of the many regulars, was negotiating with a customer. Shelby gripped my arm as they crossed the road and ducked behind a building to complete their transaction.

"Don't worry, Shel. It's nothing."

I turned up the walk to my building. But as I worked the main door lock, I noticed Shelby hanging back at the sidewalk. "Good joke, Anna. Now, let's get out of here, okay? This place gives me the creeps."

"It's not a joke, Shelby. This is it. My apartment is on the third floor."

"You've got to be kidding."

"I'm not." Her horror stung like a slap. "You haven't even seen the place."

"You're right. Forgive me. It just wasn't what I was expecting. I want to see it, Anna. Please."

"It happens to be terrific."

"I'm sure it is. You always had a wonderful eye."

Reluctantly, I led her through the lobby crammed with mannequin parts and packing materials. We rode the cluttered gunmetal cage to the third floor, though it felt to me like sinking. Soiled by Shelby's disapproval, my proud new home seemed shabby and depressing.

She strode around the loft with a studied smile. Made the right canned noises. But I knew she found my baby ugly, nonetheless. "Lots of room," she said. "It's charming really."

"But?"

She caught her lower lip between her teeth. "But I care about you, Anna. This isn't safe. You've got no security, not even a decent lock on the door. And the *neighborhood.*"

"If you're talking about the hookers, they're not a problem. They mind their own business." I let my scowl say the rest, *unlike you.*

"It's not the hookers I'm worried about. It's what goes with them: drugs, pimps, guns, disease, turf wars, dirty money, reckless men in heat."

Like Harvey? I was dying to say. But I held my nasty tongue.

"This may come as a shock to you, Shelby, but not everyone can afford a white-glove doorman building with hot and cold running help. I'm not a fancy Park Avenue psychiatrist like you. I'm a hack photographer, and this is what goes with *that.*"

"There are other answers. Better ones. I can help you track them down. I'd be glad to."

"You're missing the point. I like it here. I don't want a different answer."

"It's all part of the same old pattern, my friend. Same old death wish."

"If you feel so unsafe, maybe you should go."

"Since you feel so angry, maybe I should."

"Fine. I'll see you to the car if you're too afraid to walk around this horrible, scary, dangerous neighborhood alone."

"That's not necessary."

"Neither is any of this," I shot back.

She stopped at the door and fixed me with a look of weary regret. "Call if you need anything."

"Yes, Mom."

"Look, Anna. No matter who else you may push away, I'm not going anywhere. You're stuck with me. For good."

As the door shut behind her, I clutched my ribs against the pain of regret. Stubborn pride glued me in place. Shelby had to be wrong. Otherwise, I was.

I stood inert, listening to her fading footsteps followed by the slow, whining descent of the lift. After I was sure she was out of the building, I hurried to the bedroom window. Hidden by the curtain, I peered down at the street.

Shelby slid away, passing like a cool black swan through a shimmering pool of lamplight. My eyes ached as she drifted back into the darkness and shrank out of view.

Fighting tears, I worked up a nice fresh head of indignation. This was my place and this was a perfectly fine neighborhood. Shelby had some nerve to criticize what she knew nothing about. Brooklyn was a foreign country to her. What right did she have to look down her perky little nose? Her native land was Sutton Place. Her native tongue was forked.

Suddenly, something moved across the street. I stared hard, but I could not bring it into clear focus. My imagination served up the glint of malevolent eyes, feral teeth flashing behind a smirk, a large slumped figure with long, ratty hair. He was the shape and size of Dixon's weird friend Spook. A chill of fear blew through me.

My camera bag was in the living room. I slipped on the telephoto lens and hurried back to the bedroom window. But in the moment I was gone, the figure had vanished.

My eyes must have been playing tricks as usual, molding demons from the shadows. I chalked up the illusion to Shelby's nattering about evil and danger. I added that to the list of bitter grievances against my friend. Counting the gripes, I drifted off to sleep.

Chapter 19

Ted Callendar issued a broad, squeaky yawn. "Sorry."

"Don't be. Those are my sentiments exactly." Clu stood and arched her aching back. She, Callendar and Griffey had gathered two hours before for a late-night brainstorming session around the dining table of her Central Park West apartment. Given their respective schedules, ten P.M. was the earliest they had been able to get together. Clu had never imagined that running in place could be so exhausting.

She raised her legs like a geriatric Rockette, trying to ease the cramps. Through the window she spied the glow of lights from the Museum of Natural History. Tonight, she would fit in neatly as one of the exhibits, relict of a dim, vital age.

Her thoughts scrolled back thirty years. Clu and her husband, Joseph, had bought this stately six-room home in 1972, when the city real estate market had slumped in a seemingly bottomless trough. Clu smiled wistfully, remembering how they had congratulated themselves as prices finally picked up and they watched the value of their meager investment multiply. Back then, Clu had dared to be deliriously happy. She had dared to believe that she and her young spouse were blessed with a fine start and a bright, boundless future.

Whoever saw to such things had slapped her with the cruelest imaginable punishment for that innocent hubris. The love of her life had succumbed in his sleep to a massive heart attack. Clu had awakened the morning after his thirty-fifth birthday to find Joseph stiff and cold beside her. Her fingertips still burned with the memory as she gazed at his beaming young face in the portrait over the mantelpiece.

"You want to quit, Clu? If you like, we can get some rest and try again early tomorrow," Callendar said.

"No. I think we should stick with it awhile longer. You okay to go on?"

"Yes, but Griffey looks to be another story."

Griffey slumped in his chair, snoring lightly, with his chin resting biblike on his chest.

Clu eyed him fondly. "He'll catch up after he catches a couple of winks." She trained her weary gaze on Ted. "Let's go over your psychological assessment next."

Callendar fortified himself with a fistful of jelly beans from the crystal bowl in the center of the table. "Julie Jameson's killer fits the anger/retaliatory murder profile." He pointed to a crime-scene photo of the dead child as she lay in her bed, surrounded by frills and flowers. Angry shock warped her fine features and her limbs were cocked at odd angles. She looked, for all the world, like a broken doll.

Callendar traced the mosaic of bruises on the little girl's chest and neck. "This is typical of the explosive acting-out we see in anger/retaliatory sex assaults or killings. The victim sustains multiple injuries, often inflicted in exactly this rhythmic percussive pattern."

"Why is that?" Clu asked.

"This profile type gets tremendous satisfaction from the homicide, an enormous catharsis. He enjoys the hurting so much, he gets quite literally carried away with it."

"You keep saying *he*," Clu chided gently.

"Or she," Ted conceded. "The instances of women committing anger/retaliatory homicides are rare but not unheard of. And obviously, the woman who called me had some highly personal connection to the crime. But still, I must admit I see our central suspect as a male."

"My gut says it's a woman. Specifically, the woman on the tape," Clu said.

"Perhaps we should chalk that up to artistic differences for the time being and move on." The mild suggestion came from Griffey, who had cracked a red-rimmed eye.

This was no surprise to Clu. Griffey's intelligence so far outshone anyone else's that the man remained superior even in a sleep state. "Point well taken, Griff. Go on, Ted. Please. Let's agree to use the masculine pronoun for the time being and keep all our possibilities open. Our purpose is to beat the clock, not get bogged down in silly differences."

Callendar nodded gravely. "Historically, the anger/retaliatory murderer has a pattern of estranged relationships and a tendency toward pathological attachments to women. He's hugely possessive and demands total power and control. When the victim somehow disappoints him, as she inevitably does, the killer reasons that she deserves to die."

"So he feels no guilt," Clu observed.

"No guilt and no remorse. That's one of the things that makes him so devilishly hard to catch," Ted said. "Immediately after the crime, he might be perfectly charming and relaxed. I remember one case where the perp left the scene of an ax murder with his clothing covered in blood. He washed his hands and face, threw on an overcoat to hide the worst of the gore, hailed a cab and went to the company Christmas party. There, he had a couple of drinks, chatted with colleagues and flirted with the woman he had selected as the next object of his highly dubious affections. Nobody noticed anything at all odd about him. There was a parade of incredulous character witnesses at the trial. If he hadn't bragged about the killing later, I honestly believe he would have gotten off."

Clu doodled on the legal pad she had put out to jot down ideas on. She drew the crude, faceless figure of a woman. She penciled slash marks for the pelting rain. In the legendary storm on the night of Julie Jameson's murder, all sorts of odd behavior might have been overlooked. She remembered Hurricane Queenie very well, indeed. It was one of those events that stuck with you for the length of your days. You could recall where you'd been, what you'd feared, how you'd waited for the forbidding monster to arrive.

She and Joseph had been newlyweds at the time, and the storm had stranded them at home. They had made a makeshift dinner of what little they had in the house, taped the windows and let mighty nature take her course in a variety of ways.

But despite the mitigating pleasures, despite the melting comfort of Joseph's strong, young arms, she remembered the frightening ferocity of that night. People were absorbed with basic safety, in seeking shelter and protecting their homes. There was no reason to presume that the killer had acted deceptively calm in the wake of the killing. More likely, whoever strangled that little girl simply raced through the forbidding tempest unnoticed.

Clu liked Ted well enough, but he saw the forensic universe as a neat series of psychological profile types. He was determined to hang everything on that, even if it required hacking the edges off the facts to make them fit. As a hardened veteran in the human viciousness business, Clu no longer held much stock in any such tidy view. People were animals, after all, capable of endless fresh and daring forms of misbehavior.

"I believe you mentioned that there were elements of the power/assertive type of killer as well?" Griffey observed.

"Only insofar as he left the victim faceup with her eyes uncovered. Ordinarily, the anger/retaliatory murderer will arrange the body in a more subjugated pose. Often, she is turned facedown or has her head covered."

Callendar straightened his stack of notes. "That's all I've got. You?"

By now, Clu was tired of hearing her own voice, sick of their maddening impotence. While they sat around, sifting cold ash, the next victim's hourglass was running out of sand.

Still, she could think of no better alternative than to keep going through what little they had. At least that was something. "I did an exhaustive analysis of the caller's articulation patterns and vocal rhythms. I can say with some assurance that she has spent significant time in the American South, but she has also lived in an urban cosmopolitan setting, either here or abroad. She was well educated in a classical, finishing-school sort of environment. Again, that might have been here or Western Europe. But even that doesn't account for her extremely cautious linguistic processing."

Clu held up a graphic analysis of the call and pointed to the extended time lapses between each carefully wrought phrase. "I'd bet that your caller had years of speech therapy for an articulation problem: a lisp, perhaps, or some other childish sound substitution. She probably came from a family where such imperfections were not tolerated. I don't envy her childhood, privileged though it might have been. From all indications, she was and remains locked in an emotional straitjacket, a timid soul, obsessed with external appearances."

Griffey scratched behind an ear. "Can you estimate her age?"

"Sixty-five, plus or minus, " Clu said.

"About the same as the victim's mother," Ted put in.

"Yes, and I understand that several of the other criteria match as well, but your caller was not Bertie Jameson. There's no question in my mind," Clu said firmly.

Callendar scowled. Clearly, he was no more convinced by Clu than she was by him. Sadly, nobody won in a Mexican standoff.

"Anything else?" Griffey prompted.

Clu closed her eyes and kicked around the dark, musty corners of her mind. "This is speculation, mind you. But I did pick up something not quite right in the way she sounded; maybe an early case of emphysema or some other lung disease. So she's likely a smoker or spends a lot of time around one."

"Couldn't that account for the respiratory stress you talked about?" Ted asked.

"No, this is something else. For as long as I can remember, I've been able to pick up subtle signs of illness from a person's voice. It's an instinctive thing, not hard science by any means."

It was also not always a blessing. She had caught an off-note in her husband's tone on the day before he died, but Joseph had refused to take her seriously.

There you go again, my love. Listening to the fairies and the elves.

If only she had been more insistent. If only—

"That's all I've got for now," she said. "Your turn, Griffey."

"I've asked George Farlow in London to have a look at the tissue scrapings from under the victim's fingernails and the few trace fibers found at the scene. George is a wizard at dealing with old material. Best in the world, especially in cases like this, where lots of hands have been involved and the probability of contamination is murderously high. Unfortunately, there's no rushing the kind of precision we need."

"What have you heard from Quilfo, Ted?" Clu asked.

"Nothing so far. But he has put out feelers all over the city, which will hopefully stir the pot."

Quilfo had agreed to spread the word to his fellow officers. They were to report anything they heard on the street about the Sleeping Beauty Murder, no matter how far afield the rumor seemed to be. A striking number of cases, even cold hard ones, were broken through simple word of mouth.

Sadly, the only noise so far had been from C. Melton Frame, who seemed determined to parlay the situation into still more media attention for himself. Despite the Arcanum's strict edict against discussing work in progress with the press, Frame had been issuing tantalizing hints about the case through his publicist. Mention of his "giving Sherlock Holmes a run for his money" had appeared on page six of the *Post*. The blowhard would stand on anything, including innocent victims, to raise his head above the crowd.

Clu sketched an open grave filled with question marks. Then she scratched out the drawing with large angry lines. "There has to be something more we can do."

"I suggest we take another read through the file," Griffey said.

Each of them had a folder containing every DD5 on the case. The detectives' reports detailed everything from Bertie Jameson's frantic call to 911 on the morning after the murder to the latest routine follow-up on the case by the precinct in charge almost a year ago. All of the lab and autopsy results were included, crime-scene photos, witness interviews, hard leads, anonymous tips.

Like the others, Clu had been through the reams of pages many, many times. She had sorted and annotated the information, trying to make some sense of it. The exercise had earned her nothing but intense frustration. But given the urgency of the situation, she was more than willing to have at it again.

She glanced across the table. Griffey divided his papers into tidy, even stacks, then shuffled them like playing cards. He cut the deck, setting the top half on the bottom. Finally, he rotated the entire pile and gazed at the documents upside down. Slack-faced with utter concentration, he began going through them, one by one.

Clu watched with unabashed reverence. The man engaged in stunning mental gyrations, death-defying feats of analysis and synthesis. Reluctantly, she turned to her own copy of the file.

For the next fifteen minutes, the only sound in the room was the dried-leaf rustling of pages. Then Clu caught a near inaudible hum. She looked up to find Griffey squinting at one of the crime-scene shots through a magnifying glass.

"Interesting," he murmured.

Clu paused with a page in midair. Callendar's head shot up, as well. "What, Griff? What do you see?"

Griffey pointed to a tiny dark spot. "That faint mark there, on the child's neck beneath the ligature line. What does it look like to you?"

"A bruise. I counted thirty-two on the body, made by the knuckles of a closed fist. It's consistent with the rhythmic assault pattern I mentioned earlier."

"That's what I presumed, as well, Ted," Griffey said. "The coroner referred to multiple contusions followed by the strangulation that caused the child's death. With that in mind, I took a harder look at this particular mark over the hyoid bone. It's different from the others. Have a look."

Clu stared at the pink oblong blotch under the magnifier. Ted Callendar peered over her shoulder. "It's a thumbprint."

"It is, indeed," Griffey said. "It would appear that whoever strangled the child did so manually first and then applied the ligature."

"That makes no sense, "Clu said.

Griffey smiled ruefully. "Murder rarely does."

"Now, the million-dollar question is: What, if anything, can we learn from that print? Skin is a poor print vehicle in the best of circumstances, and what we have here is a very old image of dubious quality." Griffey turned to Clu. "Do you think someone at Latham can extract any meaningful information for analysis?"

"Honestly, I don't know, Griff. I'll check with Evidence first thing tomorrow," Clu said.

"Excellent. Meanwhile, Lyman has agreed to get his pals in D.C. to start compiling the whereabouts of the principals in the case."

"You're a step ahead of me as always, Griff," Clu said. "I was just about to suggest that. I'd say we have more than enough to interest the FBI."

Callendar chuckled. "That doesn't take much these days. Since RICO took out most of their favorite suspects, most of those poor souls are itching for action. Quilfo tells me a couple of Feds have taken to hanging out at the Cold Case Squad, hoping for vicarious thrills."

"I imagine this thing will get their blood pumping," Clu said gravely. "One proven lunatic on the loose and Lord knows how many potential victims."

The grandfather clock struck one A.M. Solomon Griffey pushed back from the table. "If you are in agreement, I'd suggest we call it a night. We have our work cut out for us tomorrow, to be sure."

Chapter 20

I spent much of the morning fighting with myself. At least a dozen times I picked up my cell phone to call Shelby, but decided against it. I wanted to sulk awhile, wallow in deep, satisfying resentment. Shelby's clear intelligence and forgiving nature would spoil everything.

Still, I felt terrible. No matter how fierce our disagreement, Shelby remained my best and most important friend. I picked up the phone once more, but I still could not bring myself to dial.

When I heard my phone's tinny rendition of "Ode to Joy," I lunged for the thing, hoping it was Shelby calling to capitulate first. But no such luck.

"Hello, sweetheart. Glad I caught you. Is everything all right?"

"Yes, Uncle E. How about you? Have you gotten things straightened out?"

"Not yet, but I will. I will."

I wasn't used to hearing my uncle so somber and absorbed. He sounded thick with worry, totally disconnected from his inner elf. Or maybe it was simply a bad connection.

"Are you all right, Unc? Feeling okay?"

"Yes, Anna. Just a little tired, I guess."

"Come home, then. Get some rest."

"I will, sweetheart, believe me. Just as soon as I can. Meanwhile, you're sure you're okay? There's nothing you need? No problems?"

"Not unless you count this stubborn uncle of mine, wearing himself to a frazzle."

"Don't worry. I'll be fine as long as I know everything is going well with you."

"It is. You take care, please. Talk to you soon."

From downstairs came the sound of Moshe Price flogging his troops. "Tell me, David. Did you go to school to learn how to be such a *klutz,* or does it come naturally?"

"People drop things. It happens."

"People dock people's pay for dropping things. That happens, too."

"Look, I'm shaking. I'm trembling."

"All I get from you is big-mouth back talk and busted merchandise."

I grabbed my camera bag, suffered the perilous descent down the rear stairs and ducked out. At this hour, a sole hooker strode up and down across the street, tapping entries into her PalmPilot. Bolly, the homeless artist, perched on the corner on a salvaged bar stool, sipping a cappuccino. A lanky gray-haired woman pushed a toy poodle in a gleaming English pram. This was prostitution and vagrancy New York style. This was walking the dog. I had an entire dictionary of fresh rules and confusing idioms to learn.

I snapped a couple of shots, but I could not muster my usual enthusiasm for the work. The argument with Shelby hung on me like a yoke. So did my week of forced exile from Burlingame Media. After the debacle with the drug heist, if I happened upon something that looked like a story, the only rational response would be to ignore it.

The empty days stretched before me like a huge desert sprawl. I did not do well with unmarked time. Left to my own dubious devices, I tended to ramble and lose my way. Despite Shelby's assertion, this was not deliberate. Trouble did not always announce itself with flashing caution signs. At least, it did not to me.

Two blocks away, I came to a schoolyard. Small kids dashed about in a giggly game of tag. A large group huddled in a ragged circle, playing dodgeball. Through the lens of my Canon, I caught the spray of silken hair, cheeks flaming, eager fingers grasping chunks of sky.

I crouched low and aimed my lens through the twisted diamonds in the wire fence. Children in their natural habitat were the most fascinating creatures, studies in raw, unfettered response. I focused on a plump, freckled girl in a white shirt and plaid jumper. Her front teeth were chipped. Unruly red hair spilled around her squat features like carrot juice. In the nanosecond it took to advance the film, her face went from jubilant to grave, from hopeful to horror-stricken. A loving glance dissolved in an acid wash of spite.

My spirits rose. Here was a perfect project to pass the time. I envisioned a trail of sequential shots cataloguing the full range of human emotion. Click, and the little girl showed me one after the other: envy, anticipation, remorse, revulsion, hope, elation, commotion, surprise. Happily, I snapped away. The camera was magical, indeed.

A shadow bloomed before me. "Can you take my picture, lady? Please?"

"I will in a minute."

"How many is a minute?"

"Sixty seconds."

"One-two-three-ten-*sixty*. Okay. I'm ready now."

"I understand, sweetie, but I'm not. You'll need to wait a little while, okay?"

Carrotop's face was a flower in accelerated time lapse, Silly Putty with an attitude. I wanted to catch every pliant wiggle of her features. I had an odd sense they held some crucial secret, that they could reveal something rich and profound.

My little tormentor refused to quit. "How 'bout I take your picture, then? Can I, please? Pretty please, huh?"

"Not right now."

"I promise I'll be very, very, *very* careful. I would never drop your cambra."

"If you wait patiently, I'll let you. Okay?"

Her voice went coy. "I know what you are: a photo-toe-gographer."

"I'm a *photographer,* yes. And right now I'm very busy working."

"I had my picture taken before lots of times. Mommy took me."

"That's nice."

"I even had my picture taken with Goofy once and once with Elvis Parsley. And you know what?"

"What?"

"I'm going to be a photo-tah-grapher when I grow up. Just like you."

"That's nice, but I need you to move over just a little bit, okay? Photo-toe grabbers can't have people blocking their light. That's very, very important."

I was still riveted on the redheaded girl, willing this pesky little gnat to fly away.

The child's voice curled in a whine. "How come you're taking Amanda's picture a hundred kazillion times and you won't take mine even once? That's not fair."

"If you go play awhile, I promise I'll take your picture later, and I'll let you take some, too."

"But I want you to take it *now!*" She started wailing like a car alarm, drawing a stampede of worried adults. Splayed thighs and spread haunches blocked my view of the carrot-haired girl.

"What happened, Cindy sweetie? Are you hurt?"

The child spoke on grand tics of grief. "She's a mean old lady and she only likes A-man-da."

The larger shadow moved closer; slim denim-clad legs blocked my view. "I'm sorry, I'll have to ask you to leave."

"Just a few more minutes, please." I couldn't bear to stop shooting now. The rubber-faced girl kept showing me fresh moods—more than I knew existed. I needed to register them all.

The other teacher shielded her eyes and squinted down at me. "Anna?"

Startled, I recognized Drake's pixie friend Monique. I stood quickly. "You work here?"

"I teach the kindergarten. This is the most amazing coincidence. I was talking about you not ten minutes ago, saying how great it would be if we could get people like you from the neighborhood to come in and run workshops for the children."

"Sounds like a great idea. I'd love to."

"You mean it?"

"Absolutely. My dad introduced me to photography when I was younger than these kids. Sad to admit, but I can't think of anything that's given me close to as much pleasure. Sharing that with these guys would be fun. Anyhow, maybe there's a future Ansel Adams or Cindy Sherman in the bunch. I'd be proud to say I knew them when, helped them get started."

"That's wonderful. You can't imagine what a difference it would make. With the budget cuts, we're down to bare bones. No real art program, no music to speak of, barely any PE. When would be good?"

"I'm between assignments this week, so I'm pretty free."

"Perfect. I believe you could be the antidote to twenty-seven cases of acute spring fever. Twenty-eight, including mine. We could start right now if you're up for it."

"Now's fine." Carrot Juice twirled at the edge of my vision. I hated to miss a single shift of her kaleidoscopic face.

Monique flipped the latch and opened the gate in the fence. The kids clamored close, reaching and pleading as I entered the yard.

"Can I be first?"

"No, it's my turn. I called it."

"I called it firster."

"No, me!" Cindy, the aspiring photographer, asserted her priority by shoving a smaller boy to the ground. Upturned like a turtle, he filled his bony chest and went my mother's favorite shade of crimson.

"Places, children," Monique called with crisp authority. The kids scrambled to sit in tidy, silent rows. "Ms. Jameson is our guest and we need to show her our very best manners."

"Yes, Ms. Sharon," they chorused sweetly.

"Good. Now, I'm going to give each of you a number. When your number is called, you can come and work with Ms. Jameson. While you're waiting for your turn, we'll have storytelling time."

She tapped each child lightly on the head as she counted aloud. Between rows, she offered me a brief, whispered course in kindergarten management. "The smartest thing anyone ever taught me about teaching is to ignore rotten behavior and catch kids being good. Even the most dedicated monsters act appropriately once in a while, even if it's only by accident. They get better and better if you reward them with praise right away."

"I wish someone would explain that to my mother."

She counted off another row of heads. "Fairness is a big issue. Kids this age are hypersensitive about what they consider justice and equity. They want their share, or maybe a little more, especially when it comes to attention."

"Sounds like kids my age." I pulled my guilty gaze away from Carrot Juice.

Monique tapped the final boy in the last row. The toothless towhead radiated pride as if he had won Olympic gold. "I'd suggest you work with two students at a time, if that's all right with you," she said. "You can show each one how to take a picture of the other."

"Excellent idea. It'll be much easier for them to shoot someone the same size."

"Okay, number one and two, go with Ms. Jameson."

Two flame-cheeked hellions scrambled to their feet and rushed me like guided missiles.

"Easy, Ben and Rusty. Slow down," directed Monique. The boys stopped short, then continued toward me in exaggerated slow motion. "Amanda, please come up and be our first storyteller."

My attention swerved again to little Carrottop as she rose from the center of the seated pack. Triumph registered on her pliant face. Smugness yielded to a wince of self-doubt. Before I could snap a few quick shots, my little charges took me firmly in hand. They pulled me across the yard toward the school building, a four-story red-brick structure, vintage 1950.

"Gimme your camera," demanded the dimpled moppet called Ben.

"I'm gonna take pictures of doggie poop," Rusty giggled.

"You're a silly poop-head yourself," Ben observed.

"Am not."

"Are so."

While I waited to catch the little beasts being good, I locked on the telephoto lens and caught a few more shots of Amanda as she made her recitation to the group. I caught a few disconnected scraps of what she was saying, but the story registered clearly in her ever-shifting expression. Her eyes stretched in extravagant anticipation of her forthcoming birthday, then sparked with fear as she reported that her grandfather was gravely ill. If Grampy didn't get better in a hurry, a promised trip to Great Adventure might be postponed. Her lip trembled with grief, then curled in resentment. Worse than that, the old man might get to go to actual *Heaven,* while her parents refused to take her to an amusement park in *New Jersey.*

Talk about not fair.

Rusty tugged at the leg of my navy pants. "When do I get to take a picture?"

"Can we please use the camera, lady? Promise we'll be good." Ben's look glowed with angelic sincerity.

I took out the old Polaroid I used for test shots. While Rusty mugged, I showed Ben how to see through the viewfinder and hold the camera steady as he clicked. Both boys watched bug-eyed as the glossy image materialized. Through them, I relived my first mystical contact with the power of light and film.

When his turn came, Rusty took up the Polaroid with great solemnity and peered unblinking through the lens. His tongue bored into his cheek in intense concentration. "There," he said in triumph as he snapped the shutter. As the likeness bloomed, he eyed it reverently. "That's the very bestest thing I ever did."

"It's an excellent job," I told him, feeling his wonderment and pride.

Introducing kids to this endeavor I so loved felt like one of the very bestest things I'd ever done, as well. I worked through story time and the nature lesson that followed. After that, all the kids except the ones assigned to me went inside for math readiness and computer work. I felt like a carbonated kid myself, discovering the myriad joys of the camera all over again. Time passed with such dislocating speed, I was incredulous when Monique appeared at the classroom door and tapped her watch.

"Only time for two more before dismissal," she said. "Can you come back tomorrow?"

"Absolutely."

"Great. You're a huge hit with the children."

"It's mutual."

While I waited for the next pair in line, I made a mental list. I'd run out of expensive instant film four groups before. The others had seemed happy enough waiting for results. I planned to drop the film at a one-hour place on my way home so they could see their shots tomorrow.

My mind was spinning with enthusiasm and ideas. After everyone had a turn, I would give each pair a chance to play with candid shots. They could record a daily picture diary, chart their growth in handmade albums and create picture stories.

"We're ready now, Ms. Jameson."

A plump, putty-faced boy stood waiting. Behind him, a petite blonde girl studied the ground.

"Hi. Are you ready to take pictures?" I asked.

"I'm ready." The boy posed with an exaggerated smile and his fists planted gamely at his waist. His teeth looked like a picket fence with several missing posts. The little blonde averted her face.

"What's your name, sweetie?" I coaxed.

"I am Oliver Matthew Steven Weller-Durst," the boy said. "Wanna hear me spell that?"

"Sure."

"T—H—A—T," he said, giggling.

"What's your friend's name?"

"She's shy."

"Shy? That's an unusual name."

The girl's delicate frame shook with mirth.

"So tell me, Shy, have you ever taken pictures before?"

"I'm not *Shy*. I'm Viviana."

"Really? You seem a little shy to me."

She giggled again, but still, she averted her face. I dangled my Canon as bait. "Come here, Viviana. Look through this special window and tell me what you see."

She edged closer and held out her hands. Slowly, she turned toward me.

My throat clamped and my heart hammered viciously.

Caught at the right light and angle, the child looked exactly like my sister. Then she moved and the disquieting illusion fell away.

Chapter 21

Phil Stanton was on the phone, ordering supplies from the phone book–sized catalogue on his desk.

"That's the package of graphic pencils on page one nineteen, not the box on special on one seventy-two. I presume those are medium leads? No? Then maybe I'll take the medley you feature on the insert. And why don't you add a few packages of those nice-colored folder tabs. I like the assorted colors, self-sticking type, but with the natural glue surface, not the peel off."

Clu caught his eye and tapped her watch.

Stanton held up a finger and returned to the catalogue. "Now when are you going to get more of those lovely accordion paper folders with the Velcro closures? Quite honestly, I find the new plastic version somewhat off-putting. So antiseptic."

He listened and then chuckled dryly. "Yes, yes. Isn't that always the way? My theory is that they have a discontinuation committee that meets whenever I've settled on something I particularly like. Various companies have ceased production on my favorite accordion folders, shaving cream, golf balls, gym shorts and aftershave. It's uncanny."

"Please, Phil. This is *important*," Clu said.

"Excuse me," he told the phone. "This is important, too, Dr. Baldwin." He sighed mightily. "Now, where were we? Oh, yes. I'd like to apply a small credit I have with you people. It's from about a year ago, something under ten dollars, but every bit helps, I always say. Can you look it up? Certainly, I'll wait."

Clu opted not to. She pressed the switch hook, disconnecting the call.

Stanton glowered at her. "That was highly unnecessary, Dr. Baldwin. Now I shall have to repeat the entire transaction again."

"I'm sorry, Phil, but I need your help and time is of the essence."

"I hesitate to state the obvious, but disrupting my call is hardly an effective way to predispose me to help you."

"All I need is ten minutes. This has nothing to do with playground politics or our inalienable constitutional right to dislike one another. It's a matter of life or death."

His look brightened. "Yours?"

"Sorry to disappoint you. It's about the Julie Jameson case. We have reason to believe that the killer may be planning to strike again."

"We? Who, pray tell, would that be?"

Clu winced. She hated to play her ace of trumps so early in the game, especially given that it involved the cause of Stanton's seething envy. He had been angling for an invitation to join the Arcanum for years. When he was passed over yet again and Clu was asked to join, he took his boundless frustration out on her. "The Arcanum is looking into the child's murder. We've discovered something that falls within your area of expertise, Phil. We could dearly use your input."

Phil leaned back in his studded leather chair and laced his fingers behind his doughy neck. "Are you saying that the Arcanum lacks an evidence expert? Astonishing."

"The group's charter limits the membership to thirty, as I'm sure you know. We often look to outside sources for help."

"And when those sources prove valuable, do you exalted souls ever deign to extend a membership invitation?"

"If you agree to help us, I'll make the recommendation the next time there's a vacancy. No promises, no guarantees. That's the best I can do."

"I am a seasoned, respected professional, Dr. Baldwin. If your silly little group requires my expertise, they should recognize the value of my participation. It hardly seems reasonable that one must wait around for a current member to move to another country or the afterlife."

"It's not my decision, Phil. All I can do is make the recommendation. Now will you help or not? There are certainly other evidence people I can ask."

He tapped an impatient cadence on the desk. "What have you discovered?"

Clu showed him the thumbprint on the crime scene photo of the Jameson child. Perched on the stern wooden chair opposite his desk, she waited.

For several minutes Phil squinted at the magnified image. His broad face warped with distaste. "Unconscionably poor quality. Not to mention pitiful evidence management. These photographs should have been stored in clean plastic sleeves. They have been exposed to damaging light rays and ambient pollutants."

"Can you do anything with it?"

He filled his chest and exhaled a long, noisy stream. "Normally, this would be simple. Print analysis today has been refined to rapid, pinpoint science. You've never shown much interest in my department's work, Dr. Baldwin. Perhaps you'd care to see the current state of our art."

"As I explained, Phil, there's a time problem."

"I assure you, none of your precious moments will be wasted. Come along." He led her through the rear office door to a large, garishly lit laboratory. Everything was computerized, digitized, spewing dizzying patterns and ever-shifting shapes. Sharp halogen beams struck the polished-steel surfaces and speared the light shards streaming through the blinds.

Phil crossed to a ponderous machine near the window. "Normally, we capture the sweat and sebum that produce a latent print on the glass faceplate of a scanning device similar to this one. The system we've developed uses a vector analysis of the data at a minimum effective resolution of two thousand dots per inch. From there, we make several passes to optimize and clarify the image. Basically we're converting raster pixels, which are the horizontal scanning lines in a computer image, into vector lines, which can be used to classify the prints. The system is cheaper, faster and far more reliable than individual analysis by even the best print expert."

Clu set her thumb on the faceplate. "Unfortunately, we don't have a live suspect; we have a faded old photograph of a print. This is all very interesting, Phil, but I don't see the relevance."

"Patience, Dr. Baldwin. Given that the investigators did such a slovenly job of gathering and preserving this evidence, our only reasonable approach is a classical dermatoglyphic analysis, or as you may know it, scientific study of the palmer and papillary ridges."

"Fingerprint analysis, you mean."

"In layman's terms, yes." He inserted the photograph into a high-powered magnification unit. "Parts of the print are obliterated. Likely the subject's skin was overly damp. Still, it would seem to fall into the whorl pattern."

"Reasonably common."

"True, but in the palmist view, the subject with this type of configuration tends to be ruled by inescapable needs and desires. He's typically selfish and suspicious, willing to ignore basic societal rules when it suits his warped sensibilities."

"You honestly believe that? Palmistry is not exactly hard science."

"Maybe not, Dr. Baldwin, but it is based on extensive clinical observation. The best practitioners develop quite the hand feel, so to speak. Over many decades of study, several highly respected palmists observed that the whorl pattern in fingerprints appeared disproportionately in criminal populations."

Clu nodded wearily. "Interesting. Now, what if anything can we do with that print?"

Phil spewed air like a ruptured balloon. "All right, then. I'll charge right to the point, if you insist. We've developed algorithms to extrapolate from partial or damaged print information, which can then be run through a fingerprint database such as CAL-ID or AFIS."

"That's wonderful."

"It would be, but in this particular case, I don't think we could yield reliable results. The problem is twofold. First, the image itself is flawed and faded, but additionally, our analysis would require an enlargement, which paradoxically would magnify the distortion."

"So we're back to square one."

"Not exactly. I believe I have enough information here to make a reasonably reliable visual comparison."

Clu groaned. "So you're basically saying that we'd need to have a print to compare it with. What good is that?"

"Simple," he said. "I can compare it to the exclusionary prints the lab techs must have taken at the murder scene. Even incompetent boobs such as the investigators on this case would have followed that basic procedure. With any luck, you'll find them in the evidence room at the precinct."

"Excellent. I'll get our man in the department on it right away."

Stanton's face lit with a puckish grin. "Obviously that little club of yours could use some genuine expertise, Dr. Baldwin, not to mention some younger, more nimble and energetic minds. Embracing the future demands a willingness to move on and make bold, courageous changes, don't you think?"

Clu sighed. "Quite honestly, Dr. Stanton, at times like these I try not to."

Chapter 22

I dropped off the film at a one-hour photo shop on Berry Street, which was cleverly named One-Hour Photo; then I headed for a market down the block. Energized by my teaching debut, I decided to throw an impromptu dinner party. Monique was free, as was Dixon. I was about to call the others who had helped me fix up the loft, but my brain balked when it came to Dixon's weird friend Spook.

I kept catching glimpses of the mechanic, or a figure shaped like him, lurking in the shadows, following me around. Knowing that this might be a product of my imagination did not make me any more willing to invite the creepy character back to my home. Instead, I decided to limit the guest list to two.

I tossed a package of linguini in the cart along with plum tomatoes, mushrooms, Parmesan cheese, fresh basil and assorted other spices. Trolling the aisles, I added a sourdough baguette, olive oil, a wedge of runny Camembert, pistachio nuts, a tin of butter cookies, chocolate chip ice cream, strawberries and whipping cream. I bought coffee and other basics to stock my vacant pantry: sugar, licorice whips, Oreo cookies, diet cola, marshmallows, honey nut peanut butter, maple syrup, potato chips.

After picking up the developed film, I trudged home, struggling under the weight of four ponderous bags. The checkout clerk had piled them so full, I could barely see where I was going. To make things worse, it started to sprinkle as soon as I left the photo shop.

Quickly, the rain intensified and the wind picked up, lashing straps of saturated hair in my eyes. Soon the grocery bags were soaked and threatening to disintegrate.

By the time I reached my street, I was in similar shape. But weather, like many things, is subject to highly personal interpretation.

Bolly, the homeless artist, was in the middle of the street, dancing jubilantly in a yellow slicker, hands cupped to catch the pelting downpour. When his palms filled, he juggled the water with manic glee. Three of the regular working girls huddled beneath an awning, watching his performance with ill-disguised disgust. Anxious to get inside, I sprinted down the block.

Muddy runoff sluiced across the walk. Cradling the sodden bags, I fished through my cluttered purse for the key. As I found it, I felt a harsh jab at the small of my back. My head filled with overwrought aftershave. A breathy rush invaded my left ear.

"You look real hot, baby. How much?"

Turning, I found a brawny ape in a Michigan State football jersey and sweatpants. The rain drenched his cropped greasy hair and streamed down his square, pitted cheeks. His broad neck tapered to a comically small head and his outsized shoulders shadowed absurdly narrow hips. He looked like a parade balloon gone awry.

I stifled a laugh. "Excuse me?"

He pumped a fist in obscene suggestion and snaked his other hand around my waist. "Little Johnny wants to come out and play. So how much?"

"Are you nuts? I'm not for sale. Get away from me."

As I wrenched free, one of my bags tipped, spewing sacks of chips and cookies on the flooded walkway. The maple syrup followed, and the jar broke, bleeding sticky amber in the mud.

"Look. I haven't got time for games, baby. Tell you what. I'll settle for a blow job."

"If you don't get lost, right now, I'm calling the police."

His face screwed in pained concentration. "Okay, a hand job, then. But that's my final offer."

I pulled out my cell phone and jabbed 911. As the call rang through, he backed away with his hands in the air. "Easy, girl. Whoa. I'm going. I'm out of here."

His pale blue pickup was parked on the opposite side of the street. After he unlocked the cab, I scooped up what I could of the wet, fallen groceries, worked the lock and slipped inside.

Before I could shut the door, an enormous burst from behind sent me staggering. I collided with a trash bin filled with mannequin parts. The bin overturned, scattering its grotesque contents. A cracked skull caught me hard in the breastbone. A disembodied hand raked my arm.

I was pinned between the ape in the football shirt and the trash, finding it hard to tell them apart. Using what little leverage I could muster, I butted the slobbering jerk away. He slipped on the wet floor and went sprawling.

"I told you to leave me alone. Get this through your thick skull: I am *not* a whore. Now get *out* of here!" I railed.

He burst to his feet and lunged at me. "I'll teach you to tease, you bitch."

He struck like a sprung trap: hands, teeth and hot, venomous rage. I couldn't free a limb to knee his crotch or poke his dark, furious eye.

Even as my fear grew, my fight was running out. My muscles quavered and burned. A defeated grunt escaped me.

"Good," he rasped. "Now you're ready to play my way, aren't you? You be a *real* good girl, and nobody gets hurt."

His steel grip devolved to a crude revolting caress. He nuzzled my neck and squeezed my breast, sparking pain. The harder I fought, the more ferociously he clutched me.

Desperate, I went slack.

"That's right, baby. You just relax and leave everything to me."

I forced myself to stay absolutely still as he pressed me to the concrete floor and pinned me with his suffocating weight. Groping down between us, he untied the knot at his waistband and worked the damp sweatpants down his hips.

He snickered. "You won't sell, I'll take the free sample."

As he fumbled with his pants, I focused on his warped, ugly face. When his eyes strayed to the left, I arched my right fist to catch the mangled bridge of his nose.

But he was too quick and too strong. He caught my arm with hideous force and pinned it painfully to the ground.

"Try that again and I'll break it."

"Get *off* of me. Let me go!"

"Shut the hell up."

He writhed against me, moaning low.

"No!"

I was trapped, immobile, sinking beneath the fear. Moshe Price and his crew were gone for the day. No one on the street was close enough to hear me above the striking rain.

I kept struggling on instinct. He tore at my saturated blouse until the buttons popped. Then he fumbled with the button on my jeans, forced down the zipper. Gulping for breath, I fought dizziness.

"Stop. Don't!"

Suddenly, his weight eased. Then a voice boomed. "Let the lady go, scumbag. Get down. That's it. Show me your hands. Now spread them. Are you okay, Ms. Jameson?"

Squinting through the fluorescent glare, I saw Detective Al Elisson looming overhead like an elephantine angel. Rising shakily, I fastened my jeans and wrapped myself as best I could in the wet, ruined blouse. I was shivering so hard my voice came in sharp, breathless bursts. "I am—yes."

My attacker turned on the angry defense. "Bitch asked for it. *Begged* for it. If she changes her damned mind, it's not my fault. I know my rights."

"I'm sure you do. And we're going to see to it that you learn your wrongs," Elisson said mildly.

He took off his giant baseball jacket and draped it across my back. I felt his body heat, smelled lime-scented cologne and wet leather. "My partner's outside. I'll hand Prince Charming over to him and be right back. Wait for me here."

"Okay."

Steering my assailant by the elbow, he ducked out into the storm. Through the rush of rain and wind, I caught low, grave-toned murmuring. Then came the angry smack of a car door and the fading growl of an engine down the street.

The detective returned, flecked with rain, and mopped his face on his sleeve. "You all right, Ms. Jameson? Want me to take you to the ER?"

"Not necessary. I'm a little shaken up, but otherwise fine."

He frowned. "I have to tell you, you don't look so fine."

"Maybe not, but I am thanks to you. Not to sound ungrateful, but may I ask how you happened to show up exactly when I needed rescuing?"

"Magic of modern electronics," he explained. "FCC requires that all cell phones have a GPS chip set that transmits your location by satellite whenever you make a nine-one-one call. Dispatch relayed your location and put out a broadcast. Harry and I happened to be in the neighborhood. He lives nearby."

"I didn't even think the call went through."

"Obviously did. Dispatch heard enough to decide it was worth sending us around to check things out."

"I'm grateful to you, Detective, though I have to admit, you're not exactly how I pictured my guardian angel." He was more the way I pictured a cozy den or a favorite sweater. Familiar in a way I was still unable to place.

He smiled his crooked smile. "Common misconception. We come in all sizes up to triple extra large. The wings and halo are optional. Personally, I find they get in the way. Your apartment's upstairs?"

"Third floor."

"Lead the way. I'll carry your stuff."

"That's not necessary. I can manage."

"Do me a great big favor and indulge me just this once, Ms. Jameson. Will you do that for me, please?"

Elisson collected the scattered groceries in the shredded remains of the bags. I led him up the creaky elevator and down the hall to my loft.

"Can I offer you a cup of coffee? A beer?" I asked.

"Coffee, if it's not too much trouble."

"Not at all."

While I put up the pot, he strode around. He continued his patrol as I ducked into the bedroom and threw on dry sweats. From the bedroom, I could hear him muttering, clacking his tongue in crisp disapproval.

He accepted the mug with a frown. "Can I give you a couple of pieces of advice, Ms. Jameson?"

"I don't suppose I can stop you."

"This place violates every safety rule in the book. It's a break-in waiting to happen. You need good strong window locks, a heavy dead bolt on that front door and the back door needs to be replaced altogether. Given that it opens out onto a common roof with easy access from the fire escape, you should install a metal security door that locks from the inside only." He gazed out over the roof at the river.

"If someone wanted to get in here, to get at you, his biggest problem right now would be deciding which way in to use. He could tie up a boat at the dock, walk up to the back of the building and climb the fire escape."

"I hear you. I'll take care of it."

"Or he could simply stroll in through the front door, take the elevator and let himself in. A butter knife would open your front door."

"I *said, I'll* take care of it, Detective."

His tone sharpened. "Do that. And from now on, try to take better care of *yourself,* will you, Ms. Jameson? Cops don't need you to churn up business. There's never any shortage of eager victims and sick creeps who are more than happy to take advantage."

"I didn't ask to be attacked."

"In a way, that's exactly what you did. You don't use basic common sense, you're asking for trouble. It's like those stupid girls out there, walking the streets. They get hurt; they expect the cops to fix it. Sorry, but as far as I'm concerned, it's a self-inflicted wound."

"I don't appreciate the comparison."

"So be it. The fact remains that if you invite problems, you're probably going to get them. I don't know what part of Dixieland you come from, but you're in the big bad city now. You want to stay healthy in this town, you can't afford to act like a rube. Look around before you approach your building. Have your key in hand and close the door quickly once you get inside, so no one has a chance to push in behind you. Never, ever open your door to anyone unless you're one hundred percent sure it's a good guy. Figure anyone who comes into this place could be casing it for a break-in or worse. Sizing up ways to get in and out undetected, learning about how you live, studying your fears and anxieties, calculating where you might be most vulnerable."

"I understand."

"That includes repair people, salespeople, even some you might consider friends. Once someone knows where and how you live, he's got a great big advantage."

I thought about Dixon's mechanic friend. The man had invaded my space. I had watched him make a mental map of the apartment and of me. I was angry with myself for allowing that, ashamed of my foolish compliance. I should have turned the creep away, rude or not.

"I was bringing home groceries, Detective. Minding my own business. I hardly think that's reckless behavior."

He scowled. "Turns out it *was* reckless behavior. That's why I'm here."

"Really? I thought you dropped by to give me a lecture."

"Nope. I'm throwing that in, no extra charge." He made another circuit of the loft, checking for more things to criticize. Peering out the window front, he found what he was after. "Also, you should get your landlord to install better fixtures at the building entrance. And stronger bulbs. Criminals hate good light as much as photographers love it."

"Fine. Now if you'll excuse me—"

His face softened. "Sorry if all that came across like a scold. I just don't like to see innocent people getting hurt."

"Me neither. This may come as a shock to you, but even dumb rubes from Dixieland have the capacity to care about themselves."

He winced. "Sorry about that, too."

"Apology grudgingly accepted. Actually, I didn't think my accent was all that obvious. I took elocution classes with Miss Penny Proffitt on Saturdays for years to conquer that dreadful drawl. Then, Miss Proffitt didn't exactly sound like the Queen of England, now that I think of it."

"I have an ear for accents, even the slimmest ones. Yours is barely detectible, honestly."

"Good try, Detective. Anyway, I hear you. I'll be careful."

"You can't be too careful, Ms. Jameson. You've seen for yourself what's out there. And that guy is a prince compared to some. I spent most of the morning cleaning up after a much nastier character. Guy's committed four break-in rape/murders in the last two months."

A moth of fear fluttered deep inside me. "I haven't read anything about it."

"That's because he's a chameleon, and chameleons are hard as hell to catch. They show no definite pattern, so the crimes are recorded as separate incidents. They slip beneath the radar screen that's thrown up for serial crimes, which makes their lives much easier. One of the killings was in Manhattan, one in Queens, one in the Bronx and one in Westchester County. The perp used a knife on one girl, another was suffocated, one was strangled and one was bludgeoned to death with a lamp. The vics were all different, too: one slim white nurse's aide in her thirties, one teenaged Hispanic unwed mother, one African-American honor student at Columbia and one very lapsed Catholic girl who was working as a topless dancer in a strip bar uptown."

"Then how can you be sure it's the same perpetrator?"

He shook his head, chuckling. "Harry keeps asking the same question. So I'll tell you what I told him: experience, gut. Call it what you will. I've been following the case very closely, and I just know we are dealing with one very clever, very slippery, very *bad* boy."

"I hope you're wrong."

"I'm not. Sooner or later he's going to run out of fresh ideas, or he'll start to repeat some unconscious piece of the crime, leave a calling card. They all do eventually. When that happens, the press will turn him into a cross between the devil and Brad Pitt. He'll be front-page news, a big-deal celebrity, man of the hour." He fixed me with a hard, heavy look. Then he slugged back the last of his coffee. "But until that happens, nobody has a clue where or how the son of a bitch is going to strike next. So take care of yourself, will you, Ms. Jameson? Characters like him have incredible radar. They hone in on the slightest weakness and take full advantage."

I handed him his jacket. "Thanks again for the rescue."

"Stay out of trouble. That's all the thanks I ask."

"Don't worry. You won't be hearing from me."

He shrugged. "Not for a thing like this, I hope. But the offer stands. If you need anything, I'm only a phone call away. In fact, I can help you with the locks and all if you'd like. My partner does security installations on the side. He's better than anyone you'll find in the Yellow Pages."

I led him firmly to the door. "I'll keep that in mind, Detective. Good-bye."

Chapter 23

Dixon heaped his plate with the last of the pasta primavera and a giant slab of butter-slathered bread. He tossed back the last of his second beer and reached for a third.

"Anna is a natural-born teacher," Monique told him. "I've never seen the kids more excited about anything than her photography lessons."

"Don't ask me to teach those little guys about print journalism, Monique. To be honest, I'm afraid of the competition," Dixon said.

"Of course I wouldn't ask you. Those little ones are sensitive. They scare easily."

"Now you've gone and hurt my feelings," he said.

"I believe that would take power tools," Monique observed.

Dixon's eyes narrowed as he flipped the cap off his Sam Adams dark. "What's up with you tonight, Anna? How come so quiet?"

I shrugged.

"You have been sort of distant. Are you feeling all right?" Monique asked.

"Fine."

"Come on," Dixon coaxed. "Fooling a lowly reporter is one thing, but you can't put anything past a crack professional observer of human behavior like Monique. The woman can juggle two dozen five-year-olds with one hand tied behind her back."

I twirled a forkful of linguini, again and again. "I told you, I'm fine."

Monique set a restraining hand on his arm. "Don't push her. If there's something Anna wants to say, she'll say it."

"I'm not pushing. I'm encouraging her to get whatever it is off her chest. We're your friends," said Dixon gently. "You can trust us."

My eyes stung and tears streamed down my cheeks.

"That's good," he said. "Talk. You'll feel better."

I bit my lip, but the words strained for release. "Some jerk pushed in behind me when I came home from the store. He took me for one of the whores, even though I was drenched from the rain and had my arms full of grocery bags. I told him to kiss off, but he wouldn't take no for an answer."

Monique's hand flew to her mouth. "My God, Anna. That's awful. We should get you to a doctor. Call the police."

"No. It's okay. When he refused to leave me alone, I dialed nine-one-one. Thankfully, the cops showed up before he could—"

"Smart thinking," Dixon observed.

"It was that same detective who was working the drug bust and pulled me off the street."

"The Goliath look-alike?" Dixon asked.

"Yes. He happened to be in the neighborhood."

He frowned. "Fascinating coincidence, don't you think? Something tells me big John Law has something more on his mind in your case than public protection."

"Jesus, Dixon. The man saved my skin."

"Don't mind him," Monique said. "He makes your basic paranoid look overly trusting."

"Most paranoids are," Dixon insisted.

Monique ignored him. "You didn't need to do all this, Anna. We could have made it another time."

I mopped the tears with my napkin. "No. I'm glad you're here."

"Can we do anything?"

"There's nothing, honestly. I'm all right."

"No, what you are is amazing. You pick yourself up after a thing like that, pull yourself together and cook this delicious dinner. I can be leveled for hours by a violent movie," she said.

"That's because you've never had to deal with it in real life," Dixon said.

"Since when does living through a violent attack make it any easier?" I challenged.

He raised his hands. "Whoa, easy. I didn't mean that at all. I was talking about myself, being a reporter. After a while, you see enough, you get a little numb. It stops affecting you quite as much. That's all. I wasn't talking about what happened to you today or . . ."

Bristling silence filled the room. I let it steep awhile, gathering electric force, and then I stared hard into his eyes. "Or what, Dixon?"

His gaze swerved away. He could not bring himself to look at me.

My neck heated. Obviously, he had learned about my sister's murder. I imagined him studying up on me, reading the sordid details of my family's private hell in a handy report from Burlingame's research department.

I wondered how detailed the dossier would have been. Did he know about my precocious little nervous breakdown, my chess games with Dr. Eiseman? Did this man know that I took hormones to control my heavy, irregular periods? Had he uncovered my persistent, infantile fear of total darkness? I still slept with a night-light. Wouldn't my colleagues be amused?

"Or what, Dixon?" I demanded again.

"Or any other disturbing behavior you might have been exposed to in your life. People get desensitized. That's all I was trying to say."

"Is it?"

"Yes. It was a general statement. Not about you."

Monique stood and started clearing the table.

"I'll do that," I said.

"No, you sit and relax. Talk to Mighty Mouth. I'll clean up."

Dixon held silent until she was out of the room and our words were lost in the rush of water from the sink. "It wasn't about you, Anna. That's the truth."

"But you know."

His face pinched with regret. "About your sister? Yes, I do, but it's background noise, ancient history. What I care about is now. And you."

"I don't like being the subject of your so-called research. It's like rifling through my drawers. Worse than that."

"I looked you up after the boss saw your work and mentioned your name to me, way before you showed up. As a reporter, it's something I do routinely. Curiosity is essential in this business. So is digging around under the surface. You know that as well as I do."

"That doesn't make it right."

His shoulders hitched. "I didn't tell Burlingame about your sister. I would never tell him or anyone."

"Why not?"

"Because I can imagine how it would feel to me, to lose someone close that way. People shouldn't be tossing it around as a curiosity."

"Scruples and empathy? What kind of behavior is that for a journalist? You'd better watch out, mister. Our colleagues have worked long and hard to win recognition as ruthless, cold-blooded, coin-operated parasites with ice-sculpture hearts."

He held out a hand. "Forgive me?"

"I need to see the file, Dixon. I need you to get it for me."

"There's nothing in there you don't already know."

"I want to see it anyway."

"Research doesn't like files to circulate."

"Get them to make an exception. I don't want to wait until I'm out of exile."

"It could take a little doing. But if you really want to take a look, I'll figure something out."

"Do that."

"Then will you forgive me?"

"I'll try."

I took his outstretched hand. His grip was so warm and comforting, I held on a beat too long. Then I recoiled in clumsy confusion like a kid caught fishing around in her mother's purse.

He pulled at his beer and acted seriously nonchalant. I kept glancing at him, meeting his pointed gaze, playing eye tag.

Dessert was ice cream and cookies, most of which went down Dixon's throat. How I envied the man's metabolism. My every indulgence slid directly to my hips. I've often thought that I might as well bypass my sluggish digestive tract and apply the calories topically.

Monique brushed sugary crumbs from the table into her palm. "This has been great, but you guys will have to excuse me. I'm pooped. Must have something to do with spending most of my time in the company of five-year-olds. I find myself watching cartoons, wanting nap time and going to bed obscenely early."

"I can relate," I said.

"Thanks so much for dinner, Anna. You still on for tomorrow?" she said.

"Definitely. I'll be at the school first thing." I looked at Dixon pointedly. "I should probably turn in soon, too."

He refused to catch the hint "There's something I want to talk over with you before I go."

I saw Monique out and dawdled near the door. Dixon sat inert, listening, until the creaky gunmetal lift hit bottom.

"What is it?"

He motioned for me to come closer.

My pulse was a sledge. I had a long-standing policy of not getting personally involved with anyone at work. But Palmer Pruitt, my sole colleague for the last ten years, had been far from a serious temptation. Dixon was a different story: sensitive, funny, wise and smart. After my earlier run-in with the groping goon downstairs, I ached for the kind of comfort I suspected he was willing and able to give.

I moved a few tentative steps closer. "What?"

He patted the chair beside him.

"No, you come here."

As he slowly approached, a suggestive grin played on his mouth. His lips were full and well defined, and I wondered how they would taste. How would his lanky form meld with my abbreviated roundness? What about lighting, set design, costuming, dialogue, props? First times were fraught with so many intimidating unknowns.

Then, he stalled at a respectful distance. "I'm sorry for what happened to you today, but it gave me an idea that's going to blow Burlingame away. A sure way to smear Mayor Conley."

"I don't understand."

"We do a feature story on the flourishing sex trade right here on your block. I'm thinking of a photo essay with sparse, very pointed text. We go for high impact, no holds barred. Tight shots of the girls with a focus on select body parts. Close-ups of approaching johns. Money changing hands. With any luck, we can catch license plates from out-of-town, men with wedding rings and guilty expressions, underage kids, maybe even some nice shocking holy types."

I had noticed more than one black-clad Orthodox man negotiating on the street and at least one car with clerical plates. "I've seen a couple of those."

"Excellent. We'll need to record some nice suggestive action, stuff we can run on the front page. I'm thinking of silhouettes through car windows. Clinches in the shadows. Nothing too graphic, but clear enough to tell the story."

"I still don't understand how any of that would harm Conley."

"Hizzoner has made a huge noise about cleaning up the city. Number one on his hit parade has been keeping anything to do with sex out of the public eye. He's gone after naughty billboards, sexy shopwindows and anything that he counts in his very broad definition as 'public lewdness': cleavage, heavy handholding, felonious potty mouth—you name it."

"I've seen stories about that, but I took it as a joke. Politician talk. Sound and fury, signifying nothing."

Dixon nodded enthusiastically. "It is a joke, but a dangerous one. The hell with free speech and civil liberties. All Conley cares about is throwing his weight around. He also throws around all sorts of bullshit statistics, claiming that he's made the city a safe, sanitized, G-rated place. The righteous indignant folks, and there are plenty of them, eat it up and flock to the voting booths."

"So we show that his cleanup claims are phony, at least around here."

"Exactly. You can catch everything we need right out your window, from the privacy and convenience of your very own home. I'll caption the shots, and then we present the whole thing to Burlingame as a canned feature. The boss has been looking for something like this to embarrass the mayor with for weeks, but he's been barking up the wrong trees. If we can pull it off, we'll be golden."

"I don't know, Dixon. I have a proven anti-Midas touch when it comes to Burlingame. Everything I've tried to do for him turns to mold. Maybe you should take it to someone else."

"No way. This one's all yours."

"It won't work. Burlingame is so angry with me; I've been banished twice. If I so much as showed my face around the Flashlight Building, I think he'd happily toss me out the window."

"It's not a problem. I'll see to what needs to be done at that end. You just take the pictures."

"Something will go wrong. It always does."

"Start tonight and get the rolls to me as quickly as you can. I'll take care of everything from there."

"I don't know. I have a bad feeling about this."

He looked me hard in the eye. "Listen to me, Anna Jameson. Your luck is about to change."

Chapter 24

The seventeenth precinct of the NYPD runs from Thirtieth to Fifty-ninth Street, Lexington Avenue to the East River. Officers on the squad are charged with protecting the rights and enterprises of the area's sixty thousand law-abiding workers and residents from the six thousand others each year who stray across the line.

The station house, a run-down, flat-faced building, sat in the center of the block on the north side of East Fifty-first Street. Clu waited for Phil Stanton outside, in the shadow of Old Glory, tapping her annoyance on the rain-darkened pavement. Her eyes ached from lack of sleep and the hours she had spent staring at small, faded print. The mildew and dust in the basement property room had inflamed her hypersensitive sinuses. Poking through the grim detritus from the Sleeping Beauty Murder had inflamed her sensibilities, as well. How could a promising, innocent life be reduced to this? Decomposed remains and open questions. Clu felt stiff, sore, discouraged and generally out of sorts.

Still, her biggest headache at the moment was Phil Stanton. The man was infantile and annoying enough under ordinary circumstances, but in his current state of profoundly exaggerated self-importance, he was positively insufferable. It was like trying to deal sensibly with a runaway blimp. The only reasonable recourse was a well-aimed dart.

Russell Quilfo had arranged for them to get rapid access to the battered file box that contained many of the fabric snips, trace fibers, nail scrapings, suspect objects and other goodies that the crime-scene technicians had gathered in the Jamesons' apartment shortly after the child's body was discovered.

Once again, Quilfo's good name and contacts had served the Arcanum well. He was one of the society's few solid tethers to the real world, where tidy academic theory often proved laughably inadequate to account for the all-too-common unthinkable acts Clu had come to think of as *normal human sadism.*

Griffey, Trupin and Ted Callendar had joined her several hours earlier in an interview room to sort through the gruesome souvenirs. The three of them had worked with painstaking deliberation. The artifacts were, for the most part, poorly catalogued and perilously preserved. Many, many careless fingers had probed through the box in the three decades since the killing. Amid the official plastic bags and envelopes, they had come upon a scatter of coffee grounds, a tube of cigarette ash, a greasy sandwich wrapper and a wad of crumpled Kleenex. They did not wish to add to the contamination or risk undermining the fragile remains.

Griffey had spotted a tiny visible corner of the print cards, which had been wrapped, inexplicably, in the soft frilly nightgown that Julie Jameson had worn at the time of her death. The garment, along with the child's flowered underpants and a pair of pink furry slippers, had been inserted into an airtight plastic evidence bag and sealed.

Callendar and Clu had been anxious to have at them, but at Griffey's gentle insistence, they had left the prints undisturbed. That was over an hour ago, an hour and twelve minutes, to be precise. Clu had paged Stanton immediately, and he had responded with facile assurances that he was on the way. Then, so were Christmas and St. Patrick's Day.

She walked to the corner and fixed her angry sights on the approaching traffic. Several cabs breezed by, and a trio of buses snaked past in a conga line before the light changed.

No Stanton.

Her temper rose to a roiling boil as she fished out her cell phone and keyed in his beeper number. She hung up and waited.

Nothing.

In a mounting snit she reentered the station house. As friends of Russell Quilfo's, they enjoyed VIP treatment. Precinct commander Captain Jeff Goldstein had installed them in the briefing room and offered them full use of the station house facilities, including unlimited cups of poison coffee.

The desk officer, a wiry young Latina, shot Clu a wary look as she passed. "Everything okay, Dr. Baldwin?"

"Has anyone called for us? A Dr. Stanton, perhaps?"

"No. Only Lieutenant Quilfo, and I put him right through."

"If Stanton should call, I'd like you to put him through, as well. Actually, I'd like you to put him through terrible things. Flaying would be nice. Tar and feathers. Whatever you think."

"Yes, ma'am. I read you loud and clear."

Finally, Phil bumped through the door, squiring Sadie Olbetter. They were flushed and giggling.

"Here we are," Phil announced.

"Lead us to the evidence." Sadie raised an imaginary lance and prepared to charge.

"You're snockered," Clu observed. "How charming."

Phil attempted to look harsh. "We are certainly not *snockered,* as you so crudely put it, Dr. Baldwin. We are ever so slightly relaxed."

"I hope you're not too *relaxed* to see clearly and make reasonable assessments, Phil. As I explained, this is not a game."

Sadie plunged her chipmunk voice into a lower register. "This is not a game," she intoned. "I am not a crook."

Phil joined her in a fresh round of hysterical tittering.

"Come on, Phil. Let's get to it." Clu pointed sternly to the bench beside the door. "Wait over there and think happy thoughts, Sadie. Your buddy will only be a few minutes."

Stanton pouted. "I do not see why Dr. Olbetter cannot come along. She can add her astute observations." The words sagged from his booze-thickened tongue.

"We need her to guard the door, Phil," Clu said dryly. "Very important job."

He trailed her to the briefing room, where the podium and dozens of folding chairs had been pushed aside and a scarred rectangular table brought in for their use. Captain Goldstein had also provided the overhead projector and screen, a laser pointer and notepads emblazoned with the NYPD shield.

Griffey, Ted, and Trupin were still picking through scraps of evidence from the battered box marked JAMESON, JULIE ANN.

"Sit, Phil. Have some coffee." Clu poured him a cup of the acrid sludge. "Dr. Stanton went out and got himself a wee bit overly relaxed," she explained.

"That brew will put the starch back in your spine," Trupin predicted.

Stanton took a hesitant sip and sputtered, coughing, dousing his clothes with muddy spray. "Oh my. That's dreadful."

Clu tossed in a handful of sugar cubes and stirred furiously. "Consider it medicine, Phil. Come on. Drink up. Yummy, yummy."

Stanton choked down most of the three cups she pressed on him, and his look sprang from woozy to wired. "All right. That's enough. Let me have a look at those prints."

Clu retrieved the plastic bag containing the child's nightgown with the print cards inside. "We went through the evidence file and found these. We left everything exactly as is until you got here. Any suggestions?"

Stanton took the bag gingerly. "Only that we indulge in a moment of prayer. Why in heaven's name would anyone store the cards this way? Clothing tends to be contaminated with body oils and fragrances at best. Any fool knows to segregate worn garments from other evidence."

"Apparently some fool did not," Callendar said.

As Stanton split the seal, a noxious smell wafted from the bag. Scowling in revulsion, he set the evidence box on the floor and dumped the contents of the plastic bag on the table. Using the tip of the laser pointer, he unfolded the child's ruffled gown and regarded the sodden clump of index cards inside.

"Ruined." He prodded them apart, wrinkling his nose against the malodorous yellowed mess. "Completely useless."

"Maybe not," Callendar said. "I didn't see a mention of this anywhere, but if the child wet herself, we might be looking at the motive. One of the parents might have gotten enraged and lost control. It wouldn't be the first time by a long shot. Enuresis is a common trigger for child abuse."

"But why wouldn't someone have picked up on that years ago? It doesn't compute," Clu said.

Stanton rose in disgust. "Certainly it does. What do you expect from common law enforcement types? Civil service buffoons and muscle-heads with authoritarian personalities. They overlook glaring inconsistencies and crucial facts all the time."

Griffey smiled at him thinly. "I fear we are all guilty of that at times, Dr. Stanton. I am quite confident that tests will demonstrate that the urine on that gown and cards is nowhere near thirty years old. Given the vivid color and the pungency of the scent, thirty days would surprise me."

Clu rubbed her weary eyes. "Which would mean that someone destroyed this evidence deliberately. But why? If they wanted to get rid of the prints, wouldn't it have been more sensible to simply make them disappear?"

"If destroying evidence was the only purpose, yes," Trupin said. "My guess is that whoever did this intended it as a quite literal show of contempt."

"There must be some way to figure out who's had access to this box in the past month," Clu said.

"I doubt it," Griffey said. "I checked the log when we came in, and there were no entries for the Jameson file in the past couple of years."

"Yes, but there must be a master log of people who use the evidence room," Clu persisted. "Any one of them could have taken a detour to the Jameson file."

Griffey tapped his thumbs together. "I'm sure there is, and certainly we can have a look at it. But I strongly suspect that whoever did this took pains to mask his identity. Obviously, he would wish to have his contribution remain anonymous."

"I agree with Griffey. I'm not hopeful." Trupin returned the ruined prints to the box and closed the lid. "Apparently, your caller was correct, Ted. Someone is playing a very sick, very dangerous game. And so far, he's at least one critical move ahead of us."

Chapter 25

Through a stingy gap in the curtains, I stared down at the street. I had gathered extra lenses and film and all the nerve I could muster. Despite Dixon's facile assurances, I understood that I was treading a dangerous line. Someone could glance up and catch me recording behavior they would rather keep to themselves. You never knew what a desperate, threatened character might do in reprisal. I had learned that the hard way with the jerk in the football shirt earlier today, and I could still feel the hot warning gaze of the drug lord as he leered at me from the police cruiser. Still the risks seemed a reasonable trade-off for the chance to redeem myself with Burlingame.

I had taken every prudent precaution: dimmed the lights as low as I could bear, arranged the curtains to camouflage any flash off the lens and dressed in dark clothing.

The earlier downpour had scrubbed the air and polished the pavement to a cool obsidian glint. Warm air tumbled in from the river and collided with the night chill, raising thick puffs of fog. Spectral swirls danced in the conical street beams. A distant ship's horn bleated low.

At first, I saw no one. Then, sweeping the shadows through the telephoto lens, I spied a bulky shape at the corner. Squinting hard, I caught the primal, rhythmic motion of a locked pair of hips. A head tossed back in mock passion, then rock stillness.

Moments later, half the bulk split away and skittered like a naughty pup toward the VW bug across the road. The other half stroked her spongy nest of teased red hair, smoothed her spandex skirt and ambled back to pose in the murky lamplight. She lit a cigarette, and the match blaze set her small, blunt features in garish relief. Her slim lips drew tight as a miser's purse, the raisin eyes hard as flint. She pulled a Wet-Nap from the top of her knee-high boot, split the foil and wiped her mouth and hands. She followed that with a shot of clear liquid germicide, which she rubbed onto her palms and up her round pale arms.

Soon, another girl emerged from the courtyard between my building and the next. Geisha swirls of skunk-streaked hair cradled her skull. She wore a feathery stole in cotton-candy blue over a cropped black strangle-tight dress. Poised beneath a streetlight, she tugged a gold mesh pouch from her clutch bag. She frowned at her image in a gilt compact as she dabbed on fresh lip gloss and rouge. She brushed on extra mascara, tidied her sculpted brow and patted a blush-stained powder puff over all. Next, she sprayed her neck and wrists with scent from a small flowered atomizer.

While I snapped her, catching every phase of the ritual primp, two more girls appeared. A john on foot strode away with hooker number one. The pair ducked into a doorway, where they blended into the murky shadows. Four minutes later—not a second more—the woman emerged, jamming folded bills in the abyss between her breasts. She used another scented wipe and more germicide.

This was prime time on the street. Rush hour. I counted six whores, but soon a Volvo wagon crammed with boisterous drunks pulled up and peeled off all but one. They stuffed into the car like circus clowns, riding laps with their heads ducked to avoid hitting the roof.

The remaining girl stood, clutching her scrawny ribs. Through the lens, I zoomed in on her. Her lip quavered and tears spilled from her soft green eyes. She was clear-skinned under the doughy makeup mask. Her body was lithe and long-limbed. She looked painfully young, no more than a teenager. I ached to scoop her up and tend her like a broken bird.

Several of the women straggled back, laughing in boisterous whoops. A newcomer turned up, loud and brash, trying to claim a slice of the crowded territory, and a fight broke out. I kept clicking away, scooping up the images. Flashing teeth and limbs flailing. Jutting hips and glint-eyed fury. Then came the promising haze of approaching headlights and all the whores sprang back into business mode. They straightened up, posed in the brightest arcs of street-light and smiled. The new girl claimed a space at the tepid periphery of a light pool. The others hooted in nasty delight as she was passed over several times. But finally her turn came and the joke died of natural causes.

I had gone through the two-dozen rolls I had set out. When I went to retrieve more from the store I kept in the refrigerator, I was stunned to discover that it was nearly two A.M.

Back at the window, I noticed that the sad little bird had hooked a worm. I watched the pair through the camera's long lens, but I did not press the shutter. The last thing that kid needed was the kind of publicity this shoot could bring.

Her dainty hand looped through the arm of a buzzard-chinned man with gelatinous jowls and a monk's tonsure. Her green eyes darted nervously as she steered him across the street toward the courtyard. As they neared my building, I caught his smoker's growl interspersed with her timorous trill.

"You have to wear one, mister. Okay?" she said.

"One what?" he asked coyly.

"Protection. You know. Here. I have all kinds. Flavors, too. You can pick."

He snickered. "You just hold on to those, baby cakes. Might come in handy on a rainy day."

"No. Honestly. You have to use one. Otherwise, I can't."

"Sure you can. Watch."

They were directly under my window now, too close to the building for me to see.

I heard scuffling, muffled grunts. The drone of a passing car muted her peeping cries.

"Stop that. Don't! You're hurting me."

"Cut the crap, girlie. I'm not in the mood."

"I can't. I mean it. Not this way."

I cast around for something to do. I considered calling the cops, but playing white knight to streetwalkers was not high on their list. Turning on the light might distract him for a moment, but it could also bring some very nasty unwanted attention to me.

"That's it. No more games. Now move!"

Her cry was an icy spear through the stillness.

Soundlessly, I slid the window higher. If I dropped something, it might distract him long enough for her to flee. I pulled loose a dangling tar paper strip.

Struggling, they slowly edged toward the courtyard. They were still too close for me to let go. A capricious wind could send the scrap hurtling directly at them. The sharp edge could gouge an eye or slash an artery. There was no way to assure that it would not hit the girl.

"That's better. Now shut up and stay still."

"Please, no."

I held the tar paper out over the sill. The cool breeze stroked my trembling fingers. As I was about to let go, I heard the strike of fast approaching footsteps.

A voice thundered, "You heard the girl, fat man. Let her go."

"Buzz off. I paid good money and I'm going to get what's coming to me."

"Oh, you'll get what's coming to you all right."

"Why don't you mind your own damned business?"

"This is my business. The girl belongs to me. She's all mine. You dig?"

The bald man snorted. "You expect me to be impressed by that bony little skirt? She's barely worth the price of admission."

"No. I don't expect you to be impressed by that, fat man. I expect you to be impressed by *this*."

I heard a sharp crack, then mewling. "What did you do that for? You broke my nose, for Christ sake."

"Just that? Let me try again."

"No, don't. No more. Please."

The bald man broke into a labored run and took off whimpering down the street. The pimp, a towering figure in a cowboy hat and a long canvas coat, squired his baby whore across the street and saw her safely ensconced beneath a prime streetlight at the center of the block. He ran his finger across her cheek like a threatening blade, and the girl shivered. With a chilling smile, he turned and strode away.

Silently, I shut the window. All of a sudden, I was weary to the bone.

Chapter 26

Lyman Trupin exited the cab near the Fifty-ninth Street entrance to the Roosevelt Island Tram. He walked one block over and three down, glancing back at intervals to make certain that he had not grown a tail. His moves and instincts had been honed to razor sharpness by a four-decade stint in the service of national security. Retirement had done nothing to dull his edge.

Angling the bill of his baseball cap to shade his face, he stopped at a bagel store near the corner. When his number was called, he selected a dozen assorted, still oven warm, and a half pound of cream cheese with chives. His former colleagues would provide the coffee and entertainment.

Turning east onto the cross street, he slowed to a leisurely pace and fixed his level gaze straight ahead. The dark sedans lining the road were official government vehicles, connected to the top-secret communications center halfway down the block. In a few of the cars, working agents slumped behind the wheel, feigning sleep. Others stared at the morning paper while they monitored field tests or awaited relayed orders to deploy. In this age of hair-trigger information exchange, their operations had taken on an air of pinball frenzy.

Operatives out of this center were trained to be invisible, and for over a decade they had remained so to the many area residents who passed each day on their way to school or work or whatever. Once in a great while, a rumor flared about the anonymous, windowless, pale brick building: that it must be an underground clinic or a porn film studio or an illicit lab producing designer drugs. But each theory had lost momentum and died with encouraging speed. By nature, people were lazier than they were curious. Underground operations had capitalized on that simple understanding since the dawn of espionage and subterfuge.

Trupin had no intention of encouraging a fresh round of questions with his presence here. He had always maintained the lowest possible profile, even during his six-year tenure as Bureau director. Despite the serendipitously public turn his career had taken, he remained very much a private man, most comfortable in quiet surroundings, simple circumstances, and conservative garb. His costume of choice was a dark blue or charcoal business suit, a starched white shirt, a club tie and the sort of proper, unforgiving oxford shoes that would have made his dear departed mother smile. Some in the department had speculated, not entirely behind his back, that Trupin must have a waterproof version of the outfit for bathing and a sterilized one for sex (not that anyone truly believed he indulged).

Clad as he was that morning in the sports cap, jeans and a bright blue golf shirt, he was all but unrecognizable. Even Marjorie, his wife of thirty-five years, had blinked hard when he appeared in the kitchen for breakfast. She had quipped that he must be going off to see some young girl, taking his show on the road, as she cunningly put it.

Trupin had always maintained a strict policy of keeping her uninformed about his work. Top-secret information was not suitable for pillow talk or

any talk. Still, given her impeccable instincts, she often came uncomfortably
close to the mark. Margie was a brilliant, beautiful woman, and sexier than hell,
even after thirty-five years. And yes, they indulged with shameless panting
frequency. To this, Trupin attributed his positive outlook, healthy heart and
unwavering focus on the golf course.

A small art gallery and frame shop abutted the communications center.
The clerk, a slender blond agent with a dense French accent and an eye for
impressionist oils, answered the bell. He checked Trupin's credentials, taking
nothing for granted, and led him to the rear of the shop, where a connecting
door vanished amid the jumble of canvases, tools and mitered lengths of wood.

Trupin passed through a slim cluttered corridor to a security antechamber
on the other side. There, a young female agent with cropped butterscotch hair
and balloon breasts checked his ID again.

"It's an honor to meet you, sir," she said.

Trupin trained his eyes well above her horizon and nodded crisply. "Have
the others arrived?"

"Yes, sir. All but Mr. Frame."

"I suspect Mr. Frame will be late for his own funeral."

Another young agent led him to the largest of several command rooms,
where Clu Baldwin, Solomon Griffey, Ted Callendar and Russell Quilfo were
watching special agents Bell and Weller set up. There were globular devices and
clear suspended screens and a staggering number of computers, flashing complex displays.

"*Monsieur, le Directeur,*" said Nate Bell, a reed-thin young Sinatra clone.
"Welcome, sir. Come in. Take a load off."

"Thank you, Agent Bell. How have you been? How's the family?"

"Kids are getting big. So is the wife. You know the drill."

"I do." Trupin glanced at the equipment, then at Nate Bell's portly sidekick.
"And you, Agent Weller?"

"Can't complain. How's it hanging with you, sir?"

"I'd say we're about to find out."

Melton Frame breezed in as they took their seats. He posed at the head of
the conference table with his hands splayed on the smoked glass and his chest
heaving for grand dramatic effect. The surface held a reflection of his roadkill

toupee and sagging buttermilk mustache. "Oh my. Hope I didn't keep you waiting, but I promised to do a piece with Matt and Katie on the morning show and it just went on and on and on—"

"Sit please, Melton. We're just about to begin," Trupin said.

"This one, you must see. They put me on with that dreadful critic Bill Nadler. He tried to bait me, but I was positively crushing, if I do say so myself."

"These good people have worked overtime to get us the information we need. Let's not take needless advantage of their generosity, shall we?" Griffey suggested.

Frame pulled a bagel from a bag and slathered it with cream cheese. "Is that coffee I smell? I would absolutely kill for a decent cup. That swill they make at the studio ought to be illegal."

"Should be ready in a few minutes," said Bell. "But no guarantees you'll find it any more to your liking."

"Now, on Oprah, they know how to treat their guests. Some of the finest espresso you've ever tasted. Fresh biscotti and croissants to boot. It's no wonder that gal has trouble keeping off the pounds."

Clu's teeth ached from clenching. "Let's begin, shall we?"

"But forget Letterman. What a pack of pikers. You can hardly get a decent glass of water on that set."

Bell and Weller crossed to the front of the room, sidestepping Frame like a piece of cumbersome furniture. The two agents had been partners for over twenty years, close friends as well, and most viewed them as an inseparable set. Other operatives at the center referred to them as Mutt and Jeff or, on off-days, Jekyll and Wide.

Nate Bell slipped into his standard role as narrator, while Weller worked the controls. Everything in this facility was next generation, up to the minute, state of the art. Coming here, in Trupin's mind, was akin to watching a James Bond film. He didn't expect much in the way of polished plot or inspired performance, but the special effects were superb.

Weller tapped a touch pad and a clear globe-shaped display lit with dozens of broken lines and varicolored lights.

"Each light represents one of the principals or suspects in the Jameson case. At Director Trupin's request, we cast the broadest possible net, tracking a number of subjects who were dismissed by investigators for good alibis or lack of probable cause."

He flipped to another display, this one a large flat panel that appeared to float magically a foot from the wall. "I'll call your attention to this legend, which we established for the sake of convenience. The red lights represent family members, friends and neighbors are blue, yellow lights are for business associates and patients of Dr. Jameson at the time of the murder. Green is for workmen in the apartment building where the child was killed and various merchants and others the family dealt with around the neighborhood. That includes people that the victim or family knew through her kindergarten."

"What are the purple lights for?" Quilfo asked.

"Let's call them very long shots. Mostly, they were people falsely fingered in anonymous tips or phony confessors who called in to the special investigative unit that worked on the case. We tracked them, just because—"

Weller showed his pudgy palms. "Can't hurt."

"Hear! hear!" Quilfo said. "I've always believed in the chicken soup approach. What can't hurt might conceivably help."

Clu was counting up the black lights. "And I presume the black ones are out of the running?"

"It's been thirty years. Not surprisingly, many people involved have moved on to much greener pastures," Bell said.

"Or gone directly to Hell, no passing go, no two hundred dollars," Weller added.

While Trupin and the others studied the annotated globe, Bell elaborated further. "The lines track individual migration. We crosshatched our subjects' movement patterns with crimes similar in any conceivable way to the Sleeping Beauty Murder: child killings, stranger break-in and assault, unsolved homicides in general, home murders, summer killings, murders during storms, etcetera."

"Anything?" Griffey asked.

"No," Bell said. "We did find continuing large suspect clusters here in New York and in Charleston, where the family moved."

"That's hardly surprising," Clu observed.

"True," said Bell, "but there are a couple of interesting oddities."

Quilfo was pitched forward in his seat, squinting at the globe. "So many yellow lights around Charleston. Dr. Jameson's colleagues and patients, you said?"

Bell's eyes widened. "Why, yes sir. Exactly. More than one would logically expect. We've got our people down there looking into it right now."

"I believe they'll find an innocent explanation," Griffey said. "After they moved to Charleston, Frank Jameson went to work for Hurley Pharmaceuticals. The company had trials running on several promising medications. In New York Dr. Jameson had been an internist, specializing in cardiology. He contacted a number of his sicker patients, who elected to go to Charleston and take advantage of the studies. Many of them settled in and stayed."

"How did you know that, Solomon?" Clu asked.

"It was a small, handwritten note in the margin of one of the DDfives. Page three sixty-eight, second paragraph from the bottom, I believe. I just happened to take note of it as I was leafing through."

"Your little parlor tricks are so very entertaining, Griffey," sniped Frame. "But I don't see where we're getting anywhere with all this." He turned to Bell. "Did you people learn anything useful? Or are we just here to look at the pretty decorations and spin our wheels?"

"Actually, we learned *nothing* useful, which might be very useful, if you think about it," the agent said.

Frame slumped in a chair and groaned. "Oh goody. Now we're playing riddles. What's next—charades?"

Griffey stifled a smile. "It's very simple, Melton. If an outsider killed the child, someone with a propensity for that kind of crime, chances are that he or she would have struck again, somewhere, somehow, in all these years. Chances are we would have found some connection to similar crimes."

"So what we're probably looking at is an isolated crime of passion," Callendar observed. "Which points back to the parents yet again."

"That would not account for our caller," Clu said.

"It would if it turned out to be Alberta Jameson after all," Callendar said. "Were you able to get information on the origin of the call to my house on the Arcanum line?"

"We were. Thanks for reminding me." The rotund agent fished through his pockets and dumped his catch on the table: coins, chewing gum, breath mints, lottery tickets, lint. Finally, he unearthed a small, folded sheet of notepaper. "Here it is. We checked the call detail records through the central office database and found an absolute match in start time and duration. The woman who contacted you called from a pay phone in the international arrivals lounge at the Hartsfield Airport in Atlanta."

Callendar nodded. "Atlanta's the connecting hub for most flights in and out of Charleston. Again, I see a natural link to Mrs. Jameson."

"It was not Bertie Jameson, Ted. It was simply not her voice," Clu insisted.

"Then maybe she got someone to make the call for her, maybe even the same person who destroyed those print records."

Clu made angry slash marks on a notepad. "Why would she trust an outsider with explosive, damaging information like that? She'd be inviting blackmail, or worse."

"Maybe she has a subconscious wish to be punished, as you yourself said when you listened to the voice," Callendar observed.

"Yes, but I'll remind you, that was not Bertie Jameson talking. Anyway, if she wanted to be punished, she could simply turn herself in."

Griffey shrugged. "Maybe, maybe not. It's also possible that the answer is something else entirely, that we are missing the forest for the trees."

"Howling at the moon is more like it," Frame sniffed. "What are you suggesting, Griffey? That the butler did it?"

"I'm suggesting that we need to keep all of our options open, including the ones the original investigators closed." He smiled at Weller and Bell. "Most impressive. Very comprehensive job. Now, if you would, gentlemen, I'll ask you to indulge me. Take a look at this thing inside out and sideways, would you please?"

"We'd be glad to, sir," Bell said. "Only—"

"Only, with all due respect, we have no idea what the hell you're talking about, sir," Weller added.

"Dr. Griffey would like you to assess the data without any preconceived ideas," Trupin explained. "Assume that every suspect is still suspect and that some prime suspects may never have been placed under scrutiny at all. Don't take anything as a given. Start from scratch. We are looking at a potential suicide risk plus the threat of several other victims if our caller is correct."

Quilfo nodded eagerly. "One useful approach would be to look at current crime patterns without reference to the Jameson suspects. See if anything under open investigation matches one of the suspect movement patterns you've identified."

Griffey stroked his chin. "My thoughts exactly, Russell. Let's see who's doing what to whom."

Bell flipped off the displays. "What the hell. We'll give it a shot. Try some other approaches. A thirty-year-old cold case is a Hail Mary play anyhow."

"That's exactly where we are in this, gentlemen," Griffey said. "My British friend called to tell me that the DNA analysis yielded inconclusive results. The evidence has been compromised beyond usefulness. I'd say we are down several points in the last period and running out of time."

"Where I am is caffeine-deprived," Frame groused. "Damned coffee must be ready by now."

Trupin slapped him on the back. "Bless you, Melton. No matter how desperate things become, one can always count on you to keep your priorities straight."

Chapter 27

At seven in the morning, my cell phone blared the "Ode to Joy." Groggy, I rushed to extricate the instrument from the tangle of clothing I had dropped on the floor late the night before. At this hour, it had to be the city desk calling. Burlingame must have changed his mind and decided to reinstate me early.

The heraldic summons sounded once again. I rifled through my crumpled khaki pants, my blue T-shirt, underwear and socks. Finally, I traced the sneaky gizmo to the toe of my left loafer. I wrenched it free and connected before the call bounced into the black hole of my voice mail. Since I had moved to New York, the phone had soared to impressive new heights of unreliability. My account was with a rock-bottom-priced South Carolina operation that had worked tolerably well in Charleston but continued to bridle at the change of venue. I was stuck with ten months remaining on my contract and a two-week wait for a landline from Bell Atlantic. The virtues of change did not always ease the countless tiny tortures of adjustment.

"Anna? Thank God."

"What is it, Mom? What's wrong?"

"I had a terrible call," she murmured. "So frightening."

"What are you talking about? What call?"

"That doesn't matter now that I know you're all right. The point is I couldn't find you. Where on Earth have you been?" Her tone strengthened and grew teeth. "I tried you at the hotel Sunday, but they said you'd checked out. At first, I thought it had to be a mistake, the clerk reading the screen wrong or a foul-up in the computer. But no, I checked with everyone up to the general manager, and sure enough, you'd simply vanished without a word."

"I didn't vanish. I'm right here."

"I must have dialed your cellular phone a hundred times but all I kept getting was a recording telling me the customer is unavailable."

"My phone's been misbehaving since I got here. I'll have a serious talk with it as soon as we hang up."

"I was worried sick, thinking who knows what might have happened to you."

I wanted to tell her that nothing had happened, but the lie stuck in my throat. I could still see the dripping rage on the stranger's face downstairs; I could still feel his crude, groping fingers on my flesh. My overblown confidence had been replaced by a harsh, numbing awareness of real vulnerability. If Elisson had not shown up, who knows what might have happened.

"I hated to bother her," Bertie said. "But I finally broke down and called Shelby last night. She said you two had dinner the other evening. She tried to assure me that everything was fine. But I still needed to hear it directly from you."

I could read my mother's indictment between the lines. *You had ample time to fritter away with your friend, but you couldn't spare one second to call your frightened, aging mother and put her tormented mind at ease.*

"We had a quick bite in the neighborhood. That's all."

"Really? She said you had a nice, long talk, that it was good to catch up."

"It's only been a couple of days since we spoke, Mom. I'm not some run-away kid; I'm a thirty-three-year-old woman."

"Don't exaggerate, Anna. You won't be thirty-three for months."

"Thirty-two and three quarters, then. It still hardly counts as a dis-appearance."

"Shelby told me she'd seen your new apartment, that it's in Brooklyn."

I cringed, waiting for the exploding shoe to drop.

"She says it's charming," Bertie said. "Large and bright."

My heart swelled. Bless Shelby for not betraying me. She was my true sis-ter, after all. "It's wonderful. You should come see for yourself."

"Honestly, Anna. You know there's not a snowball's chance in Hades of getting me anywhere near that horrible city. Just the thought—"

"I can send some pictures if you like."

"That would be nice." She blew a beleaguered breath. "Well, then. As long as you're really all right, I'll let you go. I certainly don't want to take up any more of your precious time."

"Stop, Mom. I'm glad to talk to you. Anyway, you haven't told me about your frightening call."

"Oh, it's just foolishness, Anna. Not worth talking about."

"I want to hear anyway."

I could hear her weighty breathing on the line.

"Tell me."

"All right, if you insist. Some man called late the other night, after we'd gone to sleep. I picked up, but I was so disoriented, I only caught part of what he said. 'Tell her to watch herself. Tell her I'm getting closer. Closing in.'"

"Did he call you by name? Give any indication that he knew us?"

"No, sweetheart. Only what I told you. That was all."

"I'm sure you're right, then. It was probably nothing. A wrong number or someone playing stupid tricks."

"Your father never heard a thing. So who knows? Maybe I dreamed it. Maybe it was my own silly nerves playing tricks."

"Maybe so." My silly nerves played considerable tricks of their own. As my mother told the story, I could hear the low, menacing voice on the phone: I could feel the dark, approaching threat. *Getting closer—*

Bertie shifted deftly to her favorite subject. "So, you're going to be thirty-three, Anna. Hard to believe. Imagine. Dad and I had been married a dozen years when I was that age."

"Yes, Mom. Message received. You take care."

The sun stabbed my bleary eyes. Peering at the street, I saw Bolly, the homeless artist, sleeping in the shelter of his three-legged desk. One of the working girls slumped in a factory doorway across the road, smoking a slim, dark cigarette. She tapped her high-heeled foot and blew a chain of smoke rings. Every once in a while, her languid gaze swept the deserted street from corner to corner.

I fitted my Canon with a telephoto lens and zoomed close, but after a few useless frames, I gave up. She looked bored and disgusted, simply passing time. Last night's makeup had eroded to smudges and shadows. In her worn jeans and cropped V-neck, she could have passed for a disillusioned shop clerk or office worker.

I packed extra film, my most user-friendly cameras and other paraphernalia I thought I might need with Monique's class. I climbed down the flimsy metal stairs, balancing the lumpy fanny pack, an overstuffed backpack and two ponderous totes. Staying out of Moshe Price's way still seemed prudent. Nice as he could be, my landlord had a trip-wire temper that I was determined to avoid.

My fingers cramped from their desperate lock on the rails, and my eyes played dislocating tricks. The building's darkened brick facade seemed to waver in the light morning breeze, and the span between the fire escape rungs kept shifting, so at intervals I stepped down too hard or had to grope for firm footing.

Clammy relief washed over me as my seeking toe finally settled on the ground. I circled through the courtyard toward the street. But before I reached the sidewalk, Moshe Price came charging out of the building, shaking his finger.

"No wild parties, I told you. No crazy guests. You heard me?"

"Yes, Mr. Price. Why? What's the problem?"

"I want to know what went on around here last night? And don't tell me nothing. When I walked in, the building looked like something out of the Wild West. Things broken, knocked down. I haven't seen such a mess since Mrs. Graff."

My face went hot. I hadn't thought about the things that had been over-turned and broken during the struggle with my assailant downstairs. "Some jerk thought I was one of the working girls and followed me inside. He did not give up easily. I'm sorry for leaving things that way. I'll clean it up right away."

His eyes gaped. "You're all right? He didn't hurt you?"

"No. He didn't, Mr. Price. Fortunately, a detective happened by and took him into custody."

"They should lock up that stupid *putz* and throw away the key. Shame on him. Putting a nice girl like you through such a thing."

"It's okay. I'm fine now. I'll go put things back in order."

"You'll do no such thing. My men already took care of it." His look went solemn. "You go rest, take it easy for a couple of days. My Rivka can come by and look after you. Bring you nice warm meals."

"That's sweet, but unnecessary. I feel just fine. In fact I'm on my way to the elementary school. I'm teaching the kids photography."

"You're sure you're up to it? You shouldn't overdo."

"Positive."

"You need anything, you'll call?"

"Thanks. That's very nice of you."

"Nice has nothing to do with it. It's a rule I forgot to mention. A tenant needs something, she calls immediately. Night or day. No exceptions. Do I make myself clear?"

"You do, Mr. Price. Perfectly."

"Good," he said sternly. "And don't forget *Shabbos* dinner. You'll relax and enjoy, eat a good meal. Do you a world of good."

"Yes. I think it will."

I arrived at the school as the first of Monique's little students straggled through the door. They greeted me like a rock star, clamoring for precious scraps of attention, "My turn. Mine, Ms. Jameson! Please."

Cindy's voice jittered as she bounced around in a frenzy of enthusiasm. "Can I go again? Please can I go again now?"

"After everyone's had a turn," I told her. "Who has numbers eighteen and nineteen?"

Identical towheaded twins approached, clad in gingham dresses and white sandals. They walked in lockstep, mugging in deliberate synchrony. "I bet you can't tell us apart," they chorused.

"Maybe the camera can. Take a look."

One of the girls peered through the lens while the other posed. "Stop it, Molly. Your face is all mushed up."

I twisted the focusing ring. "Better?"

"Now her hair looks fuzzy and she has two noses."

"Move this ring very slowly until that clears up."

She worked for an instant and then passed me the camera. "It's dumb. Come on, Molly. Let's play frogs and princesses."

"You go. I want to take pictures with the lady."

"You can't do that. You have to play with me."

"No I don't. Mommy says we can each play with whoever we want, and I want to play with the lady." She eyed the camera critically. "What's this called?"

"That's the shutter release. It lets the light in so the camera can see."

"Like taking off your sunglasses in the house?"

"Pretty much."

"And what's this thingy here?"

"That tells you how many pictures you've taken, so you know when you need to put in more film."

She nodded with grave understanding. "Like when the cookie box gets empty and there's only those crinkly paper cups?"

"Exactly."

Her sister edged away and drifted aimlessly around the room. "She's the baby," Molly explained. "I'm four minutes older."

"I see."

"What does that silver whatsis do?"

"It lets you change the lens when you want to look at things a different way."

For the next hour, I worked with the few remaining groups. Then I started the rotation over again, this time explaining what *candid* meant and sending each pair off on their own in search of intriguing shots. Monique had cautioned that the idea might be flawed. She warned that five-year-olds could not be trusted to deal responsibly with valuable equipment. But the first two girls listened with rapt attention to my instructions. They marched off with my old Nikon point-and-shoot and returned ten minutes later, beaming with pride in their accomplishment.

Everything went exactly as planned for three groups. Still, Monique kept glancing up nervously from her reading readiness lesson under the broad maple tree in the yard, casting around to see where the kids and camera were.

After the next pair went off to take their pictures, she took me aside. "I hate to nag, Anna, but you don't know five-year-olds the way I do. They can be perfect angels one minute and fearsome weapons of cataclysmic destruction the next. It's a really dangerous age because they can lull you into letting your guard down, trusting them with too much responsibility. They have the charm, the moves, the intelligence, but you shouldn't be fooled."

She directed my gaze to the tiny, bisque-faced child across the room. "That's Layla. Looks like a perfect little doll, right?"

"You wouldn't exactly mistake her for the Terminator."

"A couple of weeks ago, her mom needed to get ready for an important business meeting, so she set Layla up with her favorite 'Little Mermaid' video and told her to stay right were she was until the sitter showed up.

"Ten minutes later, Mommy is in the shower and she hears a monstrous noise from outside. She grabs a towel and looks out the window. There's her precious little doll, the one who has never given her a moment's trouble, standing on the lawn in front of their brownstone, with her hand over her mouth and her eyes big as Frisbees.

"Mom throws open the window and calls out, 'What's wrong, honey?' Then she spots her brand-new Taurus wagon across the street, wrapped around a neighbor's tree. Seems Layla went out to the driveway to look for the sitter. While she was waiting, she let off the brake and put the car in reverse on their steeply inclined driveway. She has no idea why she did that. It just seemed like a good idea at the time."

"I hear you, Monique. I promise not to entrust any of these kids with a motor vehicle."

"I'd hate for them to ruin your camera, Anna. It's nice enough that you agreed to give us your time."

"It's my complete pleasure. Teaching these kids is like falling in love with photography all over again. I can't remember when I've enjoyed anything more."

"I'm sure you'll enjoy it just as much if they don't wreck your equipment. Look, I have some money left in a small discretionary fund I get from the PTA. I can buy some of those disposable cameras, and the kids can go to town."

"They'll never get the same quality prints with those things."

"Maybe not, but I seriously doubt you'll hear any artistic complaints."

"I used my father's old Ricoh when I was younger than them. There's nothing to worry about. You'll see."

My words were drowned out by a long, anguished shriek. Monique and I raced to the side of the yard. She crouched in front of Rusty, while I went to Ben, who cowered, weeping, behind the slide.

I saw no visible signs of injury, no blood or obvious bruises.

"Did you fall, Ben honey? What hurts?"

He wept inconsolably, tears streaming, nose bubbling green.

Starched with terror, Rusty backed against the swings. "You'll be mad, Ms. Sharon. You're gonna kill us dead, I know it."

"I never kill anyone dead before lunchtime," she said. "Now tell me what happened, please."

"Show her, Rusty," said Ben. "Show her what you did."

"You did it, not me."

"We can talk about that later. Right now, I need to hear what's wrong," Monique insisted.

Slowly, Rusty stood, lurching on syncopated tics of grief. His right hand was under his barber-striped polo shirt, wrapped around a firm protrusion. He raised the shirt, exposing the sorry remains of my camera, a sentimental favorite that my uncle Eli had given me for my high-school graduation. The case was cracked in two places and the film advance lever had been broken off. The lens, with its clever built-in protection, had been shattered. If Rusty hadn't explained that the Nikon had been dropped, I would have sworn that it must have been the victim of a wild horse stampede or a runaway locomotive.

"I'm sorry," Ben wept. "I didn't mean it. Honest."

Monique glared at Rusty.

"I'm sorry, too, even though it was all his stupid fault."

"That's okay." I swallowed hard. "Stuff happens."

Monique led me back toward the main group. "That's what I was trying to tell you, Anna. Stuff especially happens around these little Indians. Now I insist on those disposable cameras. I'll pick some up after school today."

"No, I can get them. I have to meet Dixon downtown anyway in a little while. With any luck, I can make it back in time for everyone to take a few shots before dismissal."

"Great, I'll get you the money."

"That's okay. I can spring for them. No big deal."

"Absolutely not, my friend. You've already made more than enough sacrifices for the cause."

Chapter 28

Clu nudged off her slippers and planted her outsized feet on the coffee table. Her wet hair dripped a steady beat onto the collar of her blue terry robe, and her skin shone from a long, determined scrub in the shower. It had taken most of twenty minutes and half a bar of glycerin soap for her to feel clean again after a dreadful half-day stint with Melton Frame.

Sheepishly, she eyed her late husband's smiling portrait. "You're absolutely right, Joseph, I brought this on myself. But somehow, that devil of a man managed to manipulate me.

"Sure, I should have known better, but I let down my guard. When he claimed he wanted my opinion on a theory he was developing in the Jameson case, I took the rotten blowhard at his word. Next thing I know, I'm stuck in his office stewing while he blathers on the phone to his press agent and his literary agent and his real estate agent and Lord knows who else. I wanted to strangle the maddening fool, but I'm not given to allow myself such sinful pleasure."

Clu pressed her eyes to stem a budding headache. When she peered up again, Joseph was still smiling in his sweet, forbearing way.

"Yes, you're right. I should have caught the joke early on and marched out of there. The problem is that this Jameson case has me thinking with half a head, at best. I couldn't bring myself to pass up anything that might prove useful in solving the damnable thing."

Staring hard, she could have sworn she detected a subtle change in the portrait, a quizzical cast to Joseph's clear young eyes.

"No, it's not just about my Grandpa Jimmy, rest his soul. Though I must admit I would dearly love to clear up the cloud over his name.

"But there's more, a personal thing. Remember when the case first broke? Everyone was talking about who murdered the little girl and why. People took sides, mostly the mother's or the father's. And when we got together with friends, the Julie Jameson murder was always a prime topic of conversation."

Pausing, she pulled a slow, deep breath.

"What you might not remember is that I never took part in those discussions. While the others sat around talking about Bertie and Frank, I sank inside myself, nursing a deep, secret ache. All I could think about was that dead child's sister, what she must be thinking and feeling. How she would ever survive."

A solitary tear traced the contours of Clu's craggy face. "The thing is, I lost a sister, too, Joseph, a nameless tiny soul who died at birth. I know I mentioned that to you, but not the details. We were identical twins, little no name and I.

We shared the womb for seven months, until my mother's body could no longer sustain us.

"I was breech, turned backwards, always the contrary one, even then. By the time they managed to pull me into the world, my twin was gone. She was dead of coming second. Dead of my getting in her way."

Clu blotted her eye with a sleeve. "Sounds foolish, I know, to blame myself for what happened at my birth. And I don't really blame myself in any reasonable sense of the word. But I can't help relating in a special way to the brothers and sisters of children who have died. When there was talk about the Jameson case, all I could think about was the sister she'd left behind, what she must be suffering."

Clu ached to climb onto Joseph's lap and bury her face in his neck. "So when that blasted Frame hinted that he might have some idea of how to solve the case, I felt compelled to hear him out. Of course, he had no theory at all except his own profound self-importance. All he really wanted was to pick my brain and find out if I'd come up with anything inventive that he might be able to claim as his own idea.

"I suppose he also sought my company because the man is an empty shell. He doesn't exist without an audience to affirm him. I'm sorely tempted to send the pompous fool a canned laugh track or one of those flashing signs they use on quiz shows to solicit applause. But no, you're right, Joseph. There's no point. He would not begin to get the joke. He has no idea how insufferable he is. I'd rather have spent my day with swarming insects. At least they have some purpose."

Clu evicted the heinous Melton Frame from her thoughts and took up the Jameson file. Heeding Griffey's advice, she tried to clear her mind of conclusions and start anew.

She considered that her basic premise might be flawed. What if the desperate woman who called Ted Callendar had nothing to do with the case? A notorious incident like the Julie Jameson murder drew countless crime devotees. The Internet facilitated rapid-fire idea exchange between interested parties, so it was possible for an outsider to have extraordinary knowledge of arcane facts in the notorious killing.

With that in mind, she played the tape again. Clu searched for signs that the caller had rehearsed or otherwise planned her emotional plea. She reran the final segment several times, trying to imagine a seasoned actress delivering the lines. *Please, Mr. Callendar, I can't go on like this much longer. You people are my only hope.*

Unconvinced, she switched off the recorder. "That woman knew the case from the inside out, Joseph. She lived it and she's living it still. I've not a doubt in my mind that if we found her, we'd have the answer to this whole bedeviling mess."

Crossing to the window, Clu gazed across the street at the tempting green sprawl of Central Park. Strollers passed in companionable clusters and pairs. She pressed close to the glass like a prisoner spying unattainable freedom or peering at a lover through a bulletproof, soundproof shield.

She trudged back to the couch and took up the file once more. She played the tape again, first backward and then at a slow forward drone. On one pass she focused on the vowels, paying particular attention to the *A* and *O* sounds, which were particularly subject to regional variation.

The exercise confirmed several of her original impressions. Callendar's woman caller was in her sixties, formally educated in a rigorous environment. Her hypercautious locution was the product of precise, demanding parents and years of speech therapy. She was suffering from acute emotional distress and a chronic, and likely serious, respiratory disorder.

As the tape spun, a single word caught her attention. Backing up, she isolated the four-syllable constellation and played it several times. *Assassinate . . . assassinate . . . assassinate.*

Studied carefully, the second *A* sound was a dead giveaway. This woman had not just spent time in the South, as Clu had originally concluded, she was Southern to the core, born and bred.

With mounting excitement, Clu thumbed through the case file once again. This time, she searched for female witnesses and suspects who came from the South.

She found one, a former baby-sitter for the Jameson children, from Mobile, Alabama, who would have been about the correct age. Flipping through the detective reports, Clu discovered two teachers from the Carolinas among the staff at Julie Jameson's kindergarten. The number grew alarmingly as the file progressed. Several residents in the Jamesons' apartment house had been reared in the South. So had a number of local merchants, relatives and friends.

One-quarter of the way through the file, her list stretched to more than thirty names. Clu plodded on with a mounting sense of futility. They were taking long shots, grasping at straws.

A Hail Mary play might be the only thing left to them, but the sad truth was those desperate attempts rarely ever worked.

Chapter 29

Dixon sprawled on a bench in the plaza in front of the Flashlight Building. Mirrored lenses blanked his eyes and his legs were splayed like one of Moshe Price's mannequins. He was muttering into his cell phone, taking notes in his leather journal, frowning hard. Behind him, the Burlingame brass flying fish spat a luminous spray into the fountain.

I ducked past the building's entrance and perched next to Dixon with my head bowed and my hand propped to camouflage my face. "Hi."

He flipped the phone shut and closed the journal. "Hi, yourself. How'd it go?"

"Pretty well, I think. There was a lot of action last night, and the atmosphere was nice and creepy. I shot thirty rolls, mostly of the girls, but I got some decent close-ups of deals in progress and the kind of suggestive stuff you were talking about. Shadows in the doorways. Silhouettes in parked cars. No priests or rabbis yet, but I guess you can't have everything."

I handed him two large envelopes crammed with film.

His face brightened. "Can't wait. I'm going to have these babies developed right away."

"Sure you are," I snickered. "Something tells me you haven't dealt with the film lab lately."

"Ah, but I have. I've had to bring in a couple of shoots from freelancers I worked with on stories. And I have learned the secret way to Earl's heart."

"Me, too: money and terror."

"Chocolate works better. Snickers bars to be specific. A few of those babies, and Earl is jet-propelled."

"Now you tell me."

He raised his shades and winked. "Stick with me, Anna Jameson. I will teach you the secrets of the universe."

"Thanks anyway."

He patted the envelopes fondly. "If these are half as good as I expect, I'll have them in Burlingame's hands by the end of the day. I've already put together the captions and text, so all I need is a couple of hours to polish the piece and package it. With any luck, we can get it up and running in time for tomorrow's metro edition."

"So soon? I was planning to do more shooting tonight, maybe for the next few nights, before we settle on which pictures to run."

"No way. We need to get in with this ASAP."

"What's the big rush?"

"We don't want someone coming in with a more damaging story about the mayor sooner. So far, there's no hint of any competition, but things move with lightning speed in this business. If we've got the goods, it's crazy to wait."

"I don't know, Dixon. I still have a bad feeling about this."

"Why? What could possibly go wrong?"

"Something, everything. Every action can inspire an unequal and disastrous reaction."

"What's that? One of Murphy's laws?"

"No. It's one of my mother's. She makes Murphy look like a cockeyed optimist."

"Well, in this case, your mother's law doesn't apply. This piece is going to land you at the top of Burlingame's list."

"Which list?"

"Trust me."

"I'm trying, Dixon. Meantime, I should go. He's probably put out orders to have me shot on sight."

Pedestrian traffic had bloomed to a midday crescendo. Workers on lunch break streamed out of the Flashlight Building. The air filled with gossip and cigarette smoke.

"Go ahead. I've got everything under control."

Still ducked behind my hand, I hurried toward the corner. I swerved around a double-wide stroller crammed with packages and kids and aimed for the subway station down the block. As I reached the head of the gloomy stairwell, a sharp, indignant voice called from behind, "Hey, wait!"

Fearful that I had been spotted by one of Burlingame's people, I charged down the stairs. Near the bottom, I almost collided with a crimson-nosed man in a tattered tuxedo who veered suddenly into my path.

He bowed low. "So clumsy of me. My sincerest apologies."

"That's all right."

"Do tell how I might make it up to you."

"Just excuse me, please." I tried to get by him, but he kept shuffling about in confusion, blocking the way.

Before I could edge past, the voice called again. "Hey, Anna. Wait up."

Glancing back, I saw Dixon bumping down the stairs in a loose-jointed trot. He caught up with me, breathless, and steered me around the chivalrous bum. On the littered landing, he passed me a thick sealed folder. "I forgot to give you this. It's the file you wanted. Research didn't want to let it out, but I talked them into it. I have to get it back soon, so please get to it as quickly as you can."

"I will, thanks."

I took the train back to Marcy Street, clutching the file on my lap. It felt heavy and dangerous. Stamped warnings emblazoned the cover: CONFIDENTIAL and EYES-ONLY and PROPERTY OF BURLINGAME MEDIA ENTERPRISES, INC. My name had been typed on the small label in the upper right corner. Someone had added an *I* before the *E* in Jameson.

I stopped at One-Hour Photos and bought the disposable cameras. Processing was included, said the plump, walleyed clerk.

"One hour?"

"Not on this. It'll take overnight."

"Why is that?"

"Just is," she huffed. "Like I said."

"How much extra would one-hour cost?"

"Dollar a roll, but you get a dollar-off coupon with every one purchased, so it would come out exactly the same."

"Sounds good to me."

She grinned broadly, exposing dull, crooked teeth. "Does. Only problem is developing that film takes a bit more than an hour, no matter what."

"How long?"

"Overnight."

I argued with her for a few minutes, trying to iron the more serious creases out of her thinking, but it was an exercise in utter frustration. Her boss made the rules according to some perverse reckoning of his own. I didn't know of any other place nearby to pick up the toss-away cameras, so I relented and paid for these.

With fifteen minutes left until dismissal, I hurriedly distributed the cameras to Monique's class. The kids scattered like buckshot, happily clicking away, until the dismissal bell ten minutes later. They gathered their things and handed me the cameras as they headed for the door.

"All used up?" Monique said.

"Amazingly yes."

"I'd be amazed if they weren't. Delaying gratification is not a strong suit at this age."

"I'll drop them off to be developed. We can spend some time tomorrow looking at the results."

"Perfect."

Back at One-Hour Photos, the walleyed girl was locked in combat with another irate customer.

"Let me get this straight," said the stylish matron in a pink shirt and platinum silk suit. "You're going to charge me two dollars to make a negative of this print, then two dollars apiece to make copies from the negative."

The girl's head bobbed up and down like a wind-up toy. "That's right, ma'am. Two dollars apiece, like I said."

"But it says right there on that sign that you only charge a dollar and a half to make copies from a negative."

"That's right, but it's more when we have to make the negative."

"But that makes no sense. Suppose I was to have you make a negative, pay for it, walk around the corner and then bring the negative back."

"Then it would be a dollar fifty a copy, like it says right there on the sign."

"Exactly. So why don't you just pretend that's what happened?" the woman suggested patiently.

"Two dollars if we have to make the negative, ma'am. Rules are rules."

The woman set her jaw and marched out.

I filled my chest as I approached the high Formica counter. "I need these first thing in the morning."

"Deposit each one in an envelope and write your name and number on the flap. The flap will serve as your receipt. No pictures will be released without a receipt. No exceptions."

"You open at nine?"

"Nine, sharp. Unless I oversleep or the train's late."

I stopped at the market for emergency junk to see me through the reading of the file. I filled my cart with ice cream, Toll House cookies, nacho chips, cream soda, Devil Dogs, Gummi Bears and white chocolate pretzels. That would be dinner. A pack of Yankee Doodles would do for dessert.

Despite the sunny day, Bolly sat on the bar stool in his yellow slicker, balancing a fly rod over the street. As I approached, he gave a tentative tug on the line and then reeled in a manic frenzy. The rod strained and dipped as if a fighting fish had gripped the other end. The artist battled, cursing, slick with sweat, until the line went suddenly limp.

He shook the pole. "Get you next time, sucker."

When I moved to pass him, he roared in a fury, "Stop right there. You'll scare it away."

"Scare what?"

"I've been working here near all day, photo lady. You can just wait a damned minute 'til I'm done."

"All right. But I only have a minute."

Soon the line began to twitch, and the conflict raged again. Bolly rocked on his stool like a hapless lookout riding the main mast in a storm. He gesticulated wildly and strained for balance as if the imaginary fish was winning the tug of wills. I set down my bundles, fished my Canon from the backpack and shot off most of a roll.

The rod went still again. The artist hopped down from the stool and bowed curtly. "That's it, then. You can go on by now."

"You caught what you wanted?"

"Sure did. Caught you." He tossed his head back and brought up a huge, bubbling laugh. There was no self-congratulation in it; not a hint of malice or nasty intent. This character was simply having a good time.

Despite myself, I was disarmed. "Can I ask you a question?"

"You just did. Want to ask another one? Go right ahead. Talk's cheap."

"What happened? How did you come to live here?"

He scratched his bristly cheek. "On this planet, you mean? Right here on Zog?"

"No. I mean right here on the street."

He eyed me curiously for a moment. Then he gazed straight up, squinting at the sun. "If you want to know the one main thing, I'd have to say that."

"What?"

"The views. And not one single appliance. One thing I can't abide, it's appliances. Truth is, they don't like me all that much, either, especially blenders. They don't like you, man, they can be *mean*."

"I see."

"Do you? Do you really see, photo lady? 'Cause there's plenty worth taking note of. Plenty you ought to open your eyes to, for your own good."

"Meaning?"

"Me? I never mean much of anything at all. Ask anyone. I'm a chigger-brain, crazy as a gnat, and glad of it. Opens the doors up, knocks down the walls. Why pay for prison when freedom is free?"

"Good question."

"Thinking is free, too, except when you got the brain fog. Then it *costs*."

"Sure. See you." I retrieved my packages and made for home.

"Good talking to you," Bolly called after me. "Nothing like shooting the breeze, photo lady. Gets the dust out. Shakes the mind loose. Clears the lungs."

Chapter 30

I stashed the groceries, stowed the camera equipment in the bedroom and perched on my swaybacked couch. I untied the file's string closure and eased out the pile of printed sheets. The synopsis of my life occupied fifty single-spaced pages. I ran their crisp, even edges along my thumb and raised a chill breeze.

The first section held a dry recitation of facts I already knew. I had been born on August fourth almost thirty-three years ago, at Lenox Hill Hospital, attended by Dr. Timothy O'Toole, who had delivered my sister Julie two years earlier. My unremarkable delivery had followed a pregnancy that had proceeded, without incident, to term.

Somehow Burlingame's hired snoops had gotten their hands on my medical records, which detailed my tendency as a toddler to middle ear infections and occasional bouts of croup. Dr. Slonim, the pediatrician we used until we left New York, had described me as a *happy, outgoing, well-nourished girl,* which I recognized as his code for silly, chubby, motor mouth.

All of my developmental milestones were detailed. So were the millstones. I took my first steps at eleven months, spoke my first words at a year and completed toilet training at two and a half, after a battle valiantly waged and nobly fought.

At three, I developed night terrors and the profound aversion to the dark that vexed me still. According to Dr. Gotthelf, who assumed my medical care after we moved to Charleston, *This was likely in response to recent family difficulties.*

Gotthelf had predicted, in his bold, round hand, that *the disturbance will pass of its own accord,* though I noticed that he had not ventured a guess as to when.

Perhaps his prophecy might prove right someday, but I still had dreams so fierce and vivid that I awoke to my own desperate screams, raking at my throat like vicious claws. I still could not bear total darkness. During the brief moments when I needed pitch blackness to manipulate film in the darkroom, I had to close my eyes and envision the brightest sun, screaming fluorescent lights, fireworks bursting against a jewel black sky.

At eight, I broke my collarbone when I turned back to talk to Shelby, who was pedaling half a block behind me, and my bicycle hit a lurking oak. I had stitches above my ear from my fall at the Halloween spook house when I was nine. I developed pneumonia at ten, followed closely by a vicious case of chicken pox, which left scars in several highly personal places. At least they had been personal until Dixon's query made them part of this corporate record that any Burlingame employee could examine in the research department upon the submission of a routine request.

My face burned as I flipped through what else a curious colleague could find out. What I had weighed during various rounds in my battle of wobbly will, that I had suffered a pregnancy scare during my senior year in college along with a case of chlamydia, that I had recurrent yeast infections, that I ground my teeth when I slept.

My school record followed—such as it was. I had shown early promise, a solid IQ and outstanding scores on the verbal and visual-motor sections of standardized tests. I had been an early talker, precocious, socially adept. But, that promise had not been fulfilled.

In school I had majored in underachievement, with a double minor in cutting-up and maddening inattention. My performance through high school had been strictly average, with the exception of seventh grade, when my obsession with my sister's case sent my grades plummeting well south of their usual mediocrity.

I had always believed that my high SATs, enthusiastic recommendations and impressive portfolio had gotten me into Duke, but now I discovered that my admission had been ensured by a major gift my uncle Eli made to the university early in my senior year of high school.

I read those words again in numb disbelief. My uncle had always doted on me shamelessly, but I had never imagined the extent to which he might

go to protect and promote my interests. I had decidedly mixed feelings
about this, if the printed speculation was true. Buying my way into a prestigious school scorched my sense of justice and self-worth, but I knew that my
uncle had nothing but my happiness and future in mind. If he had done this,
as the report alleged, I sorely wished it had never come to light. But now I
knew it, Dixon knew it, and so could anyone who might be inclined to check
me out.

Horrified, I turned to the next section. What other nasty surprise was I
likely to find?

I read quickly through my employment history, which included summer
and after-school jobs, my years at Pruitt's and all of my freelance forays. Vague
mention was made of some difficulties I'd had with a public figure, but Senator
Bedell's name and the particulars of the incriminating picture I'd snapped of
him with a young intern did not appear. Either the research department had
failed to uncover the facts, or Bedell's powers of suppression were every bit as
overwhelming as I'd thought.

No shocks there.

The next several pages detailed my social life. There was an amazingly
comprehensive list of my friends, dating back to first grade. Shelby, as a prime,
continuing player, was described in meticulous detail:

> Jameson's longtime friend and closest confidante is a highly respected
> board certified psychiatrist in private practice in Manhattan. Her husband
> is a successful corporate executive, and the couple has three healthy, thriv-
> ing young children. The family owns a spacious cooperative apartment in
> the Sutton Place area of Manhattan and a weekend home in Sag Harbor,
> Long Island, with a tennis court and pool. Informants allude to long-
> standing envy on Anna Jameson's part, which they describe as understand-
> able given the obvious discrepancies in the friends' personal and career
> accomplishments.

Informants?

Gathering my confidential records was revolting enough. The idea that
these insects had interviewed people about me left me sputtering. Worse, their

sources had no idea about the facts. Discrepancies were not the issue in my friendship with Shelby, neither was envy. Our bond was a special, irrational, transcendent thing, and it was ours alone to define or dissect; ours to honor steadfastly or trample and repair.

Ours.

Fuming, I read on. The report outlined my relationship with Kevin, beginning with our first date (a movie and ice cream afterward, his mother drove) in seventh grade. The researchers had done a deep and thorough excavation. They knew that we had gone together to the junior and senior proms and to a dreadful cotillion, where I had blown the requisite curtsy and put a heel through the skirt of my gown. They had discovered our first overnight stay together in a seedy North Charleston motel on a summer weekend after senior year. They had even unearthed Betsey Abel, the sultry blond vixen from neighboring Shem Creek, who had chased Kevin shamelessly for years. Sometimes, he'd let her catch him, and researchers had uncovered that as well, not to mention the fact that I had Betsey to thank, albeit indirectly, for my chlamydia. In fact all of Kevin's little peccadilloes appeared, including one far more recent that was breaking news to me.

Disgusted, I flipped the page. He meant nothing to me anymore. Kevin was a starting block, something to run from at top speed with extreme determination.

The next page was a blank separator. The following sheet bore a single headline: JAMESON'S SISTER'S MURDER—AUGUST 4, 1970.

The salient details of my life, birth to the present, consumed a grand total of fourteen pages; a sketchy outline of my sister's killing filled the remaining thirty-six.

This was not surprising, either. I had long understood that my most remarkable feature by far was my close, unwelcome association with a lurid, unsolved crime. Apart from being Julie Jameson's sister, I was decidedly ordinary, and that was more than fine with me. I treasured the anonymity and privacy that had eluded my family for years after my sister's death.

During that awful time, thousands, maybe millions of pages of facts and speculation about Julie's murder had appeared in print. Her story had inspired several best-selling nonfiction books, countless novels, a feature film and at least two television movies, not to mention a number of tragic copycat crimes and a few key pieces of child protective legislation.

Even after the initial flurry passed, there was no certain or permanent respite. Every so often, the phone would ring or a knock resound at the door, and instead of a friend or neighbor, we would find some parasite lurking in ambush.

Good evening, Dr. Jameson, I'm writing an article on the outrageous cost of child-sized coffins. Care to comment?

One visitor in particular stuck like a burr in my mind. On a sultry summer night when I was five or six, a prim-looking lady in a somber dress and dark cloche hat appeared on our porch. She clutched a worn, leather-bound volume in hands that were lean and tough as chicken feet. A stiff, unfelt smile hung on her face, like a sign.

My mother went to the door and stood expectantly.

Yes?

Bertie Jameson?

Yes. Can I help you?

You can't help anyone, not even yourself. A bony finger rose in accusation. *Damned you are, and damned you shall remain for all eternity.*

Then she spotted me, pressed in the shadows of the hall, sucking the comfort from my thumb.

And so shall the fruit of your womb be damned and their fruit for all eternity.

My mother's lips pressed in a resolute seam as she firmly shut the door. She did not speak another word for hours.

Through the window I watched the woman back away slowly, her dead smile broadening, features trembling with self-righteous spite.

Shame on you, came her witch voice. *Shame on you all.*

Chilled by the memory, I turned back and started to read.

JAMESON MURDER: *Summary of known facts.*
VICTIM: *Julie Ann Jameson, age five years, two months.*
Victim was last seen alive at 8 P.M., EDT, August 4, in the family home at 552 East 60th Street. Alberta Jameson, the victim's mother, discovered the child's body at approximately 9 A.M. August 5, and called emergency

services. Before medics arrived, the child's father, Frank Jameson, a physi-
cian, made aggressive attempts at "resuscitation"(Dr. Jameson's word),
contaminating the scene and destroying evidence, severely handicapping
subsequent investigation. Autopsy put the time of death at six to twelve
hours earlier.

My father had been tried for this in the merciless court of public opinion
and sentenced to lifelong recrimination and self-doubt. According to legions of
armchair detractors, he should have known at a glance that my sister was
beyond help. He should have understood that touching his dead daughter,
making a desperate attempt to revive her, constituted a mortal forensic sin. The
hail of strident criticism that followed annihilated his passion for the practice
of medicine, assassinated his optimism and hope and bowed his spine. For trying to save his beloved little girl, my dear, gentle Pop would suffer the worst
imaginable punishment, the kind inflicted without mercy from within.

Then, there was my mother.

Investigators at the scene noted several oddities in Alberta Jameson's
behavior. In lieu of any expression of grief or shock, the child's mother cor-
dially excused herself to dress, fix her hair and apply makeup. Before the
victim's body was removed from the premises, the mother began efficiently
and systematically cleaning up after a birthday party, which was held for
the younger daughter the day before. Observers commented that Mrs.
Jameson appeared unnaturally calm and competent.

My mother had been skewered for the sin of stoicism and control. She had
been reviled for this, mocked and detested.

Like most accounts, the report had been slanted for maximum impact.
The researchers' bias blazed neon clear. One or both of my parents held the
responsibility for my sister's death.

I read through the staggering list of other suspects who had been scrutinized during the investigation, including several members of my family. No
one had escaped suspicion, including my ever-ailing grandmother, Myrna, my
great-uncle Jack, who suffered from dementia, my retarded cousin Ruthie, and

Uncle Eli, who had been passing through New York with his family at the time on the way to a European vacation.

Hundreds, maybe thousands of potential suspects had been questioned. Several prime possibilities had been dismissed for lack of sufficient, sustainable evidence, not because they were innocent. I understood this, and I had several theories of my own.

Charles Manfred Theron resided at the top of my list. Char, as he had been called, worked as a handyman in our apartment building and lived in a dim basement room beside the boiler. The creepy character skulked around the building, a silent observer who would appear with startling suddenness like a burst of evil wind. All of us kids, even the smallest ones, feared him in a primal, instinctive way, even though our high-minded parents admonished us not to judge anyone by appearances. Julie, who loved most people, had a special aversion to Char, which to this day I suspect was a prescient understanding that he would do her harm. Call it silly superstition, but I have long believed that our most persistent fears foreshadow the means to our ends. Mine would come in darkness. I was eerily certain of this.

Char took off shortly after my sister's murder, on the day when Julie's body was found, before he could be questioned or detained. When detectives on the case failed to locate him, they wrote him off, claiming he had never been under serious consideration. To me, this was an obvious defense of their incompetence in letting him slip away.

Years later, I read a compelling piece by a longtime student of the crime, citing Theron as a prime suspect, as I had. The conclusion was unassailably logical. Char had master keys and easy access to our apartment. He was a brooding loner with no known friends or normal diversions. He had ample opportunity to observe Julie and fixate on her. Most compelling, a background check put him near the scene of two earlier child murders, one in Michigan, one in Vermont. The writer had also turned up a history of mental illness in the Theron family that dated back several generations. His mother and grandmother had committed suicide. An aunt and two nephews suffered from severe bipolar disease. Char himself had been arrested four times: twice for cruelty to animals, once in a bar fight when he slashed another patron with a church key, and once for making a felonious public nuisance of himself in an unnamed manner.

This was not a nice man.

As I read, my head swam with other old, unanswered questions. Even if Char Theron proved to be innocent, there were other excellent candidates the police had failed to investigate fully.

What about the man who had exposed himself two weeks before the murder in a neighborhood park? What about the crazy who scared Julie earlier that day when she got off the camp bus? And what of the countless others who had come to the apartment over the years: repairmen, meter readers, baby-sitters, cleaning people, deliverymen, clergymen, teachers, patients, acquaintances, friends?

Forgetting all those, the crime could have been the random act of an opportunistic lunatic exploiting the cover of the awful storm that raged on the night of my sister's death. My parents were the last souls on Earth who deserved to be accused. In fact they were the greater victims in the crime. Julie's suffering had been finite; theirs had continued undiminished for thirty years.

I found the reading incredibly difficult and slow. I relived the most painful moments as I had so many times before. Somehow, time did nothing to blunt the enormity of that monstrous night. Approaching the end of the report, I felt beaten and exhausted.

Those closest to the investigation persist in their belief that the child's killer will be brought to justice. Recently, an intriguing new theory has been advanced that would account for many of the open questions in this case and explain why it has so long stymied so many experts. According to—

The document ended there. The new theory, whatever it was, had been lost or removed. Wildly curious, I tried Dixon, but no one answered on his portable or at home.

I leafed through all the pages again, to be sure that the missing one was not among them. Then I tapped the papers in a neat stack and slipped them back into the folder.

Who else might know?

I took up my cell phone to call the seventeenth precinct, which still held official jurisdiction over the ancient case. But I hung up before the call went through. Years ago, I had tried to find someone at the squad who might be able to enlighten me further about the investigation into my sister's killing. My call had been bounced from desk to desk, and a series of crisp, dismissive voices had informed me that everyone from that era had moved on or retired.

I would do better to wait until I could question Dixon. He could point me to the author of the Burlingame report. Thankfully, my exile would be over in a few days.

As I stood, stiff with immobility and tension, I caught the dull thump of footsteps on the fire escape. The rear door squealed open, and a briny breeze suffused the loft.

There was silence from below. The Marv-Liss Mannequin Company had closed for the day.

I was alone, but not alone. Someone lurked behind me, unmoving, breathing low. Starched with terror, I searched for something that might serve as a weapon. Then slowly, I turned to face the intruder down.

Chapter 31

The cab reeked of incense, chicken curry and sweat. Callendar cranked down the window and breathed through his mouth to still the queasiness. After years of numbing exposure, most things went down fine with the sight of mangled corpses. But the ripe, warring aromas in the car were raising his gorge.

He opened the next folder in the pile. On top was a grainy photo of a dark-haired man. A livid scar, shaped like a lightning bolt, scored his cheek. His rap sheet ran from petty theft to the knife murder of a young hitchhiker whom he had picked up on I95 near the New York/Connecticut border. The picture of the slash victim was clipped to the back of the print. The slight, androgynous-looking teenaged boy had sustained twelve ragged cuts and several oozing stab wounds. Not pretty. The creep had copped to first-degree manslaughter and earned a sentence of eight to fifteen. Out in six and a half with good behavior, he was now suspected in the bludgeoning of a young drifter in Queens.

Callendar set the folder aside. This was a tool man with an eye for young boys. They were looking for someone who preferred to do his handiwork on little girls.

Next in the pile was a wizened old guy suspected of stalking his young victims, then bumping them off with massive doses of insulin. Cops had been watching him for years, but they still lacked enough solid evidence for an indictment. Callendar passed on him as well. He was an outdoorsman, not the break-and-enter type. Plus, he swabbed his victims' skin with alcohol before injecting them, sparing them from posthumous disease. Julie Jameson's killer had been anything but fastidious.

Callendar had been at this for most of the day, reviewing the charmers Lyman Trupin's FBI friends had unearthed for their consideration.

Bell and Weller had mined crime databases worldwide. They had searched for cases involving very young victims, anger/retaliatory assault patterns, left-handed perpetrators, size nine-wide footprints, strangulation, digital compression of the hyoid bone, murders committed in inclement weather, killers who took jewelry souvenirs, etc. The results included over a thousand homicides.

Eliminating the ones who had subsequently died or were now incarcerated and, therefore, no imminent threat, reduced the number to three hundred sixty-five. The agents had further pared the count by one hundred and eleven, who had been out of the country or in jail at the time of the Sleeping Beauty Murder.

Cooperating agencies had transmitted profiles of the remaining contenders and summaries of their crimes to the communications center. A messenger had delivered the results to the Arcanum members working on the Jameson case. They had decided to review the files independently and then meet to compare impressions and conclusions.

For Callendar, the effort had yielded nothing so far except a painful knot in his gut. So many young lives trashed. So many dreams and families shattered in a moment of vicious lunacy.

True, he had elected to be in the misery business, but he dearly wished that business was not so damned good. The depths of man's inhumanity never ceased to amaze and appall him.

Women's too, he thought as they turned onto east Eighty-fifth Street, and he saw his ex-wife waiting. Time had done nothing to blunt her anger and resentment. No matter that she had been as unhappy in the marriage as he had, maybe more so. Janice always wanted most what she could not have.

She stood under the apartment house awning in a shapeless print dress. Her frizzy brown hair bloomed in an electrified halo. Her dark eyes beamed like pistol bores through outsized metallic frames. Madison and Cody scurried out of the building as the cab pulled to the curb.

"Tell your father you have to study for exams. I'll come for you around nine, right after the lecture," Janice called after them.

Callendar stepped out to hug the kids and help them into the cab. "I'll have them home by ten as usual, Janice. If they need to study, they can do it at my place. You have your books?"

The girls nodded tensely.

"Hop in, ladies. Say good-bye to your mom."

"I'll be there at nine. Be ready."

Madison winced hard as she slipped into the rear seat. Cody clenched her steel-jacketed teeth.

Callendar's daughters were silent on the ride, as they often were when he picked them up for a visit. Janice made a point of pouring poison in their ears on the way out the door, vaccinating them against any risk of a good time. She wanted them to know that their father was a board-certified rat. Anyone who dared show him love or loyalty was a rodent by association.

Callendar had tried to make Janice understand that this brand of warfare could only hurt and confuse the kids. He had tried on his own and with the help of the wise, seasoned family counselor whom his ex had selected for them to see.

Dr. Larwin had seconded his conviction that Madison and Cody had no reasonable role in the divorce or subsequent hostilities. Children needed unconditional love from both of their parents. They flourished best with warmth and acceptance and unflinching support. They were not equipped to act as partisans or referees.

No matter how much spiteful satisfaction Callendar might get, he would never run Janice down in front of the girls. When they complained about their mother, he gently reminded them that they needed to bring their grievances directly to the source. Yes, he detested the woman. True, she never missed a chance to make his life miserable. But he refused to avenge those wounds at his daughters' expense.

"This evening, for your dining pleasure, the chef is offering several succulent *spécialités de la maison*," he said.

"What's that?" Cody asked.

"Pizza or Chinese," Madison sighed.

"*Mais non. Mon petit chou,*" Callendar insisted. "I was thinking of something different, something new and exciting. Perhaps some *je ne sais quoi.*"

"What's *chou*?" Cody asked.

"Cabbage, which we hate," Madison said. "I vote for Chinese."

"Pizza," Cody countered predictably.

"Chinese pizza it is," Callendar declared. He called on his portable and placed the orders.

Leading the kids into his shabby third-floor walk-up on West Broadway, he suffered the usual nervous pang. He had done what he could to make his apartment homey, but he recognized that homely was closer to the fact. After child support and alimony, a cramped one-bedroom was the best he could afford. For the girls' sake, he had left all the decent, grown-up stuff they had accumulated during the marriage with Janice. Callendar had furnished his place with castoffs, closeouts and bargain-bin selections.

In his pragmatic view, the things he'd picked up did the job reasonably well. You could sit on the chairs, eat at the table, rail at the Yankees on the boob tube and see passably well by the lamps. The glassware didn't leak and plates were nontoxic. He had the best possible artwork: pictures of and by the girls. Indoor plumbing. Heat.

"So what'll it be, ladies? Shall we rent a tape? Do folk dancing? Sing sea chanteys? Meditate?"

"We have to study, Daddy." Madison sat daintily on the couch with her French book. Cody plucked a battered algebra text from her backpack and sprawled on the floor.

"Wait up. There's plenty of time for that after dinner. Why don't we talk awhile? Catch up. How's school going? Have you guys decided about riding camp?"

"You heard Mom. We have exams," Cody chided.

The younger girl's eyes kept darting toward him, and then falling away. Madison refused to look at him at all.

"Okay. That's it." He wrested away the books and sat between them. "What's going on?"

Cody leaped up and grabbed for her text. "Quit it, Daddy. You want me to fail?"

"No. I want you to tell me what's wrong."

The girls exchanged a hard, meaningful look. "It's between Mom and us," Madison said. "You're always telling us to leave things where they belong."

"Is that what's bothering you, a gripe with your mom?"

Cody swayed coyly. "Sort of."

"Madison?"

"Not exactly." She threw up her hands. "Look, Dad, I don't know if you really want the truth."

"I do, always. Let me hear what it is, and maybe I can help you decide what to do about it."

The story emerged in tortured bits. Cody had been desolate over a friend's failure to invite her to a birthday party. When she refused to snap out of her bleak mood on command, Janice had invoked her own particular brand of shock treatment.

You think you have problems, imagine how I feel. I gave your father every-thing: a beautiful home, two children. I put him through grad school, worked like a dog. And he thanks me by sleeping with every bimbo he can get his hands on.

Callendar cringed. "Those were her words?"

"Yes, Dad." Madison's lip quaked and a tear slid down her cheek.

Callendar struggled mightily to keep his tone level. "I know this may be hard to understand, but marriages break up from the inside. Sometimes people simply can't get along anymore, no matter how hard they try. Sometimes husbands and wives grow apart and fall out of love. But that doesn't mean they don't love their children exactly the same."

Cody's braces gave her frown an evil glint. "So it's true."

Treading, as he was, through a minefield, Callendar chose his moves with extraordinary care. "The only true thing is that I'm your dad and Mom's your mom and we both love you very, very much. That hasn't changed and it never will."

"She said you'd make excuses," Cody charged.

"I have no excuses to make. I can tell you both without reservation that I have never done anything to hurt you and I never would. The truth is there are no bad guys in this. Sometimes things go wrong and there's no one to blame. It's hard for some people to accept, but it happens."

"Why is Mommy so mad, then?" Madison asked.

"I can't answer for your mom, sweetie. I can only speak for myself."

Slowly, the tension dissolved. During dinner, the girls sparred with normal vigor and ate with encouraging appetite. Callendar's heart swelled with love for these beautiful kids and with poison gas for the troll who had helped him produce them.

Twisting the kids' minds with that trash amounted to child abuse. In fact Janice was the one who had fractured their marriage vows, running directly back to her old boyfriend's bed after their first major fight. But that was history, and history could be revised.

After dinner, the girls settled in with their books. Callendar read through and dismissed a dozen more files. Thoughts of Janice and her grotesque accusations kept intruding. Dealing with her helped him understand what drove people to acts of lethal rage.

He opened the next folder in the pile. What appeared trapped Callendar's wandering attention immediately. On the name line was a question mark followed by a long list of aliases. By default, the suspect was referenced as John Doe.

Doe was a peripatetic soul who had lived in at least twelve states and several foreign countries, traveling at various times under U.S., French, Spanish and German passports.

With the aid of phony licenses, transcripts and credentials, he had worked a variety of jobs ranging from construction and appliance repair to physical therapist and assistant college English professor at a small liberal arts school in Maine. Students there remembered him as demanding and intense. Tenants in the Long Island building he oversaw for a year as superintendent remembered him as a quiet, hardworking soul. Coworkers on his construction team recalled a strange guy with a stutter and a strong facial tic.

Callendar's pulse quickened. He believed he could be looking at a true sociopath, who, despite their frequent appearance in movie thrillers and popular fiction, were as rare as black swans. In his practice he had seen plenty of patients with sociopathic features, but never a pure example: someone wholly devoid of conscience, genuine human connection or any capacity for remorse.

In psychiatric literature, the pure sociopath often resorted to mimicry as an adaptive substitute for any genuine emotion. He acted the part of a real, feeling person governed by normal societal rules, though in fact he was anything but. This allowed him to function freely and made him far more dangerous.

The face that stared out from the photo held strong features in a large, blocky frame. The eyes appeared clear, sharp and intelligent. His look was clean-cut, but by all indications, this man changed his personality, pedigree and physical appearance with startling ease.

That would account for his long, continued evasion of the law. So would his obvious access to extensive resources. Traveling freely worldwide with several sets of convincing papers took money and connections. This character clearly had plenty of both.

A stack of seventeen young female homicide victim photos accompanied Doe's profile. Flipping through them, Callendar was not surprised to find a striking variety of backgrounds and causes of death. He laid them out on the end table, positioning them on an imaginary map of the world. As he did so, a definite pattern emerged, the more recent the crimes, the closer they came to New York City.

Callendar shuddered, thinking that this might be what they were up against. Aside from being young and female, these victims shared only one obvious trait. The man called John Doe had come into their lives shortly before they died.

Chapter 32

Backlit by the waning sun, Dixon's mechanic friend stood inert.
He had climbed the fire escape, crossed the roof to the catwalk and entered
through my flimsy rear door. Dressed in a soiled black T-shirt and tight black
jeans, Spook looked even stranger and more off-putting than I recalled.

"What are you doing here?" I winced at the panicky timbre of my voice.
Standing straighter, I forced my tone into a lower, more commanding range.

He showed me a filthy, rusted metal device. "Got this fan motor for your
fridge. Should make the old crate run better."

He strode one step closer, then another, swallowing my space.

"You can't just come barging in here like this. You should have called first,
at least. I would have told you it's not a good time."

"Ease up. Only take a minute."

He came at me, looping a greasy string of hair behind his ear.

"I don't have a minute. I need you to leave right now."

He made a quick, feinting step in my direction, then chuckled. "How come
you're so scared, little girl? Think I bite?"

"I'm not scared. I simply don't appreciate your barging into my home." I
backed away, keeping maximum distance between us.

"It's okay. Big bad Spook's not going to hurt you. Even when I do bite, it's
real gentle."

"You can go out the way you came or through the front. But I want you to
leave right now."

He had backed me nearly to the bedroom door. Outraged, I stalled and
stood my ground. "Leave, or I'll have you arrested for breaking and entering."

He dropped the motor with a thump and saluted with his pinkie stump
aloft. "Yes, sir. Right away, sir." He turned away, chuckling meanly, and loped

toward the door. "Now I see what Dixon means about you having a stick up your butt. Regular ice queen."

I listened until the lift dropped to the main floor and the factory door slammed shut. At the bottom of my purse, I found the detective's card. He picked up on the second ring.

"Elisson here."

"It's Anna Jameson, Detective. I was thinking about those security measures we discussed."

"That so?"

"Yes. Whenever your partner is available, I'd like to get an estimate."

"You're welcome to that, Ms. Jameson, but I can tell you honestly that Harry comes way, way cheaper than any carpenter or locksmith you'll find, plus he does excellent, solid work. Truth is, he does it pretty much for the cost of materials because he likes to see people get their places secure."

"Sounds great. How soon do you think he can do the work?"

"When's good?"

"Sooner the better."

I could feel him dissecting the silence. "You sure everything's all right, Ms. Jameson? You haven't found yourself more trouble?"

"I'm fine, Detective. Just trying not to be a Dixieland rube."

He laughed. "Nice to see you're a quick learner. We're on late tonight, off first shift tomorrow. I'll check to make sure Harry's clear. If he is, I'll come along to help out, get things done faster. Unless you hear from me, we should be able to make it to your place by nine, nine-thirty."

"The problem is I'm volunteering at the elementary school. I hate to disappoint the kids."

"Wouldn't want you to. Anyway, there's no need. These kinds of jobs are noisy, and a mess while they're going on. Probably be better if you're not around. You can leave the key under the mat. We'll replace it with one that actually keeps people out. Should have everything done and cleaned up by the time you get home."

"That'll be terrific. Thank you, Detective. Should I leave a check?"

"No need, Ms. Jameson. I'll get the bill to you when I figure out exactly what you owe."

Chapter 33

The buzzer sounded as Callendar read the last of John Doe's file. He set the folder facedown at the bottom of the pile, not wanting the taint of that sick, brutal character anywhere near his daughters.

Madison stood quickly. "Must be Mom. Come on, Cody. We'd better go."

It was only eight-thirty by Callendar's trusty Timex, and his court-ordered midweek evening visitation did not expire until ten. Janice had been squeezing as hard as she could, trying to shrink the visits for spite.

The girls were gathering their things.

"No, wait. You don't need to go yet. We haven't even had dessert. I'll go down and tell your mom to go ahead without you. I can bring you home later on."

"No, Daddy. She'll be mad," Cody said.

"Don't worry about it, sweetheart," Callendar advised. "Your mom and I will work it out."

The buzz sounded again, a harsh, insistent jeer.

"Please, Dad. It's not worth a fight."

Madison's pleading look melted his indignation. "All right. Come on. I'll walk you down."

"Don't, okay? It's better if we just go," Cody said.

Callendar relented again with a rueful smile. Ferrying back and forth between hostile parents was hard enough without these bonus pressures. He kissed his daughters good-bye and hugged them fiercely. "Call and let me know how those tests go."

"We will."

"And think about what you want to do over the weekend. Maybe we can see that new space flick at the Imax. Go blading in the park if it doesn't rain. Have a picnic."

"Sounds good."

They were out the door, galloping downstairs, dainty as a herd of rhinos. Callendar slumped on the couch with his head in his hands. He was so weary of ducking Janice's assault rounds, so sad for those innocent kids.

Eager for a diversion, he dialed Solomon Griffey at home. After six rings, the old man's wispy voice came on the line.

"Why, hello, Ted. Have you finished going through the files?"

"Just about. I want to see if you came to the John Doe yet, hear what you thought about him."

"A fascinating specimen, to be sure. But by my calculations, he would have been too young to be responsible for the Julie Jameson murder. The oldest estimate of his age would put him at no more than twelve at the time of that crime."

"Murderers that young are not unheard of," Callendar said. "They executed a kid in Texas last month for a double murder he committed at ten."

"True, but in this particular case, it flies in the face of circumstance. Young perpetrators tend to commit crimes of impulse and convenience. Given a calculated break-in during a monstrous storm, I'm dubious that a child could be responsible."

"I understand it's a stretch, Griffey. But it's possible."

"Certainly. Anything is until proven otherwise. But we are dealing in calculated hunches here, and I believe we need to be prudent with those. We have neither the time nor the resources to chase very many wild geese."

Callendar sighed. "You're right, of course, but I still have a feeling about this Doe character."

"Instincts are our stock-in-trade, Ted, and I certainly respect yours. Bring it up at tomorrow morning's meeting. Let's see what the others have to say. Meanwhile, I'll have a closer look at Mr. Doe."

"That's what I was hoping for, Griffey. Thanks."

As he set the receiver down, the security buzzer blasted yet again. One of the girls must have forgotten something. Good, he would have an extra minute with them, another hug. Given his rationed visits, he treasured every crumb. He pressed the button to release the entry lock downstairs.

Soon loud footfalls sounded on the steps. Janice burst through the door.

Callendar braced for the storm. "What's the problem now?"

"The problem is, I'm sick of waiting. Where are the girls? I told you I'd come for them. Why aren't they ready?"

"What are you talking about? They're with you. They left ten minutes ago when you buzzed."

"I didn't buzz ten minutes ago, Ted." She looked around through her giant-framed glasses. "Are you telling me you just let them leave? You didn't take them downstairs? You didn't check to be sure who buzzed? Are you crazy?"

"They're not with you? You didn't see them?"

"No. I most certainly did not."

Callendar skirted her and made for the door. He raced downstairs to the street. Frantic, he scanned the block, but there was no sign of his daughters.

He raced to the corner, calling out, "Madison! Cody!"

Janice was right behind him. Her shriek split the torpid night. "Where are my babies, Ted? You'd better find them right now, you reckless jerk!"

Callendar tried to think through the reeling terror. The buzz might have been an innocent mistake, someone trying to ring another apartment or a neighbor without a key trying to get into the building. He had done that himself a time or two.

But if they didn't see their mother, why hadn't the girls turned around and gone back upstairs?

As he ran down the block, checking the few open shops, building lobbies, anything, he tried to convince himself that this had to be a simple misunderstanding. Madison and Cody must have decided to hang out and wait for their mother on the street. Maybe they didn't want to bother him. That must be it. Then they tired of waiting in one place and went for a stroll. They weren't little kids anymore. Walking well-lit city streets, especially together, was no big deal.

Clinging to that comforting thought, Callendar kept scouring the neighborhood, calling the girls' names until his throat went raw.

Janice trailed a block behind, railing at him. "I'll make it so you never see those girls again, Ted. I'll take you to court. I swear I will."

Callendar stopped and turned to her. "You have your cell phone?"

"Of course I do. I always carry it when the girls are with you, in case they need me, which obviously they do."

"Good. Use it, then. Call your place to see if they're there. If they're not, try their friends."

"Don't you dare give me orders, you reckless idiot!"

"Look, Janice. This is not about you or me; it's about the girls. Do you want to see them safe or would you rather stand around calling me names?"

"The nerve of you. You're the one who sent them out with God knows who in the middle of the night. You're the one who's out chasing skirts while I take care of them."

Callendar spoke through clenched teeth. "Chances are they just went for a walk and they'll show up any minute. Go wait for them at my place, please. I don't want them walking into an empty apartment."

"Who gives a damn what you want?"

"Go!" he roared. "Call my cell phone if they turn up."

Scowling furiously, Janice turned back, stabbing numbers on her portable phone.

Ten minutes passed—fifteen. There was no word from Janice, not a trace of the kids. With every passing second, Callendar's terror grew. He had heard all the horror stories, including some that never made the news: kids vanishing like smoke. Kids were taken and subjected to unthinkable horrors that changed them beyond recognition. Stole their future. Ruined them permanently. A second's inattention could lead to that, a momentary lapse in judgment, a blink.

Where could they be?

Desperate, he turned back and retraced his steps. He dug a year-old snapshot from his wallet and showed it to the turbaned man in the stationery store, the moon-faced Korean girl in the greengrocery, passersby. "Have you seen these kids? If you see them, would you please tell them to go to their dad's apartment right away?"

Most of those he approached reacted with odd, distrusting looks. They did not know what to make of this.

Callendar didn't, either. The clock ticked relentlessly toward an ever more pessimistic conclusion. Almost half an hour had elapsed.

He tried Janice's cell phone, but he could not get through. Out of ideas, he headed home. He wouldn't put it past Janice to conveniently forget to report that the girls had shown up safe.

That had to be it. As he hurried back, he held a picture of his ex and the kids gorging on ice cream and mindless drivel on the tube.

But when he climbed the stairs, he heard her hysterical rambling. "No, he doesn't have a clue where they are. My God, they could be kidnapped, or worse."

"No word?" he asked.

Janice dropped the phone and collapsed in a mournful heap on the sofa. "How could you do this? What's wrong with you?"

"Stop it, Janice. That's not going to find the kids. Let's try to get a grip, think sensibly."

"I want you to call the police, Ted. Right now. Call and tell them you sent your little girls out into the night alone and now they're gone."

"The police won't do anything, not about two kids their age missing for a half hour at nine clock."

She lunged at him, pounding her fists on his chest. "Do something, God damn you! You lost those girls, now you find them! Now!"

Callendar trapped her wrists. "Stop it, Janice. Get ahold of yourself. I thought of someone I can call."

He took up the phone and held a finger in his ear to hear past his ex-wife's shrieking. Russell Quilfo's wife answered at their house and told him he could find the lieutenant in his office at the Cold Case Squad in Queens.

When Quilfo came on the line, Callendar cleared the emotion from his voice and recounted the facts. His daughters had left his apartment almost forty-five minutes ago and gone missing. Friends and neighbors had been contacted, but no one had heard anything. No, they were not the types to seize a chance like that to break away and get into mischief. Madison, especially, was an unfailingly sensible, reliable kid. If Cody, who had a rebellious streak, suggested something out of bounds, the older girl could be counted on to rein her sister in.

No, they hadn't gone off to see some boy or try to score liquor or cigarettes or talk their way into an R-rated film. Callendar was sure of that. Nor was this an attention-getting ploy, as Quilfo gently proposed.

"I know my kids, Russell. They wouldn't do that."

"You're recently divorced, Ted, isn't that right?"

"Yes, but I'm telling you, they wouldn't take off to make a point. It's just not who they are."

"Try not to take any of this the wrong way, Ted. I have to ask these questions to get to the bottom of what might be going on. Kids do take off, happens every day, and ninety-nine point nine percent of the time it's nothing at all. An impulse. Or maybe it's a simple miscommunication or misunderstanding."

"It's none of the above, Russell. Believe me. Something is wrong."

Quilfo cleared his throat. "Okay. Describe your kids. I'll put out the word."

Callendar tried to think past the sizzling terror in his gut and Janice's continued harangue. "Cody has curly brown hair and big blue eyes and braces. She was wearing blue shorts and a short-sleeve ribbed shirt. She's about four-eight, eighty pounds. Madison is a few inches taller, small-boned and slim, with straight dark blond hair and hazel eyes. She had on jeans. Pale blue, I think, and a white blouse."

"Her shirt was yellow," Janice screeched. "And Cody was wearing a short blue skirt. Jesus Christ! You don't even know what they look like. Put me on, damn it. Let me tell him."

She wrenched the receiver from Callendar's hand and began raging into the phone. "This man should be arrested for what he did. He should go to jail for negligence and child endangerment, you hear me?"

Janice went still for a moment, listening with a hard, contentious frown. Then she began a fresh diatribe. "Make a record of this, Lieutenant. If anyone hurts one hair on those babies' heads, your friend is going to pay for it—big time. Now, here's an accurate description. Cody is four feet ten inches tall and Madison is five-one. And— Oh, thank God!"

She dropped the phone and raced to the door. There stood Callendar's daughters, huddled together with tears streaming down their dirt-smudged cheeks.

Callendar picked up the receiver. "They just walked in, Russell."

"They're okay?"

"Upset, but yes, I think so."

"Go find out what happened. If there's anything we should know, call me back."

"Thanks. I will."

Janice fussed over the girls, wailing.

"Hey, you guys. Where were you? We were worried," Callendar said gently.

Madison wept into the crook of her folded arms. Cody spoke on anguished tics. "I'm sorry, Daddy. We shouldn't have gone, but he said he was a friend of Mom's. He said she was holding a table at this ice-cream place a couple of blocks away and that we were supposed to go with him to meet her."

Callendar went cold. "What happened?"

"He kept walking and walking. We said we wanted to know where the place was, and he kept telling us it was just another block, just another block. Come on, don't be so lazy. Your mom is waiting."

Janice's hand flew to her mouth. "Oh my God. Did he hurt you? Did he touch you? What did he do?"

"Calm down, Janice. Let her talk. Tell us what happened, honey," Callendar urged.

Madison found her voice. "He stopped at this playground. He told us to step inside the fence and close our eyes, that he had a surprise for us. I got really scared, and I ran. But he caught Cody before she could get away. I stopped and yelled for him to let go of her, but he wouldn't. I didn't know what to do. I was so scared."

Cody shivered with the memory. "He held me so tight, it hurt. He said he'd let me go after he gave me something. He shoved me inside the playground fence and locked it from the inside. It was dark and empty in there, really, really scary."

"It's all right now, sweetie," Callendar soothed.

"He turned me around so my back was to him, and then he started to whisper in my ear."

Callendar stroked her hair. "What did he say?"

The child shuddered with the memory. "He said I should tell you to back off about Sleeping Beauty, whatever that means. He said you better mind your own business, that this was a warning and next time he couldn't guarantee what might happen. Then he shoved this—this *thing* in my hand."

Callendar could barely breathe. "What thing?" he forced himself to ask.

Cody reached into the pocket of her short blue skirt and retrieved a small beige envelope. With quivering fingers, she handed it to him.

Callendar opened the flap and poured the contents on the table. Eleven white alphabet beads had been strung loosely on a small elastic thread. They spelled *I dam nosy doc* in black block letters.

Cody laughed nervously. "What a dummy. He doesn't even know how to spell damn. It's with an *N*, isn't it, Daddy?"

"Sure, sweetie. In this case, it would be." He did not tell her the rest. The extra *N* had been left off on purpose, because it did not fit. Callendar, who had a knack for such things, recognized that the letter string was an anagram. Arranged differently, the eleven letters spelled his daughters' names.

Janice dropped onto the couch, clutching her abdomen. "This is all your fault, Ted. All you think of is yourself. The hell with your family. The hell with everything but you."

Callendar silenced her with a dangerous look. Then he prodded his daughters to tell him everything they could remember about the scary man who had made them take the walk.

Chapter 34

Dixon called before eight, fizzing with excitement. Burlingame's response to our photo essay had been overwhelmingly enthusiastic. By incredible luck, one of the johns I had caught on film turned out to be Beau Fippinger, a popular deputy police commissioner and an outspoken supporter of the mayor's anti-sex campaign. Catching Fippinger on film soliciting an unholy favor from a low-end whore was, in the humiliation game, a grand slam home run.

"He wants us to come in right away and be available for follow-ups and rewrites, which is amazing. The boss almost never involves lowly reporters in production decisions."

"I'm supposed to work with Monique's class this morning."

"So you'll go tomorrow. You can't turn this down, Anna. Call her. She'll understand."

"Okay. I will. I can be ready in fifteen minutes."

"Great. I'll meet you at the train."

"Oh, and Dixon, two things. First, the last page of the report on me was missing. Any idea what happened to it?"

"You mean the new theory about who committed the crime?"

"Exactly. The page was gone. What did it say?"

"No idea. That page was missing when I saw the report, too. I meant to ask about it, but it slipped my mind."

"Can you check with research for me?"

"Sure, I'll call as soon as we hang up. What else?"

"I had a weird experience with your friend Spook. He came to my apartment late yesterday afternoon and let himself in. When I asked him to leave, he got testy. He said I had a stick up my butt, that I was an ice queen. He claimed he was quoting you."

"Me? Not hardly. My guess is he didn't know what to say, so he tossed out the first stupid junk that came to mind. Sorry that happened. Spook's a true marvel with his hands, but social graces are definitely not his strong suit."

"That's the understatement of the year."

"I'm sure the guy's harmless. But I'll talk to him and see it doesn't happen again."

"Thanks. I'd appreciate it."

As soon as I clicked off, my cell phone sounded again. This time it was my uncle Eli.

"Hi, sweetheart. I hope I didn't wake you."

"You didn't. Actually, I'm headed out in a couple of minutes. Big, exciting doings at work. How about you? Have you made any progress with the embargo mess?"

"Getting there," he said wearily. "I'll straighten things out sooner or later, honey. Whatever it takes."

"Sure, Uncle E. You always do. Listen, I hate to be short, but I really have to run."

"Of course. Go. I'll speak to you soon."

I showered quickly and then threw on my navy interview suit and pumps. Too jittery for the harrowing descent down the fire escape, I summoned the lift.

On the main floor, Moshe Price stood waiting. "You're feeling better, I hope? No more trouble with that *putz*?"

"Everything's fine. Wonderful, in fact."

His eyes narrowed, assessing my clothes. "What? You're going to a party?"

"No. I have a meeting with my boss."

He nodded with fervor. "The boss takes an interest in you, this is good. You look fine. Very professional."

"Thank you, Mr. Price. That means a lot, especially coming from a successful businessman like you."

A pink flush spread out from his beard. "A young person appreciates good advice, this is rare thing. Smart."

"I do appreciate it. Oh, and I wanted to let you know that a couple of men will be working in the apartment this morning, putting in new locks and stronger doors. So if you hear anything, it'll be them."

"Good. You'll tell them to send the bill to me."

"That's not necessary."

His look went fierce like a killer teddy bear. "Nobody tells me how to run my building. The bill comes to me, and that's that."

"Thanks, then. That's very sweet."

"Sweet has nothing to do with it. It's business. My building, my bill. That's all."

"I understand. Good talking to you, Mr. Price. I'd better go."

"Likewise," he called after me as I hurried out. "Go slow. You don't want to fall and hurt yourself in those shoes."

I spotted Dixon pacing nervously at the Marcy Avenue station. The train pulled in as I hurried up the stairs, wobbling awkwardly in my heels. He blocked the door, and I squeezed through as it strained to close.

Rush-hour riders jammed the car. Dixon and I were forced together, clutching the same upright rail. I enjoyed the press of his arm against mine, the random bump of his lean, muscled thigh as the train jolted across the bridge.

His hair was still damp from the shower and he smelled of shampoo and lime-scented shaving foam.

When the doors sighed open at our stop, he played offense, clearing a path with his lanky arms. We threaded our way through the streaming masses, climbed the stairs and emerged around the corner from the Flashlight Building.

Burlingame's office had left our names at security, and we were passed through quickly to the executive elevator at the rear of the building. Arthur Selkowitz had been cued. He met us at the elevators and ushered us across the broad reception area to the boss's suite.

Two men and two women flanked Burlingame at the conference table. I recognized Paul Jurovaty, *Chronicle* president, and Rob Cameron, who headed the media group's editorial department. The women were unfamiliar.

Burlingame chewed his unlit stogie. "Look who's here: Dennis the Menace and Little Orphan Annie. Come in, kiddies. Take a load off."

We sat, exchanging glances with the gathered suits.

Burlingame tipped his bulldog face toward the attractive, snow-haired woman at his right. "Meet Meryl Lubin, chief in-house counsel. Amazing lady. And she's a lawyer through and through, if you know what I mean. She can say no in twenty-seven languages for more reasons than you can imagine. She's our resident party pooper, always on hand to make absolutely sure no one has any fun."

"That's what you pay me for, Mr. Burlingame," she said affably.

"Yeah? Well, don't let this go to your head, but you're a bargain compared to Susie Q here." He made a flourish with his hand. "Meet Susie Q. Shnogg, boys and girls, our chief outside legal counsel. The Q is for queen of retainers. Quickest billable hour in the East. Most lawyers know how to charge, but I think Susie taught those characters in the Light Brigade. You bill by the word, Suze, isn't that so? Or is it so much per syllable? I'd bet you really like working with people who stutter."

Ms. Shnogg pursed her lips. "I charge for listening also, Stewart."

"That's what I like about you, dragon lady. You don't miss a trick. And neither do our little geniuses here. Tell them what you came up with, smart-ass. I have to say this is the kind of moment that makes me proud as punch to be in this grand scum-sucking business, working with fine, upcoming young scum-suckers like you."

Dixon grinned broadly. "Aw shucks, boss. You're going to make me blush. Anyway, Anna deserves most of the credit. We were talking about the thriving sex trade in certain Williamsburg neighborhoods, and that led naturally to Mayor Conley's phony claims that he's cracked down on the kind of activity and cleaned it up. A photo essay struck us as the way to make the point with highest impact."

Selkowitz perched near the door. On cue, he approached the table and passed out early mock-ups of the piece. The story would command a front-page full-color Metro section lead plus a two-page midsection spread. Dixon and I traded surreptitious grins.

"What I'm looking for is a quick, ballpark read on our downside," Burlingame told the lawyers. "When this thing hits, all hell is bound to break loose. Not only do we make the mayor look like the lying son of a bitch he is, but we've caught his main man on the police force with his pants literally down." He pointed to the john in the lead picture. "That naughty boy is Beau Fippinger." He paused for effect. "*Deputy Commissioner* Beau Fippinger, in case you haven't been following his hellfire-and-brimstone op-ed pieces in the *Times*." Burlingame beamed when that revelation drew the predictable gasps.

Ms. Lubin set the mock-up down. "If you want my gut reaction, this is a very high-risk move. What's to stop them from claiming that Fippinger was working undercover, conducting a sting?"

"Deputy commissioners don't work undercover or under covers, for that matter. An even if they did, law enforcement officers do not consummate their stings."

"I'm with Meryl on this," said Ms. Shnogg. "Taking on City Hall is one thing. You're asking for major trouble when you smear a popular cop, especially for indulging in a little private recreation between consenting adults."

Burlingame sneered at Fippinger's picture. "Turns out it wasn't as private as he thought. Look, I hear you. Plenty of New York's finest and other uniformed hacks will be pissed at us when this breaks. I know the drill. Some of our delivery trucks will get ticketed or towed; Sanitation will accidentally on purpose trash some annoying percentage of our papers. A few Burlingame employees will get hassled, maybe arrested for trumped-up offenses. So we'll deal with it. No big thing; not considering the jump in circulation I'd bet this brings."

Lubin's face darkened. "Minor mischief and harassment may not be the end of it, Stewart."

"True. I fully expect Conley to hit back, fast and hard, with everything he can lay his hands on. I want to be ready for that, and wherever possible, to nail him with a preemptive strike. But I'm not running away, Meryl. This is way too much fun."

"I could try to get Hizzoner or one of his mouthpieces to make a statement supporting Fippinger before the piece runs," Dixon said eagerly. "I could call the deputy commissioner as well, draw him out about the wages of sin. He's always quick with a handy sound bite. I shouldn't have any trouble getting him to dig himself into an even bigger hole before the story breaks."

"I love it!" Burlingame howled. "Listen to this kid. Is he a baby genius, or what?"

The attorneys pored over the pasteup, vetting every word. "I don't see any particular red flags in the text," Attorney Shnogg said.

"Me neither, aside from the obvious ones we've already discussed," said the in-house counsel. She fixed her piercing sights on me. "I presume these photographs are strictly on the level, Ms. Jameson?"

"Of course they are."

"That's good. Because one thing this organization cannot afford is another Telsey situation."

The lawyer allowed a moment of silence to let that sink in. Serena Telsey's apple-pie reputation and her spanking new Miss Universe crown had been tarnished severely by a *Chronicle* photo and accompanying piece that claimed she had been arrested several years earlier for child molestation while working for an affluent Park Avenue family as an au pair. The picture, which showed the beauty queen in handcuffs, turned out to be a fake. The jury awarded her one million dollars in compensatory damages and slapped the *Chronicle* with a twenty-five-million-dollar punitive fine. The case had been overturned on appeal on a procedural technicality, but no one wanted to go through a harrowing mess like that again.

Burlingame smacked the table. "That's it, then, ladies and gentlemen. We're good to go." He dipped his chin at Dixon and me. "Stick around, kiddies. We're going to let her rip in the Early Metro, but I want you available in case we decide to run follow-ups later on. I've arranged for you to have a vacant office for the duration."

"An actual office? With four actual walls and a door?" Dixon said. Burlingame was known for planting almost everyone in a cubicle surrounded on three sides with four-feet partitions for easy administrative oversight.

"Four walls, a door, a plant and a window. Now get the hell out of here, smart-ass, before I change my mind."

"Yes, boss. Thank you, boss. My mom will be so proud." Dixon saluted.

He turned to me. "Consider yourself out of the doghouse, kid, at least for now. Go see Walter in the executive dining room. Tell him Uncle Stewie said he should load you up with milk and cookies. I suspect you're going to need your strength once the fireworks begin."

Chapter 35

The Arcanum committee reviewing the Sleeping Beauty murder case convened in the Calibre Club solarium at 6:30 A.M. Hazy sunshine spilled through the glass. Towering ferns fluttered in currents stirred by the ceiling fan. A solitary waiter passed in stately silence, pouring tea and coffee from ornate silver pots.

Frame was late as usual, and Callendar elected not to wait. Last night's scare with his daughters still weakened his knees and shot iced acid through his veins. He had lain awake all night, reading evil omens in the shadows, wallowing in guilt and unfettered fear.

Clearly, Julie Jameson's killer or someone with inside knowledge of the crime had nabbed his kids. Callendar accepted full responsibility for allowing them to fall in harm's way. The fact that they had sustained no major injuries except to their confidence and trust did little to alleviate his agony. His girls had been in a depraved criminal's hands, utterly vulnerable.

Nor was he convinced that the worst of the crisis had passed. Russell Quilfo had arranged for a twenty-four-hour detail to keep a protective watch on Janice's apartment and on the kids when they ventured out, but Callendar knew from long, ugly experience that nothing was ever one hundred percent sure.

His throat was painfully dry, but he did not trust his unsteady hand with the brimming water goblet in front of him. From across the table, Quilfo caught his eye and passed an encouraging nod.

Callendar's voice broke as he took the floor. "My daughters were lured away from my apartment last night and taken to a deserted park. Their abductor instructed them to transmit a message to me. I was to mind my own business and stop looking into the Sleeping Beauty Murder. He said that this time was a warning. If I did not back off, he would do my kids serious harm. Then he sent them home with this." He poured the string of beads from the envelope onto the table.

"Rearranged, the letters spell Cody and Madison, my daughters' names."

A brooding gloom descended. Clu was first to break the silence. "Maybe it's time for us to step aside and pass this to the authorities. What do you think, Russell?"

Quilfo pressed hard at the bridge of his nose. "I've been giving it a lot of thought since I heard from Ted last night. In fact, I've thought of little else. Unfortunately, my conclusion is decidedly mixed. On the one hand, it's dead wrong for anyone in or connected to the society to be placed in jeopardy over a case we choose to review. Laying lives and safety on the line is well beyond our charter. But in this case, we face a particular conundrum."

He turned to Callendar. "I ran the situation past several of my colleagues, Ted. Frankly, they're dubious that we can churn up any official heat about the Julie Jameson case, especially on the basis of some anonymous character making threats. I called in markers to arrange for your girls to have protection until we clear this thing up, and they will have that, but launching an expensive investigation will take a lot more than my say-so."

Clu was incredulous. "That makes no sense, Russell. If the man who threatened Ted's children wasn't involved, how would he know that the Arcanum was looking into the case?"

Quilfo tapped the table nervously with his pencil eraser. "I can't answer that for a certainty, but as we all know, despite our strict confidentiality policy, a member might happen to talk about what we're doing out of school."

Frame sauntered in as if on cue. "Morning, all. Sorry to keep you waiting, but I had a call from the White House, and you can't believe what a chore it is to get our fearless leader off the phone. That man certainly loves to hear himself talk. He goes on and on, ad nauseam, about absolutely nothing at all. It's amazing really. You'd think he'd have better things to do than bother those of us who are actually occupied with matters of importance. Why I—"

Griffey preempted the rest of the blowhard's self-congratulatory rant. "We've already called the meeting to order, Melton. Something has come up which makes it doubly urgent for us to proceed quickly. I'll be glad to fill you in on what you've missed as soon as we finish up."

"No, you will fill me in right now, Solomon. I can't make a reasonable contribution unless I have all the information before this committee. In any event, I do not appreciate being kept in the dark."

"Then you should have arrived on time," Griffey said.

"I told you, I was talking with the president."

"So you did."

"You may have heard of him, Griffey. Leader of the free world. That president."

"Yes, and I am precisely as impressed as the circumstance dictates."

"Well. If that's your attitude, I may as well excuse myself."

"We'll certainly respect your decision, Melton," Griffey said.

Frame stood, stroking his droopy mustache. "You are all witnesses. That man deserves to be officially sanctioned. Perhaps asked to resign for unbecoming conduct. Now I am leaving this meeting, and I shall not return until I get a proper apology."

He waited expectantly for the show of support and indignation that failed to follow. Turning on his heel, he strode in comical slow motion toward the door. When that, too, failed to draw any response, Frame had no choice but to make good on his threat.

As soon as the door shut behind him, Clu picked up the dropped thread. "All right, Russell. I'll concede that someone may have leaked the story about our review of the case. But what about those beads?"

Quilfo frowned. "If one piece of inside information was spilled, who can guarantee that the drip stopped there?"

Grim-faced, he propped on his folded forearms. "There's something more that we have not considered, and that's the simple power of word of mouth. Even if the broken bracelet was kept from the press, there's been ample opportunity for some insider to reveal that detail. Countless people in the department knew about the missing beads. So did the Jameson family and close friends. It's more than likely that some insider mentioned it to some outsider in all these years."

"None of this resolves the immediate issue, Russell," Griffey said. "We must assume that the man who accosted Ted's daughters poses a serious threat. Doing otherwise would be highly imprudent. Now, what shall we do about it?"

Callendar filled his chest. "Whatever you decide, I can't ignore the threat to my kids. I need to bow out of this matter. I hope you understand."

Griffey set a hand on his shoulder. "Of course we do, Ted. Your first consideration must be your children."

"Yes."

"You must be aware, though, that it may not make a bit of difference whether you bow out or we all do. If someone sees you or us as a continued threat, he may act in some retaliatory way nonetheless."

"I understand that, which is one of reasons I've decided to excuse myself. I have confidence that Russell's people will do a good job, but I'll feel better if I'm around to keep an eye on the girls also."

"Do it then, Ted. There'll be lots of other cases. The Arcanum will be glad to have you work on those," Trupin assured.

"I hope so, Lyman. Thanks." Callendar rose and left the room.

After he was out the door, Quilfo spoke again. "What about the rest of you? Are you in on this or not?"

"In," Clu said quickly.

"Don't get me wrong, Dr. Baldwin. Just because there may have been an information leak does not mean that the threat isn't real. If someone out there is intent on intimidating us into dropping the case, what happened to Ted's kids may well be a gentle preview."

"I'm in anyway, Russell," Clu said. "If I had family to worry about, perhaps I'd feel differently, but quite frankly, I have no intention of being pushed around by some bully who preys on little girls."

"My sentiments exactly," Griffey said.

"Mine, too," Lyman Trupin said.

"What about your wife, Lyman?" Quilfo asked. "If what happened with Ted is any indication, our subject is not above assaulting innocent bystanders."

"Marjorie would not want me to retreat from a situation like this. Quite the contrary. Plus, she hasn't exactly been spared from risk over the years, given my line of work."

Quilfo nodded. "Obviously, my wife and kids have lived with the threat of nasty fallout, as well. This is business as usual."

Griffey set his jaw. "We're in agreement, then. Now, how shall we proceed?"

"I've been thinking about that as well," Quilfo said. "I believe we need to consider deliberately worsening the leak."

"Go to the press, you mean?"

"Yes. Without directly violating society policy, we can use department contacts to plant a few well-placed hints. We can highlight one member's name to draw this man out, offer him a focus. I can have my people ready to jump in the minute he makes a move. "

"If one of us is to act as bait, I would like to volunteer," Griffey said.

"I'm a better choice," Clu said. "This character sounds like the type to take full advantage of a poor old widow lady."

"That hardly describes you, Dr. Baldwin," Quilfo said.

"It will to him. Go on, Russell. Sign me up. We have a detailed description of the man we're after from Ted's kids. It doesn't sound as if this guy is capable of slipping under doors or through keyholes."

Clu read from a handwritten note. "These are the older girl's words: 'He was about Daddy's age, I think, but he was at least a head taller and really big.' "

"Ted had them look at several pictures from the files the FBI collected for us," Clu explained. "They couldn't make an absolutely positive ID, but both girls reacted strongly to John Doe."

"I'm not pleased to hear that," Griffey said. "There are certain creatures one prefers not to encounter under any circumstances."

"I understand what we may be up against, Griffey." Clu peered over her granny glasses at Quilfo. "I'm counting on you to put good officers on this, Russell, not the deaf or nearsighted ones."

Quilfo's face drew in a mock frown. "That doesn't leave all that many options."

"I'm sure you'll work something out, Lieutenant." Clu got to her feet. "Let's get to it, gentlemen. This thing has gone on far too long."

Chapter 36

The Early Metro had gone to bed, but the edition carrying our explosive story would not hit the streets for at least an hour. Dixon and I sat in the office, fidgeting with nervous anticipation. We kept starting disjointed conversations that flitted out of our jittery brains. Both of us jumped when his cell phone sounded.

Listening, Dixon went grave. "I see. Can't you contact him? Ouch. That's terrible."

I gestured frantically for a sign, but he waved me off. My heart started stammering. Something must have gone wrong with the story.

"What, Dixon?" I whispered insistently.

He cupped his ear to block me out. "How long do they think? Jee-zus. Sure. I understand. You'll let me know. Thanks." Flipping the phone shut, he blew a long, slow breath.

"What is it? What's wrong?" I demanded.

"That was a friend of mine from research who agreed to check on the missing last page from your report. Turns out the guy who wrote it left Burlingame a month ago to set up a bed-and-breakfast in Vermont. When my friend tried to reach him at the forwarding number he left with personnel, she got his wife. Seems he was out walking the dog, and a pickup truck swerved, knocked the guy down and took off. A couple of kids saw the hit, but they couldn't get the license number and the cops haven't been able to track down the truck. Poor guy's been in a coma ever since. Prognosis isn't good."

"That's horrible."

"It is. But then, I suppose when your number's up—"

I thought of my sister, whose number had been up at the tender age of five. Touching the case, even now, seemed to carry some sort of lethal jinx. Churning inside, I moved toward the door. "If you don't mind, I think I'll take a walk."

"Sure. Go ahead. I'll hold down the fort."

I followed the WALK and DON'T WALK signs, angling vaguely northeast, and soon found myself outside Maitland's Gun Shop, to which my uncle Eli had arranged to ship my pistol.

I wandered in and strode around. My run-ins with Spook and the jerk in the football jersey had put me in a beleaguered state of mind. Dixon's story of the hit-and-run victim had shaken me further. Still, as I looked at the cases full of weapons, I remained convinced that having a gun around was a ludicrous hedge against violence or uncertainty.

As I turned to leave, the gray-haired clerk came out from behind the desk with a neatly wrapped package. "I was wondering when you'd be coming in, Ms. Jameson. Everything's all set. Here you go."

"How did you know who I was?"

"From your picture. Mr. Jameson sent one for the license. Now you enjoy that little beauty. But treat her with respect. She's far more powerful than she looks."

"I know that. To be honest, I'd rather not have it around."

He smiled knowingly. "Exactly what Mr. Jameson predicted you'd say. My orders are to introduce you and get you two off on the right foot. I can arrange for lessons if you like. There's a range downtown I particularly like."

"I'll think about it. Meanwhile, why don't I leave the gun here?"

"Nope. She's yours, and you need to take her home. You'll get used to her, Ms. Jameson. Wait and see. Before you know it, you'll come to think of her as a friend."

I preferred my friends softer and far less lethal. Thinking of which, I stuffed the package deep in my purse and wandered to the stately Park Avenue apartment house where Shelby kept her office. I pressed her buzzer at exactly ten minutes to the hour, the moment when therapy sessions normally drew to a close. Freud would have considered this the overt manifestation of my repressed unconscious need. I preferred to chalk it up to dumb luck, a handy concept that did not require ten years of deep, expensive analysis.

Shelby was slow to buzz me in, and my heart sank as I realized how badly I ached to see her and clear things up between us. Desolate, I turned away, but as I moved to cross the broad, flower-lined street, I heard my name.

Shelby leaned on the sill and called out, "Hey, Anna. Come back. Come in."

Dark paneling and muted lights gave her office a hushed, soothing feel. Bookshelves crammed with psychiatric texts and nineteenth-century novels backed a Regency writing desk. A cordovan leather chaise capped by a cozy afghan and stuffed animals spanned the center of the room.

She wrapped me in a hug "What a nice surprise. I'm so glad to see you."

"You too. Sorry about the other night. I guess I'm a little hypersensitive about the loft."

"No. You're a *lot* hypersensitive about it. I wasn't criticizing your place at all; it's bright and quirky and charming and wonderful, just like you. I was just concerned about your safety."

"Then you'll be glad to hear that I'm having better doors installed, and new locks."

"Good. But I'd feel even better if you installed a twenty-four-hour guard or two, and a couple of pit-bulls."

"Not necessary. You know me. I can be pretty nasty if need be. Almost pit-bull quality."

"I can't argue with that."

I hugged her again, enjoying her bony solidarity and the curly tickle of her hair. "Contrary to what you think, I'm pretty fond of myself most of the time. I'm not being self-destructive. I took that place because it was the best I could afford."

Her look was dubious. "I hear you."

"Yes, but that doesn't mean you believe me. I've known you long enough to speak the language. In Shelby-speak, *I hear you* means I'm not going to argue with such nonsense. I got that from you and I use it all the time."

Her mouth tugged in a tiny grin. "I hear you."

"Thanks for putting in a good word about the apartment to my mother, Shel. You calmed her down beautifully. I owe you more than one for that."

"Good. Next time my mother gets on my case, I'll refer her to you."

"Handling each other's mothers. That's my idea of a perfect friendship."

She went serious. "Listen, Anna. In the interest of full disclosure, not all of my reaction to your loft was pure and selfless."

"I don't understand."

"The truth is I'm a little envious, my friend. Maybe more than a little. The whole world is available to you, choices I couldn't begin to make anymore. Having kids is a wonderful thing, and I wouldn't trade them for anything. But on some level, I wish I could be on my own again, living and doing exactly as I please, answerable to no one but myself."

"It doesn't exactly work that way, Shel. I may not have three kids and a Park Avenue practice, but I'm not exactly a free agent."

She eyed me curiously. "Says who?"

"I can't rattle off a list from the top of my head. But there are plenty of major constraints on me."

Her look was dubious. "I hear you." The buzzer sounded. "Damn. That's my next appointment, a multiple personality. I've counted six so far, each one more obnoxious than the last."

"Do you offer a group discount?"

I slipped out through her small reception area, past Shelby's multiply obnoxious patient.

Back at the Flashlight Building, I found Dixon at the desk, jotting notes, barking orders and juggling several of the calls at once. The five available lines kept flashing red, bleating with harsh insistence.

He winked at me as he picked up yet another line. "That's perfect. Have someone take the statement and relay it to Cameron. He's planning a special letter-to-the-editor page completely devoted to this."

Another line flared.

"Excellent. Pass that along to the executive suite, will you? Burlingame is going to love it."

With every call, Dixon's ebullience grew. During a momentary break in the action, he burst from his chair and danced me around the room in a manic waltz.

"Whoa, easy, boy. So happens I use those feet on a daily basis."

"You won't believe what's going on, Anna. It's incredible. Huge names are lining up to rag on Conley. Some of his staunchest, longtime supporters have jumped ship. A citizens' group is calling for his resignation. The guy comes across looking like a lying hypocrite, and that's the biggest sin a public figure can commit. No one really minds if you're a crooked slimeball, as long as you're up front about it."

"What's next?"

"Burlingame's still cooking that up with the powers that be. I have some relay instructions in the meantime. Otherwise, he wants us to sit tight."

"What's your best guess?"

His shoulders hiked. "With the way this thing is snowballing, the sky's the limit. We've already had feelers from producers on two out of the three network news broadcasts, plus a couple of the key talk shows. Lord, how I love fireworks. And it's not even the Fourth of July."

Dixon dove for another call. I sat facing the desk and tried to absorb the dislocating chain of events. This story was growing like the blob, beyond control and reason.

His fingers splayed in a victory sign. "That was Sary Maitland, the gossip columnist for the *Inquirer*. She wants to know if the *Chronicle* has any comment on a report from an anonymous source that Deputy Commissioner Fippinger was fired from his last job for conduct unbecoming with two of his assistants' wives."

"Sounds like a very friendly guy."

"Indeed." The phone rang again. "Scandal Central," Dixon answered jauntily. "You name him, we'll defame him." As he listened, his grin fell away. "That's nonsense, Mr. Burlingame. It has to be a desperation play. Or some kind of mistake."

He held the receiver away from his ear, and I caught the roar of Burlingame's raging fury. "There's no goddamned mistake. And I don't want to hear your opinions on this or anything. Just send your goddamned playmate up here. And tell her to make it quick."

The color had leached from Dixon's face. "Come on. Boss wants to see us."

"He said me."

"Then he's having a pronoun problem. This is our piece. If there's a problem, we're in it together."

I followed him out, scurrying to keep pace with his long, hurried stride. "What happened, Dixon? What did he say?"

"I'll tell you on the way. We'd better hustle. Keeping him waiting is a very bad idea, especially when he's in a mood like this."

We took the elevator to the lobby and transferred for the express to the executive suite.

"Fill me in, Dixon. What's wrong?"

"Apparently, there's a problem with the story. Fippinger's filed suit. That's all I know, but I'm sure we're about to hear all the gory details."

A cold front had blown in with striking speed. Passing assistants looked away, as if the mere sight of us might pose some serious risk. Burlingame's receptionist set her jaw as she waved us through.

Burlingame huddled with the lawyers at the conference table. Spotting Dixon, his grim look darkened even further. "What are you doing here, smart-ass?"

Dixon took a seat. "If there's a problem, it involves both of us, Mr. B."

"Here's how it works, boy wonder. When I want to see you, I'll say so. *Capisce?*"

"Yes, but we worked together on this, Mr. B. It's our joint responsibility."

"Would you look at this? Chivalry isn't dead after all; it's just stupid and suicidal. Now get the hell out of here and wait downstairs."

"It's okay, Dixon. Go," I told him. "Please."

After he left, Attorney Lubin passed me a set of papers. "Have a look at this, Ms. Jameson."

The document was a libel action, which had been filed with record speed. Burlingame Media was named, as were the *Chronicle* and myself. The documents also contained a motion for injunctive relief, ordering the paper to cease publication of its "malicious, damaging, and unsupportable" allegations at once and print a retraction.

Attorney Shnogg sat back and folded her arms. "Care to comment?"

"Only that it's ridiculous. You saw the picture. How can he claim our piece was unsupportable?"

"Fippinger swears that the picture was a fake, that he was nowhere near your neighborhood last night."

"Then he's lying."

Shnogg passed me the morning edition society page. "On the embarrassment scale, this one is over the top, Ms. Jameson. This happens to be a shot one of our staff photographers took at a PBA fund-raiser last night at the Waldorf. You may recognize the smiling gentleman at the center of that jovial group as none other than Deputy Commissioner Fippinger."

I stared at the picture. "This must have been taken earlier."

"Maybe so. But we have impeccable independent confirmation that the fund-raiser didn't break up until nearly one A.M., and that Fippinger was there until the bitter end. Afterward, he met with a leadership coalition in an upstairs suite until the wee hours. Apparently, the commissioner will attest to that as will several religious leaders and a couple of highly respected judges."

My head was spinning. "All I can tell you is I did not fake that picture or any picture. I would never do such a thing."

"Save the lies for the courtroom, where they belong, kid," Burlingame snarled.

"It's not a lie, Mr. Burlingame. I simply shot what I saw. I never even heard of the deputy commissioner until your staff identified him. Anyway, what would I possibly hope to gain by pulling a stunt like that? It's insane."

"Is that the way it is? You're planning to plead insanity? How about a Twinkie defense? Or raging hormones? Go ahead. Let me hear. Lord knows I can use a good laugh."

"I'm not pleading anything. This is a mistake, plain and simple. I did nothing wrong."

"You're going to fry for this, kid. Extra crispy," Burlingame rasped. He turned to the lawyer. "Cut to the chase, mouthpiece. What's our downside?"

"Hard to say. But I think you can minimize the bleed if you comply with the request for injunctive relief and issue a prompt retraction."

"I'm allergic to retractions. You know that. Every damned one we print damages our credibility. Let's hold off awhile and see how this plays out. I'd rather see us bleed a couple of bucks at the other end than come in with our tails drooping now."

"I'm afraid it could be more like a major hemorrhage. You haven't been shy about your feelings toward the mayor and his friends, Stewart. If you don't back off in some official way, it'll be hard to avoid the appearance of malicious intent."

Lubin nodded. "I agree. A retraction would be embarrassing, but far from fatal. Our competitors have had to deal with much worse. Think of that plagiarism scandal at the *Press* last spring, which involved a rather juicy conspiracy. All we have to do is retreat from one employee's unscrupulous behavior." Her stern gaze lit on me.

"Let's make sure that's what this is before we dive headfirst into another shallow pool," Shnogg advised.

"The only one going in headfirst is Little Bo Peep here."

Shnogg shot him a warning look. "We intend to find out precisely what happened, Ms. Jameson. We have been checking it out through every conceivable avenue since the moment this came to our attention. You're free to go now, but please make sure you're available by phone. You'll hear from us as soon as we have further information."

"Don't even think of trying to run out on this, kid. If you do, I'll track you down and see that you pay full price plus bigger interest than you can imagine," Burlingame warned.

"I have no intention of going anywhere, Mr. Burlingame. I did nothing wrong."

"Nevertheless, I'd advise you to consult an attorney, Ms. Jameson," Lubin suggested. "This is a very serious matter."

Burlingame swatted the air in disgust. "Get out of my sight. You're putting a new hole in my ulcer."

I rode to the main floor, then up again to see Dixon. He was on the phone, still fielding calls. Spotting me, he wound up quickly. "What's the story?"

"The deputy commissioner is suing, claiming the picture was a fake. He was at a fund-raiser at the time. Everyone but the Pope is willing to attest to it."

"Jesus, Anna. You faked that picture?"

"Of course I didn't. How could you even think such a thing?"

He eyed me strangely. "I don't know what to think."

"Thanks for the show of support, pal. It's just what I needed."

"Look. My head is on the block here, too. If the piece goes down, I go with it."

"I'm the one being accused, not you. I'm the one named in the lawsuit."

"Don't worry. They'll get to me, sooner or later," he said miserably.

"Maybe you deserve it, Dixon. Doing the piece was your idea and you brought in the shoot. You were the one who had control of those pictures. Maybe you faked Fippinger's shot, hoping to make a bigger splash."

"You know me better than that. I would never do such a thing."

"No, and neither would I."

His clear eyes fixed on mine. "You're right. I'm sorry. Of course I believe you."

"Good. I believe you, too."

"Fine, that's settled. Now how do we convince the rest of the world?"

"You know how things work around here. Who, besides you and me, had access to those rolls? Who had the means and know-how to pull off a thing like this?"

"I could name dozens of people. But why would anyone want to fake that picture? I don't get it."

"I don't, either, but we have to assume that's what happened. Now, we're both supposed to be investigative journalists. Let's pretend this is someone else's mystery and figure the damned thing out."

Chapter 37

By the time I reached home, my building was deserted. Riding the lift to three, I slipped off my pumps and suit jacket. My pearls and earrings followed. Slipping them in my purse, I spotted the wrapped pistol. Quickly, I pinched the clasp, anxious to have the weapon out of sight so I could pretend it into benign nonexistence. I had neither the time nor the energy to deal with it right then.

The detective had propped an envelope in a cast-off mannequin hand outside my door. Inside, I found new keys and a note. Elisson and his partner had completed all the work except to my new rear door, which needed a replacement for a faulty cylinder. Either he or Harry would come back as soon as they secured the part. I was not to worry about settling up, we could see to that later. Meanwhile, he had heard about my "little problem" with the deputy commissioner's picture and the threatened lawsuit, which had already hit the news. If there was anything he could do, I should call.

The detectives had left things pristine and strikingly secure. In place of my flimsy door locks, fierce metallic protuberances now clamped on their muscular receptacles like mad dog's teeth. The windows bore heavy-duty locks, and four-inch nails fastened the frames to the sills. A dense steel penitentiary-style slab blocked the rooftop entry. No wicked wolf could huff or puff his way in here. At least I could eliminate the fear of a casual intruder from my worry list.

My next pressing need was legal help. My uncle Eli struck me as the best place to turn for a recommendation, but I was bumped to voice mail when I tried his cell phone. Eli's portable line rang all over the world, and normally he answered no matter what the time or circumstance. I presumed he must be in some heated meeting and could not afford to be disturbed.

Hanging up, I rummaged through my other possibilities. As an independent contractor, not on the official company payroll, I did not qualify for union or in-house legal help. Dixon, for all his contacts, did not know of any lawyers with suitable specialties aside from the ones who worked for Burlingame, and they would be busy defending the company from me.

Shelby's contacts tended to be platinum-banded, jewel-studded types, and strictly out of my price range. I shuddered at the mere idea of what a defense against these charges might cost.

Taking up the phone again, I dialed Detective Elisson. His resonant voice broke with static and background noise.

"It's Anna Jameson, Detective. We have a bad connection. Let me call you back."

"No. Don't do that. I'll call you."

When my phone sounded moments later, his muffled words were blunt. "It's hard for me to talk to you from here, Ms. Jameson. You're not exactly Miss Popularity with the boys in blue right now. The deputy commish has lots and lots of friends on the force. Fiercely loyal friends. He was not the right guy to take on, to put it mildly."

"I didn't take him on, Detective. If the shot of him with that prostitute was faked, someone else did it."

"Yes. I know that."

"You do?"

He laughed at my blithering surprise. "Subtlety and subterfuge are not exactly your style, Ms. Jameson. You're more the bull-in-a-china-shop type, if you don't mind my saying."

"In this case I don't mind at all. In fact, I appreciate the vote of confidence."

"You've got that, for what it's worth. And I'm willing to help, as I said, but given the mood around here, we'd better keep that strictly between you and me."

"The one thing I need right now is a lawyer. Can you recommend anyone?"

"There are plenty of suits with briefcases out there, but you want someone really smart, capable of steering you through stormy seas. My guess is Fippinger and his friends are going to hit you with everything imaginable."

"I know. That's why I'm anxious to get good advice as quickly as possible."

"Let me think about it awhile. Ask around. I'll call you soon as I have an answer."

"Thanks. If you don't get me right away, keep trying. My phone's been acting temperamental."

"I'll find you when I have something to report, Ms. Jameson. Don't you worry about that."

Chapter 38

Clu poured two fingers of Glenlivet, dropped in a couple of cubes from the bucket on the sideboard and clinked her tumbler against the glass over Joseph's portrait. Her ever-smiling, perpetually young late husband stared back with his wide blue, unflinching gaze.

Clu wanted to shrink to a miniature, point her toes and dive into those opalescent eyes; she ached to join her beloved in some cotton-candy afterlife of perennial sunsets, lilting music and luminous clouds. But she would settle for anything with him. A blink. A breath.

No one suspected the depth of her loss and loneliness, and as someone who hated mewling in all forms, she was glad of that. Since Joseph and then her parents died, all in the space of one year, Clu had built a high, barbed fence around her feelings, buried them hard and deep.

"So, Joseph my love. What do you think of your little darling now?" Sipping the single malt, Joseph's poison of choice, she recalled his magical ability to make her feel graceful and small. No matter that her rangy frame stretched to six feet and change and clumped around on size eleven feet. No matter that she had large, coarse, poker table features and had always been accepted unquestionably as one of the guys. Around Joseph, rest his soul, she had been a little darling, delicate enough to catch a breeze and fly.

"Look, Joseph. Here I am, right smack in the middle of page six of the *Post*. Would you believe it, me in the midst of all those genuine celebrities? Listen to this. 'Look for big breaking news in a very old, very infamous murder case. A reliable source reports that Dr. Clu Baldwin of Latham Forensics has fresh information that might bring the killer to justice at last. Kudos, Clu. The world is waiting."

Clu turned the column around for the picture to see. " 'The world is waiting.' Pretty impressive, don't you think? And look, my love, I got more space than Trump's latest strumpet did, more than Leonardo or Madonna. Wouldn't Sister Bernadette from Perpetual Sorrows burst with pride? Remember how she loved everything to do with celebrities, my love? Remember how she used to hide the transistor radio earphone under her wimple during catechism to catch the soaps?"

She sipped again and made a sour face. "Hell no, Joseph. I'm not frightened. What's to be frightened of? Certainly not checking out. Everyone has to do that, sooner or later, like it or not. It's nature's way. Sweep the dust aside and make room for the new ones.

"Was it so bad for you? Tell me that. You certainly looked peaceful enough, lying cold as a mackerel beside me. Gray as lead."

Clu leaned closer and dropped her quivering voice. "Can I tell you a dreadful secret, Joey love? I thought you were teasing me at first, playing one of your little jokes. I kept begging you to move, to say something, but you just lay there with that smug little smirk on your face, like you knew something I didn't.

" 'Please, love, stop,' I said. 'You're scaring the bejesus out of me.' Lord, how I pleaded with you. But still, you wouldn't listen, wouldn't move. Finally, I got so mad, I took you by the shoulders and shook you something fierce. I kept shaking, hard as I could, until I heard something snap."

Clu shivered hard, remembering. "I can still hear it—that snap.

"For the longest time I was convinced I must have killed you. I knew it had to be my fault, no matter how the doctors explained to me over and over, as if I was too slow to understand, that you'd been dead for hours. Taken in your sleep by a major heart attack. Myocardial infarction, they said. But I couldn't get it through my skull. To this day, those words put me in mind of an Irish jig, something light and energetic with a beat. 'My O'Cardial infarction. Sure and you're the apple of my eye.'

"Of course, I knew on an intellectual level what had really happened, that the rigor had already set in and that's why I got that awful noise when I tried to rouse you. But smart as I'm supposed to be, I couldn't make myself accept it. There was an argument raging inside my head for years, the cool, quiet, reasonable side against the part that screamed with guilt and pain. The only way to stop that battle in my mind was to get really angry with you, Joseph. The nerve of you to leave me like that. The nerve of you to break all those happily-ever-after, fairy-tale promises. The nerve."

Clu settled on the couch for a good cry, one of those deep, unfettered, healing soaks that she had not enjoyed for years. But she found that she could not enjoy this one, either. She muffled her mouth with a throw pillow to keep the guard outside from overhearing. Bad enough that nice young officer had to spend his night alone in the hallway, watching her door. He didn't need to listen to her blubbering like an overgrown baby.

Clu hauled herself up and dumped the rest of the Scotch down the kitchen drain. She was not made for hard drink. Instead of devilish merriment, liquor turned her to maudlin thoughts and brutal attacks of the woes.

Enough of that, she told herself sharply. She washed her face in the kitchen sink, dried off on a dish towel and pinched a bit of color in her cheeks.

She put the kettle up to boil, and then walked the long, narrow hall to the door. She knocked. Though she felt a little foolish rapping from the inside like a spooked prisoner, she did not want to startle the nice young cop on guard.

"Yes, Dr. Baldwin? Is there something you need?"

Clu opened the door, as she had been instructed, to the limits of the security chain. "I'm making tea, Officer. Would you like some?"

"No thanks, ma'am. That's okay."

"How about a Coke, then? I have diet and regular. Or maybe a ginger ale?"

The cop could have passed for a gangly twelve-year-old with his tawny curls and curious expression. The collar of his uniform shirt stood out from his long, slim neck, and his sleeves were too short, as if he was still growing so fast, his clothes were powerless to keep up. His manner was sweet and poignantly deferential, as if he found himself in the presence of something ancient enough to inspire his youthful awe.

"A regular Coke would be great, if not too much trouble."

"No trouble at all. Would you care for some chips with that?"

"Sure. Thanks."

Clu fixed the snack and ferried it back to the door. She balanced it on a small entry table to unfasten the chain. "There you go."

Officer Nolan, as his ID declared, snapped to his feet and took the tray. "Thanks so much, Dr. Baldwin. But I honestly don't want you to go to any more trouble on my account. Just go about your business and forget I'm here."

"I've become quite talented at forgetting things, Officer Nolan, but in this case, I'll respectfully decline. If you need anything, another snack or something to pass the time or to answer nature's call—"

He glanced at the empty milk carton at his feet. "Thanks. I'm all set."

"I see. You take care, then."

"If you don't mind my saying so, Dr. Baldwin, I've studied your work on voice printing and linguistic analysis. It was a particular interest of mine at the academy. I'm a big fan."

Clu stifled the smile. Wait until Joseph heard about this. Not only was she scoring ink on page six, but she had snagged a cute young groupie, as well.

"That's very kind of you, Officer, not to mention courageous. I'm afraid my writing tends to be a trifle technical and dry."

"Not to me. I must have read your article on semiotics and psychosis a dozen times. Fascinating stuff."

"I'm glad you think so. Many would consider it an insomnia remedy. Let me know when you finish with that snack, and I'll come for the tray."

"Sure, I'll knock softly. If you're busy, just ignore it. I'll make sure nothing happens to your things."

"I'm not worried about them in the least. And thank you, Officer Nolan, for guarding my castle door."

"It's my pleasure, Dr. Baldwin. An honor actually."

Inside, with the door firmly shut, she allowed the smile to bloom. What a lovely turn this dismal evening had taken. That nice young man had plodded through her dense academic ramblings and found them of use. Perhaps others had as well.

How nice.

Clu had begun to review her life and do the final sums. By most measures, her existence did not amount to much. She had no surviving family, no children and precious little legacy aside from her highly specialized body of work.

But perhaps she had touched a student or two, set some thinking in a fresh direction. And perhaps that counted for a bit more than she'd dared to consider.

She winked at Joseph's picture. "The ego deprived of a feast can thrive on a diet of crumbs, my love."

Energized, she sat before the rolltop desk in her study and reviewed the Julie Jameson file yet again. On a legal pad, she listed the known facts and open questions.

A left-handed, explosively aggressive intruder had murdered the Jameson child in her bed. The perpetrator had entered the family's apartment during a ferocious storm and stood dripping rainwater on the carpet while he watched his victim sleep.

There had been no sign of forced entry, and the doorman posted in the lobby had seen no strangers enter or leave the building. A closed-circuit camera monitored the only other entrance to the apartment building, a service door at the rear.

Normally, that rear door was locked after business hours, but early on the morning after Julie Jameson's death, it was seen lolling open by a resident out walking her dog. The handyman, Charles Theron, swore that he had locked the door at five P.M. sharp, as he always did. A building porter named Albin Marks confirmed Theron's story, claiming that he had watched the handyman lock that rear door with a key. Under further questioning, Marks stated that the handyman had tested the lock in his presence and confirmed that it was secure. Because of the raging storm outside, they were doubly careful, both men attested. Of course, they could have concocted the story to cover what turned out to be a deadly omission.

Question, Clu wrote. If the door was locked as Theron and Marks alleged, who might have opened it between five P.M. and the next morning? Who and how?

Question: How had the intruder gained access to the apartment without forcing the front-door lock?

Also: Why would a murderous assailant stand watching his intended victim sleep for ten or fifteen minutes before doing her harm? What was he doing and thinking during that time? Why would he raise his risk of detection by lingering at the scene?

Clu imagined a lurking stranger, the little girl coming awake. Vividly, she conjured the child's desperate cry in the tense trill of a frightened five-year-old.

Who are you? What are you doing here? Mommy, help!

Fact: The parents slept in the adjacent room, with their bed positioned no more than six feet from the child's. Only a slim plasterboard wall separated Julie from her parents. Yet Bertie and Frank Jameson heard nothing of their daughter's final struggle.

Fact: Parents, especially mothers, demonstrate particularly keen sensitivity to the sounds of their children's distress. As early as three or four weeks after birth, studies had shown that new mothers respond with a classic fight or flight response to their infants' cries, especially cries of pain. Blood flow is shunted from the extremities to the core, protecting vital functions while the body mobilizes. The characteristic adrenaline surge yields a quickening of the pulse and heightened sensory acuity. Extraordinarily rapid and effective responses often result.

Fact: Frank Jameson was a seasoned, practicing physician. Years of emergency calls and specialized training would have conditioned him to awaken quickly from even the deepest sleep, especially in response to an apparent crisis.

Did the parents fail to hear Julie? Did they hear her and ignore her? From the signs of desperate struggle, it was highly unlikely that the child had remained silent during the attack.

Clu's thoughts scrolled back to Ted Callendar's caller. In her mind, she heard the voice again: the masked Southern accent, the subtle signs of a respiratory disease. The woman had also suffered from crushing guilt that caused her to refer to the murdered child in a distant, dissociated manner.

And why was that?

Clu's pulse raced as the reason came clear. She connected to the Internet and tested her suspicions by remote. *Bingo.*

Frantically, she leafed through the file until she came to the transcript of the woman's call. Reading it now, all the pieces slid into place with sickening smoothness. Why had none of them come to this before?

Clu went to the living room. Facing Joseph's picture, she blew a kiss and winked. "Imagine it, Joseph, this old girl has figured out whodunit in a thirty-year-old case. Tell Jimmy for me when you see him, will you, darling? Finally, my dear old granddad may be able to rest in peace.

Amen.

She explained aloud how she had come to the identity of the woman caller. Clu detailed where that conclusion had led her and how she had confirmed the startling truth. She imagined she saw the gleam of pride in Joseph's eyes.

Exhilarated, she dialed Griffey's number. The phone rang eight times before she gave up. Either he was out for a constitutional or enjoying an evening snooze.

The machine answered at Ted Callendar's house. He was probably planted outside his daughters' home, keeping vigil like Clu's young guard.

Frantically, she dialed Russell Quilfo and Lyman Trupin, but recorded messages greeted her at both numbers. Melton Frame was out of the question. Clu would sooner take the answer to her grave than give that insufferable ego case a chance to run with it to the press.

She dialed the others again, but there was still no response. Clu forced herself to settle on the couch with a stack of professional publications and wait a full half hour.

Before the time elapsed, she heard a timid knock at her front door. Setting her journal aside, she went to retrieve Nolan's tray.

Giddy with delight, she opened the door. "All done with that, Officer? Can I get you anything else?"

She stopped as if she had hit an unseen wall. Instead of her nice, young admirer, she faced a brutish stranger.

"Who are you? Where's Officer Nolan?"

The intruder did not speak, but his lips warped in a lazy smirk that told her everything.

Desperate questions massed in her mind, pressing for release like a panicky mob. But before she could squeeze out the first of them, the stranger's hand came up and she spied the glint of a blade. Slicing heat crossed her neck, followed by a sharp, sparkling pain. Air rushed at the base of her throat, followed by a sticky burst of warmth.

She knew the impertinent term for that lethal slash from ear to ear, the gaping arc of flesh. Homicide cops and morgue ghouls called it the second smile.

Her breath escaped in a rasping stream. Her strength ebbed, and she drooped with maddening slowness toward the floor. She could see the darkness rising up, wavering nearer, a giant maw, waiting to swallow her whole.

The stranger watched until she crumpled to the checkerboard tile. Then, humming a brisk, happy tune, he wiped his blade and slipped away.

Chapter 39

The address Elisson gave me matched a soaring structure of granite and dark tinted glass. At eight P.M., the lobby was deserted. A pile of sign-in sheets sprawled on the security desk. The first after-hours visitors had filled in all the requisite information: name, person to be visited, time in and out. Later arrivals had scratched illegible, partial information or resorted to dubious jokes. According to one, Mickey Mouse was in the building, meeting with the big cheese upstairs.

Dean Winkler's office was on the eighteenth floor. He answered when I rang the door to the locked suite. The lawyer Elisson had recommended was an affable, handsome man with dense pewter hair and steel-toned eyes softened by a spray of laugh lines. He had doffed his tie and suit jacket and opened the collar of his rumpled white shirt.

I followed him to a generous corner room. He motioned me toward the leather visitor's chair and sat behind the mahogany partner's desk. Artful family pictures graced the inlaid leather top: children sloshing in a puddle, a young woman cradling an infant in her arms. Several beautifully composed enlargements lined the walls. There was a humorous stadium scene where all the seats were empty except for one sleeping man at the extreme left of the last row. Beside that was a group shot of eight highly contented-looking cows.

"Are you the photographer?" I asked.

"I took the pictures. But I'll leave it to professionals like you to claim the title," he said.

"You're very good, Mr. Winkler."

"Blame that on the subjects. My picture-taking abilities are all about patience and happy coincidence."

"So are everyone's. Thanks for agreeing to see me so soon. Detective Elisson said you're the best attorney around to advise me in this matter."

"He only gave me a rough sketch of the situation when he called. Why don't you start at the beginning?"

He listened raptly while I spoke, jotting an occasional note.

"They told me they were doing everything they could to get to the bottom of what happened," I said finally. "Meanwhile, I feel as if I'm sitting around with my head on the block, waiting for the blade to fall."

"How long have you worked for Burlingame?" he asked.

"It's only been a few days; and I'm not officially on the payroll yet. Any assignments I get are paid on a *per diem*."

He frowned in thought. "Who, besides you, had contact with those pictures?"

"I gave the exposed film to a reporter named Dixon Drake, who took them to Burlingame's film lab for me. From there, I honestly can't say what happened to them. The lab is far from secure territory. A zillion people have access. Any one of them could have been responsible for faking that shot."

"Yes, but it would take a degree of technical know-how. Isn't that right?"

"True. But at a place like the media group, plenty have that."

"What do you hope to achieve at Burlingame, Ms. Jameson? Career-wise, I mean?"

"At the moment, survival would be nice. I'd like to avoid losing any essential organs, especially my pride."

His dark eyes sparked with amusement. "What did you hope to achieve before all this hit the fan?"

"Am I right in assuming that anything I say here stays strictly between you and me?"

"Absolutely. Our communications are protected by attorney-client privilege."

"Then the truth is, deep down I hoped for international recognition and respect, giant rewards and maybe just the teeniest bit of immortality."

"Honesty. How refreshing." With a nod, he cut to the chase. "At this point, your only reasonable course of action is inaction."

"Do nothing?"

"There's nothing to do. What you've described amounts to a game of hot potato. Somebody did something to someone and everybody wants to pass it along as quickly as possible so they don't get burned. You're a perfect scapegoat, so you catch the flak."

"I've never been anywhere near perfect at anything, Mr. Winkler. Why this?"

"It's simple arithmetic. You had access plus motive, which adds up to a nice big target on your chest."

"What motive? What could I possibly hope to gain by faking a picture of a powerful public figure who was bound to defend himself with both barrels? The whole thing makes no sense."

"It could be argued that bringing attention to yourself, even negative attention, could further your career. Many people believe the old saw that any publicity is better than no publicity."

"Sure, and I could have been inspired by sunspots or orders from a golden retriever. Both of those are just as logical. Maybe more so."

His smile was kindly. "Relax. I'm on your side."

"It's pretty hard to relax with the police force and my boss busily heating the tar and plucking the feathers."

"Try meditation. Maybe recite a soothing mantra. Here's one that works beautifully for me." His face went slack, and his eyes drifted shut. "I will show those bastards. I will show those bastards. I will . . ."

"I can relate to that."

"Use it then, Ms. Jameson. I suspect it's going to come in handy before this thing is resolved. The fact is, you're a perfect target because of what you do have and what you *don't*."

"Meaning?"

"You're not officially an employee of the media group, so it's easy for Burlingame to distance the company from you and you from it. Also, you're a relative unknown, so any fanfare is likely to die out sooner. Perhaps most important, you don't have a lot of big muscle behind you, or so Burlingame believes. He expects you to roll over or put up your dukes. Either way, you lose."

"I'm afraid you've lost me."

"You come across as looking guilty at worst, and at best, you appear to be on the defensive. They're trying to maneuver you into a classic no-win situation, Ms. Jameson. It's like putting someone on the stand and asking when he stopped beating his wife. Any answer is the wrong answer. Saying nothing is the only way you can hope to win. Then, after you're vindicated, you get to make the bastards swallow their words with the condiments of your choice."

I drew my first deep breath since I left Burlingame's office. "Sounds wonderful. But what if I don't get vindicated?"

He pulled a fresh sheet from his legal pad. "That is part of your homework assignment, Ms. Jameson. I want you to devise comprehensive contingency plans. Go through all the worst-case scenarios and imagine all the positive responses you might have to them. I encourage clients to prepare for the worst and expect the best. That's the best way to feel empowered, plus it tends to get the irony gods off your case."

"Sounds like a tall order."

"Wait, I'm going to make it taller. I want you to do all that right away, tonight would be good, then I want you to kick this whole unpleasant business to the back of your mind. It has to run its course, and no amount of worry on your part is going to change that."

Despite everything, I had to smile. "That's like telling me not to think of elephants. The harder I try, the more those big gray wrinkly animals are going to stampede through my mind."

Standing, he extended a firm, steady hand. "It's mind over matter, an exertion of your will. You'll be amazed to find what you can do when necessity dictates, Ms. Jameson."

"I hope you're right, Mr. Winkler. What do I owe you for today?"

"There's no charge for the consultation. All you owe me is that homework. If this matter winds up in litigation, we can discuss my fee structure."

"Thank you."

"Go home and get to it, Ms. Jameson. I'll be eager to hear how it goes."

Chapter 40

A pack of preteen kids crowded the video games, zapping aliens, shrieking insults and raising a shrill rash of noise. Callendar worked his eyes across the sprawling lobby of the East Bay Multiplex, tracking unseen evils of his own.

Janice had insisted on taking the girls out to celebrate the conclusion of their final exams. Callendar's suggestion that she reconsider—given the circumstances—had brought a predictable response.

The girls and I will not be held prisoner because you like playing Sherlock Holmes with that stupid club of yours, Ted. You created this mess, and you'd better go fix it. Meanwhile, I intend to spend a nice evening out with my daughters. Period.

Callendar had tried to reason with her. All that mattered was their daughters' safety, which could be best assured by keeping them close to home until the danger passed. With Quilfo's man, a solid veteran of the force named Jon Fiorito, posted outside the apartment door and Ted stationed outside the building as a first line of defense, the kids would be protected.

But Janice wasn't buying. She reminded him with the subtlety of an armored tank that his protection had proven sorely inadequate. She accused him of trying to redeem himself with needless heroics.

I know how to take care of them even though you obviously don't, Ted. Plus, we have this stupid cop following us around, whether we like it or not. Now, why don't you take a hike? I don't appreciate your stalking us, too.

The feature in theater seven let out. People spilled through the doors and headed for the exits and the rest rooms. By conservative count, Callendar had observed ten similar exoduses in the last two and a half hours. Naturally, Janice had selected the longest-running film in the fifteen-auditorium complex, which stretched to nearly four hours, including previews of coming events. Naturally, unknown to him, she had called ahead and reserved seats for the popular show, banking on it being sold out before Callendar could buy a ticket. So he was consigned to the lobby and the alien-zapping hooligans and the interminable wait.

This marked the perfect end to a perfectly awful evening, which had followed a strikingly horrible day. First, he had waited outside the girls' small Upper East Side school while they took their exams. The civilian security guard, a burly dimwit, kept questioning his presence as if Callendar were a loitering pederast instead of a concerned father. Every half hour or so, the jerk went off like Old Faithful, spouting hot air until Callendar reasoned him into another brief period of calm.

Still, seeing his girls again, bubbling with eager relief after their tests, had made that all worthwhile. So was hanging around outside their apartment house all afternoon, dodging kamikaze nannies wielding baby prams, yapping dogs and Janice's elderly neighbor, Mrs. Feder, who took the opportunity on spotting Ted to tell him exactly what she thought of him for leaving Janice utterly destitute and seriously ill.

Callendar had listened politely, clenching his teeth. Janice could lie all she liked and gullible, well-meaning people like Mrs. Feder were welcome to swallow her garbage whole. God bless America.

Afterward, he had gnawed on a stale street vendor pretzel and a tepid Sprite, while his ex-wife and daughters dined in opulent elegance at his ex-favorite Italian restaurant. Janice had co-opted Da Maria as she had everything she could lay her malignant hands on after the split. She had told Mama Maria that Ted had fathered not one but two love children between Cody and Madison.

Fiorito, the cop assigned to protect them, had taken a place at the bar and sucked down pasta and veal parmigiana, courtesy of the taxpayers, but Janice threatened to raise a scene if Ted so much as thought of doing likewise. Not that he was anxious to risk having Mama Maria poison his chicken piccata. That woman could be almost as fierce as his ex.

Next, he had trailed Janice, the girls and Fiorito to the movies, where he discovered that the show they were going to see was sold out.

The video gamesters went wild as one player registered a record high score. Callendar's eye darted to the screen, where exploded monsters, spewing green guts and Windex-blue blood, littered an eye-popping galactic battleground.

By Callendar's watch, the feature had more than an hour left to run. He hoped the girls were enjoying it thoroughly and that Janice hated every minute. That would provide some small compensation for his endless wait.

Another feature ended and a crowd of viewers spewed from auditorium ten. From the snuffling and streaming tears, Callendar could tell this one had offered a classic Hollywood ending.

"What a terrific film," one woman wept miserably.

"Best I've seen in years," sobbed her companion.

The video kids gave up and left. Callendar perched against the deserted snack stand and watched the empty escalators twirl. Aside from a solitary clerk behind the ticket counter, he was alone.

He watched the clock, which appeared to move in perverse slow motion. Callendar was not, by nature, a patient man. An entire day of crushing inactivity left him jangling with nervous unease.

He pulled out his cell phone to play a quick game of "snake" and found the message symbol flashing on his display. Dialing in, he was surprised to hear that four voice mails awaited him. Almost no one ever called except the girls, and they would be upstairs in theater six for yet another hour.

The first call was a wrong number, Julio looking for Louise, not happy that she hadn't shown up yet. Next was Clu Baldwin sounding strangely giddy and coy. *Call as soon as you can, Ted. I have something very, very interesting to tell you.*

Next came a series of odd sounds followed by a jarring hang-up. Maybe it was Julio again, getting even more anxious. After that came a barely audible message from Griffey, also requesting him to return the call as soon as possible. Something in Griffey's timorous tone moved Callendar to call him first.

He dialed three times before the connection was made. The phone rang once, then again. Griffey was notorious for taking his sweet time getting to the phone. One of a vanishing breed of die-hard holdouts, he had no answering machine.

Callendar listened to the third distant ring and the fourth. He shifted his phone to the other ear, settling in for a long wait. But before the next ring, a commotion from above grabbed his attention.

No shows were scheduled to let out before the one Janice and the girls were watching, but suddenly a frenzied mass of people charged down the escalators, pushing and shouting. Callendar read the shocked terror on their faces.

Rushing toward the doors, he tried to intercept fleeing patrons. "What happened? What's going on?"

A tattooed man in a tank top shoved him aside. "Out of my way, asshole! Move!"

He set himself in the path of a young couple racing toward the street. "Please. What happened? My kids are up there."

"Bomb threat," said the girl. "No one knows where. You'd better get out."

He made his way toward the escalators, searching desperately for his daughters, struggling against the panicky exiting mob that threatened to trample him.

"Let me by, goddamn it. I have to get my kids."

Finally, he reached the moving stairs. He bounded up the ascending side, scanning the frantic faces that passed on the way down.

Where were his girls?

A raving throng massed at the top of the down ramp, shouting for the people in front to hurry. People were screaming, praying, weeping. One pasty-faced woman clutched her chest and swooned.

Finally, toward the back of the crowd, Callendar spotted Janice's frizzy hair. He barreled through the pressing hordes to reach her. Liquid with relief, he saw that she clutched one of his daughters in each arm.

"Thank God."

"What are you talking about?" Janice railed. "There's a bomb in the theater. We can all be blown to kingdom come any minute!"

"Calm down. Follow me." Callendar stepped behind her and steered the three of them toward the up escalator. "Hold hands." He stepped on first and led them down, training his eyes ahead and timing his steps to outpace the stairs' ascent. The girls followed, Madison clutching his hand and leading her little sister with reassuring calm. Janice brought up the rear, shouting and bitching all the way.

"Are you crazy? Are you out of your goddamned mind? We're going to get killed."

"Ssh, Mommy. It's okay," Madison said.

Once they had all reached the bottom, Callendar guided them firmly toward the door. Outside, they faced a screaming swarm of fire engines, emergency vehicles, police cars and an armored van marked HAZARDOUS MATERIALS—KEEP AWAY.

A team in full protective gear rushed in with a trio of bomb-sniffing dogs. Cops cordoned off the sidewalk fronting the multiplex and evacuated the other stores in the block-long strip.

Callendar wanted to see the girls safely home. But Janice bounced in record time from raw hysteria to burning curiosity. "This is exciting. Let's wait and see what happens."

He glanced nervously at the milling crowd. This was not exactly a secure environment. "Where's Fiorito, Janice?"

"No idea. I haven't seen him since they made the announcement to evacuate. Some guard," she huffed. "Lucky thing I know how to keep an eye on these kids."

His ex-wife's attention was fixed on the commotion across the street, flashing lights, rescue workers scurrying about. Now the TV news vans were starting to descend.

"Look, girls. There's News Channel Four, and Eyewitness News. Maybe they'll interview us."

"We need to get out of here, Janice. It isn't safe," Callendar rasped.

She jutted her pointy chin at him. "Go before you wet your pants, Captain Courageous. We'll be just fine."

The girls cowered together. They were far more worried about the threat of explosion here than inside the theater. Janice would not budge, certainly not at his suggestion. Callendar saw no choice but to be vigilant and wait this out. Slowly, he maneuvered her and the kids closer to the front of the crowd, where several cops in uniform had gathered.

Deliberately, he engaged the nearest officer in conversation. "Have they found anything yet?"

The cop, a short Hispanic man, pressed his two-way radio to his ear. "There's no bomb. Looks like the scare was a deliberate cover-up."

"For what?"

"Sorry, sir. That's all I can say for now."

At that, a blond talking head from one of the networks posed before a cameraman in the middle of the street. Callendar strained to hear as she spoke into the microphone.

"I am surrounded by people who were evacuated from this theater moments ago after a bomb threat was called in to FBI headquarters. At this time, investigators have ruled out the presence of an explosive device inside, but they did find the makings of a highly explosive story."

Her jade eyes widened. "After determining, with the aid of specially trained dogs, that no bomb was present, police on the scene made a horrifying discovery. A man, believed to be an off-duty New York City police officer, was found dead in the theater showing the latest blockbuster from that red-hot hit machine Cinemagic Films.

"The cause of death is not known, but according to a police spokesperson, foul play has not been ruled out."

Frowning, she listened to an update through her earphone.

"This just in," she said. "We have learned from reliable sources that the fallen officer was, in fact, murdered. Further, the assailant left a message on the body, though we don't know its contents at this time. We'll have further details for you as this chilling story unfolds. For *News Views* this is Lisa Kaplan reporting. Back to you in the studio, Gail and Richard."

Callendar's heart was going nuts. He caught the uniform by a sleeve. "The dead officer. Was his name Fiorito?"

The cop's face went tight. "How did you know that? What's your connection to this, sir?"

"It's a long story. Look. My name's Ted Callendar. I'm okay. You can check me out with Russell Quilfo at Queens Cold Case."

"I know Quilfo. I'll do that." He made the call. "All right. It checks."

"What was the message on the body?" Callendar asked.

"I don't know, Mr. Callendar. As of now, they're not letting that out."

Chapter 41

Back home, I settled on the swaybacked couch to tackle my homework assignment. Attorney Winkler's encouragement had put me in a fighting frame of mind.

Eyes shut, I conjured a grotesque pageant with all my worst fears competing for the crown. Contestant number one was the hoary troll of failure. Vividly, I saw my worthlessness stripped naked and forced to strut in the harsh public glare.

Stewart Burlingame could brand me as unscrupulous, smear me in his many publications as a lying cheat. With ease, he could ruin whatever slim chance I still had to work in my chosen field.

Big deal.

A few weeks ago, before my uncle Eli called at Pruitt's to report Burlingame's interest in hiring me, I had faced the same long, daunting odds. True, working in the photo studio fell far short of my dreams, but most things did, including, as I had come to learn the hard way, the way dreams sometimes played out in reality.

Photography was what I did, not who I was. I could find another occupation, if it came to that.

I thought of teaching. Working with Monique's class had been absorbing and fun, even if it had cost me a prize old camera and a bit of dignity. It occurred to me that I could set up workshops for aspiring photographers of various ages, maybe run them through one of the Ys or the public schools or an adult education program.

As an alternative, I could print my best work and try to sell through galleries. Or I could put together a book of related pictures, have someone, maybe Dixon, do the text and try to interest a publisher. Nothing was to stop me from pursuing several alternatives at once and see which proved the most satisfying and successful.

Next I considered the gruesome prospect of having to slink home in humiliating defeat. That one was not pretty, either. My mother would treat me like an exasperating dolt who had failed to follow the simplest, most logical instructions. There would be smug looks and gossipy snipes from so-called friends and neighbors.

Then, none of that was new.

Eventually, the wagging tongues would move on to fresher, juicier targets. Eventually, even Bertie would weary of clacking her tongue in dismay.

Then again, I could choose to live elsewhere, make a fresh start in an entirely new place. The whole world was open to me, a universe of choice and opportunity. Shelby was right. I might not have everything, but I had that freedom.

Bolstered by the thought, I turned to the legal worst-case scenario. According to Winkler, the chances of Deputy Commissioner Fippinger winning his lawsuit were slim. As a public figure, he would be required to meet the Sullivan standard, which meant that he had to prove that I had acted with malicious intent.

Even if the court awarded damages, Fippinger could not take what I did not have. The same was true for Stewart Burlingame, who might attempt to reduce the paper's exposure by filing suit against me. In this rare case, my sorry financial circumstances could prove to be a perverse advantage.

Winkler seriously doubted that any criminal charges would be brought. Courts gave great latitude to the media, especially where public people were involved. Proving a deliberate fraud would be virtually impossible.

I cast around for further worries, but found none. Though the large, ugly Fippinger mess was far from resolved, I felt oddly relieved. Winkler was right. Facing down my worst fears had shrunk them to manageable size.

Part two of my assignment proved no harder. I resolved not to think about elephants or anything at all. And as soon as my weary head crushed the pillow, I drifted into a hard, dreamless sleep.

Chapter 42

Callendar met the others outside Clu's building on Central Park West. Following Quilfo, they pressed through the mass of curious residents and reporters clotting the sidewalk. They crossed the gracious lobby and rode the elevator up in somber silence. The night's unthinkable events hung on them like a suffocating shroud.

Yellow crime-scene tape papered the hall, and the white tiles in the checkerboard marble floor were pink-tinged with blood. A chalk outline marked the spot where Clu's bloody corpse had been found. The crude rendering reminded Callendar of the crayon tracings his little girls had made of their tiny hands in preschool.

A barrel-chested plainclothes detective greeted them at the door. Quilfo introduced him as Jeremy Heckerling, veteran head of homicide for the twenty-fourth precinct, which spanned much of the Upper West Side.

"I'm still combing the place with the MCDU, Russell, so I'll have to ask you not to touch anything," the detective said.

Quilfo sought affirming nods from Trupin, Callendar and Griffey. "Don't worry, we know the drill."

"If you spot anything that looks to be of interest, let us know," Heckerling said. "This one's shaping up to be a major puzzler. The doorman saw nothing peculiar and neither did any of the other tenants. This is not the kind of building someone can slip into easily. Whoever we're up against knows his stuff."

"How's Nolan?" Quilfo asked. The young officer assigned to guard Clu's apartment had been strangled and left for dead.

"Docs can't say yet. He's in intensive care at Saint Luke's, still unconscious. Until he comes around—*if* he comes around—they won't know whether he suffered any permanent brain damage."

Quilfo set a reassuring hand on Callendar's back. The others had induced him to come along and add his thoughts to whatever else this visit might reveal. "Don't worry, Ted. No one is getting anywhere near those girls of yours. Houdini couldn't break through the security around them."

Callendar was a coiled spring. "I'm sure that's true, Russell, but I'm still anxious to get back and be near them, silly though that may seem."

"It doesn't seem silly in the least," Griffey said gently. "We're all terribly upset by this, Ted. Upset and worried sick. It would be inhuman to feel otherwise."

Four technicians from the Mobile Crime Detection Unit canvassed the living room, searching for fibers, hair and latent prints. The scene had been photographed and descriptions of findings recorded in minute detail on tape. Surfaces had been dusted and the carpet and furniture mined for every bit of trace evidence. Whatever they found that looked at all significant had been transferred to evidence bags, then sealed and marked to ensure a clean chain of evidence.

Otherwise, everything lay exactly as the first officer on the scene had discovered it. A bottle of Glenlivet sat on the sideboard beside an ice bucket and a pair of silver tongs. A dirty tumbler lolled in the sink along with a dinner plate striped with crumbs and dried gravy. On the counter lay a half-empty sack of tortilla chips and an empty can of Coke.

Next, they filed into Clu's bedroom. The evidence techs had finished with the room, leaving the dresser drawers agape, spilling their conservative contents. The closet was in obscene disarray and the canopy bed had been stripped. The Arcanum members filed through in awkward silence, uneasy with this violation of their dead colleague's private space, uneasy with everything about this horrific situation.

The society's mandate was to take an arm's-length look at long-unsolved crimes. Their involvement was intended to be academic and theoretical, despite the grisly nature of the subject they addressed.

But this case had trampled every conceivable line. One of their members had been murdered. The children of another member had been menaced, and the officers assigned to guard them now numbered among the victims.

Griffey coughed to clear the raw emotion from his tone. "I see nothing unusual here. If you're in agreement, gentlemen, I suggest we have a look at Dr. Baldwin's study."

Griffey led the way to the dark paneled study across the hall. Clu's reference library and favorite novels lined the walls. Her papers were neatly stacked. The Julie Jameson file rested agape on her rolltop desk beside a legal pad scrawled with notes.

With his fingers laced behind his back, Griffey squinted down at Clu's notes. He read her list of facts and questions aloud. Then he studied the page to which the file was open: the transcript of the mystery woman's call in to Ted Callendar on the Arcanum line.

"I suggest we all read these notes and try to follow Dr. Baldwin's line of reasoning," Griffey said.

Griffey tracked Clu's list of questions and answers: There had been no signs of forced entry into the Jameson apartment. While the back door to the building was found open early on the morning after the crime, employees might have neglected to close it despite their self-serving testimony to the contrary.

If a stranger was responsible for the murder, why would he have increased his risk of discovery by waiting around for ten or fifteen minutes dripping on the carpet before the fatal attack?

Perhaps Clu believed that the circle of rainwater had been a diversionary ploy. The killer could have collected the water and dumped it on the rug to confuse investigators. Or he might have had some other unknown reason for saturating the carpet.

Try though he did, Griffey could not make a coherent connection.

The parents' failure to hear Julie's distress cries had clearly stricken Clu as highly significant. Evidence showed that the Jameson child had struggled violently with her assailant. Logically, the little girl should have made some sound loud enough to arouse her parents, especially considering any mother's instinctive sensitivity to a child's distress and her father's training as a physician.

That is, unless she recognized and trusted her killer until the last desperate moments of her life.

From this, Clu likely had concluded that the parents or someone close to the family committed the crime. Griffey had listened to the message she'd left on Ted's machine shortly before she died. From her ebullient tone, Clu obviously believed she had unraveled the vexing puzzle of Julie Jameson's death.

Much as he wished that was true, Griffey saw several immediate problems with her apparent train of thought. It was reasonable to assume that even the most desperate screams could have been drowned out by the ferocity of that night's storm. Further, the murder followed a party during which both parents admittedly had consumed more wine than they were accustomed to drinking. Frank Jameson was not on call that night and between the alcohol and the oppressive effects of the hurricane, he may well have been less responsive and vigilant than usual.

Griffey remained unconvinced, and as he glanced at the faces around him, he saw that the others had a similar reaction.

"I see what she was getting at," Callendar said, "but still leaves too many unanswered questions. Dr. Jameson wore a size eleven shoe and the mother was a six, but the killer's footprints were a nine. Also, both Dr. and Mrs. Jameson are right-handed and a left-handed person murdered Julie. The parents can't be responsible. It doesn't add up."

Lyman Trupin frowned. "As you describe it, that's true. Still, I wish I knew exactly what Clu was so eager to report. She knew all the facts as well as anyone. I seriously doubt that she simply jumped to some old, indefensible conclusion."

Quilfo shook his head. "Unfortunately, we have no way to find out what she was thinking."

The rest of the apartment yielded no further revelations.

Heckerling saw them to the door. "I'll keep you posted if anything else turns up."

"Same here," Quilfo assured.

As they stepped into the hall, Quilfo's cell phone rang. "Quilfo speaking. Yes, good. What was it?"

Hanging up, he fixed his somber gaze on Callendar. "That was my office. They just got word on the message that was left on Fiorito's body in the theater."

"What was it, Russell?" Trupin asked.

"I'll tell you, but it has to be kept strictly confidential."

"Of course, "Griffey said.

"And Ted, you need to keep cool. Everything is under control. You must believe that."

"I'm cool as they come, Russell. I'm frosted. Now tell me, goddamn it."

"All right. The message was a string of alphabet beads tied around Fiorito's neck. It said, 'The sisters next.'"

Chapter 43

Moshe Price hurried out to meet me as I left the building. "I saw in the paper about you. About that business with the cop and the lawsuit," he said sternly.

My landlord's reaction was a problem I had left off the list. "None of it is true, Mr. Price. I expect to have it straightened out very soon. Please don't worry."

"Who's worried? I say, good for you. Those *kurveh* and their customers are a pox on the neighborhood. Maybe now they'll move somewhere else."

"Maybe so, but that wasn't the point. The story was only meant to show that the mayor's cleanup claims aren't true."

"Of course they're not. Who expects truth from a politician?" His eyes narrowed. "So now you're a big famous celebrity, you're still coming to *Shabbos* dinner?"

"Definitely. I'm looking forward to it. What can I bring?"

"Only your appetite. I'll come for you at six sharp."

"Thanks. Is there anything I need to know? Any special rules?"

"Yes. You're supposed to eat and relax, plenty of both. You can do that?"

"I think so, Mr. Price. I'll try."

The door to One-Hour Photos was locked, but I spotted the walleyed clerk in the office at the rear of the shop. According to my watch, it was ten past nine. I knocked. When she did not respond, I rapped harder.

Sporting a bilious look, she raised her index finger. I was to wait.

I gave her a few minutes' grace, then caught her eye and tapped my watch face.

Finally, she lumbered to the door and worked the lock.

"I'm here to pick these up." I handed her the receipts. "They should have been ready yesterday."

"Wait right here." She disappeared into the back office. I heard odd scuffling, muffled voices. Soon, I caught the plodding approach of footsteps. But instead of the clerk, two uniformed cops rushed me with drawn guns.

"Show me your hands, lady. Do it!" barked the beefy young officer whose name tag read Anderson.

The other, a grizzled mug named Riccardi, shoved me against the counter and patted down my sides."

"What is this? What are you doing?"

Riccardi read my Miranda rights. Then Anderson waved a picture under my nose. "You took this filth?"

I could not make out the subject. It looked vaguely like a walnut half, but the shot was blurred and taken at too-close range.

"No. I'm sure I didn't. What is it supposed to be?"

The younger one chuckled dryly. "Go ahead and play innocent. Won't make a bit of difference. You're nailed, you pervert. You're toast."

"I don't know what you're talking about."

"You got some nerve, you hypocritical bitch," Riccardi said. "Those bullshit charges you trumped up against Beau Fippinger are chump change compared to this."

The clerk ventured out of the office and stood in the doorway. "It's really, really disgusting what you did. I called the police right away, soon as I saw."

"Would you please tell me what this is about?"

"It's about kiddy porn, lady. It's about taking close-ups of a little girl's privates," spat Anderson. "Talk about sick."

Now the picture came clear. "This is all a ridiculous mistake. I've been volunteering with a kindergarten class, teaching them photography. I gave the kids disposable cameras and let them go off to take candid shots. One of the children must have taken this."

"Sure. That's perfect. Blame it on a little kid," the beefy cop snarled.

"I'm telling the truth. Call Monique Sharon at Parkway Elementary. She'll back me up."

"Why? Is she in on this, too?"

"Don't be ridiculous."

"I wouldn't think of it." Riccardi wrenched my hands behind my back and clamped on handcuffs, forcing them tight enough to stem the circulation. "We're playing this strictly by the books, missy, chapter and verse."

A curious crowd had massed outside the shop. Hot with outrage and embarrassment, I ran the gauntlet to the squad car at the end of the block. Anderson drove to the station house with Riccardi in the shotgun seat.

I was read my rights again. Anderson booked me before an audience of jeering cops.

"Serves you right, you lying bitch."

"You're the whore, baby. Anything for a buck."

After I was printed, photographed and pumped for information for the intake form, Riccardi muscled me toward a holding cell at the rear of the precinct house.

"Is there an officer around named Elisson?"

"What are you yapping about?"

"Elisson. He's a detective. I'm not sure out of which precinct. Works undercover."

"If that's so, why would I be discussing him with you?"

"I don't want to discuss him. But if you see him, would you please tell him I'm here?"

"I'm not your errand boy, scum-ette," he said. "Send your own messages."

"Fine, I'd like to make a call then, please."

"Okay. But you only get one."

I called Monique's school and told the secretary that it was urgent. I heard kids giggling in the background, shrieking in delight, apparently unaware that the world had spun out of all rational control. Soon Monique came on the line.

"Anna, where are you? Is something wrong?"

Riccardi fixed his rheumy eyes on me as I gave her the lurid details.

"Oh my God. I'm so sorry. You poor thing."

"I'll be all right. Do you think you can figure out who took those shots?"

"Absolutely. Shouldn't take me more than a few minutes to get the culprit to confess. Where are you? I'll come down and straighten this out."

"That would be wonderful."

I settled in the cramped dismal cell, reading the graffiti on the wall. Bunny would love sweet cakes forever. Tina thought cops sucked the big hairy. Jesus loved me, no matter what.

A guard approached and opened the holding cell door. "Come on, Cinderella."

I stayed put. "What now?"

"You've been bailed out. Now, if I were you, I'd haul ass before someone changes his mind."

In the crowded waiting room, I looked around for Monique. Instead, I spotted Meryl Lubin, Burlingame's chief in-house counsel. She greeted me with a grim look and a solid handshake. "You're free to go now, Ms. Jameson."

"I don't understand. Why are you helping me?"

"I'm acting on instructions from Mr. Burlingame."

"Burlingame? I don't get it. Anyway, how did you know I was here?"

"Your friend Monique Sharon contacted Dixon Drake. Mr. Burlingame's office had already spoken with him, trying to reach you. We agreed to secure your release while Ms. Sharon arranges for the child who took those pictures to be interviewed under appropriate conditions."

"And that's it?"

"Yes. I believe you can consider this matter closed. I'll see to it that the charges are properly dismissed and the records sealed."

"You still haven't told me why Burlingame would want to help me all of a sudden."

"There's a car waiting outside to take us downtown. Mr. Burlingame would like to see you as soon as possible. He'll explain everything."

"Thanks anyway. I've had more than my quota of fun and games for one day."

Before I reached the door, she tossed a tempting lariat of words.

"We know that you didn't falsify that picture of the deputy commissioner. We're not sure yet who is responsible, but you're officially off the hook."

"I would never have been *on* the hook, unless you people hung me out to dry there in the first place, Ms. Lubin."

"You're right, of course. And Mr. Burlingame is very anxious to make amends. This is a rarity, Ms. Jameson. Believe me. Seeing Stewart Burlingame grovel is a once-in-a-lifetime opportunity. You'd be foolish to pass it up."

I couldn't help but smile at that. "When you put it that way, I'm inclined to agree. Which is your car, Ms. Lubin? Lead the way."

Chapter 44

A stooped, fleshy man awaited us in Burlingame's suite. He had an overall colorless appearance, like furniture left to fade in bright sun. Attorney Lubin introduced him as Milosz Radik, the *Chronicle*'s new photo editor.

"He comes to us by way of *Newsweek* and the *Los Angeles Times*," she explained. " Milosz, I'd like you to meet Anna Jameson. She's the photographer who shot the prostitution piece."

"A pleasure. You do fine work," he said.

"Where's Mr. Burlingame?" the lawyer asked.

Radik showed his callused palms. "He said he'd be right back."

"Why don't you set up in the meantime?" Lubin suggested.

He extracted his laptop from a canvas bag and placed it on the conference table beside a flat-screen display.

From the same bag, Radik extracted several envelopes. The first contained the front-page shot of Deputy Commissioner Fippinger with the prostitute.

Burlingame entered in a haze of blue smoke. "Everyone's here. Let's get going."

Radik pulled up a scanned image of the shot. "Our typical process today is to scan and digitize the analog images that come in on film. That allows us maximum flexibility in paste-up and composition."

He tapped the keyboard and an image file appeared. With a few clicks, he isolated a key section and enlarged it until the individual pixels registered as rows of brightly colored rectangles.

"Look here." He shifted to another area of the image. After enlarging it even further, he tracked the beam of a laser pointer over an area where the colors shifted abruptly from bright to dark. "You can see here that two images have been combined. *Composited* is the term for it."

Radik opened another envelope. "The compositing was done at the digital level. I can tell that from anomalies in the underlying code. If you'd like, I can show you the detail, but it's rather technical."

Burlingame flapped away the opportunity. "Keep it in English, Slav-man."

"Yes, sir. I'm quite sure that the alteration was made in my department, on our proprietary software. There are signature features, which are also quite technical. Suffice it to say they're about as distinctive as fingerprints. Acting under the assumption that the whole thing was concocted in-house, I checked the photo morgue. I found this."

The picture he passed around was identical to the image of Fippinger from the front-page shot. For emphasis, Radik brought up a screen that displayed the two likenesses side by side. Next, he superimposed one on the other. They were identical.

Burlingame puffed his stogie, filling the air with hazy currents. "What joker did this?"

"I don't know, sir," Radik said. "It could have been virtually anyone on my staff or a number of others who might have access to my equipment. Of course

I take full responsibility. This happened in my department, on my watch, as you say it."

"Very noble," Burlingame sniffed. "But it doesn't solve my problem. I need name, rank and serial number. I want his head on a plate and his balls in a sling. Go get him, Radik. Now!"

"Believe me, Mr. Burlingame, there's nothing I want more. I'll get back to you as soon as I have more information."

"Make it quick. Use whatever it takes, thumbscrews included. We need damage control and fast."

"Yes, sir." The photo editor packed up and left.

Burlingame sucked his cigar so his cheeks dented and a fat coin of ash dropped in his lap. Brushing it aside, he muttered angrily. "This is definitely not my day. Bad enough I have to deal with that crap, but now I get to eat a plate of crow."

"Go on, Stewart. It'll do you some good," Lubin said.

"All right, Ms. Mouthpiece. I'm biting, I'm chewing. Look, kid. I jumped to the wrong conclusion. So forget it."

I waited for the apology that did not come. "Is that all?"

He looked surprised. "What more do you want—blood? I said I screwed up. End of story."

"It's not that simple, Mr. Burlingame. You accused me of something I didn't do. You caused me considerable embarrassment and much worse. I deserve an apology at the very least."

"You are some piece of work, kid. I have to tell you."

"Actually, you don't have to tell me anything. Not anymore. I've had enough."

I strode out and crossed the broad reception area. I felt stronger and lighter than I had since I first set foot in these offices. Anything had to be better than dealing with that insufferable man. I could toss out my fishing line like Bolly and see what I caught.

I exited the Flashlight Building amid the trickle of mid-afternoon visitors. I filled myself with crisp, clear air and felt a dizzy rush of optimism.

My cell phone sounded as I approached the subway entrance. Burlingame's central switchboard number registered on the caller ID.

Expecting Dixon, I pressed the button and started talking. "Hello, Mr. Drake. You're invited to a liberation party at my place tonight. Make it seven o'clock. You bring the wine, and I'll provide Chinese takeout and an official Stewart Burlingame dartboard. How does that sound?"

Burlingame answered in his grating growl. "Not very original. But definitely better than voodoo dolls. Damned things actually work. Gave me actual hemorrhoids, plus a migraine you wouldn't believe."

My temper heated again. "What do you want, Mr. Burlingame?"

"Just hear me out, kid. Okay?"

"What?"

"I'm no good at apologies. Truth is, I can't stand being wrong. Everybody has a blind spot, and that's mine. Also, I'm a tough old son of a bitch and nasty as they come. Nobody likes me. Even *I* don't like me very much. But I run a damned fine operation, and from where you sit, that should be all that matters."

"What's your point, Mr. Burlingame? I need to make a train."

He chuckled appreciatively. "You're good, kid, feisty. You've got the makings of a serious contender, a good eye and great big *cojónes*. That's the ball game. Believe you me."

"And therefore?"

He whistled low. "You got me sweating here, kid. Seriously. My pits are damp and everything. Okay, what I'm trying to say is that you've earned yourself a place on the *Chronicle* staff. In a couple of months, when we launch *Upshot,* I'll probably move you over there. Or maybe we can work out some kind of time-share arrangement. We'll see. Point is, you do good work and I like the way you handle yourself. So report to human resources tomorrow, and they'll fix you up."

"I'll have to think about it."

"What? You need me to throw you more bones? All right. I'll go five thousand more on the base pay, but that's my absolute maximum."

"I'll let you know, Mr. Burlingame."

He blew a breathy rush. "Jesus. All right. I'll toss you another five bills up front. Call it moving expenses. But don't go blabbing it all over the place. I don't want everyone beating the drums, stirring up the damned unions."

"I told you, I'd have to let you know."

"You've got a week, kid. One week, and that's the end of it. I'm too damned fat and old to jump through more hoops than that."

Chapter 45

From the lobby of Janice's building, Callendar stared at the street. He was soaked and shivering in the air-conditioned chill, but still grateful to Sam, the doorman, who had taken pity and finally allowed him to enter the building despite his ex's shrill demands that he be barred.

All he cared about was keeping his girls safe, which he could do better here. From his perch, Callendar commanded a clear view of anyone who entered through the side door or the central rotating glass. He had half a minute or so to size up each person who strode the pale travertine span toward the bank of gilt-faced elevators in the rear. If anyone sparked his suspicion, he could call upstairs and warn the uniforms posted on Janice's floor. Quilfo was prepared to send in serious reinforcements, no questions asked, at Callendar's request.

Callendar kept trying to convince himself that this was a bulletproof, fail-safe situation. But the guard around Clu Baldwin had seemed secure, as well. Bumping off an armed detective in a crowded movie theater took dangerous, diabolical imagination and inhuman nerve. So did advertising evil intentions in advance. They were up against a very bold, very slippery beast.

The sisters next.

Callendar tried to pick his way through the tortured kinks in the killer's mind. The monster reveled in the stalking chase, the terror of his prey. He had a seemingly limitless repertoire of vicious behaviors and a voracious appetite for fresh blood.

Callendar trembled, and not from the chill alone.

He reviewed the security net around his daughters. He tried to peer through the killer's warped scope and search for fatal flaws in their defense.

Sam, a tall, affable man with acne-scarred skin, vetted every visitor to the building with scrupulous care. Callendar had seen the doorman respond with rapid ferocity anytime an unauthorized arrival attempted to circumvent his guard. Once, Sam had corralled the burly unwanted suitor of a teenage girl and sent the guy sprawling to the pavement like a sack of dust. A young Japanese man bent on distributing forbidden takeout menus was evicted so fiercely, he landed in the planter abutting the curb. Callendar could still picture the astonishment on that kid's face as his head came thumping down amid the daffodils.

Sam flashed thumbs-up, as if he had read Callendar's tortured mind. Callendar returned the gesture, though he knew he would feel no real reassurance until the killer was nailed and caged.

A couple hurried in with dripping umbrellas. Callendar recognized them as neighbors who had moved onto the floor in the chaotic final days before he left. A lanky dark-skinned man entered toting two shopping bags full of groceries. A dapper gent in his seventies followed, squiring a balloon-breasted girl with a three-foot drape of glossy onyx hair.

Each time the revolving door twirled, Callendar's heart stumbled. He was haunted by the warning message strung around Fiorito's neck.

The sisters next.

His daughters were sweet, beautiful kids who deserved their unlimited dreams. Their future belonged to them, not some vicious creep who liked to play games.

For a time, no one entered the building. Sam the doorman flipped open last Sunday's magazine and pored over the puzzle. "What's a seven-letter word for magnetic appeal, Dr. Callendar? Starts with a *c* and ends in *m-a*. Any idea?"

" 'Charisma' would work only it has eight letters," Ted proposed.

"That's it. The theme of this crossword is all things automotive, so it's probably car-isma. Thanks, that's been haunting me all week."

Word games.

From the outset, the killer had made it clear that he liked anagrams, devilish twists and double meanings. The beast never conveyed what he meant in clear, unambiguous terms. Everything was a game, a puzzle, and subject to interpretation.

Fortunately, Callendar had a knack for word play, too. He hurried to the security desk. "Can I borrow a piece of paper and a pen, Sam?"

He wrote out the words in large block letters: THE SISTERS NEXT.

At first, he saw no obvious way to rearrange the text. The X stymied him in several possible combinations. Angrily, he crossed out the failed efforts.

The doorman glanced over at the page. "What does that mean, the sister is next?"

"It doesn't say that, Sam. It says, the sisters next."

"Right, there's no apostrophe. Damned punctuation gets me every time."

Callendar reeled at the sudden revelation. There was no punctuation in alphabet beads. The ambiguity may have been purposeful or not. Either way, his kids might have adequate protection, but another father's child could be in mortal jeopardy.

"You're not the only one, Sam. Thanks."

Callendar crossed the lobby out of earshot and dialed Quilfo. He dearly hoped that Trupin's FBI friends knew the current whereabouts of Julie Jameson's sister. Listening to the distant ring, he prayed that they could get to the poor kid in time.

What chance would she have against the monster on her own?

Chapter 46

Riuka Price bowed over the Sabbath candles, her soft face warmed by the dancing flames. She cupped her hands and drew the warmth to her eyes. In a timorous voice, she chanted the prayer: *Baruch atah adonai, elohainu melech haolom* . . .

Warmed by the ancient ritual and the Prices' cozy home, my nerves uncoiled. Rivka's rich, honest fare furthered the mood. She insisted that I sit while she served chicken soup with matzoh balls, potted chicken and potato pancakes. She passed fresh *challah,* a sweet, braided egg bread, and Moshe poured dark sweet wine into the small crystal goblets.

More prayers followed dinner, and then Moshe and Rivka sang several Hebrew duets. His booming bass, a startling production from such a diminutive instrument, blended perfectly with her reedy soprano. Their faces beamed with simple satisfaction. They held hands.

This was yet another dimension to my improbable new friend Moshe Price. He was able to lay aside his sharp edge and his titanium rule book and open his heart to simple pleasures and spiritual peace. I recognized this as a crucial missing element in my life. Every so often, I vowed to give myself a nice Episcopalian *Shabbos.*

Price insisted on walking me home on his way to *shul,* though his small Orthodox congregation lay in the opposite direction. He poised his umbrella to shield me from the rain. He was a true person, a *mensch* in Yiddish parlance: my little protector. Outside the factory, he bowed crisply. "So you enjoyed?"

"Very much. It was wonderful. Thank you for having me."

"Anytime. *Shabbos* is for sharing. It's a *mitzvah* to open your house to friends."

"A blessing, you mean?"

"*Tov maod.* Very good. Before you know it you'll be speaking like a regular *Yeshivah bocher.*"

I smiled at him, this fierce little man. "It's easy to be a good student when you have a good teacher, Mr. Price."

"For a *shikseh,* you eat pretty good, too."

"That I do."

"You want me to walk you up? You'll be all right?"

"I'll be fine. *Shalom,* Mr. Price. Good *Shabbos.*"

"*Shalom* to you, too, Ms. Jameson. Good night, sweet dreams and peace."

My cell phone blared the "Ode to Joy" as I opened the door to the loft.

"I'm so glad to hear your voice, Anna. Is everything all right?"

The connection bristled with interference. "I'm fine, Uncle Eli. How about you? You sound strange."

"It's nothing. I'm on the way home, Anna, calling from the plane. I have some time in New York between connections. I'd like to come by and see you. Is that all right?"

"Of course. I'd love it."

I gave him my address, and he fell silent.

"Uncle Eli? Are you there?"

"Yes. Look, I don't want to alarm you, sweetheart, but I have to be direct. Someone has been calling people close to your sister's case, making threats. It may be nothing, but I want you to be very careful."

"My mother said something about a call, but she thought it was a prank."

"Maybe so. But it pays to be extra vigilant just in case. Make sure your doorman double checks before he sends anyone up to your place. And don't go out alone, Anna, especially after dark."

"I'm sure it's just another crackpot, Uncle E. You know how it is, every once in a while somebody crawls out from under a rock and plays one of these stupid games. Threats, letters. It's nothing."

"Maybe so. But please, keep your eyes open. If you see anything suspicious, I want you to call the police right away."

I approached the window and stared down at the street. Windswept rain swirled in the vacant cones of lamplight. The weather had chased everyone away, including Bolly and the whores.

"Don't worry, Uncle E. I'll be fine."

His tone sharpened. "I need you to take this seriously, Anna. Promise you'll be extra careful until I get there and we can talk about this further."

"All right. I hear you."

Hanging up, I felt infected by my uncle's unease. Normally, he was such an affable, easygoing soul. Then, I supposed a serious business emergency could set most anyone on edge.

Drowsy, I settled in bed with a book. The words began to swim out of phase before I finished the first chapter. I flipped on the tiny light near my bedroom door, settled under the covers and fell hard asleep. Random threats were no match for the soporific power of chicken soup, soothing friends and the storm.

Chapter 47

Quilfo was last to arrive at the FBI communications center. He found Griffey and Trupin in the conference room with agents Bell and Weller.

"Where are we, gentlemen?" he asked. "Any word?"

Nate Bell activated a colorful display. He pointed to a winking indicator light that trailed from South Carolina toward New York, then stalled in confusion at the city line. "We tried to reach Anna Jameson in Charleston, but her number there had been disconnected. We contacted the landlord, who told us she moved out a couple of weeks ago. He said she was headed for New York, but she left no forwarding address. The photo shop she worked in down there was closed for the day when we called, and we weren't able to reach her old boss. The landlord said Anna was planning to work in the city, but he didn't know the details. We're trying photo shops, studios and such, but very little is open at this hour."

"What about the family?" Quilfo asked.

"Her parents are not home. Neither is an uncle close to the family nor Kevin Moultrie, the young man Ms. Jameson was seeing before she left town. We did reach the home of the childhood friend who lives in New York. The friend was out for the evening, but her husband promised to pass along the message as soon as she gets in. We have an agent trying the others again every few minutes. It's just a matter of time."

"Time is what we don't have. If she's here, there must be some way to track her down quickly."

Bell sighed. "We've checked phone company records, credit agencies, charge records. So far nothing," Weller reported. "She seems to be paying cash and leaving precious little paper trail. But don't worry; we'll figure it out. We still have a few more tricks up our sleeve. You know our motto: We always get our man."

Quilfo knew the rest of the line, as well. They brought their subjects in dead or alive.

Chapter 48

A harsh rhythmic flapping invaded my dreams. My eyes snapped open. "Who's there?"

Heart squirming, I turned to the window, where slivers of streetlight pierced the darkness. Something was dangling beyond the glass, and as my focus cleared, I recognized it as a tar paper strip. Buffeted by the wind, it struck the pane with a jarring slap.

Nothing but the wind.

My bedside lamp refused to light. Stealing out of bed, I tested the bathroom switch and the overhead track in the living room. The silence had a dense totality: no refrigerator hum, no compressor noises, no restless creaking from the ancient appliances.

The power was out.

Sternly, I ordered myself not to panic. Rummaging through the drawers, I found a flashlight, but the batteries were dead. I longed for the extraordinary collection of candle stumps and matchbooks I had discarded in my zeal to get rid of Mrs. Graff's junk.

I struggled to beat back the terror looping around my neck. It was nothing, only darkness: the normal, innocent absence of light. How many times since childhood had I repeated that useless mantra? Why was mindless fear so much more powerful than intelligent reason?

Given that the streetlights had not gone out, the problem had to be in this building. Maybe it was a blown fuse or a breaker had tripped and all I needed to do was reset it. Of course, I needed to find it first.

I trained my memory on Dixon's friend Lou, who had installed the lighting. I remembered him calling from the kitchen, asking if the power was out in this place and that.

The ambient streetlight did not reach the living room, and only the distant city haze from across the river broke the darkness. Crossing toward the kitchen, my foot caught a sofa leg, and I narrowly missed knocking down the mock Tiffany lamp. Something crunched underfoot and my skin went clammy.

Imaginary horrors kept lunging at me from the shadows, sending me reeling as if I'd been struck. I shut my eyes to stop the dizzying rush of nightmarish images.

Closing my eyes, I held a mental snapshot of the room, everything still bright and comprehensible and neatly settled in its place. My fears subsided as I turned into the kitchen. The pictures in my mind were sharp and steady. I could rely on them.

I passed my fingers along the wall, searching for the faceplate over the electrical panel. I found nothing between the counter and cabinets. Nothing but the light switch broke the span of wall beside the entrance. Kneeling, I checked inside the cabinets. Finally, on the rear surface behind a precarious tower of pots, I found the plate.

I flipped every switch in the double line of breakers to no effect. Whatever had caused the outage was not in my apartment.

Outside, the storm flared. A lightning whip slashed the sky and the walls quaked in the furious grip of thunder. A sudden chill invaded the room. Strange. I hadn't touched the windows since Detective Elisson and his partner locked and fastened them with four-inch nails.

Maybe a pane had broken or a frame had separated from the building's rickety facade. With my lids tightly clenched, I walked to the rear of the loft. Pushing aside the curtains, I peered at the river, which was boiling with storm-induced chop. The window was secure. The cool air had not slipped through there.

Closing my eyes again, I crossed to the side of the living room that overlooked the courtyard. The chill worsened as I approached the window. A clean straight crack scored the pane as if it had been cut with a blade. Firmly, I dismissed that terrifying thought. There had to be an innocent explanation. The ancient glass must have been too weak to withstand the detectives' work on the lock and frame. Thankfully, though the wind pierced the hairline break, the sill remained mostly dry.

I walked blindly back to bed, settled under the covers and tried to sleep. A few more hours would solve the darkness problem. The storm weighed on me, dragging me down. Slowly, my muscles eased and my thoughts spun adrift.

A child whimpered in my sightless dream. Then came the plaint of a wounded kitten. I reached out, groping through the stew of darkness for the poor little creature, but a ponderous door creaked on its hinge and slammed shut, sealing the kitten away.

I struggled awake. That was no dream. Someone had ridden the gunmetal lift to my floor. Now someone was working the heavy metal latch. Sliding open the cranky door. Stepping into the hallway.

Mind bristling, I slipped silently out of bed and searched for my cell phone. This was no time to surrender to fear. I was alone with the intruder and the storm.

Chapter 49

I stabbed 911, cupping my hand to muffle the strident tones.

A woman answered. "Emergency, how can I help you?"

"Someone's in my building," I whispered, but my voice and my breath sounded monstrously loud.

The connection crackled with interference. "Speak up, miss, please. I can't hear you."

"Someone's broken into my building. I need you to send the police. The address is—"

The line went dead. Frantic, I hit the redial button. But all I got was the frenzied busy pulse that meant circuit trouble. I tried again, but still, the phone would not connect.

Groping in the dark, I found my purse and extracted the package with the gun. Soundlessly, I slit the tape and removed the paper.

The Lady Derringer nestled in the plump leather case. Removing it, I checked the cylinder and packaging.

No bullets.

I clutched the pistol anyway, thinking it might serve as a useful bluff. My heart struck like a sledge as I made my way to the living room and crouched out of sight behind the sofa.

At first, I heard nothing. Then, listening harder, I caught the muffled thud of deliberate steps. The sound grew more insistent as the interloper approached. He was in no hurry, taking his excruciating time.

He was nearing the door, almost within reach. Breath held, I waited for the lock to turn and the door to burst open.

Instead came a knock and a booming voice. "Ms. Jameson? It's Detective Elisson. You okay in there?"

Numb with relief, I set the pistol down. I crossed the darkened room and opened the door, admitting a welcome wash of light from the caged bulb in the hall. The detective's clothes were soaked and his sodden hair stuck out in porcupine pips.

"You got the emergency call again? Unbelievable."

"My sentiments exactly. Some people beat giant odds and win the lottery. Me, I get an exclusive crack at all your damsel-in-distress calls. Some luck. What is it this time?"

"Someone rode the elevator up to this floor. I heard him get out, then nothing."

"Didn't see anyone. Let me check." He poked around the corridor, then trained his flashlight out back, searching the rickety catwalk and the rain-swept roof. Returning, he squinted into the living room. "Whatever it was is gone now, Ms. Jameson. Want me to have a look around your place?"

"I wouldn't mind. Since you're here."

He strode in. "Mind if I put on some light?"

"The power's out. I checked the breakers. It must be something to do with the storm."

He worked his powerful flash beam from wall to wall. Crouching, he checked behind the furniture the way my father used to do to mollify my childish aversion to the dark. He did the same in the bedroom, bathroom and kitchen, searching closets and cupboards, opening drawers, poking through even the smallest, most improbable hiding places.

His patient rendering of the game deepened my humiliation, but I could not bring myself to stop him. I needed the juvenile comfort more than I cared about saving face. Like any frightened little kid, I understood that a determined monster could insert himself in precious little space.

"Everything seems okay, Ms. Jameson. How are you doing?"

"I'm fine, Detective. I told you, I was just concerned because I heard the elevator."

He stroked his square chin. "I understand. Of course you were. Want me to hang around awhile?"

"No thanks. You must have scared him away."

His head bobbed in exaggerated agreement. "Sure. I bet that's it. Still, I don't mind staying around awhile if you want. No problem. Probably save me another trip."

"You won't be hearing from me again, Detective. Guaranteed. I've had more than my lifetime supply of crises."

"Okay. If you're sure, I'll head home. My shift is over. I just dropped Harry off when dispatch relayed your call."

"I'm fine, Detective. Thanks for checking things out."

He stepped out into the hall again, squishing in his saturated shoes. "Lock up behind me, Ms. Jameson. And be extra careful about who you open your door to, will you?"

"Why is that?"

"That creep I told you about, the chameleon, has been at it again. Slit a woman's throat uptown. Killed one cop and critically wounded another. Homicide's still treating the hits as unrelated incidents, but take my word: One sick bastard is behind all of them. Anytime a character like that is on the loose, it pays to keep your eyes wide open and your doors locked."

"I will, Detective Elisson. Good night."

"Night, Ms. Jameson. Don't let the bedbugs bite."

Chapter 50

Callendar startled at the sound of his cell phone. He had been staring at the door for hours, snapping to every time a stranger approached or entered the building. His head ached, and his nerves were scraped raw.

As the phone blared again, he hit the talk button. "Ted Callendar here."

"Hi, Ted. It's Quilfo. We finally got a line on Julie Jameson's sister."

"Thank God."

"Yes, truly. She has cellular phone service with a small carrier in South Carolina. Her phone's out of service right now, but we tracked her outgoing calls and managed to get in touch with a friend of hers named Elisson. So happens he left her moments ago, and she's fine. We're in the process of posting heavy round-the-clock security right now."

"Good to hear, Quilfo. Thanks for calling."

"My pleasure. We can all use a little good news at this point."

The doorman flashed a questioning look. Callendar countered with a hesitant thumbs-up. He had seen far too much to take anything for granted. He was not willing to write off the threat until they had the beast in hand.

Chapter 51

The darkness pressed in again as I fastened the last of the locks.

Suddenly, I felt trapped by fear, immobilized.

I pulled long, slow breaths, and my mind began to clear. I should have taken the detective up on his offer. I wanted to chase after the burly cop and beg him to stay until the storm beasts stopped howling and my demons shrank in the healing light of day.

But it was too late. The elevator landed with a sickening thump and the factory door slammed shut.

I shut my eyes and forced myself to move away from the door. Clinging to the pictures in my mind, I counted off the steps and the obstacles. The distraction held the numbing terror at bay.

As I approached the bedroom, I heard the lift's plaintive rise again. Elisson must have forgotten something.

The whine ceased, and I caught the strident workings of the latch. Following that came the unmistakable sound of my uncle Eli's syncopated limp.

I raced back, worked the lock and flung open the door.

But it wasn't my uncle.

"Detective Elisson. I thought you were someone else."

An odd grin warped his mouth. "That's because I *am* someone else, Annie girl."

I recoiled. "Why did you call me that?" *Annie girl* had been a childhood pet name. My father was the only one who still used it.

"I called you that because you're like a silly little girl who doesn't know how to listen. I told you to be extra careful about who you let in here. I warned you, loud and clear. Now didn't I? And look what you do."

"All right, Detective. I get the picture. You can go now."

"I'm not going anywhere until I'm good and finished with you. And when I am, you'll be finished but good."

He slipped into the loft and locked the door behind him. Passing quickly from window to window, he lowered the blinds, stealing the last of the light. "Oh my. It's black as pitch in here and poor little Anna is afraid of the dark. This must be what it's like to be buried alive, don't you think? This must be what it's like to be six feet under in a box."

"Stop it, Detective. This isn't funny."

There was something chillingly familiar in his low, taunting laugh. "Oh yes it is. It's hilarious. You still don't know who I am. You still think I'm Detective Al Elisson, the Lone Ranger, who always shows up in the nick of time to foil the bad guys."

He shook a chiding finger. "That stuff only works in movies and comic books, Annie girl. If you want to get by in real life, you can't be so damned gullible. Haven't you heard? If someone looks too good to be true, he probably is."

"I don't understand. Who are you?"

He loomed in the inky darkness, a featureless, shadowy hulk. "I am anyone and everyone. I'm whoever I want to be or no one at all. All it takes is creating the illusion. That detective character was a pretty good one, if I do say so myself. One of my favorites."

"Why are you doing this? What do you want?"

"My wishes are simple, Annie girl. I want to see you at perfect peace. I want to help you stop all that messy breathing and moving around."

I backed away, searching for a means of escape. "Stop talking like that. It's crazy."

"But I *am* crazy. That's why they hid me away, tra-la, because I'm psychotic and a danger to others. Children especially, but any small weak thing will do. Even you, Annie Fanny. Even you." He started to hum, and I recognized my sister's favorite tune, "Someday, My Prince Will Come."

Suddenly, I understood who this man was. But it couldn't be.

"Alan?"

"That's right, Annie girl. I'm your dear, long-departed cousin. Have you missed me?"

"But it can't be. Alan was killed in a car crash in Spain. Alan and Irene were killed and Eli was injured."

"You see? People believe what they hear, Annie girl. I learned that from my old man. He said we were dead, and so we were. He blames his arthritic hip on the imaginary accident, and everyone believes him."

"But why?"

"Why not? Deception is such fun. There's no end to the amusing possibilities. I tell you I'm a detective and you swallow it whole. I tell you that Harry's my partner, and it never occurs to you that he's some two-bit wannabe actor I paid to play the part. Same with that lawyer, who wasn't a lawyer at all, just someone I paid to pretend."

Slowly, silently, I backed away.

"Even funnier, I tell you about a crazy serial killer on the loose, and you never stop to wonder why I know so much about him. You're bad at listening, Annie Fanny, like I said. If you had ears, you would have gotten the joke much sooner."

"This is nobody's idea of a joke," I breathed.

"Sure it is. And here's the punch line. I told you who I was all along. I said I was Al Eli's son. Elisson, get it? I simply changed the pronunciation to throw you off. And so it did."

His maniacal giggle made my skin crawl.

"Fine. I get it now. You put one over on me and I didn't have a clue. So you win, Alan. And now you can leave. I won't say anything to anyone. I never saw you. You're still long dead as far as I'm concerned."

He edged closer, and my head filled with his rank, musky scent. "Don't underestimate me, Annie girl. I may be nuts but I'm not stupid. The second I walked out that door, you'd be screaming to the cops, telling everyone who I am and what I've done."

"I won't. Not if you leave now. You disappear, and I never saw you. It's forgotten."

"Nothing's ever forgotten, not for good. That's the problem, little cousin. You were there; you saw everything. Sooner or later you were going to remember it. I've made a study of childhood trauma, repressed memory, all that. It was only a matter of time. That's why I had to come back for you."

"I don't know what you're talking about."

"Yes you do. Deep down, you know exactly what I'm talking about. Hurricane Queenie had knocked out the power. You woke up in the dark, frightened and confused. You called for your parents, but they couldn't hear you over the noise of the storm, so you got out of bed."

His voice sent me plunging back in time. I was that tiny girl again, picking through the terrifying shadows toward my parents' room, hugging myself to still the shivers.

"No, Alan. Stop!"

He spoke in a taunting, hypnotic lilt. "When you got to Julie's room, you saw me, though I was too busy to notice you at first."

The ancient image formed in a dislocating swirl. *Alan was standing beside my sister's bed, chest heaving, breathing in shallow rasps. Shocked by his vicious expression, I stopped cold.*

"When I turned around, I spotted you," he said. "But I had other, more pressing things on my mind. You might say I was murderously preoccupied, far too busy to worry about a mewling, insignificant little thing like you."

I felt the storm's electric chill, the damp tickly carpet beneath my bare feet. I watched Julie stir. Suddenly, she rolled on her side and moved to speak.

Before I could cry out to warn her, Alan sprang like a trap. He rushed to the bed and shoved my sister down. I heard the grunt of his fury, the bone smash of his pounding fists, Julie's muffled shrieks.

Then nothing.

"You were no threat, Annie Fanny," Alan hissed, "nothing but a scared little mouse."

He was right. Blind fear drove me away, sent me running. I raced back to bed and burrowed under the covers. I fell instantly asleep, as if I'd been struck. And the unthinkable images were buried under thick, soothing layers of denial and obfuscating dreams.

"How could you hurt her like that? Julie loved you."

"She asked for it. Damned little bitch refused to shut up, like my sister."

"Your sister?"

The laugh was a sick cackle, deep in his chest. "You should see the look on your face. Someone would think you'd seen a ghost."

"Your sister died when she was just an infant, not even a year old."

"A year was more than plenty. Stupid little brat kept crying all the time, getting on my nerves."

This was the creature that stole my sister and shattered my family's peace. This lunatic was the cause of the pain that had haunted my parents and cast a permanent pall of sadness on our home.

Icy rage seeped into my veins, edging out the terror.

"Your parents knew about this, that you killed the baby?"

"Not at first. Doctors thought it was crib death, which suited me fine. They didn't know about your sister, either. But a couple of years later, we were on vacation in Europe and I let something slip. My father wanted to turn me in, said I had to get help. But my mother wouldn't allow it, bless her heart. She swore she'd kill herself if Daddy Dearest blew the whistle. She kept carrying on until he agreed to keep quiet and pretend we'd been killed in an accident. She was pretty convincing, the old broad, even took a bunch of pills once and had to have her stomach pumped. Sliced her wrists once, too. Nice red bracelets, she had. Scared the crap out of the old man.

"So finally, Daddy set us up in Switzerland with fresh identities. I was to be carefully supervised by my mother, tutored at home and treated for my little emotional problems at a famous clinic nearby. They pronounced me cured twenty years ago. Model patient. And I was. I'd behave for months at a time. But then I'd get bored with the Goody Two-Shoes act and take a little vacation. Mother would cover for me, naturally. Such a dear, trusting lady. She honestly believed me when I came home and said I'd done nothing wrong."

"How many others have there been, Alan?"

"How much time do you have?" He snickered. "Wait. I can answer that. You have exactly as much time as I decide to give you."

"But why? Why do you do such terrible things?"

"Because it feels good. That's all that matters, Annie girl, feeling good. Getting what you want. Let me tell you about how I killed this old lady professor uptown. It was priceless. I found out that she and her amateur detective friends were looking into your sister's case, so I bugged their places like I did yours. All it takes is posing as a repairman or a meter reader and you can go wherever you like. Poof, and you're invisible. Simple as that.

"The others were pretty boring, routine stuff, but this old lady was a widow and she carried on conversations with her dead husband's portrait, if you can believe. Pretty rich, don't you think? *She* talks to pictures, and *I'm* crazy.

"Anyway, I heard her telling her dead old man that she'd doped out who killed Julie. She went back through the early witness interviews and figured out that my mother would be the best match for a woman who had called about the case. She was the right age, a heavy smoker, educated in fancy boarding schools. The professor checked via the Internet and discovered that there was no official record of our deaths, no newspaper report of our fatal 'accident,' no claim on my mother's life insurance policy. Old biddy put one and one together and they added up to me."

Soundlessly, I backed up until I was beside the sofa. Reaching down, I found the gun. I forced myself to wait as his shadow swallowed me and my head filled with his thick, threatening scent.

"So that was the end of her, Annie girl. And now it's your turn."

I brought the pistol up and struck the side of his head. Alan cried out and rocked back, staggering.

Breaking away, I made for the rear door. I could not risk the slow, cantankerous elevator. Frantically, I worked the lock and mounted the catwalk. Clutching the rails against the dislocating swirl of the storm, I headed toward the roof, but before I could reach it, the back door burst open.

A bloody patch bloomed at Alan's temple and scarlet trails scored his cheek. "You're dead, bitch."

Shifting gears, I scrambled toward the sculptor's apartment. Inside, I raced toward the studio.

Alan was not far behind. I heard him fumbling through the unfamiliar space, flinging obstacles aside and cursing in a mad fury.

I plucked a heavy pry bar from the row of draconian tools and perched out of sight behind the oxyacetylene tank. His footsteps came clearer, closer.

With every scrap of remaining strength, I swung out. But Alan caught the ponderous tool like a weightless trifle and wrenched it from my hands with scorching force.

He flung the bar aside and trapped me in a suffocating hold. "That's enough. I'm bored with this. Anyhow, it's past your bedtime, Annie girl. Thirty years past your bedtime, to be exact. I should have taken care of you back then, but I was careless."

"Get off me! Let me go."

He clamped my mouth with monstrous force. "Don't bother wasting the last of your breath, Annie girl. Cousin Alan is going to take you home and settle you in for a nice, long sleep."

Chapter 52

Anxious for an update, Callendar dialed Russell Quilfo at the Queens Cold Case Squad.

"Cold Case. Ploscow speaking."

"Lieutenant Quilfo, please. It's Ted Callendar calling."

"Hang on."

Waiting, Callender listened to the noise: phones ringing, radio blasts, shouts.

"Hello?"

"Quilfo? It's Ted. What's going on there? Sounds like all hell's breaking loose."

"That's because it is. The address that Ellison person gave us turned out to be phony, an old abandoned warehouse near the navy yard. I've got everyone I can lay my hands on working this thing. Hopefully, we'll catch a lucky break before—"

Callendar went cold. The danger had not passed yet.

Chapter 53

Alan muscled me back across the rickety catwalk through the pelting rain to my loft.

"Stop!" I cried, struggling wildly. "Let me go!"

He trudged through the darkened living room, deaf to my frenzied screams. My skin burned from the pressure of his grasp.

He dumped me on the bed, freeing me for an instant. I thrust up sharply with my knee, aiming for his crotch, but he deflected me with terrifying ease. Then he pinned me like a specimen to the mattress.

"I told you to relax," he snarled, crushing my limbs, making it hard to breathe.

"Stop it, Alan. No!"

His hand strayed to my throat, and he started to squeeze. My head pumped with dizzying pressure. My consciousness was melting away.

"Say good night, Annie girl. When you see Julie, tell her I said hello."

I was losing hold, drifting. But as the darkness folded over me, I heard an anguished cry.

"Stop it, Alan! Let her go!"

His mad hold eased.

"Who invited you to the party, you old prick?" Alan said. "Get the hell out of here."

"No, Alan," came my uncle's tortured voice. "You can't hurt anyone else. It's going to end here and now."

"The only way it's going to end is with you and the bitch in the ground."

Eli sobbed. "God help me, I should have stopped it all those years ago. I knew what you were, that you had to be locked away. But I was terrified of what it would do to your mother. I loved her so. And you, too. You're my son, Alan. Nothing changes that."

"Stop blubbering," Alan spat. "Listening to that crap makes me sick."

"I forced myself to believe her when she said you were doing fine, that she always had an eye on you," Eli said, weeping. "But in my heart, I knew it wasn't true."

"Give it a rest, Mr. Nobility. Whatever I am I owe to you. Remember that. I'm a product of your rotten genes, your lousy upbringing."

"You're right, Alan. It's my fault, all of it. Do what you want to me, but please, I'm begging you, let Anna go. She's done nothing."

"She was born. That's enough."

I reached toward the night table and grasped the bedside lamp. With everything I had, I hurled it at Alan's head.

"What the—?" He emitted a startled laugh and crumpled to the floor.

I scrambled up and caught my uncle's arm. "Hurry, Uncle E! We have to get out before he comes to."

"Go, sweetheart. I'll be right behind you."

I crossed the darkened living room and dashed onto the catwalk. Lashed by the wind, I struggled toward the edge of the rain-slicked roof.

I kept peering back, willing my uncle to appear. "Come on," I shouted toward the open door. "Hurry!"

Dropping over the side, I clutched the slick, wet rails. "Uncle Eli," I called. "Where are you?"

Suddenly, came a shattering burst of gunfire and a blaze of dislocating light.

A keening wail from inside pierced the lowering of the storm. Was it my uncle's cry or Alan's? I could not be sure.

The storm roared and lashed me in a turbulent rage. My foot slipped, and I hung by quivering fingers over the void. Panic roared in my ears, and my heart struck with painful ferocity. Another wind squall could wrench me loose and send me plummeting.

My hands were quaking, arms burning with the strain.

If I yielded to the fear, I was lost. Closing my eyes, I thought of Julie and my parents. I thought of my uncle and the monstrous secret he had lived with all these years. He had tried so hard to make things right, to protect his shattered family and atone for his son's unspeakable atrocities. I understood that he had come here to try to protect me yet again. And I knew that I could not leave him.

Shivering wildly, I pulled myself onto the roof. Braced against the storm, I made my way across the littered span and crossed the catwalk.

Pulling a breath, I entered the loft. I drew a carving knife from the block beside the stove.

Stiff with fear, I approached the bedroom, sifting the silence for a clue.

But I heard nothing.

I pictured the mad fiend playing with me, waiting to pounce. But it could be that Eli was hurt, his life ebbing away as I stood rooted by terror and uncertainty.

Then I heard my uncle's mournful sobs. "God help me. What have I done?"

Racing in, I found Eli seated on the floor, cradling Alan's massive head and shoulders in his lap. As my eyes adjusted to the stingy light, I could see that there was blood everywhere. Dark spray had peppered the wall and broad spreading blotches marred the floor.

"Uncle E?" I said gently. "Are you hurt?"

"He's dead," he cried. "Dear Lord, I had to kill him. There was no choice."

I went to hold him, to try to comfort him, but he shrank from me, weeping.

"You're right, Unc," I said gently. "You had to. There was no other way."

"So many deaths. So many innocent souls taken. And I'm the only one to blame. I should have stopped it right away. The moment I knew how sick he was. But I couldn't bear the thought of losing Irene, of her suicide. So I lied to myself. All those years. All that misery. And it's all my fault."

"No, Uncle E. You did the best you could. Alan was to blame. Not—"

Before I could speak the word, my uncle stuffed the gun butt in his mouth and squeezed the trigger. The room blazed for a horrifying instant as Eli jolted back, then fell beside his son.

NO!

The storm unleashed a fiery bolt and a clamorous clash of thunder. Then everything went dead still, and I filled the eerie silence with my screams.

Chapter 54

The Arcanum members milled about the meeting room at the Calibre Club, trading rueful glances and hushed regrets. As the appointed time approached, Griffey strode to the podium and cleared his throat.

"Before we come to order, I suggest that we observe a moment of silence in honor of Clu Baldwin, dear friend and brilliant colleague. She will be sorely missed." He swiped a tear, and his eyes glazed with private remembrances.

Melton Frame burst in. "Morning, all. You can't imagine what a time I've had getting here. I was the keynote speaker at the national leadership conference, and those people simply refused to let me leave. One party in my honor after the other. So exhausting."

Griffey sighed. "We were observing a moment of silence in memory of Clu, Melton."

Frame threw up his hands. "Well, pardon me for living. How on earth was I to know?"

Griffey returned to the microphone. "I believe that we can best honor Dr. Baldwin by proceeding with our work. All in favor—"

There was a chorus of listless assent.

"Fine. In that spirit, I'll respectfully ask Ted Callendar to take the floor and present the facts of our next case."

"I will." Callendar walked to the podium. "Before we consider the Kelly Anson murder, I'd like to add that Clu Baldwin was, in every sense, a person of courage and valor. She put herself on the line. She made an extraordinary sacrifice to help put a dangerous killer out of circulation. I'm proud to have known her."

"As are we all," Quilfo said.

Frame cleared his throat and raised his cup. The others fell silent, awaiting his sentiment. "This coffee's cold," he groused. "Now please, people. I've made a long miserable trip to get here this morning. I move that we hear about the Anson case and get on with it."

Chapter 55

My uncle Eli was laid to rest on the friends' side of St. Philips Episcopal Cemetery beside his infant daughter. The vacant grave on the other side was reserved for his wife, Irene, who would join them soon enough.

Investigators had tracked my aunt to a hospital in New York, where she went to look for Alan after he escaped her dubious supervision yet again. In the past, she had sunk into deep denial and convinced herself that he would do no harm. But this time, she'd been unable to ignore the dread realization that he was coming after my family and me.

Shortly after arriving in the city, Irene had succumbed to debilitating symptoms of her terminal disease. She was the one who had called my mother and the others, trying desperately to warn them into vigilance before Alan had a chance to make good on his lethal agenda. But there had been only one way to end the violence, and Eli had seen to that.

Despite the scandal, church officials decided to allow my uncle his hallowed plot. Or perhaps the scandal boosted him still further in their esteem. After a brief debate, it was agreed that Alan would be installed in an unmarked grave on the strangers' side of the cemetery across the street.

An enormous crowd had gathered for the brief graveside ceremony to honor my uncle. Many came out of respect, some out of morbid curiosity. Of course the press was there, trampling every last shred of sanctity with impertinent questions and requests for us to pose.

In reply, I offered them my middle finger. Then I took my parents' hands and strode away.

Bertie said nothing. In fact she had been shocked nearly mute since hearing the bizarre identity of my sister's killer.

We all were, I suppose, though my shock and sorrow was tempered by some small guilty measure of relief. I felt as if I had passed a painful stone, shed some deep, hideous obstruction.

Back at the house, I helped my mother set out the good china, silver and crystal for lunch. There would be only the three of us, but that number felt less oppressive than it had in the past.

Bertie had prepared my childhood favorites: fried chicken and all its weighty accompaniments. But my parents and I sat in pensive silence, our appetites blunted by grief.

My reticent father, strangely, was the first to speak. "Annie girl, it's nice to have you home."

"It's good to be here."

"How long are you planning to stay?"

Bertie set her jaw and gnawed bitterly at a wing.

"I don't know, Pop. A little while."

My mother sniffed. "Naturally. This place must seem so terribly dull and boring after New York."

I had to smile. "After New York, dull and boring is exactly what I need. I'm not going back, Mom, except to get my things. I'm going to work for the *Denver Post*. They saw a piece of mine and made me an offer. I thought I'd try my luck there for a while, see how I do at a higher altitude."

Bertie's face fell. "What about Kevin?"

"I told you, we're over."

"But all that time, all those years. You were engaged and everything."

"No, fortunately not everything. He was wrong for me, Mom. Trust me on that."

She cracked the wishbone, keeping both halves for herself. "I suppose it's your decision."

I cupped her hand, which felt surprisingly delicate and warm. "I promise I'll keep my eyes open. And as soon as I find Mr. Right, you get to pick the dress."

She had the good grace not to answer, but I could see her practiced wheels turning. Definitely a full skirt, plunging neckline, tapered waist. A headpiece and veil would hide the flyaway hair and satin pumps would add an illusion of height.

Despite myself, like all Bertie's brides, I would look perfect.

With a meaningful look at my dad, she pushed back from the table. "Come, Anna. We have something to show you."

I followed them upstairs. They passed my room and paused at Julie's door.

The door was unlocked. Bertie turned the knob and pushed in, unleashing a flood of sunlight. The blinds were open, and the space had been transformed. Pale paneling lined the walls, and a deep red Oriental rug capped the newly polished plank floor. There was a cream leather sofa and a pair of bright, upholstered chairs. The bookshelves along the far wall held my dad's medical books and my mother's favorite romance novels, in which every lovely heroine wound up at the altar beside the man of her dreams.

As I began to wonder what had happened to my sister's things, my eye was drawn to a pile of boxes near the door. On the side, each one was marked in dark block letters: JULE.

I was about to question the spelling mistake, when I realized that the mistake had been mine all these years. They had not called my sister Jewel, as I'd thought. It was Jule, a simple diminutive.

I hugged Bertie hard, and for once she didn't fuss about my messing her makeup or hair. "You like it, Anna?"

"No, I love it." I let her go and hugged my father. "It's wonderful, Pop. Perfect."

Bertie pressed her palms in delight. "The sofa opens into a bed. So there'll be plenty of space when you come to visit with the hubby and the little ones."

I caught my father's bemused eye and winked. "All things in time, Mom."

Her face went dreamy. "Yes, dear," she told me. "All things in time."

Chapter 56

Dixon knocked as I was packing the last of my things. "I came over as soon as I got your message, Anna. Welcome back." Stopping short, he frowned. "What's all this? Where are you off to?"

"Denver. I was offered a job at the *Post*. I've decided to try this leaving home thing again from the beginning, call a do-over."

"Why can't you call a do-over here?"

My eye strayed to the cleanly scrubbed floor and the bright blots of paint that Moshe Price had applied to cover the bloodstains. Mr. Price had done a good, thorough job, but nothing could ever erase what had happened here. "Lots of reasons."

"I hope I'm not one of them. I'm going to miss you."

"You too. You'd be one of the few reasons I'd want to stay." I counted on my fingers. "There's you, Shelby, Monique and the kids, the Prices and the bagels, not necessarily in that order." I zipped my final duffel bag. "If you get to Colorado, come and see me."

"I'll make it a point to get there, if that's okay with you."

I squelched a smile and shrugged. "Sure. That would be nice, someday, when you have the chance."

"How's next weekend?"

I could not help but smile at that. "I'm pretty clear, except for apartment hunting."

"Great. I can come help you find a place, settle in."

"Sounds good."

"To me, too." Our eyes caught and held.

Moshe Price appeared at the loft's open door. "So you're ready to go, Ms. Jameson?"

With regret, I broke the eye lock. "Yes, Mr. Price. All set."

"Sorry, I see you have company. I'll get out of your way."

"No, please. Actually, I wanted you to meet my friend Dixon Drake. I think he'd be the perfect new tenant for this place."

Appraising Dixon, Price stroked his beard. "Besides having two last names, what is it you do, Mr. Dixon Drake? You're also a photographer?"

"No. A reporter."

"You know how to follow the rules? No heavy cooking, rent on the first of the month—no excuses. No pets. No loud parties. Like that."

Dixon stared my way again. "Nothing like that, Mr. Price. Actually, I plan to be out of town quite a bit, visiting a friend."

Price's keen gaze bounced between us. "I see. So tell me, you know how to treat a *friend*, Mr. Reporter? You know to look after her, show her proper respect. See that she's happy?"

Dixon crossed the room and offered Price his hand. "Yes, Mr. Price. I promise you. I know how to treat a friend with all the respect and caring she so richly deserves."

Moshe shook his hand firmly. "And you, Ms. Jameson? You know also how to treat a friend? See he's taken care of? Make him at home?"

"I do, I mean—I know."

Price walked out, stroking his faithful beard. "A happy ending," he muttered. "This is good."